Death of an Eagle

Kirby Jonas

Cover art by author

HOWLING WOLF PUBLISHING
POCATELLO, IDAHO

Howling Wolf Publishing
P.O. Box 1045
Pocatello, Idaho 83204

For more information about this and Kirby Jonas' previous books, or if you would like to be included on the author's mailing list, point your browser to *www.kirbyjonas.com* or send a request via postal mail to Howling Wolf Publishing at the address above.

Book design by Serephin Multimedia *(www.serephin.com)*

First Edition
Library of Congress Cataloging-in-Publication Data

Jonas, Kirby, 1965–
        Death of an eagle / Kirby Jonas. -- 1st ed.
                p.   cm
        ISBN 1-891423-01-0
        1. Title.
                        Library of Congress Catalog Card Number 98-93213
                                                                              CIP

First edition: November 1998
Printed in the United States of America

Death of an Eagle

On *The Dansing Star*

From Elmer Kelton, six-time winner of the Spur Award for Best Western Novel:

"Kirby Jonas tells a gritty story of search, action, and revenge in Old Arizona when it was still a hunting ground for hostile Apaches and white outlaws, when hatreds ran deep, and vengeance was not the Lord's."

From Don Coldsmith, author of the "Spanish Bit Saga":

"Kirby Jonas is one of the best of the young writers who breath a new freshness into the traditional Western."

From Mike Blakely, author of Spur Award Finalist *Shortgrass Song:*

"Finally, a voice as real and honest as thunder rumbles from the canyons and tinderbox towns of the wild Old West. The voice belongs to Kirby Jonas. Every shining detail of *The Dansing Star* carries the stamp of authenticity and drums like the hoofbeat of a sure-footed horse at full gallop."

Acknowledgments

Over time and through varied experiences, I have learned certain things (hopefully) which have become ingrained in me. Through study and observation, and many hours of research, I have gathered extensive understanding of particular fields of which I write. It is nice to think that in these few areas I am, perhaps, an expert. But I could never stand completely alone. To be believable, any work of serious fiction depends heavily on the input and assistance of technical experts. I would feel remiss not to take a few moments to thank several of these experts. Without them certain sections of this book, although still possible, would have been extremely difficult to write.

My undying thanks goes out to my friend, the Honorable Clyde Hall. Without his knowledge of his people, the Shoshones, this book would never have been complete. To Dr. Chuck Trost, whose learning and love of birds made him an indispensable source of knowledge. To H. Leigh Gittins, whose knowledge of this area and wonderful dry sense of humor made my research a pleasure. To J. Frank Dobie, who, even though no longer with us, lives on in the spirit of the West. To brother Jamie, to Debbie, and to Mom, whose technical assistance was greatly appreciated and, at times, sorely needed. To Jessica Stallings, whose shy charm and down-to-earth beauty was the inspiration for Rebecca Woodland's character. To Steve Medellin, whose technical knowledge was, as always, indispensable. And, of course, to my friend, José Olano, for his tracking and outdoors expertise and for being the inspiration for *our hero*. José, my friend, you may very well have been born a century past your time, but there are those of us who are glad you were.

Books by Kirby Jonas

Season of the Vigilante, Book One: The Bloody Season

Season of the Vigilante, Book Two: Season's End

The Dansing Star

Death of an Eagle

Legend of the Tumbleweed*

Lady Winchester*

*Forthcoming

To José "Lucky" Olano, of course, because without you there would be no book. And to Lauris, for prepping our hero for stardom.

Part One
Flight of the Eagle

~

Chapter One

Crushed to earth beneath the giant, grizzled paw, the green April grass shoots quickly sprang back. But the brittle blades from last autumn lay fragmented and lifeless, dwarfed in the fresh ten inch-long depression—the track of a boar grizzly.

The Bear River Range above Bailey Creek was a remote kingdom, still capped with snow on its peaks and in its timbered shadows. And the eight hundred pound silver-back grizzly was its crowned ruler. He lumbered across the gentle, forested slope, over fallen Douglas fir and between the live ones whose tips pricked the lightly clouded sky. A chipmunk raced across the dampened trail, its tiny, striped body a flurry. The bear scarcely noticed it as he passed. His little reddish eyes concentrated on a grassy, sunlit patch in a saddle a hundred yards ahead.

Soon the bruin entered the sunny clearing. Standing with a soft, chill breeze off the snow banks playing in his matted fur, he tested the air. His nose was greeted only by the scent of Douglas fir, crushed grass, and molding duff, disturbed by his careless paws.

On the other side of the saddle, just before the shadows of the fir woods, a large log lay rotting, its belly embedded in a carpet of grass and fir needles. The bear's eyes were no better than man's, but his nose was incredibly keen. He smelled the decaying wood, identified the gray shape as a log, and moved forward purposefully.

On top, the log was pitted and sprinkled with moss. The bear rooted into it with his nose, and it broke apart easily. Settling himself back on his hind feet, he sank the long claws of his right forefoot into the wood, and grunting, he heaved to the side. With a soft crackle, the wood came apart, and large chunks rolled down the slope and came to rest among the new grass and fallen fir cones.

With a satisfied grunt, the bear made a quick survey of the black wood ant colony and large white eggs he had uncovered. Then his tongue went to work, picking up ants and eggs and pulling them into his black-lipped mouth. He made swift work of the meal, then reared back his great head to search for survivors. There were two ants fleeing along the side of the log toward safety, and he lowered his mouth to take them in.

Suddenly, the breeze shifted. He was poised to devour the ants when his keen nose caught something new. He whipped his head up, and his ears shot forward. He swung his shaggy head this way and that, searching the trees downslope, from where the breeze now came.

With a thrust of his forelegs, the bear came erect, his huge body standing nearly seven feet high. He watched the trees below, listened, whiffed the air currents. And then the breeze changed again, from the southwest once more. But the big bear needed only that few seconds' confirmation. Turning from the rotted log without a backward glance, he started down the slope, stepping easily over the downed timber and saplings in his path.

Young José Olano stretched lazily and let his dark eyes cruise the surrounding land. It was spring along Bailey Creek. Days grew longer, and songbirds were returning from their retreat to the south. Meadowlarks serenaded each other from the tops of sage, and sparrows flitted about the branches and bright new leaves of quaking aspen and serviceberry. A bluebird flew past, its wingbeats carrying it along with the motion of a wave. Up, then down it sailed until it seemed it would brush the sage, then up once more. In the valley, the tiny, scattered buildings of Soda Springs dotted the sagebrush flats. There, too, spring green painted the land, and the colors of April softened the hard lines of farms and ranches that dotted the hills around the town. José watched these sights with the sun warming his shoulders and a gentle breeze playing in his wavy black hair.

José Olano's Basque blood made his skin dark, and his eyes black like deep wells, with jet brows hanging over them. Fierceness gleamed in those eyes, yet softness surrounded them. His sharp nose overhung a proud mouth, his hair hung just past his collar, flowing loosely, like streams of hot molasses.

He dressed in the manner of the humble: a faded, gray wool shirt, baggy black pants, patched in several places, and battered leather shoes, their laces spliced repeatedly. Dirt smudged his face and hands, soiled his shirt. But out here there was no one to care about such things. José was sixteen years old that April—sixteen for one month now.

Over the grassy hill to his left, he could hear the tinkling of a brass bell and the occasional bleating of sheep. *His* sheep. Well, in a way. At least he was their guardian, for this, his first year as watcher of the flocks. The sheep actually belonged to Ben Trombell, who lived in Soda Springs. Trombell was a wealthy man—at least as wealthy as any José knew. He owned sheep in Nevada, and, since one month past, in Soda Springs. He prided himself on being the first man to bring "woollies" into the area.

Ever so slightly, the wind changed, and the new grass bent about José's feet. He walked over to a smooth-topped boulder and sat down, pulling a stalk of grass from between his teeth and tossing it carelessly to the earth. Reaching over the edge of the boulder, he grasped the neck of a battered guitar and lifted it onto his lap. He hadn't checked his flock for a couple of hours, for a feeling of laziness had overcome him. But the sheep sounded content, and he wanted to hear music. Even his own music. As pathetic as it might sound, only he and the sheep would hear. And the birds. As for them, "Sing along with me!" José invited exuberantly. If they didn't wish to, they could leave.

He strummed a few discordant bars. He started to turn the ivory-colored keys to change the pitch, but then he shrugged. Who was he to say how a guitar should sound? If he didn't like it he would just sing louder and drown it out. After all, the voice was what he wanted. Any human voice, even just his own.

He began to sing the fine songs of the old country, *Euskal Herria*—the Basque homeland. He thought of his mother and father, both long dead now. By this time their graves would grow tall with grass and rose bushes. What would they think if they knew where he was now, in the land of dreams? America. The Territory of Idaho. A faraway land so different from his own, yet a place with beauty at every turn. From the fir-covered mountains above him and far across the valley to the sprawling sage- and grass-covered vista and sparkling Bear River below. And last, to the rocky perch where he sat, surrounded by grass, trees, and the nodding heads of bluebells and yellow fritillary. What a land. What a dream!

The vibrant chords stopped as José's hands and voice stilled, and tears filled his eyes. Tears for many reasons. Tears of sadness and of joy. He missed his home in San Sebastián. He missed his parents, his sisters, his brother. But he was happy, very happy, to be here in the employ of Ben Trombell, sheep baron. To be in the middle of a world bigger than life, where opportunity waited around each turn.

But José's life lacked one element that would make it perfect. He ached to learn the ways of the wild lands. Sure, he lived his life outdoors. But he didn't want to just *live* there—he wanted to feel at home. He wanted to become competent as a hunter, a woodsman. Back in Guipuzcoa, his home province in Spain, there had been an old hermit who lived up in the hills, keeping to himself. Ixidro Ibarra was his name, and José had always wanted to meet him, to learn his ways. He had no desire to totally forsake civilization, but he wanted to have the choice. To go to the mountains when he wanted to or to stay in town with equal comfort.

There was one big problem with remembering his homeland. He couldn't think of home without remembering the bear. He could never get past that. The bear. That huge bear with its great, humped back, and the huge white patch on its chest. It seemed to José like that bear was larger than a horse. And it was, to a boy of five.

He remembered finding the dead cow. He remembered standing in awe at the mass of maggots that writhed in its ribcage, making a strange rushing sound, filling the air with a gagging stench. And he remembered his first look at the bear.

The bear saw him at a distance. It had probably smelled the dead cow a lot farther away. But when it saw movement, it came toward him at a lope. And José, only a child, nearly froze in his tracks. But he knew he had to run. He ran and hid in the hollow log where he had hid from Alfredo before. He hid and waited to die.

After a while, he heard footsteps nearby, then heard the bear breathing outside the log. It pushed the log around for a while, enough to scare the poor little boy nearly to death, but no more. And then all was silent. It was hours before José decided the bear had returned to the cow.

José had nightmares for years after that. And even when the nightmares faded, he still saw that bear when he thought of home. If only he could become a mountain man, he would fear no bear. He would fear nothing.

José began to strum the guitar again, absently. The wheels of his mind churned, and he thought of South America, where he had first traveled at the age of eleven, after leaving his homeland. There he joined his brother, Alfredo, and they thought they had found a home. But Alfredo was a wandering spirit, and the American West beckoned and beckoned. One November day found them on a ship bound for Texas. Then Texas led to Nevada, where the gracious Ben Trombell took them under his wing.

Alfredo and José knew nothing about sheep. The Basques who lived along the Bay of Biscay, like José's family, were either merchants or fishermen or something that supported the two professions. But Alfredo and José couldn't speak English well enough to get any other work, so with the flocks they stayed. Alfredo did, anyway.

José was the fortunate one. Trombell had felt him too young to stay out with the herders, and he took him to his Nevada home as a maid, of sorts. Sometimes a cook. An errand boy. The advantage was that from the age of eleven on José was forced to speak English. Few of his kind had yet come to America, and for a while José felt very alone. But after a year of trying to communicate with Trombell, he could hold his own in the English tongue. After two years, he felt comfortable. He even learned to read in English, through diligent hours of work, and one day Ben Trombell told him he spoke English better than many Americans he knew. That pleased José immensely.

As José lived with Trombell, his employer constantly taught him about sheep. When they bred, when they lambed. How to castrate the young rams. What price their wool brought. The difference between a Suffolk, the black-faced Irish breed, and a Rambouillet, the big white one known for its fine wool. José had never seen a Suffolk. Trombell swore the Rambouillet was the only breed worth having.

Suddenly, José laughed as his mind went back to a time three years past. He was barely thirteen. Ben Trombell had taken him to visit Alfredo and the other herders with the flocks. Trombell had told José how to catch a sheep. All you must do, he said, was run after one for several minutes. Soon it would give itself up and fall to its knees to be devoured or disposed of however its captor saw fit. José thought of himself as a smart boy, for a thirteen-year-old. He thought Trombell was playing a joke on him, but the man acted so serious he didn't tell him he thought so. Still, he knew dogs that were much smaller than sheep, and he couldn't catch *them*. Why would sheep be any different? After all, they had four legs, too. But he would give it a try, just to please Ben.

They got a sheep away from the flock, and José set out after it. The sheep dodged this way and that, trying to lose him, leading him through the brush. Suddenly, to his surprise, the sheep, now ten yards ahead of him, fell to its knees. It was so abrupt José didn't have time to stop or evade it. He ran right into and over the sheep, falling onto his face in the dirt, and the sheep flipped over and landed on its side. When the sheep realized what happened, it started to struggle to its feet. But José jumped up and tackled it. Holding its trembling body beneath him, he gasped for air.

José looked up to the sound of laughter. Ben Trombell, Alfredo, and the other herders were practically doubled over at the sheep wagon, laughing hysterically. José's face flushed hot. For a moment, he felt embarrassed, as if the brunt of some big joke. But when he thought of how he must have looked, running after that sheep and then sprawling over it, a smile broke over his face. Then he, too, began to laugh until tears ran down his cheeks.

Somehow, José had thought those carefree days would last forever. He had lived with Ben Trombell in Nevada for nearly four years. But he was soon to find he had learned far too much of the English language and about the sheep business to remain an errand boy for long.

One day, after supper, Ben Trombell stopped José abruptly when he tried to rise and clear the dishes. "I've bought a ranch up north, son. In a place called The Soda Springs, in Idaho Territory. It's cattle country and mining country, but I want to be the first to experiment with sheep up there. I need a man I can trust, a man who knows sheep, a man who knows English. But it'll be a small flock for now. I need only one tender, and Alfredo would have to stay here. I'd like you to go there with me. But I'm asking, not telling. You're old enough to join the herders here, if you'd like. But if you go with me, we'll send for Alfredo, too, when the flock grows."

That was the essence of what Trombell said, and José hung his head. Ben was like a father to him, so he couldn't refuse. The next thing he knew, on March 31, 1883, he was seated beside Trombell on a train bound for Idaho Territory.

A strange sound suddenly reached José's ears, wrenching him from his reverie. The sheep bleated loudly—bleated frantically, the way they did when coyotes ran in their midst. With an oath, José dropped the guitar and reached alongside the boulder again, this time to bring up an 1866 Winchester rifle. The brass frame was tarnished and the screws a little loose. The wood was scratched and a bit warped by the weather, and the butt plate was missing. But to José, who knew next to nothing about firearms, any gun was as good as the next.

He ran across the hill as fast as he could through the scattered sage. As he neared the far side of the hill, the bleating of the sheep grew louder, a sound of terror. Breathing in gasps, he reached the downslope of the hill, and below him saw sheep running in all directions. Several flew past, almost running into him, oblivious to his presence. Two lambs struggled to rise, knocked down in the stampede.

His head pounding with excitement, José scanned the open swale and the brushy forest edge where aspen grew thickly before giving way to fir. Suddenly, he saw the brown blur, heard the deep-throated roar in the trees below, one hundred yards away. Cold fear gripped his heart, and his face went nearly as white as the stampeding sheep. He had never heard such a horrible noise. And only once, long ago, had he seen an animal of such awesome size that moved so swiftly. Terror nearly overcame him.

Grizzly!

The bear cleared the trees, running almost straight at him, hot on the tail of a ewe. A huge right paw slashed out, and the sheep hurled through the air like a down pillow to land crying at the base of a lone fir tree. The bear closed the distance in a bound, and its eight hundred pounds smashed full force on top of the sheep as its teeth sank into its skull. All José could see under that bear was a five-year-old boy.

The bear lay on top of the sheep only for a moment. Then it stood again, poised like a spring on all fours, and swung its head back and forth, looking for other game. It whirled half about, its gaze terrifyingly intense. Blood dripped from its lips and from its matted neck.

José suddenly realized the Winchester's crescent butt was pressed against his shoulder. The rifle was aimed, cocked. Sweat trickled into his eyes and off his chin. His finger twitched. The rifle's barrel belched flame and jumped in his hands. He didn't hear the shot. For a second, he wasn't even sure he had pulled the trigger.

But the huge beast whirled, facing him sixty yards away. He could hear its heaving breaths. Foam and blood dripped from its mouth. It stared at him, and he stared back, frozen. His mouth was so dry he couldn't swallow—the only dry place on his entire body. He jerked the trigger, but nothing happened. He cursed and jacked out the empty shell casing. Again he brought the rifle up. He fired.

The rimfire .44's two hundred grains of lead had no visible effect on the bear. Had it scored? The bear took a step forward. José jacked in another round, fired again. This time the bear jerked and snapped at the front of its shoulder as if stung by a bee. It roared horribly and shook its head, showering the grass with pink foam and sheep's blood. With fierce eyes staring, the bear charged across the swale toward the trembling Basque boy, its ears laid back flat against its head. Four bounds, then it stopped. Only forty yards away now. Its eyes staring fiercely, the bear emitted the most terrifying roar José could imagine. In horror, he stared at the bloodshot eyes, nearly dropping the rifle.

He chambered a fourth round—fired. A fifth—fired. With another roar, the bear turned and raced downhill. José kept jacking the Winchester's lever and firing, no longer aiming but unaware of that fact. His mind had ceased to operate when his frantic heart took over.

The bear ran down the coulee, bits of mud and sod flying up behind it as its claws tore into the ground. At the bottom of the slope, it turned left to keep from running into a tangled patch of fir overgrown with maple and serviceberry. José ran after it, and as he came to the place where the bear turned, he saw it standing two hundred yards away, licking the front of its chest vigorously. At that moment, it looked over its shoulder for his pursuit.

On the left lifted a steep, sage-covered slope leading to the flat where José had sat earlier. On the right loomed a dark wooded area that revealed nothing past its secretive veil. Emitting one last snarl, the bear disappeared with a crash into the black timber and tangled brush. José's heart plummeted. Three hours till sundown, and a wounded grizzly stalked free, in heavy cover. He knew little about bears, but someone had told him of their vindictive tendency. They said one would creep back around in the dark on an assailant to take its revenge. That left no option to poor José, and his hands began to shake uncontrollably with the thought of what lay ahead.

Like a fly on the trail of the black widow, he must go into those treacherous woods after the wounded, grizzled beast—alone...

Chapter Two

With trembling fingers, José Olano reached into his pants pocket and withdrew five more .44 shells. It was the last of them. He fumbled two of them through the tarnished loading gate. The third one slipped from his fingers and dropped into the dark soil. He looked down at it with a sick, empty feeling, his face pale and running with sweat. When the next one also fell, he cursed and forced back hot tears. Gritting his teeth, he pressed the last cartridge into the magazine.

Stooping, José retrieved the two shells. With his jaw set and his throat tight, he pushed them in with care after the other three. Then he levered out the empty shell casing from the chamber. He eased down the hammer to prevent an accidental discharge, then stood gripping the stock and forearm of the rifle until his knuckles turned white.

A single tear finally rolled through the dust on his cheek, and he pursed his lips and bunched his jaw. He had tried so hard to hold back those tears. He looked slowly about, up the hill to his left, then back up the path he had just run. He hoped desperately to see Ben Trombell bringing him supplies. Or someone else—anyone. Fear gripped him so strongly now he couldn't get enough air, although he breathed far faster than he should. His feet didn't want to move. Or maybe he hadn't tried. Was there anyone in this gigantic, lonely world who could help him?

No. No one. He must meet the bear alone.

Again, he glanced toward the sun. Twilight lurked not far away, so down the narrow path he started, crowded by the hill on his left and the black woods on his right.

With a gasp, he drew up short. In the damp trail before him he saw the track of the beast for the first time. The biggest track he had ever seen. In awe, he knelt before it and placed his left hand inside. The print dwarfed his hand, and the marks of its claws stretched out three inches beyond the ends of the toes. He swallowed hard and squeezed his eyes shut.

What dastardly stroke of luck had brought him to this dangerous, hostile land? Why must he face this incredible beast alone? These were not his sheep. They belonged to Ben Trombell. Let *him* come and protect them. He didn't pay enough for José to go clawing through these tangled woods, with a foe mightier than ten men hidden somewhere in wait.

Inside, José laughed bitterly. Only minutes ago he had been pondering his great fortune here in this land of opportunity in the gracious employ of Ben Trombell. Now he almost cursed the man who had been so kind to him.

With that thought, he clenched his jaw. He was a Basque. And a man, too. Ben Trombell had hired him to protect the sheep, and he would not quit now. It was better to die. Besides, as he had recognized earlier, if he did not kill this beast, what would stop it from coming after him later, in the dark? Then it would be hopeless. Anyway, if he were indeed to die, he preferred to die in the daylight to dying in the dark.

Standing up from the paw print, he started on, his knees still shaking, and soon he reached the spot where the bear entered the timber. He'd never learned to follow a trail, but the brush grew so thick here a creature as large as the grizzly could never enter without leaving signs even a city slicker could read. José found the bear's entry point. Claw-ripped sod marked it, and broken branches, one of them as big as José's wrist. Dark blood smeared the leaves. At least now he knew the bear was wounded and would be weakened, however slightly. Making the cross on his chest, José pushed through the bushes.

The sun was still up, but soon the woods grew gloomy. The trunks of the firs were so big and plentiful that little direct sunlight filtered in among them this time of the afternoon. But in spite of the shade, brush and stunted aspens grew here in abundance. José could walk easier than in the heavy brush at the forest perimeter, but the undergrowth concealed what lay ahead, even twenty yards away.

José's wide eyes searched the shadows for the bear. He had long since quit watching the forest floor, relying on movement instead of any trail the bruin might have left. Its spoor meant nothing to him. No bird nor beast made a whisper. And no wind. The woods offered only the noisy cracking of branches beneath José's feet, and these sounds of his own passing he couldn't even hear.

He moved slowly, the rifle pressed to his chest. His head pivoted this way and that. He breathed through his mouth, and his jaw hung slack, except when he tried to lick his lips, which he didn't do often; he found his tongue so dry it almost stuck to them.

His eyes began to hurt from strain. He had gone one hundred yards into the woods. It would be impossible to find his way back out the path he came in, if he needed to. His breaths continued rapid—his heart pounded in his chest and in his ears. And his ears rang, partially from the noise of his own rifle shots, partially from the silence of the moment.

José walked aimlessly. He had no idea where the bear hid. He found himself in a tight corridor of firs, and a strange, dark odor blew to him. An odd, musky smell mingled with that of decaying flesh. His scalp prickled with apprehension. Unconsciously, he cocked the Winchester. It made a cold, metallic sound—yet a comforting sound, too. As he moved between the big firs his breath stilled. Without thinking, he was holding it, listening for any sound.

Without warning, a giant brown paw slashed from behind the tree to his right, scraping the bark and narrowly missing his head. José reeled back, trying to bring the rifle up. The weapon exploded in his hands. He felt himself going down, tripped by a tree root. He hit the ground hard on his back, knocking the wind from him, but he still clutched the rifle. Through blurry eyes, he looked up, prepared to see the grizzly falling upon him.

But there was nothing.

Then, farther up the tree, he heard an angry chattering. Bewildered, he looked up through the interwoven branches to see a red squirrel on a limb, scolding him excitedly. It had been transformed by the magic of a boy's imagination into a bear's paw.

The front of José's pants felt warm, and he looked down. They were wet. He didn't want to laugh, but he did, hysterically. He laid his head back in the damp duff and let his laughter take him until finally he lay sobbing, his forearm shielding his eyes from this hated forest.

The frightened squirrel had moved far up the tree by now—luckily for it. José would have shot it if he could, for the scare it had given him. But then he guessed the feeling would be mutual, if squirrels reasoned that way. The little rodent's heart probably beat right then at twice its normal rate after the sudden shot that had thundered through the woods.

If only José knew how to track an animal! And more importantly to shoot better! The bear might have already been dead then. But José wasn't a mountain man. Maybe he never could be. What was he doing out here?

José sat up and wiped his tears with his shirt sleeve, streaking his face. He reached up and roughed the back of his hair, shaking fir needles loose. Some of them fell down the back of his shirt, but he didn't care. He began to push to his feet with the butt end of the rifle against the ground.

A mighty roar shook the trees to their roots. José's heart skyrocketed as he whirled to his left and fell again. He glimpsed the mighty mass of bone, muscle, and fur that towered over him. He saw the yellow teeth bared and the amber claws set to destroy him.

And then the beast fell upon him, nearly half a ton of frenzied hate, before José could rise or defend himself. He lifted his arm to protect his face and felt a tremendous force upon it. He screamed and opened his eyes. The scream was enough to startle the bear into letting go of his forearm. But now the huge, black mouth came at his head. He smelled the most horrible stink of his life, a stench of warm, rotting flesh that must rise from the depths of the bear's innards.

José reacted instinctively, bringing up his right fist to smash the bear in the end of its nose with all the might he could muster. It was like striking a peeled green squash—moist but unyielding. Yet the huge beast fell back, not from the force, but in pain, and gave a horrible roar.

José rolled away and struck a tree trunk. Frantic, he clawed against the furrowed gray bark, fighting to his feet. He turned to run but felt a blow to his right side. Its force sent him hurdling through the air like the sheep he had seen earlier. A fallen log, one end suspended about three feet off the ground against another trunk, caught his fall, ripping the air from his lungs, and he felt something give way in his side. He fell across the log and tumbled over the other side, landing on his back.

With desperation, he pushed to his knees, gasping for air through burning lungs. He looked across the trunk into the pig eyes of the grizzly, eight feet away. It roared again, canting its head to one side, and José saw with a falling of his heart the rifle lying in the duff at the bear's feet. He also glimpsed the front of the bear's chest and neck, matted darkly and glistening with blood.

His eyes shot this way and that, searching for some weapon. There were no rocks, but a gray branch about four feet long and three inches around jutted from the tree trunk. He glanced back up at the bear. It stared at him and swept its great claws across the ground before it, sending pine needles and bits of mud flying. Then, with another deep-throated growl, it struck the rifle, launching it through the air to land ten feet down the log from José, on the opposite side.

Suddenly, the bear clamped its jaws and charged. As it did, José grasped the dead branch in both hands, in spite of the horrible pain in his left forearm, and threw all his weight against it. The wood cracked and gave way, and he fell forward against the log. Before he could recover, the bear threw itself on him, its right paw across his back, its left front leg burying his head, its teeth seeking a hold in his side.

Thanks to the bear's awkward position, José was able to wrench free, and he felt the flesh rip away across the small of his back. He cried out in pain and lost his hold on the club. As the bear came up on its back feet to dive over the log, José dropped to his side and rolled. The bear arrived on the other side of the log as José rolled from underneath it. No time to rise! Like in some twisted nightmare, he crawled toward where the rifle had landed. When he placed his weight on his left hand, he heard a strange crackling noise, then pain exploded through him and he almost fell. He glanced down at the awkward slant of his forearm. Then, to the side, he heard a roar and the scraping of bark. The bear coming back over the log! He felt the shaking of the earth as the beast's weight slammed the log against it.

Three feet from the rifle José lunged. With the rifle barrel now in grasping range, he felt both huge paws close on his hips. The bear tried to get its mouth over his back, and its teeth skimmed his shirt but didn't sink in. It ripped back with both paws, and he felt tremendous pain along his hips. With a cry, he fell forward and down. It was just enough to loosen the bear's hold and enough so his fingers touched the cold, precious steel of the rifle barrel.

He tried to clutch the barrel with both hands, but the left one wouldn't close. He felt a crushing weight on the small of his back, and claws sank into his skin. He couldn't roll over to face the grizzly. All breath rushed from him, and he felt hot blood flood into his face. Complete desperation surged through him. He couldn't breathe! He couldn't move!

Everything became still. It seemed his senses had stopped working. He heard only a loud, persistent ringing, as if someone had fired a cannon next to his head. Even the growls of the bear seemed a faraway, imaginary thing in an unreal world.

Suddenly, he felt warm wetness on the top of his head, then warm breath, and even though he faced the other way the fetid odor rushed over him. He dropped his head just as the teeth clashed behind him, and then, more by reflex than by thought, he brought his head sharply back up.

The force of his skull smashing into the bear's nose made it rear back. José rolled onto his back with the rifle in his right hand. He brought it high and struck the bear, and the already weak stock broke over the top of its skull. The bear roared, spraying José's face with hot spittle.

Seeing his last chance, José shoved backward, attempting to get under the log back to the other side. But on this end the log bellied nearer the ground, and at the moment when he thought he had bought brief salvation, he wedged beneath it. His head and arm were on the opposite side with the rifle, his chest tight against the wood, his lower body entirely exposed to the bear's fury.

With one dying hope, José opened the lever of the Winchester then slammed it shut. He screamed as he felt the bear's teeth sink in below his left knee with a crackling sound. With a groan, he stuck the barrel of the rifle back under the log and pulled the trigger. The bear released his leg and let out a roar. Its claws clutched, ripping him from under the log, pulling him toward it again.

As he cleared the log, he jacked in another round, and when the bear's face came at his, he stuck the end of the Winchester into its chest and fired again. The bear drove forward against the rifle barrel and nearly rammed its splintered stock through José's wounded side, tearing an agonized scream from his throat. José felt and smelled the warm, putrid breath flood over him, and he knew his fight was over. He had no more to give, and with a whimper he gave himself over to the beast.

The huge, warm muzzle touched José's mouth, its foulness turning his stomach. He felt the claws of both feet dig into him at either side of his neck. And then he felt the massive slump of the bear on top of him, and the breath rushed from him again.

The bear emitted another growl, but the power had gone from the mighty voice. The next one was even softer. José blinked his eyes open just as the bear's head slammed against his face, its mouth dripping blood and saliva. In horror, he pushed with his good hand against the side of the great head, and it lolled to the other side, the tongue dropping out. Its red pig eyes were open, and like in a dream José watched them lose their sight. Slowly the pupils dilated, and when very large, almost hiding the irises, their growth ceased. The bear drew in one more deep breath, as if settling down to sleep, and then a final sigh seeped from its bloody nostrils, and it was dead. Its muscles quivered for a time, and the side of its mouth twitched as if trying to open.

The two giant paws rested on José's shoulders, their pads like sandpaper where his shirt had been torn away. Its entire weight rested on him, and he could feel the tremendous body heat and the hot, sticky blood that oozed onto him from its chest. The bear smelled of the musky odor José had scented earlier—the smell of carrion, dust, tree sap, urine, and raw animal scent like weeks-old sweat, all churned together.

José was smart enough to know he was hurt badly, but just how badly he had no idea. He realized he must get out from under this weight, just so he could breathe freely. But how? He looked about him, but from this position he could see little. On one side, the underpart of the log and a few bushes beyond; on the other, the massive head. Turning back to the log, he reached his right arm underneath it and pulled. He felt himself budge. He tried to move his left arm, but it was unwilling. He laid down his head, sucking air. Fortunately, he had fallen in moist earth and vegetation, which gave a little beneath him. The claustrophobic terror which gripped him began slowly to give way to a dull shock and pain in his entire body.

José forced himself to stay alert, and for the next twenty minutes he squirmed and fought and prayed. The loose vegetation beneath gave him an edge, and at last he lay with his chest and abdomen free and breathed in the sweet smells of the forest. Squirrels chattered through the woods now, he noted with a weak smile. And a warbler twittered overhead. Flies began to swarm around him and the bear, buzzing annoyingly. He swatted at them a time or two, but the attempt to chase them off was futile, so he gave up. He lay there and breathed and wondered what he would do next.

He had already tried again to move his left arm, once he freed it of the bear's weight. It was broken. And he knew the rest of him was a mess, too. He had to get to the creek to wash himself, then somehow bandage his wounds.

After ten minutes' rest, José started to pull his legs free from beneath the bear. That should have been the easy part, but blood loss and the struggle had sapped his strength, and it took him half an hour to finally wrench himself free. When he tried to move his left leg, the *only* time he tried, the pain was almost unbearable, and he grew dizzy. He could hear the soft crackling of bone ends as he tried to ease it back in place. It was obviously broken, and he recalled feeling almost relieved as he pulled it past the bear's ribcage. Perhaps his own struggle from under the bear's awesome weight had set it for him.

With all his might and tears streaking his face, José pushed his injuries from his mind and reached out to grasp the base of a chokecherry. He would get to Bailey Creek if he had to drag himself all the way.

What seemed hours later, he opened his eyes and looked through the trees at the western sky. Sunset was near, and the air in the woods was cold on his half-naked body. His broken arm and leg throbbed. He was weak from loss of blood. He had moved one hundred yards from the fallen grizzly in the past half hour. Five hundred yards remained down to the creek. He wouldn't make it, and he knew it, and with a ragged sigh he sank into unconsciousness, his face resting in the mountain soil.

Chapter Three

The horse was a winner—lean and long muscled, with a coat the color of morning sunshine and a flowing white mane and tail. Small ears and muzzle, big eyes, deep chest, short back, muscular legs and solid feet, the animal embodied perfection. That horse was not up for sale, but Robert McAllister had to have it. So he stole it.

McAllister was a gaunt-looking man—a man whose sun-bronzed skin stretched drum-tight across wide, sharp cheekbones, a large-muscled jaw and cleft chin. Though not ugly, neither was he handsome. His eyes were too stormy, his brows too heavy and ragged, his skin too ruddy and wind-blown. His face and piercing eyes resembled a wall of sandstone, with two voids where patches of overcast sky showed through. And no softer were the bristly mustache and the dust-colored whiskers peppering his jaw. Scars marked his face and long, callused hands, and his nose was crooked—the features of a fighter.

At two o'clock in the afternoon, the ranch yard twenty miles northeast of Soda Springs was quiet. Robert McAllister lay in silence in the grass and sagebrush a hundred yards away and watched the house. Drapes were drawn against the spring sun, and nothing moved. In the corral behind the barn, the big yellow horse stood dozing, head drooped. Now and then it whipped a fly with its tail or flicked an ear. Otherwise, it made no move.

Patiently, McAllister waited. He had learned patience from the Shoshones, lying for hours in sun or biting cold, unmoving. He watched the horse, admiring the smooth, powerful flow of its muscles, the way the sun shone off its coat, the curves of its intelligent head.

He had been relieved of his own horse by thieves, three days ago in the freighting town of Blackfoot. Afoot, he had trudged along the lonely trail between Blackfoot and Soda Springs. Then along came the rider on the big yellow horse, a gentleman, by his mode of dress, with silvery gray hair and neatly trimmed muttonchop whiskers. He wore a striped gray wool suit and side-buttoned shoes with a deep shine only thinly obscured by a film of dust. A flat-brimmed gray hat of finest beaver felt perched atop his head, and a brand-new Winchester Sporting rifle with checkered pistol grip and forearm rested across his thigh.

McAllister wasn't a man who bowed to the so-called upper class. Facts be known, he detested them—them and what their greed was making of his beloved wild country.

Bringing in their towns and railroads. Killing off the game, wiping out millions of acres of forest. He avoided those with means, but in this case he made an exception. When the man spoke, he hid his disdain and replied as politely as he knew how, hoping for a longer look at the palomino horse. He had to admit the fellow certainly had taste in horses, and he was proud of that fact.

The horseman, who introduced himself as J.B. Trace, stopped beside McAllister and lifted off his hat, wiping his sweaty forehead with a red silk handkerchief and letting his dust sift down over McAllister's already powdery clothes. He replaced the hat and spoke with McAllister, mostly of the horse.

McAllister looked the animal over while he rested beside the road. It was a Kentucky horse, Trace said, descended from a bloodline well known for endurance and speed. McAllister commented and asked questions and politely nodded his head. He was like the big tomcat, glancing now and then at the little girl's pet canary, its stomach growling, its cunning mind planning its next move behind a mask of indifference.

When Trace at last bade him farewell and trotted along the road, McAllister had already made his decision. He wanted this horse. It was not so much anything Trace had said, but more the judgments he had made on his own. And if Robert McAllister wanted a horse, he got it—one way or the other. So with his saddlebags and rucksack slapping against his leg, and a Sharps carbine in his left hand, he started at a ground-eating lope after the rider.

McAllister's legs and his insides knew the meaning of endurance—knew how it was to run for hours on end, non-stop, tracking quarry or outdistancing pursuit. The weight of his rifle, the bags, even the rucksack was nothing to McAllister, who lived and hunted every day in the wild lands. He wore moccasins with thick rawhide soles, perfect for running, and his legs, like pistons, moved effortlessly.

It was only three miles from where J.B. Trace left McAllister until he reached the man's spread. McAllister stayed out of sight, following by track alone. When at last the pointed roof silhouettes of the ranch came in sight, he went forward at a crouch, hiding in the sagebrush where he could see both the house and the corrals. His keen eyes instantly picked out the yellow horse, unsaddled in a corral beside a barn, eating contentedly from a pile of hay.

McAllister lay low in the sagebrush to watch for activity. He wanted to get an idea who lived in the house. If he had to, he would spend part of the night here on the ground, using his back for a mattress and his belly for a blanket. That would give the horse a chance to rest, and he could ride him away under cover of darkness, without fear of being seen.

But an hour later his plans were changed by Trace. The front door of the house creaked open, and Trace stepped into the sunlight. He scanned the yard, then patted his belly and stepped off the porch, walking toward the barn. McAllister tensed. Would he saddle the yellow horse and leave again? He held his breath. He couldn't wait here forever. If Trace rode away, who could tell when he would be back? McAllister would just have to leave on shank's mare—his own two feet.

Trace went inside the barn, and after what seemed an eternity he came back out leading a saddled bay. McAllister's breath caught. Was Trace really going to ride out without the palomino? The luck seemed too kind.

But sure enough, Trace climbed onto the bay, and saying something to the yellow horse as he passed, he rode out of the yard toward the eastern mountains. McAllister just lay there, pressed to earth, the new grass pricking him softly in the throat. This was too perfect to be true.

Still, his caution made him wait another twenty minutes, peering closely at the house. When nothing moved, he crawled forward, dragging himself by his elbows, pulling his scant belongings with him. He went slowly, peering from the house to the corral. Twenty feet from the horse, it finally noticed him and whinnied, trotting to the corral bars for a better look. McAllister crept behind a pile of logs and waited, watching the house through a hole between the logs. When no one moved after ten minutes, he continued to the corral.

He spoke to the horse in a soothing voice. He reached a hand out for its inspection, and it sniffed cautiously, then touched it exploringly with its lip. At last, it allowed McAllister to raise his hand and scratch the bridge of its nose and its forehead and big round jaw.

With that introduction, McAllister climbed between the rails and stood before the horse, talking softly all the while. The horse seemed to have no fear. It nuzzled his chest as if looking for a treat and allowed him to rub its neck and chest.

In the barn, he found a saddle and bridle and two heavy wool blankets. He hefted them and carried them outside, resting them over the top pole of the corral. The horse offered no fight when he put the bridle on. It took the bit like it was sweetened with sugar. The same went for the blankets and saddle. He tied his rucksack and the saddlebags behind the cantle, slid his Sharps carbine into the boot.

At last, McAllister stood in the shadow of the barn's eaves and studied the house, the yard, the grassy land. Nothing moved except the ever-present meadowlarks whistling cheerily from sagebrush perches.

Turning to the horse, McAllister took its reins close to the bit and slid the corral bars to one side, allowing a place just wide enough for them to slip through. He led the horse on out and went slowly away from the yard, watching for the rancher.

He led the horse for half an hour before mounting, not wanting to make his silhouette any taller than necessary. When far away from the ranch, he turned to the horse and again spoke softly. He patted its powerful shoulder and caressed its flank, and then he placed his foot in the stirrup, letting it feel his weight. The horse stood perfectly still, twitching its ears.

McAllister was pretty sure of this horse by now, but a man didn't take chances on a strange horse. To prevent the horse from being able to buck or run before he was settled solidly in the saddle, he cheeked it, taking the cheek band of the bridle in his left hand and turning its nose toward him. This had the added advantage, in case the horse did try to move forward, of making it come nearer to its rider, its momentum almost swinging him into the saddle.

In this case McAllister swung aboard with no fight. To the horse, he was just as much its master as the true owner. With a smile, he touched his heels lightly to its ribs, and they moved out at a long walk.

Sitting on the horse's back was like riding a dream. It moved smoothly, cradling him far above the grassy ground. Its ears pricked alertly forward, then swung to the side alternately, keeping it constantly aware of its surroundings. Its long, powerful muscles rippled as it moved, the sun running along them like melted butter.

A shadow swung across the ground before them, and McAllister raised his eyes to search the sky. A large, dark bird soared overhead on wide, graceful wings. It was close enough to see golden light play off its head as it turned and caught the sun's rays.

A golden eagle.

McAllister felt his heart catch in his chest. What a beautiful work of art the Creator had placed in that sky! A raptor with dark eyes that could see a rabbit on the run a mile away. A bird with long, gleaming talons that spoke death to any poor creature it set its predator's eyes upon—talons that could snap a man's forearm like a twig.

Light played on the bird's head as McAllister watched it. It tipped its tail and swung to the left, turning its head this way and that to watch the ground below. It swung back to the right again, straight over him.

McAllister sighed, and a feeling of warmth stole into his heart. Oh, to be that eagle! To soar free in the heavens, unbound by any limits of earth or sky. To brace the sun and high, buffeting winds undaunted, to float effortlessly, to know and see all.

He imagined himself as that eagle, doing as he pleased, in fear of no man, no beast. Challenging the updrafts of Hell's Canyon of the Snake River or the daunting winds of the high plains. Swooping down at breakneck speeds only to catch himself and rise again effortlessly. That was the way to go. The eagle knew the meaning of freedom. It was free from the fetters of the world, making its own way. It was not banned from Earth, however. It could come back as it pleased, then sail away once more into its dreams—and McAllister's...

As he gazed, another one appeared from the north—the first one's mate. It never ventured too close, but its slow circles paralleled the first one's. Why couldn't people be that way? Why couldn't a man and woman pair up but still enjoy their freedom? The male eagle wasn't tied down. He soared as he always had. But McAllister had seen men who were fool enough to marry, and happy as some of them might pretend to be, it was plain who ruled *their* roost. McAllister chuckled to himself, causing the horse to turn its head curiously and look at him from the corner of its eye. He patted its neck. At least he and the eagles and this horse were free, and being on top of the palomino was the next best thing to flying on wings of his own.

The Creator had found McAllister the wrong body when he put him on this earth. Of that he was sure.

As he watched, the two birds, on some silent signal, began to flap their wings, and within minutes they melted into the blue expanse. McAllister rode on.

Not far ahead lay the town of Soda Springs, once a stopover for travelers on the Oregon Trail. McAllister had spent plenty of time in the surrounding mountains. Long ago, he had been stationed there as a trooper at Fort Connor. It had been years, but he had heard it was now a peaceable valley. Unlike the last warriors, the Apaches down south, the Shoshone and Bannock had stopped fighting. Those red eagles had been killed or caged.

Yet Soda Springs was no longer simply a stopping place on the Oregon Trail, tucked insignificantly away in its little corner of the world. Now it was a tourist destination, where travelers came from all over the globe to enjoy its summer climate and effervescent springs. No longer his kind of place. It didn't matter anyway. With this horse, he couldn't stay. Too many people would recognize a horse of that caliber, and he would be a wanted man. He must head for Wyoming Territory, where he might find safety.

The flat report of a rifle racketed across the prairie, and McAllister spun in the saddle. Behind him, not more than three hundred yards away, came five horsemen on the run, rifles in their hands. McAllister's heart leaped in his chest. But a grin lightened his whiskered face, revealing a missing eye tooth. Those horses couldn't catch him. He was a horseman in the truest sense. Not only a proven rider but an excellent judge of *le cheval*. He had carefully chosen the Kentucky mount beneath him and felt certain it could have no rival in the valley. Had he been a gambling man, he'd have put his money on this horse.

McAllister slammed his heels into the horse's ribs, and it broke into a gallop. The big horse was rested and ready to show off. Even with him holding back a touch on the reins, it quickly left pursuit far behind. McAllister didn't need to look back, but he did, and the riders lagged five hundred yards behind. He grinned and let out a whoop.

Across the valley they charged until they had gone two miles. Then McAllister began to pull the horse in, pacing it. Had it been up to the horse, it might have run all afternoon, to the point of collapse. But a slower lope was called for now, a pace that would eat miles and leave the mediocre horses and their riders only a memory. There were few animals in that country like the Kentucky mount; there was little need for serious race runners in a community that consisted largely of farmers and ranchers. But McAllister had need for one.

On bore the afternoon, and the sun slipped toward the far horizon. The next time he looked back, the horsemen were gone, so he slowed the palomino to a gentle trot. He came to a narrow wagon road with a farm nestled beside it, hogs rooting and chickens scratching in the yard. The smell of new bread taunted him—a homey smell, comforting in an odd sort of way, though McAllister had no memories of home that were comforting.

The farm fell behind as he rode off into the sagebrush, leaving the road. He kept to the edge of the foothills, where junipers and an occasional fir thrust up like sentinels. They went at an easy trot toward the ridges of the Bear River Mountains, visible beyond the sagebrush- and juniper-covered hills on his right.

Soon they passed a small horse ranch with seven or eight animals grazing nearby.

McAllister looked at them thoughtfully. When his pursuers reached this place, they might trade horses. And even though his was by far the better animal, it had already traveled a long road and might be overtaken by fresh stock. "Well, boy. Guess we better take 'em with us," he said to the horse, and he turned it toward the herd.

But as he did, two horsemen appeared from behind the ranch house, walking their animals slowly toward the herd. They were three hundred yards away, but both looked his way and waved a greeting. McAllister waved back. The two riders came toward him at a trot, and for a moment McAllister held his ground. He didn't want to seem rude by ignoring range manners and not greeting the men. They would surely think that suspicious, in an era when few strangers might be encountered in a day. An unhurried traveler would stop to chew the fat and exchange lies. Yet he didn't want them to recognize this horse or hold him back long enough with aimless talk for the other riders to catch up. He looked back in the direction from which he had come. There was no movement, but he couldn't take any chances. With a shrug, he continued on at a canter. When he looked back later the two men were riding back toward the horse herd.

He traveled perhaps another two miles. A large round ridge squatted above the sage ahead of him, and beyond it lifted a cloud of dust. Soon, the buildings of Soda Springs began to appear in the distance, their roofs reflecting the descending sun. Where the cloud of dust rose, he made out the herd of cattle creating it, moving through the outskirts of town.

Soon, he came to a spring bubbling from the earth. Still in sight of several scattered houses, a mile away on the outskirts of town, he stopped the horse and climbed down to fill his canteen and sip of the water. It tasted of soda, like others from which he had drunk in that area. He remembered two of them: Steamboat Springs, named for the peculiar sound it made like a high-powered steam engine, and Beer Springs, which some claimed tasted like flat lager beer. He didn't care for the taste himself, but it sort of set the mouth watering, and he was hungry as a vulture in the Garden of Eden anyway.

He rustled up a hunk of jerked venison from deep in a saddlebag and gnawed off a bite. Tasteless and old—and dusty now, after being lost in the dark of his gear for untold days. As he gnawed on the jerky and let the horse rest, he scanned the road for movement. Soda Springs, touted as a resort in national and international magazines and journals, would be coming into its popular season. He must be on the lookout for tourists venturing out to this spring. He had no desire for anyone who might identify him later to see him on the stolen horse.

But he saw no travelers, leisurely or otherwise. The only movement discernible was the varicolored form of a hawk that soared high above the sage on seemingly unmoving wings. With the water tasting as it did, McAllister emptied his canteen, and he mounted the horse again and rode on. There was plenty of sweet water in the mountains ahead without settling for something that tasted like it should have been draining into a privy.

Warily, he searched for a way to skirt the town. Civilization at this point meant only trouble, for this horse would be recognized. It looked like he could avoid the main part of town by leaving Soda Creek, the stream he was following, and veering sharply to the east. That would put him on a fairly straight path toward the town of Montpelier, then on to Wyoming or the Utah line.

He didn't know why he turned around. Maybe it was that sixth sense developed in him from years riding the wild country. But turn he did, just in time to see a group of riders closing on him rapidly. One of the horses, a paint, stood out glaringly in the group. It was one of those he had seen grazing near the ranch house. So his pursuers were on fresh mounts. And the two cowboys must have joined them, for now there were seven instead of five.

With an oath, he whirled in the saddle and kicked the horse into a gallop. The animal was still game, and it charged along the stream bank, straight toward Soda Springs. The race was not so one-sided now, for McAllister's horse had put many miles behind and the others were fresh. He turned to look back, and although the distance had initially stretched out between him and the posse, it appeared the palomino had reached the limit of its speed, and the other horses were staying with him now.

The town's first scattered shacks were only half a mile away. He couldn't see any way around the edge of town and back toward the mountains without a significant detour, so he kept the horse pointed toward town.

The horse breathed loudly now. Its eyes were wide and its ears flat against its head, as if held there by the wind whipping at their faces. He had thought it before and now he yelled it out, by way of encouragement to the horse. "You shore got bottom, you son of a rattlesnake. Get me outta this, an' you'll have a week's rest an' a mountain o' clover comin'!"

He turned in the saddle. He knew now if he didn't reach the river and the mountains soon he could lose this race. The riders were less than half a mile behind.

He flew past the first house, whose startled occupant stood up from her garden work to gaze as he passed. The shacks and cabins became more regular, and up ahead he saw a girl playing in front of one. He thought about stopping and snatching up that girl as a hostage. He wouldn't hurt her, just use her until he reached safety and then let her go. But he swore at himself reproachfully and stared at the tow-headed child as he galloped past. He was ashamed that thought had entered his head. He had never hurt a child, physically *or* emotionally, and he wasn't about to start now. Some places a man just had to draw the line.

There was no way to avoid the main part of town now. McAllister saw that with a sinking heart. As Soda Creek veered off, he kept going, right into Dillon Street, the town's main thoroughfare. Gritting his teeth in anticipation of a run-in with a horse or wagon, he yelled as loudly as he could as a warning but didn't check his speed. He couldn't afford to. Fortunately, the street was almost empty. He galloped along it at full speed, now and then veering to miss a wagon or a tied-up horse. And then he was out of the bowels of Dillon Street, and the buildings of Upper Town swiftly began to fall behind him. Those of the lower town were far off to the right, and ahead sagged the remains of old Fort Connor, most of its logs stripped away for cabin walls, firewood, or fences.

He rode like the wind, pushing the big palomino for all its worth. Somewhere ahead lay the Bear River. He hadn't remembered it being so far, but time plays tricks on the memory. He didn't remember the foothills looking so damn desolate, either. Few trees to hide in, just bare sagebrush hills with isolated hillsides and draws full of brush and aspen. Even the closer mountains were bare. That would be the work of the cussed railroad, logging for ties. They were infamous for stripping the country. But he was Robert McAllister. Trees or none, he would find a way to lose the posse.

The horse's sides heaved mightily now, its breaths sucking in and out in great, ragged gasps. It stumbled once, seemingly on nothing, but caught itself. It ran right through a stand of tall sage. Its legs and neck sawed back and forth with its movements like a machine, but less smoothly than before—a machine running out of steam.

Then ahead McAllister saw the tips of trees that marked the river. Two hundred more yards. If he could make it across, then up through the desolate foothills to the far timber the railroad hadn't been able to reach, he would be free. Not a white man alive could catch Robert McAllister in that terrain. The Shoshones had taught him how to vanish like a wisp of smoke.

Although the big horse's breaths came in gasps, it didn't seem horribly weakened yet. The animal had the staying power of a wolf, the best of its many virtues at the moment. He just hoped they made the river. That was his only chance. He still had enough of a lead on the posse that if he could make the river he might escape with not only his life but the prized horse besides.

The sage flats dropped out from under foot abruptly as they neared the river, and the horse stumbled and barely caught itself. Glancing off to the right, McAllister grimaced at the black basalt outcrop, only yards away, that fell off sharp to the river. If they had come out there, they would never have made it. They would both have broken their necks and more in the fall to the river's shore.

Where they did come down, it was steep, but not bad in comparison, and it lacked the rocks. Leaning backward, the horse steered down the hillside, dodging left and right to miss the big clumps of sagebrush in their path. McAllister bore down on the stirrups and held on, staring at the river. It was at its mightiest with spring run-off—sixty yards wide at this point, maybe four or five feet deep and running swiftly.

He gazed downriver, searching for some place to make a getaway, some way to throw the posse off. A quarter mile distant the river bent north after a tall, rocky bank shouldered into the stream. If he could make it to the other side of that bend, he would be out of the posse's sight momentarily. He might elude them then, use his trickery to slip up some unlikely looking draw.

But first he had to make it across the river while he still had time. Ahead of him was an island, twenty feet into the river. Willows too thick to negotiate wove together its entire length, and he steered the horse toward it. If he could get on the other side of the trees, they would offer him some protection from the posse's rifle fire as he tried to swim the river.

With a startling gush of ice cold water, they plunged into the river, sending spray in every direction, soaking McAllister up past his knees. After the initial plunge and upsurge of water, McAllister saw the river wasn't deep here, for the horse was able to stay on its feet, and it lunged across the water to the island. As they reached it, McAllister spun to check for the posse, and they still were nowhere in sight. He had made it! In seconds the mass of willows would cover his escape, and the other bank looked very near him now.

But he didn't see the other horse. There was no way to avoid the collision.

He was concentrating on the far bank of the river and what lay in-between. He was worried about the depth of the river, and how the palomino would take it in its weary state. The horse was crashing through the willows on the point of the island, the only crossable place along the entire forty yards of overgrown land, and it was doing fine. He had no reason to look at the willows. But suddenly, as if out of nowhere, a brown horse appeared, coming out of the thick willows to their right like it hadn't a care in the world. It stopped before him, too startled to move even if there had been time.

McAllister had just a split second to see a young girl of perhaps fifteen on the horse's back, her eyes wide and mouth opened as if to scream.

Chapter Four

The horses came together like two steaming freight trains.

With a grunt of surprise, the palomino slammed the brown one in the left shoulder, sending it stumbling sideways. McAllister knew he would go down, so he kicked his feet free of the stirrups. But there was no time to prepare for falling to his advantage. He flew over the top of his horse and struck the other one square in the head, and together the four of them splashed into the fast-moving current.

Though dazed from the impact and shocked by the cold, McAllister sputtered out of the river, and next came the girl's horse, visibly shaken. They stood in only two feet of water at the edge of the island, but the girl was no longer in sight. While the yellow horse struggled against the current to rise, McAllister leaped to its side and jerked out the Sharps carbine, then pushed himself away from the saddle to avoid being stepped on in its struggles.

Something crunched through the willows to his right, and he whirled, raising his rifle hip-high as he thumbed back the hammer. Another horse stood there snorting, wild-eyed, a young boy on its back. With eyes as wide as double eagles the boy stared wordlessly at McAllister.

With a surge of hope, McAllister splashed through the water the several yards to the boy's horse and grabbed its reins just as it began to rear back. He came around the horse and yelled harshly. "Get off! Get off the horse now, boy!"

When the boy only sat dumbfounded, McAllister reached up and took hold of his arm, jerking him from the animal and flinging him into foot-deep water at the edge of the willows. McAllister threw himself onto the bare back of the horse, a red roan, and whirled to look in the direction of the posse. They still hadn't appeared over the edge of the bluff, but he knew within a minute they would be upon him.

Whipping the horse around, he kicked it in the ribs. It slipped on cobblestones beneath the water and almost fell, but managed to keep its footing, and they plunged into deeper water. At the back of his thoughts, he caught the boy's frenzied voice from the island. "Help! Help her! My sister! Mister, please help her!"

Against his better judgment, McAllister yanked back on the reins and steered the horse to the right, turning his head to look back. He followed the boy's extended finger with his eyes to a form that floated down the stream away from him, now about ten yards away. It was the girl. Apparently she'd been knocked unconscious, but there was nothing he could do that the posse behind him couldn't. In fact, it might be just the break he needed. He could make his escape while they were busy saving the girl, assuming she wasn't already dead. "Sorry, boy!" he yelled. "I got my own bacon to save." And he reined the horse back toward the far bank.

But then his heart sank. Escape was so near he could feel his freedom open out before him like the gates of Heaven. But he couldn't let that helpless girl go. The water was swift here, and if he didn't grab her while he could, she might sink and never be found.

Cursing his stupidity, he whirled the horse and started downstream after the girl.

Even with spring run-off, the river wasn't over four feet deep. The roan seemed to be used to moving in deep water, and it swam in great lunges, closing quickly on the girl. Just as they reached her, her arm came up out of the water, then her face, and she sputtered and tried to scream. She started to go under the current, but McAllister reached out and grabbed her by the arm, pulling her to him and losing hold of his carbine in the process.

The water grew swifter now, so he let it carry them as he held onto the girl, her head just out of the water. Then he hoisted her almost effortlessly from the muddy river onto the bony crest of the horse's shoulder, and they turned toward the far bank.

The girl began to cough violently, and he held her loosely around the middle and let her. She spat up half a cup of water, then began to cry. The frightened sound nearly wrenched McAllister's heart from his chest. He could hardly stand to see a young one suffer.

As the water slowed, the horse regained sure footing, and then it was out of the water and stumbling onto the bank, splattering mud with its hooves. Once on dry ground, McAllister wheeled the horse around. He looked back upriver, and, as he had feared, the posse was just reining in around the shaken boy.

One man raised a rifle abruptly and fired, and McAllister heard the bullet slap into and whine away from a rock at the river's edge. Then a second man—McAllister recognized J.B. Trace—reached out and knocked the rifle out of the first one's hands. A heated argument ensued, in which McAllister surmised this young woman was the main concern. She was probably the only reason the rest of the posse didn't open a barrage on him now.

Whipping the horse about, he galloped downriver a ways through the brush, then wheeled again. The posse was three hundred yards away, as yet still undecided about crossing the river. No one else had tried to fire at him, and he expected they wouldn't. Most men with any gun savvy wouldn't attempt a shot at that range without a decent rest, especially with the girl there. J.B. Trace stood on the ground, checking over the yellow horse.

"Get down, girl," McAllister said suddenly. "Don't want you to get hurt." With his hands on her waist, he started to lift her up, but she closed her strong little hands over his and turned her head and torso around, her striking green eyes gazing up at him. Their glances held for a long moment in which he feared his rough-hewn face would be indelibly printed in the girl's brain. And for the first time he saw what a truly beautiful young creature she was. Even with her chestnut bangs plastered to her head and her green eyes bloodshot from the muddy water and from crying, she was a sight to behold. Robert McAllister was a rock-hard man of firmly guarded emotions, but he knew he would never forget the beautiful, fragile young face of the girl whose life he had saved.

"Thank you, sir," the girl said softly. "Thank you for helping me. I won't forget it." Finding no appropriate response, McAllister just nodded and lifted her from the saddle, letting her slide to the ground along the side of the horse. She turned and walked slowly toward the posse. She had gone only twenty yards when the first of the posse's horses entered the river.

For a moment, McAllister watched the horses slip into the stream beyond the willow island, and he thought how exceedingly easy it would be for a man of his marksmanship to kill three or more of them as they started across the main part of the river. But he was not a killer, especially of dumb, innocent horses, and besides, his carbine lay somewhere at the bottom of the river. With a jerk of the reins, he spun the roan about, his feet dangling free along its sides, and kicked it into a hard gallop toward the bend in the river.

It didn't take long to realize he couldn't go far and fast enough on the boy's horse to get out of sight of the posse while still on the bank of the river. So the first side draw he came to that was overgrown with aspen and brush, he turned the animal up it.

Soon, he moved into a pure grove of aspen, the new green leaves shimmering in the afternoon light, glowing translucently. Not far behind him, the posse would have made it across the river. He looked down on the shabby, bare-backed excuse of a horse beneath him. Its backbone protruded like a dull knife edge, and his backside didn't have much meat to protect it. The animal's ears were large, its eyes small, its muzzle big and loose-hanging like that of a bull moose. All in all, it was not much of a horse, not like he needed to help him escape the posse. But he knew one small boy would miss this horse very much.

With a sigh, he patted the roan's neck, then slipped off its side and slapped its rump hard, sending it down through the trees, back toward the river.

He had nothing left to carry, nothing to hinder his speed and progress through the trees. Only his pistol, possibles pouch, belt knife and clothes, consisting of a rough-woven gray cotton shirt, faded brown corduroy coat, and buckskin pants. His carbine was lost, and his rucksack and saddlebags were still on the yellow horse. He thought of that horse wistfully, then started up the hill through the aspens, taking care to leave little sign of his passing.

Figuring the posse would expect him to go south, where timber was nearest, he headed east, crossing into two more brushy draws as he climbed toward the high country by a more unlikely route. The third draw was choked with grass, thick stands of aspen, and long stretches of thickly interwoven mountain laurel, or buckbrush. With a backward glance toward the river, he started up through this jungle.

He heard and smelled the sheep long before he saw them. They exuded a strong, musky odor that hung like a sickness in the air wherever they grazed in any number. As he continued up the hill, he began to see them scattered about in the aspens. They ran away in terror.

Hoofed locusts, as they called them in Nevada, were not courageous. Yet these seemed more frightened than normal. Perhaps they ran half wild here, but that was unlikely in a land full of bears, cougars, coyotes, and wolves. Sheep were next to defenseless, and a flock couldn't survive long on its own. He shrugged and continued up the ridge.

When he saw the end of the trees ahead, he slowed down and peered about carefully. He guessed a herder was probably nearby, unless this flock had wandered off. But it would be stupid to assume that. Mutton punchers were notorious for an eagerness to shoot at predators—or a man foolhardy enough to stumble up through these trees noisily.

A few yards farther on, he spotted the wagon. Its white canvas top shone through the trees. And where there was a camp a meal waited. Any jerky he might have had left was in his saddlebags, so unless whoever owned the wagon was generous, he would go hungry.

"Hello the camp!" he greeted. Silence. "Hello up there!" Only the bleating of sheep and the chirping of sparrows answered him.

Cautiously, he continued up the hill until a shrill neigh stopped him short. He waited, then called out again. In a moment, he heard a thumping noise accompanied by that of a jingling chain, the sound of a hobbled horse on the move. It came around the side of the wagon, a big, stupid looking animal, mahogany bay with a bald face. Again he yelled toward the wagon, and no one answered.

McAllister walked the rest of the way up the ridge, left the aspens behind as he came onto a sage-covered flat, and stole cautiously to the wagon, peering inside. No one. Just some scattered boxes, cans, utensils, and bedding.

A few yards away he saw a fire pit and went to it. Its ashes were cold except for the heat of sunlight absorbed by them. He walked back to the wagon and rummaged around in it as far as he could reach, his hand coming back with a cotton sack stuffed with biscuits. Taking another look around, he ate one of them, ignoring its stale taste.

He left the wagon and walked around it to the horse, which had gone back to grazing peacefully. There was a saddle nearby, but he tried to locate a rifle and had no luck. He walked over to the bald-faced horse. It allowed him to come right to it and raised its head to look curiously at him. He reached out slowly and stroked its neck.

"How old are you, boy? Looks like you seen some territory." He started to pull back its lips to age it by its teeth, and the horse jerked back. "Just a little head-shy, are yuh? Guess I shouldn't look a gift horse in the mouth." He laughed at his own humor. "Well, that's what you are. A gift horse. Unless yer master's layin' somewhere watchin' me through rifle sights. What say we ride, boy? I've a powerful urge to get outta Idaho an' see some o' Wyomin'." The horse looked over at him boredly, and he chuckled. "Don't even care, do yuh?"

Saddling the horse and gathering some food in a sack, he made one last careful search of the surroundings, then started away, wanting to make time before the herder came back.

He rode across the flat away from the wagon, then started down a gentle slope. He hadn't gone far when he drew the horse up short. His eyes, always wary, had picked up the body of a dead sheep at the base of a Douglas fir. Against his better judgment, he rode forward. The sheep lay on its side, a large flap of hide torn back to expose flesh. Large holes pierced its skull, and one eye protruded grotesquely. This was a bear's doing.

McAllister climbed down and studied the ground. It was grassy and brushy. There was nothing to be seen here, to the untrained eye. But McAllister saw things others wouldn't.

The green grass around the dead sheep was mostly erect, except for the blades that had been torn or chewed off short. But last year's growth was broken where weight had been upon it. He began to move around the dead sheep in slow circles, trying to distinguish the path of a large, determined animal from sign of many smaller ones grazing aimlessly.

That was when he saw the blood. There was a splatter of it, dried now but not old, on the tips of a crushed sagebrush. Another tiny drop flaked off a clover leaf under pressure of his thumbnail. A story was coming together here—the answer why the herder had deserted his camp. A bear had attacked, scattering the flock. That explained why the sheep he saw were so skittish. The herder had wounded the bear, judging by this blood. He knew it wasn't sheep's blood—the sage gave that away. Whatever had left it had been taller than that sage, had run over it and knocked it half down, and that was no sheep.

Curiously, he followed the herder and bear down a draw. He could see the man's path, where the grass was broken over in the direction they had gone. And the bear's sign was also distinguishable, for a bear, like most animals, places its toe down first, knocking grass down to point in the direction from which it has come.

The horse was skittish. It had been ever since McAllister neared the dead sheep. He had to keep soothing it with soft-spoken words, tugging it on behind him. He turned to it now. "Sorry, boy. I'm a curious man. Guess that's my downfall. Get on a trail with a story like this, I just don't wanna stop." As he spoke, his eyes intermittently scanned the ground and the landscape ahead. He half expected the herder to come back and run into him. Or the bear.

He walked bent over and could see the trail plainly. The bear had been on the run when it left. It came down hard every jump, and each time it left a splotch of blood. He at last found a spot of soil in the path, unobstructed by vegetation, and here he took one glance at the track. He could have judged by the claws, their tips three inches from the bear's toes, but he didn't need that to know. This was a grizzly bear.

McAllister stood and looked about him long and hard. He drew his revolver and put it on half cock, then opened the loading gate, dropping the five forty-four cartridges out in his hand one by one. He blew through the pistol's chambers and through its barrel, making sure there were no obstructions. Then he reloaded it with the five shells, filled the empty chamber under the hammer with a sixth from his cartridge belt, and dropped it loosely into its holster.

He knew better than to follow this trail. No matter who may have won the battle, it was likely to mean trouble for him at the end. If the bear had triumphed, it was wounded and probably still furious, and the slug of a Colt .44 had better be placed precisely to bring down a wounded grizzly. If the hunter had won, he would come back to discover McAllister with his horse. What was McAllister to say then? "I was just bringing you your horse so you wouldn't have to walk back?" That wouldn't wash. Any man with nerve would probably kill him, or die trying. But he had grown up tracking with his grandfather, then for a time with the Shoshones. Tracking was a love. A fever, in a way. It was in his blood. He had to see what was at the end of this trail. So he continued on.

Besides, he had to admit it wasn't only curiosity that drove him on along this trail. The fact that this bear had been wounded probably meant the herder had a rifle, since most men wouldn't think of shooting a grizzly with a pistol. McAllister needed a rifle. And it wasn't like he was above stealing, even if he had to get the drop on the man with his pistol to get the rifle away. Perhaps he'd have to fight the bear, too, if it had killed the man. But he'd done that before too.

When the trail led into the timber, he tied the horse at its edge and slipped through the veil of brush. The man's path deviated from the bear's, as if he wasn't even aware it had passed there. The man had continued on the easiest way while the bear had crashed into deeper growth.

He moved very quietly, his pistol drawn. What a fool he was! He looked back toward where he had left the horse. He should leave now, before it was too late.

But it already was…

Chapter Five

Glancing ahead, thirty yards away, Robert McAllister spotted a man on his face in the forest undergrowth—a man horribly covered in blood. The man was dead, by the look of him. That left the big question: If the man was dead, where was the bear?

The hair stood up on McAllister's neck, and goose bumps popped up on his skin. He moved toward the man but kept his eyes on the woods. At ten yards, McAllister drew up short and stopped breathing to keep himself perfectly still. Was it his mind playing tricks, or had the man's ribcage expanded with a breath? Three seconds went by, and then the movement came again, very slightly. McAllister looked at the bloody form in disbelief.

Moving ahead once more, he reached the body. The body? A callous way to think of it maybe, but considering the condition it was in it could hardly be called a man. Reaching down, perhaps a little roughly, he took a handful of curly black hair and tilted the head upward.

His heart jumped, and he stared and cursed. Damn, but he had been a thunderous fool to come here! This hunter, whom he had assumed a full grown man but small in stature, was only a boy. And dying or not, he couldn't just leave a boy here alone. He must provide some comfort for what would probably be the lad's last living moments.

McAllister had two priorities. He must keep an eye out for the grizzly, if by chance it was still alive, and he must try to learn the extent of the boy's injuries. With both goals in mind, he placed his pistol close to hand, then began a painstaking examination of the bloody form.

His head, miraculously, was almost untouched. A few minor scratches, some smeared blood from elsewhere. What was left of the boy's shirt he cut away carefully with his bone-handled belt knife, revealing bruises, and gashes opened up by grizzly claws. Much of the blood staining the lad's shirt and the ground had come from these wounds, but the bleeding had mostly subsided now. Flies swarmed the coagulated wounds, lured by the first smell of blood.

When his gentle probing reached the lacerated hips, he grimaced. A good portion of the pants was torn away, and here the flesh hung loosely, sticky and thick with flies. McAllister tried to brush them away, but when they *did* leave they quickly returned. Some of them refused to go at all. Shaking his head with pity, McAllister forced himself to continue down the legs.

Below the left knee, blood soaked the pant leg. McAllister slit it from that point down through the hem and examined the leg closely. There were tooth marks there, swollen and black, and the entire area was an angry scarlet hue. He barely moved the leg, stopping when the boy began to whimper, but already he knew. He had heard the grating of bone ends against each other, and he clenched his teeth and looked away distastefully. The leg was broken.

Last of all, McAllister examined the arms. The right one was fine, the left broken. With care, he turned the boy onto his back and made a quick search of his belly and chest. Though soaked with blood, there was only one wound there, where it appeared the boy might have landed on a jagged branch or something. Numerous coarse brown hairs mixed with the blood and stuck to the boy's chest and face. The bear had been that close—right upon the boy. This massive amount of blood didn't belong to the boy. The belly wound wasn't bad enough to bleed that much. The blood belonged to the bear. Somewhere not far away that bear lay dead.

There was half an hour of daylight left when McAllister stood. He realized he had to make a camp and treat the boy's wounds. Then, if he was still alive in the morning, he could decide what to do with him. And if the posse hadn't caught up by then...

After collecting supplies from the sheep wagon, McAllister cared for the boy's wounds the best he could by firelight, washing them with whisky he found in the wagon and binding them with pieces of sheet. He straightened the broken arm and leg and splinted them with sections of fir bark, lashing them snugly in place.

With a sigh, the man sank back on his heels. He had done all he could now. The rest was up to the boy. Easing him onto his back again, he covered him with the two blankets and stood up. Back in the woods a great-horned owl hooted its eery *hoooo-hoo-hoo, hoo-hoo.* Its night hunt would soon commence. In the sky there was no moon, and a multitude of stars flickered, dangling very near the earth.

Curiosity had always been a weak point for McAllister. He looked at the boy, whose face sparkled with sweat and whose inner body works now fought a raging battle. The fire crackled softly, tamed by the cool night air. The horse moved quietly in the bouncing shadows, concerned only with a night's meal. And McAllister's mind churned with the need to see the grizzly, to know beyond any doubt it was dead, that it wouldn't come again in the night.

Going to the lantern, he picked it and his Colt up, and with one in each hand he started along the boy's back trail. It was easy to follow the path he had torn in his struggle to get out of the woods.

He hadn't gone far, though for the boy it must have seemed miles, when with a start he drew up short. There in the grass, its little eyes dully reflecting the lantern's glow, lay the grizzly, its breath forever stilled. Even lifeless, just a shell, its awesome power shook the man like a blow. It sent a chill up his spine knowing this magnificent beast had walked these woods only hours before, that its mighty roar had shaken the forest, that just for a moment the young lad must have known surely his death was imminent. Now it was a lifeless shell like the broken logs around it, once also masters of their realm.

McAllister pictured greasy bear steaks broiling over an open flame, dripping fat and sizzling angrily. It made his mouth water, so he took his knife and set to work.

The bear's hide was prime, a soft underlayer of brown with long, gray-tipped hairs. It would bring a good price. McAllister grunted and struggled and swore until he managed to push the bear over, and it rolled onto its back with a rustle of brush. Then he carefully eviscerated it by lantern light and pushed the innards away from the carcass—all except the heart, which he kept.

Reaching into the body cavity, he sliced the tenderloins carefully away from the spinal column, and then he rose. He stood over the bear and gazed down, eery-looking in the lantern light. In one hand he clutched his knife, in the other the slabs of meat, gore running between his fingers and dripping to the ground. His eyes picked up the lantern light, made him appear almost demonic as he stared at his fellow wild creature.

"Well, cousin, you lost this'n. Killed by a button." He shook his head, his features softening somewhat. "I hope he can take yer strength an' yer strong heart. He's lived an' he's conquered. He's made hisself a mighty warrior. May your spirit be with him."

A night breeze came up, ruffling the hair curling from beneath McAllister's hat. About him the trees rustled and dead fir needles rained to the forest floor. On the hill, a coyote yapped, then another, and soon the night was filled with their chorus. McAllister looked around, breathing deeply of the cold forest air. He sheathed his knife, then reached down again and brought the bear's heart out of its body cavity. Picking up the lantern and carrying heart and tenderloins, he made his way back to the fire.

In the morning, McAllister was able to more carefully treat the boy's wounds. He washed them with a tea of sagebrush leaves, then crushed leaves and roots of the yarrow plant to make a poultice and bound the wounds up snugly again. This done, he wandered down once more to the scene of yesterday's battle. In the daylight, the scene was like an open book to McAllister, although to the average man it would have been as puzzling as in full darkness. He saw the entire story unfold. He found the broken stock of the Winchester rifle, then its working part. It had been underneath the bear's body the night before. The rifle was poorly cared-for. Its riflings were corroded by black powder residue, it was dappled with rust, and some of the screws in the receiver were working loose, as happened frequently with brass. But it was a repeating Winchester, and as such worth saving.

He laid the two halves of the rifle aside, then went to the bear and carved off the backstraps from the top of its back. He sniffed these cuts, and even though still tepid, they had no foul odor. Afterward, he finished skinning the beast and cut the hide loose from the head.

The remainder of the meat would feed magpies, coyotes, ravens, maybe wolves or other bears. McAllister was not a wasteful man, yet he didn't see this leaving of meat as waste. On the contrary, *taking* it would be wrong. That would deprive nature of its fair share. To survive in the wilderness, a man must always give back to the land even as he takes from it.

He rolled what was left of the carcass off the hide, then deposited the cuts of meat on top of the hide and folded it in half. Hoisting the unwieldy package to his shoulder was a trick, but a bear hide is thin, and lightweight but for its layer of fat. The weight of the meat inside was the only real challenge. When he arrived at camp he built a fire and filled a pot with water from Bailey Creek, which ran by in a meadow below them. Into the water, he cut the bear's heart in little chunks, sprinkling this with salt. He left it to boil and settled down near the horse for a much needed nap.

Later, he awoke to the soft snuffling of the horse's muzzle in the grass. Stretching, he stepped to the dying fire and plucked a piece of meat from the steaming pot. His hard, callused fingertips hardly felt the heat. He popped the chunk into his mouth without waiting for it to cool; his mouth, like his hands, was callused, conditioned by years of scalding black coffee or steaming food that had to be wolfed down, either to get his fair share or because he was on the run and couldn't afford to relax and eat slowly. The meat was watered now, not quite tasteless but only half as flavorful as it had been earlier. The broth would be strong. Taking the pot from the coals, he walked over and set it down near the boy. He sat at the boy's head, letting it rest in his lap, and dipped a spoonful of broth out of the pot.

After blowing on the broth to cool it, he raised the boy's head with one hand, placed the spoon to his mouth and trickled it slowly between his lips. On the fourth spoonful, the boy groaned softly. McAllister stopped and waited. He looked down at the young face, the sweaty upper lip that quivered now, the facial muscles drawn tight with some unconscious battle raging. Then the face relaxed and the wrinkles around the eyes disappeared.

McAllister spooned broth into the boy until he thought he had drunk as much as his weak body could hold. At last, he eased his head down gently and stood away from him.

It was afternoon, and the sun shone down through the treetops. But even with the sun out, it was still April, with a spring chill on the breeze. McAllister had moved the boy half into the shade of a huge fir whose heavy boughs hung over him, and he sat beside him, scraping the bear hide with a chunk of slate rock. Grease covered his hands. Friction and the dappling of sunlight turned it to jelly wherever he scraped with the rock. The musky, oily animal smell of the hide was strong, but not unpleasant.

Flies buzzed and swarmed thickly about him, darting at his face, then away. Some of the more brazen ones landed on his cheeks, his cleft chin, his sweaty brow. He had given up fighting them or trying to figure out their motives. With the bear hide at his feet, why did they insist on landing on his face? He guessed maybe he smelled riper than the hide.

Finally, he stood up, his legs stiff. He stretched them and tried to stand up straight. There was one spot, down in his lower right back, that always limbered slowly. An Indian friend had dug a bullet from there, leaving a mass of scar tissue. But no one had dug the slug from the soldier who shot him. It wouldn't have done him any good.

After walking about the camp to loosen up, McAllister came back to the boy's side and knelt down. He picked up the whisky bottle, plucked the cork from its mouth. He started to raise it to his lips, then paused. He looked down at the boy. He shrugged and put the bottle to his lips.

"Damnit." With a sigh, McAllister lowered the bottle without tasting its contents. "I guess I don't need this bug juice like you do, boy. How're yer scratches doin', anyway?" He spoke just for the sound of his own voice.

He undid the boy's bandages and checked his wounds. The yarrow and sagebrush tea were working their miracle. Nodding with satisfaction, he reapplied yarrow, put on new dressings, and wrapped the wounds again.

It was time for another meal, so McAllister built up the fire and set the pot over it again. "Gonna have some more broth." He looked over the pot at the boy. "Hope you like broth, boy." He paused and rubbed his chin. "You know, I'm gonna have to come up with a name fer you if you don't wake up. Can't keep callin' you 'boy' forever."

A smile turned the corners of his mouth up, and he stood and walked back over to plop down beside the boy. "I think I got just the name. I'm gonna call you 'Lucky'. 'Cause yer the luckiest boy I know. Most people don't live to tell 'bout hand to hand battles with Griz. As fer me, I hope I never get the chance to spin a yarn like yers. Unless I'm lyin', o' course. An' I don't lie."

He chuckled. A man had to get mighty lonely to talk to himself. But he hadn't had a friend to talk to in months. Maybe a year, and even then no real friends. Time sure slipped away and left a man wondering where it all went. Anyway, in the months gone by he'd done an awful lot of talking to himself. He was the only one who would have cared to listen.

McAllister's face softened when he looked down at the boy. Lucky. He thought of his own childhood, his rough, miserable, hated childhood. This boy had to be about the same age he was when he left his home in Arkansas to wander. He had seen a lot before even wandering "Out West." Mississippi, Louisiana, Missouri. Steamboats and freight trains, and men as tough and unyielding as the rivers and oxen they ran. Gamblers in tailored suits that would shoot a man quicker than you could blink an eye, and loose women who could stab a man even faster. Grubby hobos with boot knives soiled with blood and ingrained lunacy in their eyes. Brawny bullwhackers with a string of profanity that would make the devil cringe. An unforgiving learning ground with rugged, wild men for teachers, and the elements, too. The elements taught him to kill a deer and take its skin to keep from freezing to death on a bitter, frosty night. They taught him to avoid the sun, embrace the night. Of course, he was a night owl out of necessity anyway. Night was when chicken coops and vegetable gardens were most invadable, left untended— and his human teachers had taught him to steal. And to kill.

What had this boy been through? Any of the same? Or had he a father and mother who cared? Grandparents? Friends? Well, if not then he had a friend now, at least till he healed and Robert McAllister rode away on the owl hoot trail.

Later, McAllister walked off along the creek to get a better look at his surroundings. He watched deer feed across the far side of the meadow from the creek. He didn't need the meat, so he enjoyed their presence, then watched them walk away. When he returned to camp, he pulled open the tarp to check the boy.

He found a pair of dark eyes looking back at him.

Chapter Seven

José Olano's world was black—black and spinning crazily as if he had gone into a cartwheel and couldn't stop. Like the time some neighborhood bullies rolled him down a hill in a wooden barrel—dizzying, helpless. He shook himself, groping about in the black. He could feel nothing, not even the ground beneath him. He felt like throwing up to rid himself of the nausea in the pit of his stomach, but he couldn't. An oppressive heat weighted him down, tiring him, pushing him against the earth like massive sacks of grain were piled on his chest. Sweat trickled down his face, down his chest and neck, ran into his eyes.

Suddenly, light began to appear in that hopeless, stygian universe. A gray, dim light at first, then subtly colored with green—leaves. And red. Red dripped from the leaves; it was blood. He had the sudden, sickening feeling the blood was his own.

Then like a ten foot cyclone a huge brown beast reared up before him, fangs bared, claws slashing the air. The grizzly bear! He struck at it, but something seemed to catch his hand in mid-air, as if his arm traveled through honey. By the time his hand reached the bear's nose, it had slowed almost to a stop, and he watched in horror as the bear caught his fist in its mouth and shook it violently. When he jerked back his arm, the hand was gone!

José screamed and turned to run. Tangled branches clutched at his clothing, his face, impeding his travel. He plowed through them the best he could, then turned. The bear was almost upon him, gnashing its teeth, roaring horribly. Then it was on top of him, its ponderous weight pressing him into the earth.

He screamed again and opened his eyes. For a long time, he lay perfectly still. Above him shone a bright white light. Nothing more. Had he died? Was this Heaven? There was no bear. No horrible weight. No blood dripping off leaves. Only that bright light and total silence.

Slowly, the rate of his breaths tapered off. The pulse pounding at his throat calmed until he could no longer feel it. He closed his eyes, but darkness flooded in again, and he quickly opened them, afraid the grizzly would return if he allowed the blackness to remain.

Awareness seeped into his brain like a slow trickling of water. This was not Heaven. This was Earth. He was still alive, and he could breathe. There was no bear upon him. No dark, cold, friendless forest surrounding him. He realized the bright white above him was sunlight shining through a wagon tarp. Somehow, miraculously, he must have crawled back to his wagon. But how did he get inside? He had no memory of it. He only recalled crawling away from the bear and the last helpless moment on the forest floor when he realized he would die.

He remembered suddenly the sound of crackling when he put his weight on his left arm and the excruciating pain of it. Grimacing, he raised his arm to inspect it. With dismay, he saw the crude bark cast around it, and for a moment he only stared. Then realization came. He had been rescued. Ben Trombell must be somewhere nearby! God had answered his prayers.

He heard a scrape on the tailgate of the wagon from outside. The noise startled him, and he tried instinctively to sit up. What if the bear had come back after him? Feeling the horrible pain that clutched his rib cage, he gritted his teeth and fell back. He opened his eyes again as the rear tarp parted.

There stood a man. It was not Ben Trombell, but a rough-looking fellow with cloudy gray eyes, an unshaven jaw and crooked nose, all shaded by a dirty, battered hat. They stared at each other, and for a long moment neither one spoke.

Finally, José saw the man's lips part. He seemed to be looking him up and down smugly. José had been around the world enough to have a mistrust of human kind, and this rough character looked to be the sort that would cut a man when down, take all he had, and leave whistling a tune. But something in the man's cool eyes spoke something different: the look of mercy.

"Well, well. Lucky's back from the dead."

For several moments José remained silent, unsure. From the way things looked he guessed it was this man, instead of Ben Trombell, who had saved his life. "Where am I?"

With a grunt, the man climbed up into the wagon and crouched down at José's side. "In yer wagon. Down by the crick." Silence for a moment, while the man studied José's eyes with a calm, curious gaze. "The name's McAllister, boy. Robert McAllister. We got a heap o' catchin' up to do, an' I reckon we c'n start with yer name. I just been callin' you 'Lucky'."

That struck José as a bizarre nickname to grant someone who had just been mauled and nearly torn in two by a grizzly bear. Maybe it was the man's idea of a joke. "I am José Olano."

"José, huh? Maybe I'll call you Joe," said McAllister thoughtfully. "Sounds more American."

José tried to push to a sitting position, feeling the blood rise hot into his cheeks. "My name is José, not Joe. I am a Basque."

McAllister squinted his eyes quizzically. "A Bask? What the hell's a Bask?"

What a fool! thought José. He sank slowly back, his arms weak. "I am from Spain."

McAllister stroked his chin thoughtfully with his thumb and forefinger. "Yeah, it seems I heard somethin' 'bout the Bascos. Mutton punchers—sheepherders. A feisty bunch."

"I am from San Sebastián, where the people are fishermen," corrected José. "Not sheepherders."

McAllister chuckled. "A feisty bunch," he said again. "How's yer arm feel?"

José looked down at the bandages. "It feels fine. Did you fix it?"

The man shrugged. "Don't know that I fixed it, but I did doctor it some. You were in a mighty bad way, Lucky."

José flashed his eyes at the man. "My name is José. Why do you call me Lucky?"

"'Cause you lived through a grizzly bear attack. In my book that makes you mighty lucky. I think I'll just call you that. Lucky fits you fine."

This time José ignored the name, hoping it would just go away, or that this brazen fellow would not be around long enough for it to matter. He wanted to go back to Ben Trombell, back to his sheep. "Where are my sheep?" he asked. "Are they fine?"

"Fine? They're stubble jumpers! Tarnation. They're scattered from hell to breakfast. Pack o' wolves roamed through this mornin'. Ain't heard much since, but it wouldn't surprise me if you seen the last o' them critters."

A feeling of despair seized José's insides. His sheep, gone. It couldn't be. Ben Trombell had entrusted him with that flock. If they were gone, he would never trust José again. He covered his eyes with his right hand, biting his lip. Could a dream fly away so easily, washed away with the blood of a flock of sheep?

José heard the rustle of McAllister's clothing as he stood up, and he looked up at him. McAllister was watching him, eyes soft. "Hard times, Lucky. Why don't you go back to sleep a while? Yer gonna be weak until I c'n get some solid food down yer gullet. I'll get us a fire goin' an' roast you a couple steaks. Then you'll feel better."

José tried to sit up again but fell back. He tried rolling to the side first, and that, too, failed. He looked up pleadingly at McAllister. "Can you help me to my feet, mister? I have to find those sheep. Their lives have been entrusted to me."

"Listen up, boy," McAllister growled. "Even if I wanted to help you up you wouldn't stay. You lost a hell of a lot o' blood, an' yer leg's broke. A six-year-old baby could whoop you now if he'd a mind to. Now lay back down an' quit worryin' 'bout those damn range maggots while I go whip up a little feast for us. An' if you don't want any, I'm hungry enough for both."

With that, McAllister turned and jumped down from the wagon box, drawing the sheet closed behind him. José lay on his back, unable to rise, his jaw clenched helplessly. A tear rolled down his cheek.

Not much later, the scent of scorched sage drifted in to him on the evening breeze. He savored the fragrant smell. He opened his eyes. For some time, though his eyes were shut, he had been aware of a gathering gloom inside the wagon, and now he saw the day had nearly passed. Dusky shadows wavered like purple haze in the interior of the wagon. Soon night would be upon him, and here he was, far from his homeland, helpless, with a strange, brusque man his only company. It was going to be a long night.

Now and then, a knot popped in the fire, and he could see the dim orange glow of the flames dancing to and fro outside the wagon tarp. He saw the shadow of the man moving in front of the firelight, preparing a meal or whatever he was about. José noted with amazement the man's total silence in his movements. José's only awareness of him was the shifting of his shadow—that and the comforting sense someone was near, especially someone as seemingly self-sufficient as Robert McAllister. Whatever the man's faults might be, José found himself feeling secure while he was near, something he had not truly felt since coming here.

Ten minutes later, the tantalizing odor of roasting meat penetrated the darkness inside the wagon. José drew that scent in so deeply it hurt his ribs, but he didn't care. He felt like he hadn't eaten in days, and his stomach began to rumble. He savored the fragrance and closed his eyes, and outside the fire died low.

He had started to doze, but the creaking of the wagon springs and its gentle rocking startled him awake. He looked up to a glaring bright light as Robert McAllister swung over the tailgate bearing a lantern and a tin plate. "Supper's on, Lucky. Ain't much variety, but I hope you like it."

McAllister set the lantern and plate down nearby, then wadded up a blanket, and without a word bent and lifted José's head, easing the makeshift pillow beneath it. He squatted and sank to a sitting position on his heels beside the boy, picking up the plate again. Upon it were stacked five juicy steaks on one side and a pile of bite-sized pieces on the other. He handed José a fork. "I'll hold the plate while you dig in. I cut yers up, since yer one-handed for a while."

Forgetting his manners, José grabbed the fork and stabbed a chunk from the plate, popping it unceremoniously into his mouth. It was flavorful, and not bad-textured either. Not like any venison he had ever tasted before, but still good. He followed it up with three more chunks in such quick succession that McAllister, eyebrows raised, pulled the plate out of reach.

"Now ease up, boy. Yer gulpin' like a starved bear cub. You won't be so lucky anymore if you stuff yer face so fast you dam yer flume. Take yer time. If you eat all that ther's plenty more where it came from. More th'n you an' me c'n eat in three days."

With these words, McAllister stabbed a jackknife into one of the uncut steaks and bit a large chunk out of it, chewing appreciatively. In a moment, he spoke around the mouthful. "I don't blame you much, boy. That's mighty good grub. We're eatin' better'n most rich folks do. An' by the way—I thank yuh."

José's chewing slowed, then finally stopped as he stared questioningly at McAllister. "Thank me for what?"

"Why, fer the meal. I only cooked it. Yer the one killed it."

Slow realization came to José. It was for good reason this was not like any venison he had ever eaten. It was grizzly bear meat. He started to chew again, this time thoughtfully. A creature that had tried with all its might to kill him was now nourishing him back to health. As he chewed, his mind again wandered, and soon he found himself beneath that terrible weight once more, his breath crushed from him.

"That didn't last long," José faintly heard McAllister speak. "Thought you was hungry."

José forced a smile. "I... I am. I was just thinking." He chewed the last of his bite and swallowed, looking back down at the plate that McAllister still held in a rock-steady hand. He felt a cold sweat on his forehead, and he pushed all thought of the bear away. He forked another piece of the meat and started to bring it to his mouth, then paused. "I haven't been very polite. I want to thank you, mister. You have been kind to me. You saved my life. I hope I can pay you back."

McAllister nodded and quickly glanced down at the plate. "Don't worry 'bout payin' me back, Lucky. Most folks woulda done the same."

There was that name again. Lucky. José thought about it for a moment, then smiled shyly. It wasn't that bad, he supposed. And this Robert McAllister wasn't that bad of a man.

The next morning when José awoke, soft sunlight filtered in through a slit at the foot of the wagon. He lay for a moment enjoying the trill of songbirds outside, listening for sounds of Robert McAllister moving about. He heard no such sounds.

At first, the sudden fear gripped him that McAllister had decided to move on. But he was quickly comforted in remembering how utterly silent McAllister was in his movements. And along with that comfort came the reassurance of yesterday about the integrity and inherent goodness of this man McAllister. Maybe he was not always so caring for others. From his looks, José believed he could be a hard enough man. But for some reason he had decided to take José under his wing, and José knew instinctively he would not desert him until he could get by on his own.

José began to exercise his muscles, one body part at a time. He was amazed how much better he felt after sleep. And surely the previous night's meal also helped. He eased up onto his right elbow and looked around. McAllister had slept on the ground, but apparently he had come back some time that morning, for the wagon box had been tidied up, blankets folded and things placed in some semblance of order. It was a nice change, for José wasn't one normally inclined to tidiness, in spite of—perhaps *because* of—his experience as a maid for Ben Trombell.

José managed to struggle to the tailgate of the wagon, and he parted the wagon sheet and looked outside. About fifteen yards away, seated on the ground with his back to an aspen trunk, McAllister sat silently carving on a four-foot-long tree limb. José watched him for several minutes as his fingers deftly wielded the knife, eyes intent on his work. It was a picture José would never forget: this tall, rugged man leaned against the tree, seeming so much a part of nature it was as if he were born in that very spot. And like the tree McAllister was covered with scars and rough bark on the outside, but full of vigor and life on the inside.

McAllister had moved camp, José saw now. They were camped alongside Bailey Creek, with its crystal-clear water chuckling over stones smoothed through the years. The man had found an ideal spot nestled down amid tall aspens and juniper. Bushes and long, lush grass grew beneath the trees and all along the creek bank, and songbirds twittered among the tree branches. A gigantic Douglas fir with tangled, spreading limbs guarded the wagon.

Suddenly, McAllister's hands stopped moving, and his eyes fixed on some distant object across the creek. José tried to follow the invisible route of the man's gaze. He had to start over three times, looking first at McAllister, then following his eyes out across the meadow, before he discovered the object of his interest. It was a big black bird that soared in the distance, powerful wings gracefully suspending it on the air currents. José watched for a time. He knew what it was: a turkey vulture, familiarly known as a buzzard. To him it meant only death. Or impending death. But he was fascinated by the bird's graceful, perfectly controlled flight, how it could turn in circles while seemingly making no movement of its wings or tail, as if controlled by God Himself.

The vulture finally disappeared in the fir trees on the opposite slope, and José looked back at McAllister. His eyes were once more on the project before him, his knife expertly slicing away chips of wood.

José sank back into the wagon box and leaned against the tailgate. He felt weak just from his movement of several feet, and he wanted only to rest there for a moment. He had moved too much for the comfort of his wounds and hoped the throbbing would soon subside.

McAllister's voice from directly behind him made him jerk forward with a start. He turned his head and looked at the man, who said with a slight smile, "What'd you think o' that bird?"

José sat wordless for a moment. "What bird?"

"Ah, come on, Lucky. The one in the meadow!"

"How did you know I was watching?" José was astounded.

"Felt it. Man learns to sense those things in the wild country. You watched me for a while cuttin' on that stick before then, too."

José sat silently amazed. He wished he could learn some of this man's abilities. He looked toward where the bird had disappeared. "It was a vulture," he asserted, proud of his knowledge of at least one aspect of this wild place. "My boss told me about them."

McAllister looked over quickly at José and leaned his head back a little. "Well, I'll give you this, kid, it sure did *look* like a buzzard at that distance. But that weren't no buzzard. That was a golden eagle—the surest, most beautiful piece o' grace that ever rode the sky."

José thought McAllister was mistaken, but he dared not say so. Instead, he looked thoughtful for a moment, then said, "That sure looked like all the buzzards I ever saw. How can you tell it wasn't?"

"Well, boy, I'll tell you. Couple things. First off, I knew by the silhouette. The wings of an eagle come out perty near straight, if you see 'em dead on. The wings of a buzzard swing up a little in a V shape, like they're pointin' at the sky, and their wing feathers separate more. They look like big fingers. If they're far off, you c'n also judge by the comp'ny they keep. It's not a pat rule, but buzzards usually run in a crowd. One or two partners, anyway, an' I've seen as many as thirty together. An eagle, he's a lone hunter. Once in a while you'll see two right together, but they gen'rally keep a little distance from each other. One bird's not as likely to scare away whatever they're huntin'. An' what a buzzard's huntin' don't scare away easy," he said with a sly look.

José gave a little chuckle and looked off in the direction the bird had disappeared. As much as he wanted to believe he was right, he had to concede. McAllister seemed knowledgeable, and he had been around a long time. There was no way José could be aware of such minor details. That made him wonder how many of the other "buzzards" he had seen were actually eagles.

McAllister went back to his work for a while, then returned later and carried José from the wagon. After a breakfast of bear meat, which José ate ravenously, he went and picked up a long, sturdy-looking stick that leaned against a tree. It was the branch he had been carving on earlier. A fork on one end of it had been chopped short and padded with a piece of bear hide. He walked over to José and leaned down to place the stick near his hand. "I made this for yuh, Lucky. A crutch to kinda help yuh hobble around camp, when yer of a mind to."

José's eyes misted slightly, and he dropped his gaze to the implement and fingered its newly exposed wood, touching the silver-tipped hair at the fork. "Thanks." He wanted to say something more, to show his appreciation for this man's care, but he didn't know how.

McAllister waved his hand dismissively and sat near his aspen tree to cut big chunks of bear meat into the pot. From the shade of a nearby tree José watched him. Close to noon, McAllister's task was done, and great hordes of flies swarmed about the canvas sack on the ground. McAllister dumped salt liberally into the pot, then poured water over the pieces of meat to create a heavy brine. Into this mixture he sprinkled several handsful of brown sugar, then set the pot aside.

He turned at last to José, who was watching him curiously. "A couple days, that meat'll be cured. After that we're goin' inta Soda Springs an' get you back to yer people. I figger by then you'll be strong enough to travel the two or three miles in."

José looked up quickly at McAllister. A sick feeling came over him, and he dropped his eyes to the ground. "I can't go back to Ben Trombell. He won't ever trust me again."

"Well, you sure can't stay here."

"Could you help me find those sheep, mister?"

"First, stop callin' me mister. Second..." There was a lengthy pause. "I went lookin' for yer sheep this mornin' while you was asleep. Thought I'd help you out with yer boss. They're gone, boy. The ones that ain't strewn through the woods, ripped open an' bloated, have skedaddled prob'ly clean back to Nevada—where they belong. Them wolves had a heyday, boy, they shore did. They ain't used to an animal just layin' out its neck to 'em, an' I guess they just went crazy. I counted at least fifty dead sheep. Sorry, Lucky."

José closed his eyes, his throat tight. He had let his charges down, and worse, he had let down Ben Trombell. He could never go back expecting a job. How would he hold his head up before Ben? From that time on, José Olano would be alone, after McAllister drifted on. He would be left to face the world on his own, no longer trusted by his only friend, Ben Trombell. His only asset was the fact he could speak English, but he knew nothing other than sheep, and how to cook and keep a house clean. And after living outside with the land he just couldn't see himself ever working in confined spaces again. He was intimidated by the land, its elements, its wild creatures. Yet he still wanted more than anything to learn its ways. Unfortunately, he couldn't do it alone. Nature would kill him first. But there was one man who could teach him. One man José felt would know the wild country better than anyone he had ever met. Robert McAllister.

José's throat was tight when he looked up at McAllister. He fought to hold back tears as he met his eyes. "I can't ever go back to my boss. I lost his whole flock of sheep. And I don't have any family anywhere. Could I stay with you?"

Robert McAllister laughed loudly, a forced laugh, and slapped his knee. The laugh died immediately. "No way, boy. I ride rough trails. This here's the longest I'm likely to stop in one spot for the next five months, an' that's only 'cause o' you. I don't make a habit o' stoppin'. An' I won't. Stayin' with me would git you killed, don't you see? No, it ain't the life for a pup."

"Please, mister, I won't be any trouble. I just want to learn how to live out here. I won't hold you down. I'll just go wherever you go."

"Oh, no you won't. An' if you ask again I'll take you to town tomorrow. So forget it."

As McAllister spoke, he had his back toward the meadow, and he hadn't looked that way for a time. José looked away from him, feeling sick at this rejection, and his eyes fell upon a group of horsemen riding slowly down the meadow. "There's some riders," he said with surprise.

The cat-like way Robert McAllister whirled about astonished José, and he looked up at him in wonder. McAllister took only a moment to study the approaching group, and then he laid a strong brown hand firmly on José's shoulder and looked into his eyes. "Those men're after me, boy. They're out an' about to find an' kill me, an' shore as hell they'll string me from one o' these trees. I need yer help, 'cause I shore can't fight 'em all."

This was the closest to pleading José could ever imagine McAllister sinking, and he felt pity for him. He didn't even stop to wonder why the riders were after him, for McAllister had saved his life. He had to help him if he could.

"I'm hidin' in the wagon, boy." He drew his Colt. "If they find me, I'll send six of 'em to hell, but shore as yer born I'll buck out, too." With those last words, and no further request for José's assistance, McAllister went calmly to the wagon. He walked slowly, so as not to draw the posse's attention, and climbed inside, easing the tarp shut behind him.

José sat silently until the exact moment he knew the first posse member spotted him. Then he picked up his crutch and struggled to his feet, leaning against the tree for support. Several of the men were pointing his way now, and they rode toward the camp. Their eyes swept the trees. José knew the look of fear, and he saw it in some of the men's wide, darting eyes. They looked as he must have as he closed in on the grizzly.

The obvious leader of the bunch, a burly man with silver-gray hair and muttonchop whiskers, reined an astonishingly beautiful palomino horse in at the edge of camp, and the other men followed suit. The leader looked at José suspiciously, and his eyes again scanned the camp, this time very closely, before coming back to rest on José.

"Afternoon, boy. What happened to you?" He indicated José's bandages. Before José could respond, the man charged on. "My name's J.B. Trace. I own the Circle T ranch, over toward Blackfoot. We're scouring about for a horse thief that might have passed this way two days back. When he came by, he'd've been on foot. And he's worth two hundred and fifty dollars to anyone that points us to him. Seen any strangers?"

"Yes."

Trace looked quickly at the men to either side of him, then back at José. "How long ago?"

"Two nights ago."

"Say where he was goin'?"

"He said to the Territory of Wyoming," José responded. "He walked off that way when he left." He pointed in a general southeasterly direction.

"What was his name? Did he tell you that?"

"Sure." José's mind churned, and he hoped his face was convincing. He called upon all the skills he had learned at fibbing to his parents and teachers as a child. He at least owed McAllister a good try, and if he could steer these men another way it would surely prevent several of them from losing their lives, too. The only name he could think of was that of one of the deckhands from the ship on which he had sailed to America. "His name was Jensen. He seemed like a real nice man."

"Well, he's not!" retorted Trace. "He's a damned horse thief! And a dead one, should I catch up to his thieving hide. What does this gent look like?"

"He's about as tall as you but has lighter hair. He was wearing buckskin pants and—"

Trace whipped around to one of the other men. "That sound like the fellow you saw?"

The man hesitated, looking at José. "Well," he said finally, "It's not much, but I guess it matches what I saw. You saw him, too. What do you think?"

Trace growled angrily, "My eyes aren't what they used to be. I couldn't say." He glanced suspiciously over at José's horse, which stood chewing a mouthful of grass and watching the proceeding nonchalantly. Then he turned back to José. "Now you wouldn't be lyin' to us, would you, boy? About him leavin'? Why would a horse thief head out on foot when he coulda taken your horse? For all it's worth," he added derisively. "You know, two hundred and fifty dollars could buy you a hell of a good time somewhere. Or maybe even a train ticket back to Mexico."

"I'm not from Mexico," José responded angrily. "I'm from Spain."

Trace obviously wasn't interested in the location of José's homeland and was already speaking before José had finished his sentence. "Who else is with you, boy? You ain't makin' this camp all by yourself, busted up like you are. And you didn't tie off those bandages, either."

José's mind raced, but he spoke nonchalantly. "My father's with me. He went off hunting this morning."

Trace stared at him, his eyes indecisive. He almost seemed angry José had been able to respond. "What's in that wagon yonder?"

José's heart leaped, and he felt a rivulet of sweat run down his face from what had beaded up on his forehead. His mouth was dry, as if someone had sprinkled it with corn starch, and he stammered for words.

"Uh, n—nothing's in there. Just my gear and some food. And a couple of blankets."

"Bartlett?" Trace ignored José and turned to a younger man at his side. "Go check it out. Henry, Chester, ride around on the other side of that wagon in case some yellow jackrabbit comes streaking out. And damn the hanging, boys. If you see anything move that doesn't look like gear, food, or blankets, shoot it to hell."

Chapter Eight

José's knees turned to jelly, and he felt himself start to fall. He caught his balance against the aspen and wiped the sweat from his face on the bandages of his arm. He darted a glance toward the wagon, thought better of that, and jerked his eyes back to J.B. Trace and the others. Trace eyed him shrewdly, and a knowing smirk spread his whiskers. He turned and nodded to a fourth man. "Price, you get on over there with Bartlett. I have a strong feeling there's a bobcat in this cage."

José's eyes widened. He thought his heart would stop. At the moment, he was thankful his leg was broken and he couldn't run. Otherwise, he probably would have, and he didn't want to display that kind of fear. There was no doubt in his mind, however, that McAllister had spoken the truth. When the wagon cover parted, men would die. José knew instinctively McAllister wouldn't be taken while he had the strength to resist.

It seemed an eternity as the four riders started their horses toward the wagon. It probably felt like forever to them, too. José watched them through blurred eyes, his nerves stretched taut as he waited for this valley to explode with gunfire. The horses seemed to move so slowly. Each rider had his cocked weapon in hand. They seemed to know their lives hung in the balance. Henry and Chester rode to the front of the wagon as instructed. Bartlett and Price stopped at the foot, and Bartlett turned his head to look uncertainly at Trace. Beads of sweat glistened on his cheeks, and the corner of his mouth twitched.

"Well, man?" shot out J.B. Trace. "Open the damn sheet, and let's see what's about."

Bartlett's Adam's apple bobbed conspicuously, and the skin of his face tightened. He glanced over at Price, then back at Trace and wiped a hand across his whiskered jaw. "Listen, Trace, that palomino's yours, not mine. Twenty dollars ain't enough to die for. You wanna look in that wagon, you just go right ahead."

With those words, Bartlett turned his horse and moved across to José's left, coming momentarily between him and Trace. As Trace came back into sight, José's eyes lit on his face. His skin had reddened, his eyes narrowed. "Why, boys, I guess we discovered the real jackrabbit, and it wasn't inside the wagon!"

José dared a glance toward the wagon. Price was watching Trace, and Henry and Chester had also come back around to see what was happening. José glanced back at Trace. The big man glared around him at the crowd. "Well, I guess I shouldn't have sent a boy to do a man's job. Especially a boy with yellow down his shirttail."

With an oath, Trace hefted a long-barreled scattergun from its resting place on his saddle horn. He cracked it open, peering at its twin shells. Then he slammed it shut with vigor. He smiled smugly at the crisp latching sound, and he glanced around him at the posse again, then started his horse for the rear of the wagon.

The day fell darkly upon José and the scene before him. It was as if a tent had closed around them, shutting out the rest of the world—leaving only impending doom and the question of how many men would ride away from here with their trophy and how many would never ride away. His heart pounded in his head like a nine pound hammer dully contacting the bark of a fir. He wiped his eyes again and made ready to sneak off, if he could. These men would take him and hold him as an orphan and the harborer of a criminal if he stayed here.

Trace reached the wagon, and without hesitation he took the edge of the canvas in his sunburned hand. He paused and drew in a deep breath. Then his harsh voice broke the stillness.

"You dirty son of a—" His hand flung the cover aside and a round from the shotgun exploded in the still afternoon, then another, and from the front of the wagon a horse screamed. Trace's horse reared back, and he lost his grip on the shotgun and dropped it while he fought to bring the horse under control, beating its neck with his fist.

The two riders at the front of the wagon came churning away in confusion. Henry's mount twisted and spun, slamming into Chester's horse and nearly knocking him off.

By this time, Trace had drawn a handgun from his coat pocket and jumped down from his mount, holding its reins in one hand. He returned to the wagon's canvas and tore it aside, and for a long moment he peered in. José half expected to hear shots from McAllister's gun, but there were none. José couldn't believe it. McAllister had been taken without firing a shot, overwhelmed by the shotgun.

When Trace turned away from the wagon, his face was strangely white, like the chalk of Nevada's deserts. He scanned the rest of the posse for a moment with his mouth ajar, then slowly shook his head. Without a word, he climbed aboard his mount, and José saw his knees shaking as he settled into the saddle. He turned and gave José one last glance, then laid spurs to his horse's flanks and loped away, splashing through the creek and moving up the meadow. His shotgun lay forgotten in the dust where he had dropped it.

By then, Henry had gained control of his horse, and he and Chester were dismounted and examining the front of it. José looked back at the silent wagon, then at the men who were drawing near it. He couldn't go look himself. He had never seen a man murdered before, and he had no urge to now. Let these others carry McAllister away.

The first several men to look into the wagon turned now to each other, faces unbelieving. One of them swore. Another muttered something José didn't hear in an obviously angry voice, and one of the others shot a glance back at José.

Bartlett had ridden close again to look into the wagon box, and after he did he rode over by José. "Sorry about the wagon, boy. Who's your dad? We'll try and pay him for the damages. Didn't know Trace was so trigger happy."

José paused. *His dad*? Then he remembered what he had said. He wanted to ask about McAllister, but something told him to bite his tongue. He stared at Bartlett for a few moments until the man began to look at him oddly, then finally he spoke. "It doesn't matter," he said shakily. "It's an old wagon anyway."

"Well, I apologize again, son," Bartlett said sincerely. "We should've just believed you and moved on."

Henry and Chester led their horses up then. "That crazy Trace put a slug in my horse's shoulder." Henry swore. "What the hell got into the blasted fool?"

"Fear," responded Bartlett. "But *he* sure wouldn't admit it. I will, though. I wasn't dyin' over another man's horse, not for no stinkin' twenty bucks." He looked around as if begging for someone to agree.

Chester finally responded, "I don't blame you a bit. Let's get on out of here and leave this kid in peace. He's been bullied enough for one day. Besides, his dad's likely to come back here an' shoot us."

Henry looked over at Trace's shotgun, lying in the dust. "Somebody gonna pick that up an' give it back to Trace?" He looked around questioningly at the others.

Chester glanced around, too. "Hell," he said at last. "Let's leave it and get out of here. We ain't his nurse maids." He turned to his saddle.

Bartlett reached out and touched Chester's shoulder, stopping him from mounting. "Let's get together some money, boys, and pay the kid for the wagon. We'll get it out of Trace later."

"Why not just give 'im the gun?" suggested Bartlett. "Bet that's a forty dollar shotgun." When everyone seemed in agreement, he turned to José. "You can have that scattergun, kid. We'll tell Trace we took it and threw it in the river."

José dumbly nodded his thanks, and he watched as the men mounted up, then drifted quietly along the grassy meadow, finally disappearing from sight. He was left alone in the quiet afternoon, alone but for his horse and the flies that buzzed about his head and the pan of bear meat.

Finally, José turned and looked at the wagon. It was silent. The gaping dark hole where the tarp still hung open stared at him like the eye of a cyclops, daring yet forbidding him to come near and look inside. There was no place inside the wagon where McAllister could hide. Yet he had seen him enter it, and there was no way out, not without José seeing him go. The ground around the wagon was clear, but for low grass in which no one could have crawled away unseen.

But Bartlett had as much as said McAllister was not in there. Could he have hidden under a blanket and gone undetected? It didn't seem possible, yet it was the only explanation, unless McAllister was some kind of magician who could make himself invisible—or nonexistent.

Taking a deep breath, José pushed away from the aspen that supported him and put all his weight on the crutch and his good leg. He felt weak and wanted nothing more than to lie down and rest. But he had to know about McAllister, so he moved uneasily toward the wagon, struggling to handle the crutch and not lose his balance. He stopped at the edge of the box, took another breath, then forced himself to look inside. What greeted him was his blankets, lying crumpled and still on the floor with a ragged hole blasted through them. On the far side of the wagon, wood splinters surrounded a hole where the first charge of buckshot had torn through the front boards. There was no sign of McAllister and no sign he had ever been there.

Astonished, José hopped backward away from the wagon and looked over at the bay horse. It had calmed down now, after the shooting, and stared curiously at him, munching on grass. That horse seemed to do nothing but eat.

On a whim, José leaned forward and looked beneath the wagon, saw nothing but grass and a scattering of stones. As he straightened, dizziness swept over him, and he nearly fell. To prevent landing where and when he didn't want to, he eased himself to a seat on the ground, then set aside the crutch and lay on his back, shading his eyes with his right forearm.

Suddenly, he felt the hair on the back of his neck prickle. It was the same odd feeling he had sensed when tracking the grizzly. Slowly, he lowered his arm and opened his eyes, gazing up into the thickly interwoven branches of the fir which towered over the wagon.

He was about to roll over and get up to look around him, but he paused. Something about those branches above him was not right, but he didn't yet know what. It was almost as if he could see eyes gazing down on him, and the horrible picture of a mountain lion ready to pounce flashed across his mind.

Slowly his eyes focused on a hand, then an arm. Next, the pieces of an entire body, cleverly braided among the branches of the fir. At last his vision rested on the grinning face of McAllister.

By the time José's bewildered mind realized its discovery, McAllister had untwisted himself from the branches of the tree and came swinging down, lithe as a squirrel. When he reached the ground, he was laughing—this time a real laugh, not a forced one. It took José off guard, for McAllister didn't have the face of a laughing man. José just lay on his back, looking up, and then he too began to laugh uncontrollably.

Before José could control his laughter, brought on more by astonishment and relief than humor, McAllister had seated himself against a wagon wheel and sat watching José with a twinkle in his eye. José's laughter died, and he wiped away the tears that streamed down the sides of his face into his ears and hair. He sat up gingerly, holding his now aching ribs and trying to ward off another fit of dizziness.

José looked at McAllister, his voice full of admiration. "How'd you do that? I never even saw you leave the wagon."

"Well, Lucky," replied McAllister in his soft voice, "you weren't watchin' me all the time. You were watchin' them boys ride in. An' they was watchin' you. I had that tree in mind when I parked there. They call that an ace in the hole—don't know if yer a card player. Anyway, I had plans fer that tree all along, in case them boys come sniffin'. An' they did, didn't they?"

José felt the admiration well up inside his chest. But that sentiment was soon overridden by a darker one, that of reproach. "Why didn't you tell me? You lied to me. You told me you were going to hide in the wagon, and I was scared they'd kill you. You didn't have to make me go through that. You could've told me."

The twinkle faded quietly from McAllister's eyes, and he looked at José understandingly and nodded. "I know how you feel, Lucky. I do. But you gotta understand. I been around this country a lot longer'n you, an' I've seen a lotta people who weren't near as honest or as loyal as I'd a liked 'em to be. People I believed in an' respected. An' even liked, from time to time. I learned hard lessons too many times, sometimes near hard enough to git me killed. But I don't do that no more, kid. I watch my back an' cover my tracks. I don't trust nobody till they been proved. Nobody. So don't take it personal. But now, kid, you been proved. You stood back o' me an' did everything you could to save my bacon—short o' riskin' yer own. An' if you'd a risked yer own life to save mine, I'd a thought you a fool. You don't owe me nothin'."

"I owe you my life."

"No, you don't, Lucky. I don't ask to collect debts, an' I don't remember 'em. Unless of course I'm the one owes 'em."

José lowered his eyes and picked up a handful of rust-colored fir needles, letting them sift through his fingers and patter to earth. "I want to tell you, mister, I sure was glad not to see you in that wagon. I don't know if you're really a horse thief, but you saved my life, and I'm happy you got away from those men. I hope you make it to wherever you're going."

"First off, Lucky, it's where *we're* goin', if you still wanna join me. I c'd use a honest pard that sticks by me when the goin's tough. Second, if yer stayin' with me, you gotta quit callin' me mister. Either call me McAllister or Robert. Or if those're too long just call me Gray. Shoshones gave me the name Gray Eagle, on account o' my eyes an' 'cause I admire eagles. But do me a favor: don't ever call me Bob. I ain't been bobbed an' don't plan to ever be."

José looked at the ground. He continued looking down as he spoke, afraid if he looked up McAllister would see he was close to tears. "You don't have to take me with you, mister—I mean Gray. I know you don't want to, so don't do it just because I helped you. We're even now."

"Lucky." The boy continued looking downward. "Lucky, look at me." When José did so, McAllister went on. "You did yer dangedest to throw them boys off my track. You didn't have to, but you tried to help me. I don't know why. Even after they told you I was a horse thief, you held yer ground. An' even after they told you 'bout the two hunnerd an' fifty bucks. I'm shore that's a lot more than you ever seen. I was watchin' you from that tree, Lucky, an' I seen a whole lotta me in you. I don't have any kids, but if I did I'd wish they had yer nerve. I'm askin' you to stay because I want you. I'd like to teach yuh what I know, if yer willin' to learn. I ain't askin' you to tag along because I feel obligated; I don't owe no man. But it'd shore be nice to have somebody watchin' my back that didn't aim to put a frog sticker in it first time I let down my guard."

José looked quickly away when McAllister finished his speech. He had tried in vain to keep his tears from surfacing. He wiped his eyes with his knuckles, then looked down at his lap. Finally, he looked back up. "I'd still like to go with you, all right. I'll do anything you ask me to if you'll teach me about the mountains."

"You got yerself a deal, boy." McAllister grinned and stood up. "An' the first thing we gotta do is make me a new person. I cain't keep hidin' out like this. I'll end up makin' an outlaw o' you, too, if they ketch me. It's just too dangerous bein' Robert McAllister."

He walked over near the wagon and leaned down to pick up Trace's scattergun. He patted the gun butt admiringly. "What kinda fool forgets his gun? I'm glad this one did, though. This is my ticket. This an' yer hoss, if I c'n borrow 'im."

A spark of fear struck in José's heart. "You're not going to kill somebody, are you?"

McAllister chuckled and shook his head. "Uh-uh. I figgered to trade this gun off fer some new rags an' maybe some food. Can I borrow yer horse?"

"Sure. Where are you going?"

"Away, Lucky. But just fer the night."

Again, fear clutched José's stomach. As much as he wanted to believe in Robert McAllister, the man was still a stranger, and he was not sure he could believe everything he told him. If he allowed him to leave, would he ever return?

It was not the chance of losing the horse that bothered him. McAllister had saved his life, and if he wanted the horse as payment it was the least he could give. What bothered him was just thinking McAllister might leave him friendless, not to mention with a stronger mistrust of mankind's basic nature from that time forth. It was McAllister's next gesture that laid his fears to rest. He had the feeling that was the man's sole intent.

"Take my pistol, boy, an' keep it with you in the wagon. You need it, it's carryin' six shells. An' be careful not to drop it, or it's liable to go off. On second thought..." He opened the chamber gate and removed one of the cartridges, returning it to an empty loop in his belt, then turned the cylinder so the hammer rested on the empty chamber. "Now you won't have to worry about it. I'll try to be back 'fore noon tomorra."

With those words, McAllister handed José the gun, saddled the horse, swung aboard, and rode across the meadow toward the far timber. The last time José saw him he was threading his way up into the trees, and he disappeared within their dark veil. Once again, José was alone with the woods. It would be a long, sleepless night.

At eleven o'clock the following morning, José watched McAllister leave the firs from three hundred yards farther up the valley than he had entered them and start across the meadow slowly. There was no telling how long before that the man had stood in shadowed silence and watched José's camp, making sure no one else had found it; but José had no doubt he had watched. The man was as leery as a hunted wolf.

As McAllister walked the horse across the meadow and drew near, José noted the wary way his eyes moved back and forth, scanning the trees, taking in the land as a whole and its parts individually. He also noted how his head moved very seldom from side to side, and when it did it was only very slowly, almost imperceptibly.

José smiled at how McAllister was dressed. He had traded his buckskin pants for faded bib overalls, with cracked old brogans on his feet. The same sweat-stained hat rode his hair, only he had punched the crown out so that it was rounded and showed the creases of age, worn through in one place. He had shaved the whiskers from his upper lip only, leaving a Lincolnesque week-old beard on his jaw, and he looked the part of a down-and-out dirt farmer. The beard gave him the appearance of being ten years older, and it was a cinch he wouldn't be recognized now except by someone who had seen him very close and had a chance to study his features and mannerisms. As a man who had set off to change his image, Robert McAllister was a success.

The horse's heavy hooves splashed clumsily across the stream, and McAllister drew rein in front of José. "Howdy, youngster. Know anywheres hereabouts a man might buy hisself a farm?"

José laughed. "Where'd you get all those clothes?"

McAllister swung his leg and slipped off the horse, leading it over to the wagon. As he walked, José hobbled after him. "There's a place over that mountain 'bout ten miles toward Montpelier. Just a little dirt farm. Friendly folks, though. I took off all my clothes an' walked on in there askin' fer help."

José's mouth and eyes popped open. "Really?"

"Well shore, kid. I figgered I'd git a handout if I looked poor enough." McAllister's face was serious as he spoke. He turned and lashed the horse's lead rope to the tailgate, and when he turned back around a wide grin spread his whiskers. José stared at him.

"Actually, I did take off all my clothes but my hat, an' then I wrapped up in the blanket an' went knocking on the front door, actin' all embarrassed—which to tell you the truth I was. I told the fellow an' his woman I'd been washin' up in the creek an' a wolf drug all my clothes off to eat 'em—'cause they was buckskin. It was a great story, an' they believed it all the way. 'Course, when he dragged my clothes off he taken my money pouch, too, so I didn't have any money to pay fer clothes. But they was more'n generous. I changed my mind 'bout the shotgun, too." He reached across the horse's saddle and withdrew the weapon, holding it out in front of him. "Them cowboys gave that to you. It ain't right fer me to trade, an' these clothes ain't worth that much anyhow."

José giggled again, thinking about McAllister walking up to the house with no clothes on. "You probably scared those people to death!"

McAllister chuckled and shrugged his wide shoulders. "I don't think so. They was real nice folks. Seemed perty at ease with me. They were what folks call 'Mormons'— except they called 'emselves 'Saints'. This valley's chock full of 'em. Funny thing is, you hear tell they're an awful cantankerous bunch, always lookin' fer a scrap, an' they have ten or twenty wives apiece. But these folks was peaceable as rabbits—breed like rabbits, too. An' they say most of 'em ain't got but one wife now'days, just like anybody else. I ain't sayin' their religion is true or false now, Lucky, but they seemed just like reg'lar folks to me. Goes to show yuh can't believe everything yuh hear till yuh see it yerself."

"I heard about Mormons in Nevada," recalled José. "They have their own city in Utah."

"Sure. Salt Lake City. Maybe I'll take yuh there sometime. But first, you rest up a day or two more, then we'll head on into Soda Springs. We'll meet a few more o' these Mormons."

"You think I'll be strong enough to travel then?" asked José eagerly.

"Well sure. Heck, you already look fit as a fiddle. In three days you'll be good as a guitar," McAllister winked. "Then we c'n do some travelin'."

It wouldn't be long before Fate made them wish they had ridden another direction.

Chapter Nine

Wide steel tires crushed sagebrush to earth as the old gray wagon lurched and rocked down the hill toward the Bailey Creek road. A slight breeze picked up the smell of bruised sage leaves and carried its primitive perfume past McAllister and José, seated on the creaking seat. They reached the road, and before them it made a gradual climb after they crossed the rickety bridge over the Bear River. Then out before them stretched the wide sagebrush basin.

Set against the far foothills was the town of Soda Springs, a dream child of the industrious Mormon prophet, Brigham Young. Originally settled by a group known as the Morrisites, a break-off group of the Mormons, the settlement had once been the home of Fort Connor, before the army subdued the Shoshone and Bannock tribes and imprisoned them on the Fort Hall Reservation. The Morrisites, frustrated by cold winters and short summers not conducive to crop raising, eventually moved on. The Mormons took their places and made a go of the valley, and the few remaining Morrisites were absorbed back into their mother religion.

José and McAllister could see the clustered structures of Soda Springs' two districts, Lower and Upper Town. The former, along the river, was the original townsite, founded by the Morrisites. Overlooking it on a grassy bluff stood old Fort Connor. Upper Town, on higher ground, spread away from its predecessor, a trap set by shrewd planners to catch travelers and tourists and any money they might have to spend.

Soon they began to pass occasional shacks and juniper corrals with stock standing about lazily in them. Chickens pecked in the yards and hardly paid them mind as the wagon rumbled past on the rocky road. Dogs ran out to harass them, losing interest when the horse ignored them and patiently plodded by.

From a distance, the buildings seemed to be all set at random across the sagebrush flats, as if some giant had taken up a handful of faded wooden dice and thrown them into the air, letting them land where they would. But viewed up close, the town was carefully laid out, with broad streets running perpendicular to each other like a checkerboard. It wasn't a large burg, harboring maybe three hundred souls, but room was there for growth.

As they pulled onto Dillon Street and passed the little building that served as a bank, McAllister cleared his throat disgustedly and spat, looking over at José. "There's a place I got no use for. Rich thievin' devils. 'Course I ain't got no money to put in one anyway." He spoke this last jokingly, but José could see bitterness in his eyes.

At last, McAllister drew up in front of a general store. The small establishment was built of hand-hewn logs but sported a milled-board false front. Across this were sprawled the letters, ZCMI. Several men stood on the porch talking—farmers, by their dress.

José looked over at McAllister. He was eyeing the gathering of farmers casually, but in his eyes was that ever-present look of the hunter—or the hunted. José had not yet decided which. Maybe both. He appeared mildly interested but calm, yet his eyes never stayed long in one place, nor on one face.

McAllister played out his part of the farmer wracked by too many years of hard labor under the prairie sun, with arthritis in his joints. He climbed down from the wagon slowly, then winced and rubbed his knee. He looked up at José when he hefted him down and gave him a wink. Then he straightened up, put a hand to the small of his back and stretched it.

"Hello, brother."

The greeting from one of the farmers startled José, and he glanced that way. McAllister looked over, too. When he ascertained the farmer was looking his way, he checked around behind him as if to find some other object of the man's greeting. He glanced back. "You talkin' to me?"

By now, all five of the farmers had turned and were looking from the one who had spoken to McAllister, José, and the run-down wagon. The speaker cleared his throat.

"Sure. I guess you're not from around here, ay?" asked the man in a strong English accent.

McAllister shook his head. "No sir. Come in from the Blackfoot area, actually—and before that, Kansas. I'm lookin' around fer land. Cheap land. Know any hereabouts that's fer sale?"

"Plenty, brother. Plenty." The man stepped off the porch into the dirt, holding his hand out. "My name's Brother Lee. Bertrand Lee."

McAllister shook the outstretched hand. "Howdy." When Lee looked at him questioningly, he went on. "I'm Bob Early. From east Kansas. This here runt is my son." He grinned and roughed José's hair affectionately.

Lee smiled and nodded at José. "Well, Brother Early, you're certainly welcome to the valley." He turned to the other four men with him and introduced them in turn. Then he added, "Harold McGee is the land agent around these parts. You might talk to him. In the meantime, I'll spread the word around that you're lookin' for a spot o' land."

"Obliged," replied McAllister. "Good to meet you, Brother Lee."

José looked up at McAllister. Maybe it was only because he knew the man's character, but calling a man his brother who wasn't didn't fit him. He wondered why McAllister had even said it and if the farmers had noticed how odd it sounded. But when he looked over at them they were all smiling and nodding good day to him and McAllister.

When José and McAllister entered the store, an array of odors beset them. New leather, lavender, cinnamon, mint. The clean smell of bolts of yard goods and from the pickle barrel the sour smell of vinegar, which set José's mouth to watering. Best of all was the yeasty odor of fresh bread, and José glanced at several loaves cooling beneath a towel on the long plank counter at the rear of the store. There were new shirts hanging from wooden hangers, pants also hanging to prevent the ugly crease that tended to appear in the legs after too long on a shelf. Garden implements hung on the right hand wall, buckets and boxes of hardware lined the one across from it. Next to the pickle barrel at the corner of the counter squatted a cracker barrel, and three hams and a cured leg of lamb hung by strings from the rafters. José looked hungrily from these to the bottles of pickled eggs on the counter top. It amazed him how much goodness seemed crammed into one tiny store. McAllister walked up to the counter, José leaning on his crutch and limping behind him down the narrow aisle between bolts of gingham, calico, and muslin.

The man behind the counter wore red sleeve garters to hold back overly long sleeves and a black, pin-striped vest. He had short white hair, a pointed beard, and a smile-creased countenance.

"Good afternoon to you," the man smiled. "Bread's fresh out of the oven—the missus has been working hard. Would you and the boy care to try some?"

"How much?"

"Five cents a slice, with all the fresh butter and strawberry preserves you like," replied the man with a broad smile.

McAllister wordlessly dug a ten cent piece out of his pouch and placed it on the counter, and José watched hungrily as the storekeeper sliced off two thick pieces of the steaming bread and set them on the counter beside a crock of butter and a bowl of preserves. José thought he must have gone to Heaven after all, when he took the first bite.

McAllister wolfed down his helping and glanced across the row of rifles standing upright in a rack behind the storekeeper. "I'd like to git my boy a rifle of his own, but I'm a mite short o' coin. You do any tradin'?"

The storekeeper shrugged. "Depends on what you have to trade."

"How 'bout hides?"

"We take hides, yes. What do you have?"

"A grizzly. It's green—just a few days old. An' the fur's prime."

"Well, let's take a look at it then."

McAllister nodded. "All right. Lucky, you look over them rifles. I'll be back shortly."

José needed no prodding from McAllister. He already had his eye on a brand-new '73 Winchester. Its wood shimmered like silk, its brilliant blue octagonal barrel glinted in the dim light. Before he could say anything, the storekeeper drew the rifle from the rack and passed it to him. "I saw you eyeing that, son. Nice, isn't it?"

José started to reach out his hand, then stopped and looked into the man's eyes for sign of approval. "Go ahead, son," the man insisted. "Take it. Get the feel of it." He smiled and thrust the weapon a little closer to the boy.

Gingerly, José leaned up against the counter for support and set his crutch aside. He took the Winchester in his hand. Against his palm the red walnut was even smoother than it had looked. Its steel was flawless, its case-hardened receiver coldly beautiful, with its umber and deep blue swirls intertwined in a haphazard design. He set it on the counter and pressed the butt against his abdomen to steady it, then worked the lever gently with his good hand, gazing into its inner works. He pressed his little finger into the loading gate as if pushing a cartridge home. He held it up with the barrel resting on the counter and gazed down the top of the barrel at the blade front sight, picturing a deer before him in a meadow. The crescent butt pushed firmly into his shoulder, a little too firmly, perhaps, when his finger touched the trigger—it was a touch too long. But he would overlook that minor flaw, for he had some growing yet to do. This was definitely the gun for him.

The door creaked, and José turned. McAllister came in carrying the grizzly hide, followed by a second man who looked vaguely familiar to José. The hide looked even bigger than before, awing José with a memory, and its stale animal odor permeated the close room. He found himself edging away nervously as McAllister drew near with it. He cursed himself. Would he always be a coward when it came to bears?

McAllister lay the hide across the counter. The storekeeper was looking at it and nodding his head, eyebrows raised. "Now that's a bear!" The man who had followed McAllister in nodded his agreement, staring in awe.

McAllister reached over and squeezed José's shoulder affectionately. "My boy, here, killed it in a hand to hand fight. Biggest bear I've seen in years."

"I'll bet," said the storekeeper, looking from McAllister to José and back. "Well, let me look it over."

The white-haired man began to examine the hide inch by inch, for flaws. Except for the bullet holes in its chest there was not one flaw, speaking for McAllister's deftness with a knife.

Still holding the shiny Winchester, José looked over at McAllister, who had been covertly studying the rifle. At the same instant, McAllister looked up, and their eyes met. José knew McAllister would like this rifle. But despite an understanding smile McAllister shook his head. The motion was almost imperceptible, yet there was no mistake. José's heart fell, and he looked quickly back down at the rifle. Then he laid it carefully on top of the counter and hobbled to the other side of the store on his crutch.

A minute later, José heard the storekeeper speak. "That's a prime hide. A prime hide. Your boy must be a real frontiersman to bring down a bear like that."

He meant the words to flatter, yet in them José sensed sarcasm, like he thought the story was a joke. McAllister must have caught that, too. He looked the man squarely in the eyes. "He's no frontiersman, mister. But that boy is one hell of a man." McAllister turned away, his eyes searching out José in the dimly lit room. "C'mere, Lucky." When José hesitated, he waved him over emphatically. "Come on. I think my story's in question."

The storekeeper's cheeks went a little red. "Oh, I believe you, stranger. I believe you."

McAllister looked at him, then back at José as he limped over. "See that arm? Broke clean through. Bear bite. The leg, too." He reached out and took a hold of José's shirt, untucking it and raising it to his chest. "Now turn around, Lucky. Show the man what a grizzly can do in a close fight."

Reluctantly, José turned in a circle, embarrassed by the attention. When he turned back, he saw the amazement in the storekeeper's eyes. The man who had come in behind McAllister, a cowboy by his look, also stared in disbelief, and he and the storekeeper looked over at each other.

"Well, I'll be," said the cowboy. "How'd you kill 'im?"

McAllister spoke for him. "With a broken Yellow Boy. An' damn if he ain't as much man as anyone in this valley."

"I reckon he is at that," agreed the storekeeper. "And I guess you have a gun coming for this hide. The boy likes the .38-40." He pointed at the rifle on the counter. "I'll trade for the hide and eight dollars."

"It's too much. Besides, it ain't what we're lookin' for," countered McAllister. He indicated another rifle at the end of the rack. The scars in its stock and worn spots in the bluing could be seen from yards away. "How 'bout the rolling block? How much is that?"

The storekeeper turned and looked at it, then quickly over at José. José looked away, but not before the man saw the disappointment in his eyes. He couldn't help it. He didn't want any gun other than the Winchester. And when he realized which weapon McAllister had picked out, his disappointment nearly turned to grief. It was the ugliest thing he had ever seen.

The storekeeper handed McAllister the rifle, and he turned it over in his hands, checked it out thoroughly, and nodded as if satisfied. Not until then did he hold it out to José. "Remington made a hell of a rifle there, Lucky. Sturdy and strong. It don't shoot but once, an' that's a-plenty when it's a forty-five seventy. You hit any man or beast where you should, he'll go down. No question of it."

The storekeeper's eyes flickered up at McAllister, and his face paled. "I don't think that's any way to talk, sir. I would appreciate it if you limited your talk of killing to animals, not men."

McAllister looked at the man, his face expressionless. Looking into his eyes was like staring into two deep holes full of frozen water. "Mister, there's animals, an' then there's *animals*. Some walk on four legs, but the worst ones walk on two. Ain't no worse animal than a man gone bad, an' there ain't no animal needs killin' more."

His face still pale, the store owner stared at McAllister, then looked away. "If the boy wants that rifle, I'll trade straight across for the hide."

"Throw in four boxes o' shells, an' you got yerself a deal."

The other man thought for a moment. Finally, he cleared his throat and then smiled, not at McAllister, but at José. "It's a deal, if I can shake this young man's hand."

José looked at McAllister, then at the store owner, forcing a smile. He reached out and shook the hand firmly, then held on while he spoke. "I hope you don't ever decide to shoot at a man with that, son. Folks shouldn't be killing each other or even talking about it."

José nodded and pulled his hand away. McAllister blew derisively out his nostrils and looked over at José. "There'll be plenty o' time to talk about that kind o' thing, kid." He turned back to the storekeeper. "You got a length o' rope or a long strip o' rawhide you don't need?"

"Sure," replied the man, reaching behind him and drawing out a coil of slender rope without even having to look and see where it was.

McAllister took the rope wordlessly, drew his belt knife, and cut off a four foot length, dropping the extra on the counter. With deft hands, he tied one end about the forearm of the rifle, the other around the stock behind the trigger guard. "You'll need this till you heal up, Lucky."

José took the Remington when McAllister held it out again. Its barrel was tarnished, nicked here and there, mottled where spots of surface rust had been polished away. Its finish looked much like that of the Winchester the bear had broken, in fact, only now he had seen better, in the brand new seventy-three. It was a hard pill to swallow, but he bowed his head and slung the rifle about his neck. Looking up, he thanked the man, turned, and hobbled from the store.

McAllister looked back at the storekeeper, extracting a ten dollar gold eagle from his pouch and laying it deliberately on the countertop. His index finger rested on the coin for several seconds, as if it were hard to relinquish, but then his hand fell loosely away to his side. "This is for a sack of flour, some sugar, coffee, and beans. And just so's you'll know, mister, I'm no killer, an' neither will the boy be. I don't kill for no reason— man *or* beast. If a man dies by my hand it's only 'cause he's got blood in his eye fer me."

The man nodded as he laid the boxes of cartridges on the counter. "Well, that's somethin'. Just make sure the boy knows that."

"He knows."

McAllister named off other supplies and bought a folding skinning knife as a gift for José. While the storekeeper bundled the items up, McAllister could feel the eyes of the cowboy studying him. The man had looked at him oddly when they first met, out on the porch, and although he was friendly enough, something about the way he looked seemed prying, overly curious. Finally, McAllister looked over at him. "C'n I help you?"

"What?" The man straightened up from where he had been leaning against the counter. "Oh, sorry. Was I staring? Didn't mean to. Just daydreamin'."

McAllister nodded as he took the bundle under his left arm. "Well, see yuh around." He nodded at the storekeeper, then picked up his supplies, turned and stepped out on the porch.

José sat on the edge of the porch petting a mongrel dog. Several of them had been sniffing around the wagon when he came out. They could smell the bear meat and knew where it was concealed. The Remington rifle leaned against the porch boards beside him, its barrel pointed downward and resting in the dust. "Pick up the rifle, boy," said McAllister angrily. "That's no way to treat a gun."

José obeyed, not looking over at McAllister. "Sorry," he said. He heard footsteps behind them and saw the cowboy leave the store and walk off down the street. He mulled over the man's vaguely familiar features, but he couldn't place him.

McAllister deposited the supplies in back of the wagon, then plopped down on the porch beside José, resting his shoes in the gravelly dust. "A gun c'n save yer life, Lucky, or it c'n kill you. You treat it with respect, it'll be yer best ally. But you mistreat it an' it'll turn on you quicker'n a rabid dog. Don't ever rest the bore against the ground. It might fill full o' dirt an' blow right up in yer face."

They sat in silence for a moment, José staring at the ground, still petting the mutt. "I know you ain't happy, boy," said McAllister finally. "But this gun was fer you, an' you only, an' as far as I know, all you had to pay fer it with was the bear hide. I cain't go throwin' in that kind o' money on another man's rifle an' expect 'im to still feel it's his. You gotta be able to know you own this shooter all to yerself. Besides, you need somethin' stronger than a .38. An' another thing: in the places I'll take you before this summer's over ther' ain't no place fer a perty rifle. You'll see why. So hang in there an' trust me. Someday you'll have a Winchester, hopefully a .44 or bigger. A man-size gun. Until then… Well, just trust me. Now let's go get some grub down our gullets."

They stopped to eat in a Chinese restaurant next to Gorton's Billiard Hall and Saloon. The food was different than José was used to, but pleasant and satisfying. When he and McAllister had eaten until they could hold no more they sank back, and McAllister bit the end off a long black cigar and stuck it between his teeth. He lit it, and pungent blue smoke filled the air. José coughed and looked at the cigar, twisting up his face in disgust.

McAllister grinned. "Don't like it, huh? Well, you will. Helps digest dinner mighty good. Calms the nerves. Nothin' like it 'cept maybe the clear Idaho air on a fall mornin'."

José pondered this. How could a man compare the smell of a stinky cigar to that of mountain air? He didn't say anything. Perhaps when he was older he would acquire a nose for it. For now, it just turned his stomach.

Where José sat, his back was to the room, but he was in a position where he commanded a view of the street through the hazy window. McAllister, on the other hand, had chosen to place his back against the wall, with a view of front and back doors and anyone in the room. So it was José who saw the men coming, and one of them was the cowboy from the store. Suddenly, he realized why the man had looked so familiar. He was one of those who had confronted him in the meadow, one who had hung to the back of the group. And there was a grim determination on his face now and a set to his jaw. The cowboy was in the lead of a group of twelve or fifteen men, several of them carrying firearms.

Fear gripped José so for a second he couldn't move or speak. It was just long enough for McAllister to catch the horrified look in his eyes. Like a caged animal, McAllister lunged to his feet and whirled toward the window, inadvertently slamming the table into José's ribs. José didn't even feel the pain. His fear was so intense it blocked out all other sensation. Through blurry eyes he saw McAllister reach for his Colt and start to pull it free. There were no words from the man and there would be none. He knew the only way out now was his own death.

"No, please!" José begged. "Please don't!" There was no one else in the room, no one to hear the pleading in his voice. He wouldn't care if there had been. He didn't want his friend to die. He didn't want to say good bye, not as long as there might still be a way out of a confrontation.

The mob was nearing the front door, their eyes bright with excitement, with the knowledge they were closing on their quarry. Several of them ran around both sides of the building, blocking any exit from the rear. There was no magical tree now as before, no possible way to escape unseen. Robert McAllister would go down fighting, and he would take men with him, and in the fight José knew he might die, too. But he didn't dwell on that. He only thought of being alone.

Robert McAllister, the man with eyes like hailstorm clouds. Fear was an expression his face didn't know, although his blood must race wildly now. His countenance was frozen with the thrill of impending battle. The knowledge that here was his last fight, and he must make it a good one, giving everything he had to give. Because the last battle and no other would show the true steel within, would tell the world of a man with the fury of a cougar, a heart of fire. His thumb drew back the hammer of the Colt, his eyes narrowed.

And then their eyes met and held. "Please don't fight them," José whispered. He didn't think until later how silly that sounded. "Gray, you're my only friend."

José had never seen a man's resolve completely disappear in a matter of seconds. But McAllister's did, and his eyes took on a resigned look, and with what he must have felt was a sure knowledge that he would hang for this decision he released his pistol's hammer and slid it back into his belt. Closing his eyes, he sank into his chair.

Not knowing what else to do, José sat down, too. And then a sudden, wild thought came to him, and he blurted it out at the last second. "I'm not your real son, Gray! Tell them Indians killed my mother and father and you adopted me!"

And then the door flew open and the mob crowded into the little room, shoving tables and chairs out of the way, knocking some over. Some brandished firearms, several clubs, one a pitchfork, one a blacksmith's hammer. An older man carrying a shotgun stepped to the front.

McAllister and José gazed about them in astonishment. McAllister looked at the older man. "What's goin' on? We done somethin' wrong?"

The old man leveled his shotgun at McAllister's head, both hammers cocked. "Well, we don't know that yet. Some say you're a horse thief."

"A horse thief?" McAllister repeated in horror. "Oh no. Please don't point that thing. I c'n explain about the horse. I know it belongs to my boy's boss, but we intended to take it back to 'im. We really did. Ain't much of a horse anyway."

José looked quickly over at his friend. He hadn't yet grasped the run of his talk, yet knew it was a show. He was pleading with this old man like the real McAllister would never do, like José hadn't believed McAllister capable of even pretending to do.

"You c'n take the horse," McAllister went on. "The wagon's his, too. Just let us get some stuff out of it first."

"What are you goin' on about, mister?" interrupted the cowboy from the store. "I don't trust a thing you two say. We jumped this kid up on Bailey Creek." He spoke to the crowd but continued to stare at McAllister. "He claimed he was with his pa, an' now this fella's sayin' the same thing." He drew himself up straighter. "Even a fool can see you two ain't related, and if you'll lie about that you'll lie about anything. This kid's just coverin' for you."

A gush of wind left McAllister's lungs as he glanced over at José, feigning relief. "I'm the only pa he's got. His folks were killed by Injuns a few years back in Kansas, an' I adopted 'im. We been together ever since."

The cowboy was taken aback for a moment, but then he bulled on. "That don't mean a thing. A man came through a while ago and stoled a horse from J.B. Trace, then kidnapped little Rebecca Woodland. He'd a killed her, too, if a posse hadn't caught him. I was in that posse, and I say the man was you! And whether you're his pa or not, you're still a damn horse thief!"

"Nobody calls me that," McAllister said, his eyes narrowing. "I was with the kid all week. I've never stoled—" He started to stand up, but the old man yelled for him to sit back down.

"Don't you move again, mister, or I'll take your head off. If what you say is true, it'd be easy enough to find out. Now just sit there and don't blink."

José knew any fear McAllister had displayed was a show, but his own was not. Tears blurred his vision, and as much as he wanted to he couldn't stop them.

"Yer scarin' my boy," said McAllister suddenly. "Yer a bunch of bastards."

"To hell with yer boy!" said one burly man. He reached over and grabbed José by the shirt, jerking him out of his seat. He shoved him toward the men near the door. "Get him outta here, or we'll hang him with this horse thief."

José fell into waiting arms that clutched him ungently, men reeking of the stale sweat of days of hard labor in the sun. One man spun him around and took him by the neck in a choke hold, not bearing down yet certainly not worried about his discomfort. "Let the boy go, big man," ordered McAllister from his seat, the feigned fear in his eyes turning to hard steel. "He's got a broke leg an' arm, an' besides, he's half yer size."

"Yer worried about him, you shoulda thought o' that before," growled the burly man.

"I said, let him go." McAllister's entire body had visibly tensed, and José watched him fearfully.

The man holding José chuckled. "I'm going to break the kid's scrawny neck if you don't just shut up and do as you're told."

McAllister's eyes went hard as stones, and with no more warning he came up out of his chair under the old man's shotgun, grasping the barrels and shoving them skyward. The double-barreled blast was mighty in the little room, taking them all by surprise. McAllister's momentum carried the table over onto its side, and he went over it on top of the old man.

Shocked, the crowd paused, and then they were on him.

Like a demon McAllister fought, striking everyone within range. He had the advantage of knowing he had no friends there to hurt accidentally. In the melee José was flung toward the door, and he hit it with his head, sliding to the floor with colored lights dancing in his brain. He could hear the roar of several men, cries of pain and anger. He wanted to rise, to do something to help McAllister, but there was nothing he could do.

Suddenly, a gun exploded, and José opened his eyes. Men packed the room, some standing, some rising, some just sitting and holding battered body parts. Silence filled the moment, except for the sound of ragged breathing. One man stood holding a smoking rifle. Another lay prone, unmoving, in the center of them all.

Between the legs of the crowd, José saw the fallen man. With a sick heart, he stared at the soles of that man's worn-out brogan shoes.

Chapter Ten

José's heart seemed to stop. His breathing did, too. He didn't mean it to, it just did. His fear was too strong for anything but his eyes and ears to work.

That was McAllister lying there. And someone had fired a rifle. To José, that meant they'd shot McAllister. In that close space, someone had to have been shot. The bullet had to go somewhere. And at that range... McAllister must be dead.

So what could José do? Would they send him to jail for lying about McAllister? Or should he tell them McAllister had forced him to lie? No! Curse them all. He had tried to protect McAllister because the man had saved his life. He had been forced to lie to do that, but he would do it again if he had to. Except now he had no excuse to lie. Even if it meant his dream of becoming a mountain man was over, he couldn't give up his integrity. He would just as soon be dead.

The older man with the shotgun stood back from the others. His parted lips carved a gash across his pallid face. He wasn't breathing hard like the rest of them and didn't appear to have taken part in the scuffle after being knocked down. The only sign he had been involved was a trickle of blood at the corner of his mouth. Slowly, he raised his eyes to the skinny blond man who held the rifle, blue smoke still curling out of its barrel. The blond man looked sick.

"Did you shoot him, Wilson?" The question seemed meaningless. McAllister was immobile on the floor, and Wilson held a smoking rifle in his hands. José couldn't see Wilson's face, for his back was to him, but he saw his head tilt to look down at McAllister. A few seconds passed while black powder smoke the odor of rotten eggs dissipated in the close room.

Finally, the blond man looked up. "I just meant to hit him. I didn't know it was cocked."

The burly man who had grabbed José earlier looked over sharply at Wilson. "Well, that's pretty stupid." He crouched down and placed his fingers alongside McAllister's neck. He nodded, then turned him onto his back. Between the legs of several men, José saw with sudden elation the slow rise of McAllister's chest, and he rose partway off the floor. "He ain't even shot," claimed the burly man at last. "There's what you hit." He pointed at a hole in the floor surrounded by fresh black powder burns. "You 'bout stove in his head though."

Wilson turned around, and José saw the bright red of his face as he stumbled past and outside, leaving the door open.

Color began to return to the old man's face now as José watched him glance about at the others. "Well, I didn't intend for this to turn into a brawl. Let's see what we can do for this fellow till he comes to."

"Yeah," piped up the burly man. "Can't hang 'im if he dies."

José's heart jumped, and he looked back over at the older man.

"Well, you won't be hanging anyone today, Trent. I'll turn this man over to Deputy Goss when he comes back." He suddenly recalled José's presence and looked over at him where he sat on the floor. "Someone help that boy to a chair. Can't you see he's hurt?"

It was true José was in pain. The fall had jolted him, and he felt stickiness beneath the bandages on his back. But that was nothing compared to the pain he felt as they hoisted him from the floor and carried him to a chair. Every part of his body throbbed. He was dizzy. He was nauseated. And still, he felt better physically than he did inside his heart. They meant to try his friend for horse theft—if he lived. And he'd heard they hanged men for that.

The older man stood bent over in front of José, his face only two feet away. "You going to be all right, boy? That was pretty uncalled-for, what happened." José only nodded, holding his aching ribs and trying not to look too sick. "My name's Weaver, son. Abe Weaver."

"I'm José."

Weaver nodded. "Well, Leonard there says your father stole a horse from J.B. Trace. Trace left town on the train last night for a horse buying trip to Boise, so your friend will have to be held until he gets back, unless we can solve this. But I suppose you have a story of your own. What is it?"

José took a deep breath and winced at the pain that shot through his side. As he leaned forward and clutched his ribs, the pain ebbed slightly, but he didn't let on. He needed this undisturbed moment to gather his thoughts. His story had to be good, for he was sure they would check it against McAllister's when he came to—*if* he came to. José hoped the steel of the rifle barrel hadn't caused McAllister any permanent damage. He looked up now and over at McAllister. Several men had dragged him to a wall and had his head propped up with a coat. Blood was plastered in his hair.

"He didn't steal any horse, mister," said José, trying his best to meet the man's steady gaze. "He's been with me all along, except for a couple of times going hunting."

The cowboy called Leonard spoke up. "There's no need jawin' over this, Weaver. I'm sure this is the man I shot at across the river, but I know someone who'd be positive. I'll ride out and fetch Becky Woodland into town. She's a right smart girl, an' she got herself a long hard look at the gent. She'll know him."

"Perfect," replied Abe Weaver with a nod. "Go and get her. We'll hold these two at my house till you get back."

José sighed and stared blankly at the floor. He wanted to breathe easily again, but it was no use. Whoever this girl was, she would bring McAllister down, for deep inside, as much as he had come to like McAllister, he was certain he was guilty. So he and McAllister might share a few more hours of strained companionship, depending on how far away this girl lived. But when she got there and positively identified McAllister the game was over. José put a hand over his eyes, and a tear escaped unbidden and rolled down his cheek.

Two hours later, the pair sat gloomily in the parlor at Abe Weaver's house. McAllister was stretched full length upon a window seat, his boots off, revealing wool socks worn through at heel and toe. Though the sky was slightly overcast the sun's ray's shot through the clouds and through the filmy glass of the window and warmed him gently.

José sat at right angles to the window seat in a Sleepy Hollow armchair with big, fat arms and almost completely covered in rich floral brocade except for the carved black walnut legs. But in spite of the chair's comfort, the house was cold, and he shivered as he looked longingly at the light splashed across his friend. Mrs. Weaver saw this, and she brought him an afghan and laid it across his lap.

José looked up at the woman. Her steel-colored hair was tied behind her head, and she wore a faded yellow dress speckled with once-red flowers. Her smile deepened the fine-cut wrinkles about her eyes and mouth and nose. Mrs. Weaver reminded him of his mother.

After José thanked her, she left. Now only he and McAllister remained—and Abe Weaver, who sat in a Windsor chair and looked on stoically, the shotgun across his knees.

In the corner of the high-ceilinged room towered a grandfather clock of finely carved maple. Black Roman numerals contrasted a large, stark white face, and the bronze pendulum swung to and fro rhythmically. José fancied his heart beginning to beat to its time. He watched the minutes tick by and then gradually his heart began to quicken. He sensed it and felt his stomach tighten; something was about to happen.

Horse hooves clattered on the road outside, and metal tires grated on rock. Through the window he saw a wagon rattle past. By the abrupt way its noise ceased he knew it hadn't gone far. He had only glimpsed the rig—he hadn't seen its passengers but guessed who they must be. He began to breathe shallowly and too quickly, and he looked over anxiously at McAllister.

His friend was watching him, and with a slight nod he let him know he had seen the wagon, too. He reached up and pulled the bloody rag from the side of his head and fingered his hair gently. His fingers came away clean.

McAllister sat up slowly and looked over at Weaver. "Would that be them now?"

"I suppose it would. But sit tight. They'll come to us." He turned and called out. "Mother? Let them come on back here when they knock."

"Yes, dear," came the answer.

Soon the knock came, and several voices sounded at once when the door opened. One of them was deep, grating—polite yet not friendly. Maybe it was only so because José expected it to be. He didn't want to look, but he did. He stared at the doorway through which they would come. He could feel his pulse throb along his temples. He felt his head would burst.

The cowboy, Leonard, came in first, walking in his swinging gate with his boot heels clopping on the wood floor—another of the luxuries the Weavers enjoyed. Then it seemed an eternity while a heavier pair of boots followed, moving almost ponderously toward the doorway.

A man with a full chestnut beard streaked with gray suddenly filled the doorway. A flat-brimmed, round-crowned black hat sat atop his head, and it threw into dim light a pair of green eyes that lit upon McAllister with a gaze that could have melted ice. He was dressed in a shabby black suit with a patch on one knee, and he wore no gun in sight. The man stood better than six and a half feet tall, and his shoulders and his face and his hands were very big. José gulped. He was sure the man could have torn his arms off at the shoulders.

And there, safe beneath the massive bulk of the man's arm, stood the girl.

Without realizing it, José let his mouth fall open as his eyes met hers. He had never had a girlfriend. And he had been in the hills for an awfully long time. Maybe that dictated the way his eyes received the sight before him. But José Olano thought this was the most beautiful thing he had ever seen.

Judging by the identical eye and hair color, she was obviously the big man's daughter. But as far as looks they had nothing else in common. Her locks shone softly in the dim light and curled loosely over her shoulders, framing a face with perfect ivory skin. Her dark brows were arched and accented eyes of deepest green that brought back memories of the stormy bay as José's ship sailed in off the Atlantic. And beneath a perfectly straight nose were full lips, frank and honest, and a chin proud and strong. José guessed her to be about fifteen years of age.

She wore a dark green calico dress, and though patched in several places she made it seem the attire of royalty. For one so young, she held herself quite proud and straight, and despite the modest, floor-sweeping dress, her budding womanhood was very plain. José stared at her like he had been slapped, and finally she looked away. Her eyes fell then upon McAllister.

Rebecca Woodland had a way of looking into a man's soul that didn't fit one so young in life. José continued to stare at her eyes, transfixed, and he caught the change in them when she looked at McAllister—a flicker of recognition. He glanced quickly over at McAllister. Carrying his act through to the bitter end, the man gazed at her with a puzzled look, an expression with no unfriendliness but no sign of recognition, either. Just a plain look that said to the girl, *I'm sorry, miss. I don't think we've ever met.*

The girl's eyes again darted to José's face, and for several seconds they held each other's gaze. Then she looked back at McAllister. Her eyes blinked, but not involuntarily. It was a slow, calculated action whose significance was meant to be caught only by someone already closely watching her. Her lip corners turned up, very faintly, and then that look of soft mercy vanished. She looked up at her giant of a father. "That's not him, Papa. That's the wrong man."

Leonard's eyes snapped to the girl, then up at her father, who glanced back at him. Befuddled, he looked back at the girl. "Are you sure about that, Miss Becky?"

Rebecca didn't hesitate. She gazed Leonard squarely in the eyes. "I'm positive. I remember him very well."

Leonard, face flushed, looked at Woodland beseechingly. "You two might wanna talk a mite before you leave here," he suggested, choosing his words carefully. "Gettin' grabbed like that and near drowned could be pretty scary for a youngster. Could be she needs to think on it for a while to really recall his face."

Mr. Woodland looked down at his daughter, whose eyes were already raised to him. He gazed at her searchingly, his green eyes intense. "Look again if you have to, Rebecca. Remember, girl, once we leave this house there'll be no turnin' back. If it's him, it's him, but there'll be no changin' your mind later. Think on it well."

Rebecca's lip corners turned up understandingly, and she nodded. "I know, Papa. This man is not a kidnapper." She looked back over at McAllister, and this time she smiled. "That's the wrong man. We should let him go."

Woodland turned to Leonard and Weaver. "You heard my daughter, gentlemen. You have the wrong man, and I suggest you turn him loose."

Abe Weaver had stood from his chair. He was still holding the shotgun, its barrels aimed at the floor, and he watched Rebecca closely. "You're a sharp child, Becky. And everyone knows a Woodland wouldn't lie. So I guess we got the wrong man. Thank you for your help in clearing it up." He turned to McAllister. "All right, mister. I'm sorry for the mix-up. But remember, the fight was started by you. The brutality was not my idea. You and the boy are free to go."

McAllister glanced at José, and they stood up in unison. José's back and ribs felt very stiff. He was sure his wounds had ripped open, but the thick bandages kept any blood from showing, and he was afraid to tell anyone. He wanted to leave this town as soon as he could.

"Your weapons are by the front door," said Weaver, reading the questioning look in McAllister's eyes.

He started to follow the two of them to the door, and Mr. Woodland and Rebecca stepped aside to let them pass. But McAllister stopped in front of the big man and his daughter. He was more haggard-looking than normal, his hair tousled, his forehead smudged with blood, his right shirt sleeve torn almost off at the elbow. He leaned a little, favoring one side. But his gray eyes were as bright as ever, and coolly they stared at the girl. Then he smiled. "Thanks, miss. I was in a bad way."

Rebecca tilted her head slightly forward in a nod of acknowledgment and she held out her hand to him. McAllister leaned back a bit and looked at the hand, then glanced up at Woodland. At last, he took the hand and squeezed. "Thanks again."

José followed closely on McAllister's heels, hobbling on his crutch. He was afraid to look at the girl again or at the man who towered over her, red hair and beard framing his broad face. But when McAllister stopped at the door to pick up their guns, he had to stop too, and his eyes involuntarily drifted to the girl. In consternation, he caught her looking at him, her steady gaze reading his thoughts like a book. Or so he felt. Blood rose to his face.

McAllister stuck the Colt pistol in his holster, then picked up the Remington rolling block rifle. He held it in his hands for a moment, nodding with a look of satisfaction, then turned and handed it to José, holding out his hand for the crutch he had made. "Yer a man, Lucky. You c'n tote yer own blowpipe."

José looked up at McAllister with tears brimming his eyes, and he traded the crutch for the rifle, using it, butt down, in place of the crutch. They stepped through the front door onto the porch and started down the street to find the wagon.

They had not gone far before a voice called out from behind. It was Mrs. Weaver. She hurried over to them, holding something in the crook of her arm. When she reached them, she revealed a gray flannel shirt, freshly pressed. She held it toward McAllister. "Take this, sir. I think yours is past mending." She indicated his torn elbow.

"Thanks, ma'am, you been more th'n kind."

When they got back to the wagon, all José wanted to do was leave this town. He wanted to beg McAllister to let them get in the wagon and make dust, but he didn't want to seem afraid. He didn't think that was an emotion the man would understand and one he might take as a weakness. So he held his tongue. But the moment he had an opportunity, he took it.

McAllister stood at the front of the wagon, his left hand resting on the iron tire. His eyes scanned the dusty street and its drab establishments. "Well, Lucky, we c'd go to the Hotel Sterritt an' try to get a bath, but since yer wantin' to be a mountain man, you may's well know: they don't take baths." He gave a chuckle. "Besides, I've heard stories about that place, an' they weren't pretty. Between the seam squirrels, bed bugs, an' bad vittles, they should be payin' their customers, not the other way 'round. But ther's a place up the road a piece that we need to git you, if yer wounds're ever gonna heal. So let's light a shuck outta this town. It's a mite unfriendly, an' I'm sick of all these rich folk lookin' down their nose at me."

José nodded wordlessly and let McAllister heft him onto the wagon seat. McAllister walked around and hopped onto his side and slapped the reins against the horse, and the wagon rocked out of town as dust billowed off the unwatered street.

As the wagon rolled, McAllister glanced to the southwest. "Looks like this weather's fixin' to change." Masses of cloud the color of his eyes piled up like soiled sheep's wool along the far horizon, and now that McAllister mentioned it José could even feel the temperature drop. He started to wonder if they shouldn't have stayed in the Sterritt after all, in spite of its "seam squirrels" and bed bugs.

Soon, the town disappeared behind the hills, and the wagon continued north, then gradually west. It rolled along the dusty road, and miles and miles of new spring grass and big sage rolled away on the left before struggling upward under tree-clad slopes. On the right, low, juniper-dotted hills lined the horizon. And straight ahead rose more timbered mountains, which McAllister called the Portneuf Range. José set his sights on them expectantly, eyeing the snowbanks that blanketed the canyons and ridges. To the south, the glowering clouds overcame the sky, and a stiff breeze slapped the tops of the sagebrush angrily, kicking up dust.

They made camp that night between the road and the Oregon Short Line railroad tracks, in a flat place occupied by a water tower and train stop dubbed "Squaw Creek." On all sides, minor mountain ranges could be seen, and wildflowers like dormant butterflies dotted the land.

While they lay in the wagon, José listened to his friend's steady breathing and heard the first of the rain whisper across the wagon cover. It sounded like falling pine needles at first, just a slow, loose rattle. Then it came down steadily, and soon he heard the steady *drip, drip* at the foot of the wagon, where the rain had found its way through a hole in the wagon sheet.

The wind had slowed, but occasionally a gust caught the wagon cover and flapped it loosely, allowing a soft sprinkle to touch his cheeks. It was very cold, and he realized that was partly because he was hot. The fever was returning.

The next morning they slept until nearly noon, and when they awoke the rain had ceased. After a leisurely breakfast they continued on. José said nothing about the fever, but McAllister seemed to know he was in pain, for he kept the wagon at a snail's pace, and they plodded into the afternoon. Every few miles they would stop the wagon and get down to stretch.

It was much cooler than the last week had been, much more like April should be, and the wagon wheels sloshed through puddles of mud, dragging in the deep spots. The wagon swayed and jolted, every little bump in the road offering José new pains. It hadn't been bad at first. The excitement of new country and of their recent adventures had occupied his mind. But now the thrill had worn off, and each hole or rock struck by the wheels sent pain through his wounds and through some places that weren't even hurt. His head began to throb mercilessly so that soon even the beauty of the mountains hugging them closely on either side couldn't distract him. Worst of all was his arm. An unquenchable fire burned deep inside it. Yet he couldn't say anything about his misery to McAllister. He had promised not to be a bother.

When the sun set, they were traveling along a narrow valley with the muddy Portneuf River close on their right. Beyond its banks towered jagged rocks and juniper trees, and a steep-sided bare hill blocked their view of the setting sun. Just after they crossed the river, three deer with shaggy coats darted across the road. José watched with no relish, for pain had totally overcome him.

They came to a bend in the river and swung west with it. To their left towered a sagebrush hill and more rugged, broken rocks choked with maple. It dropped steeply toward the river, where cottonwoods towered along its banks.

McAllister looked over at José as if about to say something but then paused. He watched him for a moment, then reached over and squeezed his shoulder gently. "Almost there, Lucky. Hang on for a while longer."

José tried to smile, but it was feeble. He bent forward and closed his eyes, swaying and jolting and cringing with each bump of the wagon. They turned left, away from the main freight road and the railroad tracks, and soon he felt the wagon grinding to a halt on the gravelly trail. He looked over to see McAllister watching him, his eyes soft.

"We're here, boy." He pulled back the brake to set it and hopped down from the wagon. José looked around deliriously at the slopes on both sides, ominous in the half-light. To the left and in front of them, he heard the rushing of the river and rain-freshened leaves whispering soft in the evening breeze. It was a chill breeze, smelling of juniper, sagebrush, and cottonwood, and felt good on his fevered cheeks. Across the river, several hundred yards away up the slope toward the mountains, José made out the forms of cabins separated by large stretches of open ground. Their windows glowed with cheery yellow light and smoke curled from their chimneys.

McAllister came around to his side of the wagon and saw him gazing toward the dwellings. "It's a damn shame there's people movin' in. This used to be a perty peaceful spot. I hear they're callin' it Dempsey now, after some old boy that used to run around up here." He shrugged and sadly shook his head, looking away from the houses. He held up his hands. "Come on, boy. I'll get you down."

Though dreading the feel of the man's hands against his battered body, José ached to get off the wagon seat, so he obeyed. He steeled himself to McAllister's fingers against his ribs. The man hefted him from the wagon like a child, and he leaned against its side.

Dizziness swept over him. It was as if all his healing the last few days meant nothing, and he was back where he had been when he first met McAllister. He felt like he had no control over his movements.

And then the world faded away.

When he awoke, in total darkness, he was cradled in McAllister's arms, and they were on the move. As if he weighed nothing, McAllister packed him down a slope through tangled bushes and tall grass. The sweet smell of cottonwood leaves permeated his senses. The rumble of the river sang to him gently and lapped over stones along the bank.

José suddenly remembered the pain McAllister must have been in himself from his beating. The man had practically had his head knocked in, been kicked, punched, and battered by clubs. His face was covered by red welts and bruises, some starting to turn blue. Yet José hadn't heard even one complaint from him. He swore the man would hear none from him either. At last he came to a stop and laid José down in a bed of soft grass.

"This is it, Lucky. Shuck yer clothes. I'll run back up the hill an' get the lantern an' yer rifle. Then we're gonna take a swim." José looked up at McAllister incredulously. The water had to be freezing! It was April, and the elevation was high enough to keep the water as cold as frost. But he was too tired to argue. He started to unbutton his shirt, but somewhere in the process he fell asleep, his face bathed in starlight and the last of the dying rusty light in the west.

McAllister had been gone only minutes when José awoke to the crack of a single gunshot. Then the night was still.

Chapter Eleven

There is no painkiller like fright. José came very much awake in an instant and rolled over onto his stomach. He no longer felt his ribs or aching head. Involuntarily, he held his breath as he looked up the slope where his friend had disappeared and from where the shot had come. His eyes darted this way and that, peering into the shadows.

He felt like screaming, not only in fear, but out of frustration. When would the danger go away? Would it ever? Maybe only if he left McAllister. Every time he started to relax, something else happened. It was wearing him down. McAllister could make him a mountain man. He was sure of it. But not if he got them killed first!

At last, McAllister's voice drifted down to him. "Lucky? Everything's all right. I was just shootin' at a deer."

José released his breath and plopped his head down on the soft, wet grass. Then he raised his head again abruptly. *Shooting at a deer?* How could he see to shoot? It was as dark as the inside of a horse's stomach!

An eternity seemed to pass before he heard McAllister descending the brushy slope, and then he was at José's side. He hadn't even made a noise until almost upon him. McAllister squatted down beside him on the grass. "We got fresh meat, boy," he said matter-of-factly. "Startin' with this." In the dim light, José saw him stretch his hand toward him. "Take it."

José pushed himself weakly to his knees and reached out. Gingerly, his fingers touched an object in the man's hand. It was warm, soft, and slimy to the touch. Instinctively, he retracted his hand. "What is it?"

"Deer liver. It's an Injun delicacy."

"It's raw?" said José incredulously.

McAllister laughed. "Well, of course it's raw! How would I cook it? It's still fresh and warm anyway. Ain't no reason to cook it."

José felt sick to his stomach. He wished it were light enough to see McAllister's face. Maybe he was just teasing him. "Could you—did you bring the lantern with you?"

There was a moment of silence, then McAllister sighed. "I brought it, but I was hopin' not to have to light it. Never know who's about."

José swallowed and shut his eyes tightly. He was pleased to hear the flare of a match, and he opened his eyes to see McAllister's eerily lit face in the sickly yellow light. The wick of the lamp came to life, and McAllister adjusted it up.

"There. You happy?" José wasn't, but he didn't say so. He stared at the bloody hunk of steaming organ, wishing he had never asked for the light. McAllister's face not only affirmed he was serious, it showed he must have already consumed a generous amount of the liver himself, for his mouth and chin were smeared with blood. "Well?"

Steeling himself, José reached out gingerly, taking the bite-sized hunk between thumb and forefinger. Without waiting, he plopped it into his mouth and started to chew. When the taste hit him, he thought better of this and swallowed it whole, wincing as it slid down his throat.

McAllister chuckled. "Not that bad, was it?"

José felt brave, and he didn't want to disappoint his friend. He could be a real mountain man after all. "Sure. It wasn't nearly as bad as I thought it would be."

"Good." McAllister reached down to the grass. When he stood again José saw with horror a hunk of liver big enough to cover McAllister's hand, steaming and dripping gore.

"Now gobble this down while I shuck my clothes an' go try the water." Numbly, José let the weight of the organ fall like a skinned grouse into his palm. It must have weighed a pound. He was thankful when McAllister blew out the lantern before going to the water. He didn't want him to witness his misery.

Then he had an idea. He knew he needed nourishment, but that could come as well from cooked steaks as from raw liver, and with much more satisfaction to his tastebuds. How would McAllister know whether he ate the liver or not? Feeling guilty, but not guilty enough to down a pound of steaming raw liver, José waited, listening to the rustle of McAllister's shirt, then his pants. When the man slid into the water, it surprised José how near it sounded. Was he in the river? If so, it must have bent sharply this way and was much closer than he had believed. Although McAllister hadn't gone as far away as he'd hoped, he had only one chance. Hoping the sound of the water would cover his deed, he flung the hunk of liver as far as he could out into the bushes. Then, as an afterthought, he smeared blood on his mouth and chin. He hadn't sunk far enough to eat any more than the one tiny piece of raw liver and hoped he never did.

"I'll come out an' get you, kid," he heard McAllister say. "The water feels good." Too overwhelmed to fight, José carefully shed his clothes, trying to push the pain out of his mind as he drew the cloth past his wounds. By the time he was done, McAllister was beside him, and he picked him up like so much grain in a sack and carried him down to where the water gurgled. McAllister's cold, bare skin against his felt surprisingly good after the day of being pounded by the wagon seat. His hard, muscular arms and abdomen pressed against José. There was no wasted flesh, no loose flab anywhere on McAllister's form.

McAllister picked his way carefully down over wet rocks, and soon José heard him wading into the water. He clenched his teeth, anticipating the chill of the water. There was still snow in the high country, and this water must be like ice, but he had to prove his manhood to McAllister. He couldn't let him know how he was dreading the cold.

When the first of the water touched José's skin, the shock was almost excruciating.

Not the shock of breath-stealing ice water but of water so hot it was like it had been heated on a stove. He looked toward McAllister's dim silhouette. "Hot springs," said the man simply. "It'll soak yer aches away."

Though the water was far too hot at first, and José didn't think he could stand it for long, its soothing fingers began quickly to work deep into the muscles of his legs. It was like a giant bathtub larger than any in the world, and it was free! He found himself drawn into it, and though it burned into his wounds as it soaked through his bandages, the pain eventually ebbed. He sank down, letting his skin get used to it a little at a time. And then it was up to his chin, and he sat on a smooth, round boulder someone must have rolled into the pool just for that purpose.

The hot steam wisped past his face, making him sweat, and the breeze cooled it and dried it on his cheeks. Condensation began to build in his hair, then run back down his face in icy rivulets. The hot water, swirling in slow eddies about him, had a hypnotic effect. Had it been a touch cooler, he might have gone to sleep. Instead, he began to feel light-headed. At last he heard McAllister rise from the water.

"Time to go, Lucky," he said simply. "You c'n get too much of a good thing. You need to rest yer wounds."

He carried José up to the bank again, laying him down gently. The grass was cold but felt good against hot skin. José lay there and closed his eyes. He could have fallen asleep, but the night air cooled him quickly, and soon he was shivering in the dark.

He heard McAllister stand up and slip into his clothes. Then the man walked over and knelt beside him, slowly cutting off his wet bandages. When he was finished, he stood and held out a hand to him in the dim moonlight. Wordlessly, José took it and came to his feet. He leaned against McAllister for support while he slipped his own clothes on. He found himself dressing slowly, letting his weight rest against McAllister's solid torso. It was a strange feeling, there in the dark, this man and boy who hardly knew each other, touching as if both needed the closeness to quell their loneliness. Neither one spoke, and neither had to. It was a moment in which they grew together silently, and José felt as safe as a new-born fawn with its mother.

When José had tugged on the one shoe he needed to hop around, they returned to the wagon, and there McAllister relit the lantern and had José take off his shirt again so he could redo his splint with the sheet and two lengths of board he had acquired in town. He also replaced the other bandages and resplinted the leg, then lifted José into the wagon. McAllister crawled inside, blew the lamp, and lay down beside him, and José quickly fell into a dreamy sleep.

It was the best José had slept in months. The hot water worked its miracle, and he was so relaxed he didn't awake even once but slept on past the rising of the sun. He didn't know how long McAllister was up before he awoke, but the blanket beside him was cold. He got to his knees and looked outside.

The first thing that caught his attention was the carcass of a deer with nubs of soft-looking velvet protruding from its head. It was sprawled belly up across two rocks, its body cavity propped open with a branch of sagebrush. Sight of it reminded him of his bout with the steaming liver, and he looked shamefully away. He noticed several magpies perched restlessly in a juniper tree not far away, talking and eyeing the deer hungrily.

The next thing he noticed was the hot water pools. There were several of them, and they were surrounded completely by jagged, tawny rocks from which clumps of sagebrush and grass grew. Little wisps of steam curled up lazily and disappeared in the cold morning air. Fifty yards to his left ran the Portneuf River, a rapid, shallow stream at this point, rushing noisily over a flat-worn bed of rock. And in front of him an almost vertical wall of the same tan stone rose thirty feet high, and another rock-strewn hill two hundred feet tall rose beyond, to the horizon.

Soon McAllister came from the river, which was traversed by a log bridge. He had forsaken his newly procured overalls and brogan shoes for his grease-blackened buckskin pants and moccasins. He had also shaved off his beard and looked like himself again. He saw José and smiled. "How yuh feelin' this mornin'? Get a good night's rest?"

"Sure. The best night I can remember since sleeping in a good bed."

McAllister scoffed. "No such thing as a 'good bed', Lucky. You'll learn that soon enough. The ground's the only way to go, unless it's rainin' or snowin' or such. Otherwise, you got the wind to lull you to sleep, an' the wolves to sing to yuh an' the stars an' moon to watch over yuh. Listen to that river yonder. No house ever give yuh that, did it? Just four walls an' a roof to pen yuh in." It was hard to disagree with all that beauty, but José wasn't totally convinced. Houses didn't have bears in them to rip you to ribbons, either.

Suddenly, José smelled woodsmoke. Almost instantly, his mouth began to water. "Are you cooking something?"

"Not yet, but I'm fixin' to. Git yer shoes on an' let's go to the fire."

The fire burned in a clearing that had seen much use. The grass was pressed down, ground to dust in many places. There were dead logs and large rocks set strategically as only man could have done and several large circles of rocks blackened by many campfires.

"This is sacred Injun ground, Lucky," explained McAllister. "They prob'ly don't come so much anymore 'cause it's become a place fer tourists, but it used to be this was neutral ground—a kind o' sacred healin' place. All the tribes c'd come here under truce to heal their wounds and banged-up bodies. I been here with 'em myself a time or two, back 'fore the white man killed half of 'em an' shoved the rest onto reservations. Back 'fore they was buildin' cabins up on that hill over there." With a look of disgust, he kicked at a rusted tin can near the fire. "Times've sure changed since them days."

José started to sit on one of the rocks, but McAllister stopped him. "Hey! I wanna show you somethin' before I start cookin'. Come with me."

Leaning heavily on his crutch, José followed McAllister curiously back over to where he had been lying on the grass the previous night. McAllister motioned José over several feet past. "Look here," he said, pointing at the ground. "Looks like someone shot a small animal here not too long ago."

José peered closely but saw nothing. He had no idea what McAllister was trying to show him, and though he hated to admit it, he had to if he was to learn. "What is it?"

"Come on, Lucky! Get down close. Look where my finger is."

José did so, trying to keep from putting too much weight on his broken leg. There was one tiny spot of brownish red on a leaf. "Is it blood?"

"Good, Lucky," praised McAllister, patting him lightly on the shoulder. "It is. But don't stop lookin' yet. Look close now. Which way did the animal run?"

José stared at the drop of blood, his mind churning. Then he began to look in the immediate area for tracks, those of a rabbit or something else small. Something that would point out a direction of travel to him. But there was nothing. At last he admitted he couldn't tell.

"All right. I saw yuh lookin' around fer tracks or somethin'. That's good, but you need to gather all yuh can from every little bit o' sign before yuh go on. This little drop o' blood's like a word in a book, an' yuh need to look at it close an' get its full an' real meanin' 'fore yuh go on. It's important, 'specially if yer trackin' an animal on the run in rocks. You might see hoof scars on the rocks, if it has hooves. You might even see claw marks, 'specially if it's a big bear. But don't count on it. If it's a man yer huntin', an' he's smart enough to take his shoes off, he won't leave nothin'. Even moccasins c'n give a man away, now an' then, but bare feet won't unless he lets 'em start bleedin'. So look close at that blood drop. See how it's kind of in a teardrop shape, but with a long tail? If somethin's movin' fast an' bleedin', it might look like that. If it does, it's almost a sure sign. That sharp part o' the teardrop is pointin' the way the animal ran. Now when you find this spot, you'll wanna mark it somehow. With a big stick or somethin' you might see from a ways off. Then if you lose the trail you c'n always go back."

José nodded interestedly. Forgetting his hunger, he eagerly waited to see if McAllister would find this wounded animal.

McAllister watched him closely. "*Now* you c'n look fer tracks. But if it's a big animal or even a jackrabbit it might've leaped a long ways 'fore comin' down again. So line up on that spot o' blood an' look out ahead. Where would you go if'n you was a wounded animal? Is ther' a place to hide up there? Is ther' one way where the travelin' ain't as hard as another? If the layout don't mean nothin' to yuh, just start goin' perty much straight where the tail o' that teardrop points. But keep to the side of any tracks or sign. You don't wanna spoil yer trail. Always leave it so's if yuh had to come back you c'd always track the same undisturbed trail again."

José nodded and began to follow the way the teardrop pointed. Soon he pleased himself by finding two more drops of blood, one on a blade of grass. He didn't think many people would have spotted that tiny drop. "Good goin', Lucky," McAllister smiled. "Yer on yer way to becomin' a real tracker. Now, did you notice how that blood's just barely dry? That means it's fresh. It could've been shot yesterday an' been kept moist till sunrise by the cool air an' the rain. But it's a sure fact it was shot after the rain, or it woulda been washed away."

Again, José nodded. He realized whoever had wounded this animal must have done so not long before his and McAllister's arrival. He continued on until he had gone another twenty yards without spotting any further blood. At last he turned to McAllister. "I think maybe we got off the trail. There aren't any tracks or anything. Wouldn't there be some in the dirt somewhere?"

"I don't know, Lucky. Think about it. Maybe it was a bird. A bird could've flown over an' lost that blood an' never left a track."

"Yeah," José seized gladly upon the suggestion. "I'll bet it *was* a bird."

"Somethin' that flew, anyway," agreed McAllister cryptically, then immediately continued. "So all you got to go by is the line he left you. Now go back to where you saw the last sign an' put a marker there." José did this, McAllister following along patiently. "Then go back to the first blood, stand back and line up the two. They'll make a straight line, an' that's what you follow, at least till yer perty positive ther's no more sign that way."

José followed this instruction, and it led him right back to where he had given up. Discouraged, he looked over at McAllister, but the man only motioned him on. By now, José had started to wish McAllister had never even spotted the blood. His good leg was growing weak from hopping around on it, and his bad one was starting to throb from the jarring.

They had taken only five more steps when José turned again to McAllister. "I think I lost it. If it's a bird, it could have flown a mile away."

McAllister shrugged. "You could be right, boy. If you wanna be a tracker, you best get ready fer a lot o' disappointment. Some of 'em just get away, if yer fool enough to take them bad shots. But you ain't through till the game's played out an' you've done everything you know. You can't leave an animal that might be sufferin' out there somewhere, 'specially if yer the one shot it. So get down on yer hands an' knees, keep on that straight line, an' try lookin' fer blood again. You don't find some in another twenty yards, we'll call it a good try an' go eat."

José obeyed and eased to his hands and knees, holding the crutch in his good hand and struggling forward. He hadn't crawled five feet before an object at the base of a large sagebrush drew him up short. His heart leaped in sudden recognition, and he pushed up onto his knees. "I don't think it's here," he said, not looking at McAllister.

McAllister smiled and said, "Well, let's have a look." To José's horror, he bent and peered into the brush. Then, leaning forward, he reached under the sagebrush and came up holding the dirt- and debris-covered hunk of liver José had thrown away the night before. "Well, I'll be damned," he said, looking over at José with feigned amazement. "Someone musta gut-shot a deer an' its liver fell out while it ran. I guess it's our lucky day. An' just think. If it hadn't been fer you, we wouldn't a found it."

The cool morning suddenly felt very hot to José. He was mortified he had been caught trying to deceive this man who had befriended him, and sweat began to bead up on his face. But if for nothing else than his own pride, he had to meet McAllister's eyes. He had to prove he was not cowed. With that determination, he looked over into his friend's face.

McAllister was watching him with a crafty grin, and he reached over and tousled his hair. "Kinda skittish o' raw liver, huh? Well, don't worry, Lucky. We'll get you another. Fer now, let's try some stewed."

And so for breakfast they ate liver, heart, and wild onion stew. And pure hunger made it taste almost good.

José sat across the fire from McAllister, cleaning out his bowl. He looked up suddenly. "How'd you shoot that deer last night in the dark?"

McAllister smiled. "I heard 'em walkin' first. There were four or five. Then I seen their silhouettes. Wasn't hard. Folks're way too used to lanterns 'n' such, Lucky. Fact is, people c'n see perty good in the dark if they get used to it. Maybe we'll sit out here t'night without a fire an' let you try it. If yer gonna hang around with me, you need to git used to the dark anyhow. As far as that deer, when it comes to shootin' a pistol, even in daylight all yuh need to do is point it like yer pointin' a finger. Forget it even has sights. If it's far enough away to need sights, shoot it with a rifle."

José nodded and sipped the last broth from his bowl. "What river did you say that is?"

"That's the Portneuf. Used to be a mighty fine beaver stream, before yer time an' mine both. The Shoshones call it *Tobitapa*."

The little camp on the *Tobitapa* became a school for the frontiersman and his student. José spent his days learning the ways of the land, its animals, and its native and transplanted peoples. In the evenings, he and McAllister stripped down faithfully and sank into the steaming pools. It was a sort of paradise, and only at a distance did they see anyone from the houses on the hill. But sometimes wagonloads of tourists would arrive from Soda Springs or McCammon Junction, and José and McAllister would make themselves scarce until the wagons rolled away.

The recently laid Oregon Short Line tracks ran past above the camp, and now and then a train would come chugging by, blowing its high-pitched, eery whistle at them and the Dempsey settlers. José liked the sound of it, but McAllister always seemed to change the subject whenever he said anything about the locomotives, so he started keeping his thoughts to himself.

José healed at a seemingly miraculous rate, and McAllister assured him he could thank the combination of the grizzly heart, the hot pools, and the plant medicines working their magic together, along with a mixture of clear mountain air and sparkling water. José had to believe it, for he had never seen anyone heal as fast as he was, and he had seen many injuries in his time. After four weeks he was able to grasp and squeeze objects in his left hand without pain. Soon he was putting more weight on his broken leg than he would ever have thought possible.

Each day brought new discoveries. He learned where to find game: marmots and cottontails in the rocks, snowshoe hares in the timber, and whitetail jackrabbits in the sage. He learned to hunt for deer along the water, early and late, or to flush them from their beds in the draws and in the rimrocks during the day.

He learned how to make a simple deadfall out of a flat rock and a stick, how to make a snare out of deer sinew. He learned how to spear a fish with a spear he made himself. He learned to build a fire with a flint and steel and a nest of cottonwood or sagebrush bark or cattail fluff. McAllister even taught him the more primitive bow and drill method, and he was ecstatic the first time his spark finally created a flame, after many frustrating hours crouched over his work.

To José, this was a time for dreams coming true. He had wanted to know the mountains, and everything he had dreamed of learning and more was at his fingertips. He knew more than the average person about surviving in the outdoors. Of that he was certain. He felt almost strong enough, good enough, to think about... but no. No, he was not strong enough. Not strong enough to undertake the one thing that plagued his mind some part of every day. Not strong enough to fight the one animal that caused him to wake up nights, screaming in horror.

Hunting down and killing a bear—a good, clean killing with no harm to himself, and no fear. That was a dream he might never attain. But if he didn't, he would rather be dead.

For the past two weeks, they had lived on jerked meat and wild plants. McAllister refused to let him shoot any game. José was disappointed, for he wanted to try out his new rifle, now that he could hold it in both hands. Even though it wasn't the gun he had wanted, he liked the feel of a gun kicking against his shoulder and the smell of gunsmoke.

One morning, a gray, drizzly morning José thought they would spend inside the wagon, McAllister cut away José's casts, and then the two of them went about working his atrophied leg and arm muscles, to slowly get them back in shape. Rainy days stretched on while the strength steadily returned, and before long the boy felt like he could take on any mountain.

Two more weeks went by, when it rained nearly every day, and at breakfast one day they finished off the last jerky of a deer McAllister had shot. The dark sky hung low over their heads, and masses of cloud blocked view of some mountains and faded the rest into gloomy obscurity. With depressing frequency, the rain came in curtains, dripping off their already saturated hat brims. One minute it would rain, and the next it would fade, and the moisture would hang suspended in the air, curling about the rocks and trees above them. But always somewhere in view would hang the gray curtains, drenching some canyon or mountainside, feeding some chattering creek that would eventually empty into the now turbulent Portneuf.

Suddenly, McAllister turned to José and wiped his mouth with his sleeve. "This rain ain't gonna rest, Lucky. But we can't let it keep us down. I reckon it's time you go try out that rifle o' yers. Let's walk down along the river an' throw some lead."

José jumped up immediately, not wanting to give McAllister a chance to change his mind. He picked up the rifle and a box of shells, and they set out along the bank of the river. They were walking side by side about a mile from camp. A wall of black lava jutted up to the north of the river, and lush green grass dripping with water carpeted its banks and drenched their feet as they ambled along. José suddenly looked into the river's current underneath the far bank and saw something slowly waving that didn't look like moss. He pointed it out to McAllister.

"Good eyes, boy! That's a beaver tail. An' a big one he is, too. Betcha never had beaver tail before, have yuh?"

"I've never even *seen* a beaver before," replied José. "Are we going to eat it?"

McAllister shrugged. "Well, we gotta kill it first. An' that ain't an easy chore."

He made himself a spear by lashing his knife to a chokecherry limb. Then he looked across the river, and the beaver was still there. Its tail swished slowly under the water. The rain had begun to fall again, making tiny dimples on the water's surface as it gurgled past.

"How long can he hold his breath?" asked José, astounded.

"Quite a while. 'Course he might have his head in a hollow up under the bank, too. But we better get 'im 'fore he decides to head fer a den. Tell yuh what. You stay on this bank, an' I'll just wade over an' stick 'im. You'll see it ain't easy as it sounds."

So McAllister waded across the river, and the beaver remained, apparently believing itself hidden. But just as McAllister got out of the water and walked to a spot above the animal, it sensed his nearness, and frantically it shoved away from the bank, heading into midstream.

Without a pause, McAllister held the spear up high and lunged from the bank. With incredible accuracy, he speared the beaver high in the neck as he splashed into the stream like a cannonball. When he came up from his dousing, the animal was in its last death struggle, the stick dancing crazily in McAllister's hands. Then the stick was still, and a cloud of red washed away from the deeply buried knife blade into the river.

José cheered and threw his hands into the air. "Bravo! I thought for sure he got away."

He was standing there, smiling broadly with the rain running down his cheeks, when the sudden, mud-muffled thunder of many hooves startled him, and he whirled toward the sound. He had just enough time to glimpse five Indians on horseback, coming at him in a gallop. They wore buckskin pants and shirts, those who wore any shirts at all, and they raised a yell like wild men.

"Gray!" José yelled. "Indians!"

The ground shook with thundering hooves, and José turned back as they closed around him.

Part Two
Under the Wing of Gray Eagle

Chapter Eleven

José whipped back and forth, glancing frantically from one brave to another. He was sure he was about to be murdered.

"Gray, what do I do?"

McAllister called from the water. "Just be still. I'll be right there."

At that moment, the shoulder of one of the brave's horses struck José in the chest and knocked him sprawling. He landed on his back and rolled over, coming quickly to his knees. The Indian just laughed as he galloped past, then hauled back on his reins to skid his horse to a halt.

McAllister had climbed from the river, and José heard him speak sharply behind one of the Indians. He spoke in a strange foreign tongue, and José didn't understand him, but the braves took their attention from José and reined their mounts around to face McAllister.

One Indian, a big man with broad, bare shoulders and twin braids hanging to the middle of his back, spoke then, his words a guttural mixture of sounds like McAllister had uttered. Again, the white man answered him in the same tongue.

The big Indian's eyes narrowed, and he looked McAllister up and down critically. His eyes revealed a faint flicker of change, a fleeting second when his expression turned from one of mistrust to one of curiosity. "You speak our language good. Who are you?"

Surprised at the Indian's proficient use of English, José glanced quickly over at McAllister, but the man's face was unaffected. "I'm Robert McAllister, who yer people call *Bia gwi'yaa'aishim*—Gray Eagle. I'm a friend of Captain Jim's."

The big Indian looked over at one of his cohorts. The other man nodded and said something in Shoshone, and the big Indian returned his gaze to McAllister. "You say Captain Jim? He is a good man. Why do you hunt here—on the land of the People?"

McAllister shrugged, studying the Indians coolly. "I'll tell you. But why talk here? Follow us back to our camp. We have coffee there, and lots of sugar. Beaver tail, too," he said with a smile, holding up the dripping rodent by its tail.

The big Indian grunted. "Sugar, huh? We will go then. You show us where your camp is."

"You handle our language perty good yerself."

The Indian chuckled. "Yes, better than many of you do! I was trained in the best of your schools. But you can see they didn't take the 'Injun' out of me—the 'prairie nigger', as some of you white men say."

McAllister laughed and glanced over at José. "Can you run, Lucky?"

Alarmed, José looked into his eyes. "Run? Why?"

"Don't worry, boy. I just thought we'd trot back to camp. Runnin' with 'em—not against."

José sighed with relief. "Sure, I can try."

"Good." McAllister turned back to the Indians. "My brave little friend was hurt in a fight with a grizzly bear. But watch. Still, he has his strength. He has eaten the heart of the bear that hurt him." He looked at José and winked, and after reaching over and taking the rolling block out of José's hands, he started out at a jog upriver.

José stayed with him as best he could. Even when he hurt the worst, and his arm and leg throbbed mercilessly, he knew he couldn't stop. He had to keep up with McAllister—he had to show no pain. He couldn't allow weakness in himself while these Indians could see.

At last, they reached the camp, almost a mile's run, and the Indians leaped down from their mounts, looking about at the wagon and the sodden ground around the fire's ashes, where the down-trodden grass was littered with many bones of deer and small game. "You stay here for a long time. Why do you come to the land of the People and stay?" asked the big brave.

McAllister shrugged idly. "I like it here. You have the medicine hot springs, an' I'm friends with the People. I been here many times. Once with Captain Jim, once with a friend you might know—Snow Otter."

The big Indian grunted. "I know Snow Otter. A brave man in his day. Too bad he is one of the 'progressives' now. And Captain Jim, he is well known among the People, a strong leader." He waved for the others to sit, and they did. They seemed to respect his word, and José decided he must be their chief, or a leader of some sort.

"I am called Moose Jaw by the People," said the brave. "This is Tongue Eater." He pointed toward the Indian he had spoken with earlier, a squat, barrel-chested man with pocked skin and narrow eyes pressed to a deep set by high, beefy cheeks. He was the brave who had steered his horse to knock José to the ground. Among all of the Indians, only Tongue Eater wore an eagle feather—only one—dangling loose in his hair. Moose Jaw introduced the others, and they nodded silently, eyeing the wagon. All of the others, unlike Moose Jaw, had heavy faces and bodies, with eyes set back deep behind their cheeks.

"If you'll start a fire, Moose Jaw," said McAllister, "I'll bring coffee and sugar."

McAllister climbed up into the wagon and rustled around, then leaped back loosely to the ground and brought a cup of coffee grounds and a sack of sugar, along with another of jerky strips. He held the sack of jerky toward Moose Jaw. "Here. Eat this while I skin out this critter."

The Shoshone took the sack and peered inside, then pulled out a piece of meat and gnawed off a bite. He passed the sack to another brave. Then he reached into a beaded leather pouch hanging from his belt and pulled out a nest of cattail fluff, knelt and deftly put together a fire bundle with grass one of the braves picked from beneath the wagon. Reaching into his pouch again, he took a square piece of char cloth and placed that in the center of the bundle. He pulled a piece of red flint from the bag, along with a chunk of steel, and struck the two together until sparks fell loosely onto the char cloth. The big Shoshone pursed his lips and gently blew, cupping the grass bundle about the cloth. Finally, the bundle took flame, and laying it carefully into a pile of twigs and grass the other braves had prepared, he blew again, and the fire crackled to life, quickly sucking the moisture out of the other materials.

McAllister turned from watching to reach down for the blackened coffee pot. "José. Go fill this with water, pard." José did as told, jogging over to the river, wanting to show that, even after the run, he was still strong.

This whole event was still like a dream to him—the Indians, the stomping, half-wild horses, the big Shoshone brave. He was impressed by the way McAllister handled it, as if he knew these Indians would do whatever he told them. Not once had he betrayed any sign of fear.

Turning from the water, José stared at the column of blue smoke that filtered loosely into the damp air. The Indians were seated again, legs crossed. Only Moose Jaw stood. McAllister was squatted on his heels, speaking with the other braves, using hand motions and sometimes pausing to recall a word.

José returned and placed the big coffee pot on the fire. Then he took a couple of steps back and listened, wide-eyed, to McAllister talk. There was nothing recognizable about the words. What fascinated José was the fact it was McAllister's peculiar deep, gravelly voice forming the foreign sounds. He marveled as the man's hands waved and fluttered, creating their own words.

Finally, McAllister turned to the beaver, lying on its back near the fire circle. "José, I want you to watch this close. Yer gonna be doin' it yerself soon." He slipped his knife from its sheath and cut around the hard, coarse shell of the tail, then put the knife down and snapped the tail bone. With another cut, he removed the whole tail and dropped it unceremoniously into the fire, raking coals over it with the blade of his knife.

Next, he cut into the beaver at the throat and began peeling the hide downward from a thick layer of sticky fat. With the hide removed, his last step was to eviscerate it. All this José watched with fascination. McAllister's movements were so smooth and certain. There was no wasted motion. He looked up at José. "I hope you watched close, Lucky. Next one's yers."

José just shrugged nonchalantly. "Whenever you say." He stole a quick look at Moose Jaw, finding his eyes on him, and he swung his own eyes away quickly.

Some time later, José noticed the clouds had started to break, and patches of blue sky showed through. But the cold remained, and the Shoshones had all taken blankets from their saddles and wrapped them around their bare shoulders—all except Tongue Eater, who either was much tougher than the rest or was just a fool—José hadn't decided which. As for José, he huddled into his own coat and wished the clouds away. He had had enough of rain for one year.

McAllister pulled the beaver tail from the coals. The outer shell had swollen up and charred, now resembling a layer of heavy paper, which he peeled away. José had to look closer; it appeared to be solid fat. He watched as McAllister cut a chunk off and passed it to him. José started to eat, forced to because the Indians were watching. But he saw nothing good about the flavor, *nor* the texture. It was nothing more than solid fat, just as it had looked.

McAllister watched José distastefully swallow the beaver fat, and he laughed. "That's how you *don't* eat beaver tail, Lucky. Now we'll show yuh how yuh do."

He proceeded to cut off chunks of the fat and skewer them on a little stick, placing it over the fire. The fat quickly began to sizzle and drip, and after a while it turned a golden brown color. Now McAllister passed the stick around, and the Indians pulled off chunks and popped them into their mouths. They ate and licked the grease from their fingers, smacking their lips. José was last to try the beaver tail cooked that way, and he was surprised at the now pleasant flavor. It was strange, yet good.

"There yuh go, Lucky." McAllister smiled. "An Injun treat. Mountain man, too. Fat's important when you live out in the weather all the time. Can't get too much of it."

José nodded, trying to rub the grease off on his pant legs. He noticed the Indians were rubbing it through their hair. "That's a sign they like yer grub, Lucky," explained McAllister.

After the beaver tail, two cups of coffee went around the circle. There were only the two, so everyone shared. The coffee tasted sickeningly sweet to José, for the Indians wouldn't drink it until McAllister dumped in sugar to their satisfaction.

In speaking, McAllister jumped back and forth between Shoshone and English, while Moose Jaw insisted on English. The others never uttered a word of it. José assumed they couldn't speak it. But he was thankful for Moose Jaw and his mastery of the language. He didn't know why he chose to speak it instead of his native tongue, but he was glad to catch part of this conversation, the part that, to him, was the most important, because it came from this heroic-looking warrior.

As the others spoke, José's eyes were fixed on the big Shoshone. He was an impressive specimen of manhood in any race. His shoulders were broad and finely rounded, his chin square, his eyes deep-set and dark, seeming to catch everything around him as they roved restlessly over the group, about the surrounding hills. Moose Jaw wore no shirt, only leather leggings and a breech clout and a pouch slung by a strap over one shoulder. Moccasins adorned his feet, with fringes of skunk tail trailing from their heels. They were decorated on top with intricate beadwork, bizarre floral designs in yellow, cobalt, lavender, and green. His braided hair was long and sleek and shone when it caught the sun breaking through the clouds. José studied Moose Jaw closely. If he were an Indian, this was how he wanted to be. Like McAllister, so in control of himself, of his surroundings, almost a thing of beauty—a creature of great strength and grace like the mustangs that still roamed the hills of Nevada.

Moose Jaw looked over, and their eyes met. This time José, though embarrassed, didn't look away. Their eyes held until finally a slight smile touched the Indian's lips, and he nodded. He looked over at McAllister and spoke several sentences in Shoshone.

McAllister turned and looked at José with a close-mouthed grin. He looked again at Moose Jaw, nodding, and said something back in Shoshone. When he looked at José again, he spoke something José had heard them both say, and then he said in English, "Moose Jaw jus' gave you a new name, Lucky. He says his name for you will be *Geta suande dei dainape'e.* It means somethin' like, 'Little-Man-With-Warrior's-Eyes'."

When José caught the full meaning of the words, a feeling of pride burst up inside him, and he looked over to find Moose Jaw's eyes on him. The big Indian nodded and smiled, and José smiled back.

Now Moose Jaw settled back on the wet grass, his shoulders sagging slightly as he relaxed. He looked at McAllister. "I asked before, why do you come here to hunt on the land of the People? Your land is just a small distance that direction." He pointed east.

"I like it better on yer land. The water's cleaner. The grass is taller. It's warmer. An' the animals're bigger an' more beautiful."

Moose Jaw listened to McAllister speak, and a quiet twinkle appeared and grew in his eyes. A slight smile touched his lips, and he spoke in his own tongue. "*Ene debizhi i'shambe.*"

McAllister sat still a moment, then laughed. He looked over at José, whose curiosity was sparked. "He said I'm a great liar. I guess that's a compliment."

Tongue Eater, the squat brave, spoke up then. "*Ene haganai bide'nu?*"

McAllister glanced at José, reading his curiosity. He looked back at Tongue Eater and spoke in English, for José's sake. "Where do we come from? *Tosh-y-shoke-up-ro-tosh-wa.* Soda Springs." The Indian name referred specifically to the "place of the effer-vescent waters," rather than to the town itself.

"*Hina enen dekai?*"

"*Badeheya'a. Ha'nii'i. Sogodeheya'a. Weda'a. Moppo.*" McAllister laughed, and the braves laughed, too. McAllister looked over at José. "He asked what I'm huntin'. I told 'im elk, beaver, deer, bear—and mosquitoes."

José laughed. "I think the mosquitoes are hunting us."

McAllister chuckled and translated this to the Shoshones, who laughed again and shared some other joke of their own. The camp became relaxed after that, and José felt safe, like he was part of the group.

During a lull in the conversation, José ventured shyly to ask Moose Jaw the reason why Tongue Eater was the only one wearing a feather in his hair. He had always been under the impression that it was a custom of all Indians.

"You are observant, Little Man. But you see, the feather of Eagle is a symbol that a man has 'counted coup'. He has made some kind of strike against an enemy. But we do not make war anymore. And only with war can a man count coup. Tongue Eater, he joined the Bannocks when they tried to go back to their old ways a few years ago. The whites, they called it 'the Bannock War'," he said and chuckled. "Tongue Eater counted coup there. He killed a man. That gives him his right to wear the feather of Eagle in his hair."

José shivered and looked at Tongue Eater, who silently watched him through his deep-set eyes. He quickly looked back at Moose Jaw.

"Why do you speak English so well?"

Moose Jaw laughed. "It is not so difficult, Little Man. I was one of very few grown men who agreed to go to the white man's English school and learn their language. I have an old Injun teacher at Ross Fork. He told me a man who will be a great leader should learn to talk in all worlds." He laughed again. "I guess he thought I would become a great leader."

Later, the well-roasted beaver meat glistened in the sunlight that had won its tussle against the clouds. José chewed a bite and listened to the Shoshones talk, wishing he understood them the way his partner did. Still, he laughed when they laughed, just for the joy of laughing, and watched Moose Jaw admiringly. He sat listening, basking in the welcome sunlight on his damp hair. He chewed the beaver with savor, for though it had a strong taste, meat was meat, as McAllister always said.

Early in the afternoon, three of the Indians mounted their horses and rode off. They headed south across the river, and José watched them disappear up in the junipers of the foothills. Nobody said much about their leaving, and José watched them curiously, wondering where they headed. Three hours later, he heard two shots.

Toward evening, when the sky was paling and taking on a greenish cast in the west, the braves returned. One of them was on foot, leading his horse, on which was tied a young buck mule deer. McAllister congratulated them heartily—at least José assumed it to be congratulations—and helped them unload the deer by the wagon.

Two of the braves made quick work of skinning out the deer, while McAllister took José down by the river to cut willow spits on which to roast the venison. They chose young, green branches and cut them off, then shaved one end to a sharp point. The fresh smell of the river and the vegetation after the days of rain was tantalizing, and José breathed deeply of it. The air was cold, but it felt good, and the birds had come out to make their last music of the day. José could see their drab feathers flitting back and forth in the willows and streamside grass.

"What do yuh think o' these Injuns?" McAllister asked as he whittled.

José looked up, trying to read behind his eyes in the growing dark. "What do you mean?"

"You trust 'em?"

For the first time in hours, a small doubt leaped into José's mind, brought on by McAllister's query. He sensed there was some cryptic meaning behind the question. "I don't know. I think so."

McAllister eyed him with a studying gaze for a moment. At last, he nodded. "Good. I do, too. But it ain't because they're Injuns. Don't *ever* make that mistake. You'll hear people— 'specially Easterners—try to tell you Injuns're noble as gods. It ain't true. Ther's good'uns, an' ther's bad'uns. Just like white men. You go trustin' too much, yer liable to wind up without somethin' that's yers—maybe yer hair. But Moose Jaw's an honorable one, I think. He comes across true to me. Reminds me o' old Chief Washakie. The others seem all right, too—all except Tongue Eater. I won't say he's bad, exactly. I just ain't got 'im figgered out yet. He c'd go either way. Jus' watch 'im, that's all."

They walked a ways together in silence, toward the fading light of the western sky. Finally, McAllister stopped again near a willow. "I've known all sorts of Injuns, Lucky. Mostly, the Shoshone's a good bunch. They taught me a lot, an' I admire 'em for what they know an' what they c'n do. But they got one man by the name o' Pokatilla—they call him Pocatello now, or *Paugh*atello. Whatever you call 'im, he was a hard man in his time. I guess the white man give 'im plenty reason, takin' what he figgered his rightful ground. But if you was white, best look out. He was a white man-hater to the core. Even a white man who was liked by the rest of them."

A chill passed up José's spine. "Is he still around here?"

"At the Injun agency, I imagine. But he'd be perty old now. Ain't got much vinegar left. But I hear they're callin' some little train station after him, over west an' north o' here. So I guess his name'll live on. Funny how white men are. You'd never catch an Injun namin' somethin' after a white man he figgers wronged 'im. But we do it an' don't think a thing about it."

José smiled at that strange custom. "What does that mean—'Pokatilla?'" he asked.

"Nothin'." McAllister laughed. "That's white man's name for 'im. Part o' the rations the army doles out to the Injuns is pork an' tallow. They say his name come from that. I guess it's as good a story as any, but I just know his name ain't Shoshone. They don't have any 'L' sound in their tongue."

José thought quietly about that for a minute, then grinned and shook his head. *Pork and tallow.* What a name! "So you say Pocatello hated white men just because they took his land?"

"Well, not just that. We been fightin' back an' forth fer years. Back in sixty-three a glory hunter by the name o' Connor wiped out over two hunnerd Shoshones over on the Bear River by a town they call Preston. The whites called it a battle, but don't be fooled. It was a massacre. Most Injuns ever killed in one battle by our armies. You gotta remember, when white men win a skirmish, they call it a battle. When Injuns win against whites, it's a massacre." When José just stared at him, McAllister laughed. "It was a joke, Lucky. Anyway, things like that've built up, an' Pokatilla don't forgive. I don't think I would either. Well, let's get on back to camp," he said suddenly. "My belly button an' my backbone're gettin' just a little too well acquainted."

Later, only the stars and the glowing fire lit the camp. South of the Portneuf, lights glowed from the ranch houses up at the edge of the foothills. The Portneuf wandered by, winding its way in the dark, whispering secrets among the grassy banks. There was no wind, but still the night was very cold. In the fire, sparks popped now and then, glowing in the dirt, burning quietly out. José gnawed on a hunk of bloody venison and studied the Shoshones quietly. No one spoke, enjoying their meal in silence as orange firelight flickered and lit their faces eerily.

At last, McAllister wiped his hands on his leather pants and looked over at José. "They call this *tuhea*. Or *sogodeheya'a*."

José repeated the words carefully, looking at Moose Jaw as if for approval.

The big Indian nodded. "And what you ate before," he added, "is called *ha'nii'i*. What the white man calls beaver."

Before José could say anything, he heard the raspy cry of a nighthawk veering by close overhead. Moose Jaw looked up and shook his head. He glanced over at McAllister, then back at José. "*Gi'yii'i*," the Indian said. "He cries his grief."

"*Gi'yii'i*," José repeated haltingly. It sounded like "jee-yee," with a barely audible sigh on the end. "*Gi'yii'i*," he repeated, then sat silent, waiting for Moose Jaw to go on.

"*Gi'yii'i* once was the friend of white man," said Moose Jaw. "He tried to help one of your people—a trapper of *ha'nii'i*, the beaver. But after he helped the trapper the trapper betrayed him. Now *Gi'yii'i* still cries."

"How is yer Pokatilla?" McAllister asked suddenly. "His health still strong?"

Moose Jaw shook his head. "He is an old man. He lives now on Bannock Creek, and not many see him. In not many more harvests, he will go to the land of *Da-ma-Appah*."

McAllister nodded and looked at José. "*Appah* is the father—sort of the god of the Shoshone. '*Da-ma-Appah*'—our Father. The Great Spirit. In proper Shoshone, they call him *Newi newe'naipe*."

José nodded and looked at Moose Jaw. "If Pocatello goes to the land of *Appah,* who will be your chief?"

Moose Jaw shrugged loosely, wiping his mouth. "We have no chief, as you call it. We have head men, but custom does not require us to follow anyone. We listen to who we like."

The big Indian motioned to one of the other braves to put more wood on the fire, and the brave obeyed, adding several big sticks. The fire blazed up around them. Moose Jaw chuckled. "Used to be, only *dai'bo'o*—white man—built big fires. Now there is nothing to hide. The People, too, build big fires to warm them."

He looked over at José, and a gleam came into his eyes. He glanced at McAllister. "Hey. Have you told Little-Man-With-Warrior's-Eyes about *Nenembi'i*?"

McAllister smiled mischievously. "No, I reckon I forgot. You'd best tell it. It's yer story."

Moose Jaw turned back to José. "You listen, Little Man. To something very important. Don't be afraid, for there are many of us here, but be careful when you are alone in the dark. There is a people called *Nenembi'i*. Little people. They live in the earth, and in rocks. *Nenembi'i* can be a friend, but he does not like a person who angers him. *Nenembi'i* can be mean and very silent. *Nenembi'i* can go anywhere—anywhere except in a dwelling.

"*Nenembi'i* is out there now, in the dark. If you listen close, some nights you can hear them chant in lonely places. I heard them myself once, when I was young. It scared the hell out of my horse! If they are angry they shoot you with tiny arrows. Then you will be very unlucky. Or dead.

"Our People once found a circle of old warriors sitting in council. They were still wrapped up in their blankets, dead for a long time. Their skin was dried and old, and their teeth showed through their faces. *Nenembi'i* killed them, all of them, for some evil.

A man does not anger *Nenembi'i*. If you do, and they find you in the dark some night, *Nenembi'i* will come out of his home in the earth and rocks and kill you. But if you are not dead by sunrise, then you are okay. *Nenembi'i* has no powers in the daylight. If he is caught out when dark is gone, he must wait till dark again to regain his powers."

José looked at Moose Jaw, spell-bound. A shiver ran up his spine. He looked around uncomfortably at the darkness outside the firelight. He kept waiting for the braves to laugh, but none of them did. Then he noticed some of *them* were looking into the dark also. He scooted closer to the fire.

McAllister broke the eery silence. "Don't let 'im scare you, Lucky. The *Nenembi'i*'s nothin'. It's the red-haired cannibals you have to watch. They roam by the hundreds in these hills. They'll roast you alive if they catch you. An' they can't be fought. They're mighty warriors. They can jump up in the air an' catch an arrow an' throw it back with deadly aim."

For José, the comfort of the fire had vanished. The giant grizzly was too close in his past to enjoy such stories. He stared silently into the fire and tried to think of lighter things. José looked up when one of the Shoshones said something and everyone laughed.

"Horse Killer says you should not look at the fire," translated Moose Jaw. "You will not be able to see *Nenembi'i* or the cannibals coming from the dark." José forced a laugh, feigning bravery. But he didn't look back into the fire.

Moose Jaw turned to McAllister. "I and my friends will camp there, by the river in the grass. Our People need meat, so we will stay for two or three days and hunt. You may stay here in peace, Gray Eagle. I feel you are a true friend of the People. But do not let Little-Man-With-Warrior's-Eyes wander too far away in the dark. I would be sad if he did not come back."

McAllister laughed. "I reckon he'll stay close."

In the morning when José awoke, the Indians were gone. They had gone up one of the canyons hunting, McAllister explained. It was a beautiful day, with the sun shining brightly, and they wanted to make use of it.

After a breakfast of venison steaks and wild onions, McAllister sat across from José. "I think it's time we took you out to see how yer arm's healed. Wanna shoot that rifle, bein's we never got to last time we tried?"

José straightened up. "Of course. Where?"

"We'll go down by the river. I'll start you out on sagebrush stumps."

"What about the Indians? Won't the shooting disturb their hunt?"

"It's good o' you to think o' that, kid. But I already told 'em we'd be practicin', and Moose Jaw didn't mind. He wanted to take you with him, but I told 'im we needed to git yer arm in shape before yuh did any serious huntin'."

Anxious to get the rifle in his hands, José went to the wagon and climbed inside. He took up the Remington and a box of shells and stepped back off the tailgate to the ground.

McAllister stood there waiting for him. "You ready?"

"You bet."

McAllister smiled. "All right. Let's see how that arm works now."

They went to the bank of the river and walked along it to a point one hundred yards from camp. It was a warm day, and the sun beat pleasantly on their shoulders, counteracting a cool breeze off the last of the mountain snowbanks.

"Well?" McAllister stopped short. "Looks like as good a spot as any. Know how to load that gun?"

José had watched McAllister closely whenever they went out with the rifle, and he was glad to demonstrate his knowledge. Then he looked up at McAllister. McAllister held out his hand for the rifle, and José gave it to him. After he had looked it over, José figured he would give it back. But when José reached to take it, McAllister held it out of his reach. "Hold on, Lucky. So we don't have to go an' change yer name to *Un*lucky, let's go over some things here. First, when yer holdin' this gun, you respect it like as if you were holdin' a rattler by the tail. Real careful, now. I mean *real* careful. No playin' around. No daydreamin'. You mind that big hole there like it's the rattler's mouth. An' keep yer finger away from the trigger less'n yer ready to shoot. All right?"

José nodded patiently. Though firearms certainly weren't second nature to him, he had heard these things before. He didn't feel he needed to again, but he didn't want to anger McAllister.

"I assume you know how to line the sights, Lucky. But do yuh know to squeeze the trigger slow? Don't *pull* the trigger, like some'll tell yuh. *Squeeze* the trigger. Real careful. If you pull off target, stop squeezin' an' get back on. Relax. Take a deep breath or two. Be sure of yerself. Know there ain't no way to miss, because yer name is Lucky, an' Lucky don't miss. Ever. Lucky has a single shot rifle, mister, an' Lucky has one shot to his name. Lucky puts a slug where it counts most, right to the head or the heart—the head, if possible. If there's any doubt about hittin' somethin', you promise me one thing: yuh won't shoot. Only shoot if you know fer a fact what yer shootin' at is gonna go down when yuh touch off the shot. If ther's a chance yuh might miss, yer better off savin' yer lead. There'll always be another chance. The man that keeps his head is always the man that wins, given ever'thin' else is equal. Remember that, Lucky, an' you'll do all right."

Next, McAllister had the boy load and unload the rifle two hundred times, then unload it and point it at a target, squeezing the trigger carefully and pretending to shoot it, again for two hundred times. At last, when José was wondering if he would ever get to shoot, McAllister told him to put a round back in the chamber.

"Now, there's a dead sage twenty-five yards out there. Let's start out close up." He stopped suddenly. "Hold it. Before I get you shootin' an' losin' yer confidence, let me fire that smoke pole. If we know fer a fact the sights're on, we'll know where the fault lies if you miss."

Reluctantly, José handed McAllister the rifle. McAllister took it and aimed. The barrel didn't seem to waver at all. "Plug yer ears, boy," said McAllister quietly, but before José could do so, the rifle boomed and jumped in his hands. A thick cloud of smoke filled the air, then slowly floated away with the breeze.

"What were you shooting at?" José asked. "You didn't hit the sage."

McAllister chuckled. "Shore I did, boy—a different one. Take the gun and come with me."

José took the rifle and followed McAllister along the river bank. Some seventy yards away, the man stopped at a dead sage and pointed. The tip of one gray branch was tan, where it had recently been blown away. José looked at the branch, then back to the spot where he and McAllister had been standing. His mouth dropped open, and he stared.

"One shot, one branch, Lucky. That's all you should ever need."

José closed his mouth and looked up skeptically at his mentor. "Were you really shooting at that branch?"

The warm look suddenly disappeared from McAllister's face, and José felt a chill in the air that was more than the breeze. "I never hit but what I shoot at. And I don't lie to a friend."

José swallowed. "I didn't mean… Sorry, Gray. It just seems so far away, and that branch is so small."

McAllister's eyes softened again. "Don't worry, Lucky." He clasped his shoulder in a big hand. "You'll be doin' the same before we part ways."

In awe, José walked beside McAllister back to where they had stood earlier. He looked at the branch the man had pointed out for him. It looked so close now. It seemed an unfair advantage. "Can't I try the one you shot at?"

McAllister looked at him sternly. "A man's gun hand relies on his confidence, Lucky. Yuh build yer confidence, yer skill builds with it. I'd hate fer you to miss yer very first shot with this rifle if it c'd be helped. Shoot at the close mark first."

With a nod, José turned and eyed the branch the way he had seen McAllister do. He fixed his eyes on it, then raised the rifle to his shoulder. He lined up the sights, watching the branch carefully. Then he pulled the trigger.

The impact against his shoulder was shocking. This wasn't like his .44. It knocked him back, made him wince in pain. He lowered the rifle, and when the smoke had cleared away, he stared at the tip of the branch. It was still there! "You hit it," said McAllister, beside him.

He looked over quickly. "Are you sure?"

"Shore I'm shore. Come on." He walked to the sagebrush, and José followed. There, as far to the right as it could be without missing completely, was the faint burn mark the bullet had made in passing.

"You pulled the trigger," McAllister said, looking at the scar. "You didn't squeeze it. If that'd been a man—I mean a *deer*—at two hunnerd yards, you'd a missed 'im clean. I'll tell yuh somethin' anyway. We need to saw off an inch or so from the end o' that stock, an' then we c'n pad it for yuh. When you get older, yer arms'll grow an' you'll get some meat on yer shoulders. Then it won't hurt so bad. That stock's too long for yuh now. An' another thing: we'll put some mullein leaves in yer ears to keep down the noise, too. Yuh start gettin' skittish o' loud noise at this stage o' the game, you'll never be able to shoot worth a bull's teet."

José smiled but looked down dejectedly. When he looked back up, he didn't meet the man's eyes directly. "I didn't do too well, did I?"

McAllister put his hand on his shoulder and squeezed. "Yuh did fine, Lucky. Other than jerkin' the trigger, yuh did fine. Once we do the things I told yuh, you'll be out-shootin' me every time. In fact…" He reached into his belt pouch, removing the pocket knife he had bought back in Soda Springs. "To congratulate yuh on hittin' yer very first target with this rifle, here's a jackknife fer whittlin' an' skinnin'."

Before José could open his mouth to thank him, McAllister tensed. His eyes riveted on something across the river, toward the settlers' cabins. There was a light in his eyes that caused José's heart to start pounding, and he didn't even know why.

"Now there's a feller standin' there that I aim to kill."

The big man threw another cartridge into the rifle's chamber before José could speak or see what he was gazing at.

He raised the rifle to his shoulder and squeezed the trigger.

Chapter Twelve

José pried his eyes away from McAllister and gazed searchingly, almost frantically, across the river. He didn't see a man over there—or anything else McAllister might have shot at. He attempted to follow the invisible line made by the man's eyes, but that accomplished nothing.

Suddenly, McAllister chuckled. "I got 'im, boy. Right through the head."

José swallowed audibly, staring across the river. The sickness in the pit of his stomach had blurred his eyes so he couldn't see much, but he kept staring because he didn't want to look at McAllister. Had his friend just murdered someone? Just like that, like throwing a woodtick in the fire? If he had, it would mean an end to all his mountain man training. He couldn't stay with a killer. He managed to calm himself enough to stammer, "Wh-where is he?"

McAllister looked over at José, a smirk on his face, then pointed loosely across the river. "Well, over there in the brush, Lucky. Didn't yuh see 'im settin' there?"

José swallowed, staring toward the cabins half a mile away up the slope for any sign of movement. The only movement was of several cows looking their way curiously. "I don't see anybody," he uttered at last.

"Well, here." McAllister handed José the rifle. "I'm goin' over to make shore he's dead. Hold onta the gun, an' if yuh see 'im move, shoot 'im again. An' remember, aim fer the head."

José held the rifle wordlessly, staring at McAllister in horror. He had no intention of shooting anybody, but he didn't dare defy this man, not if he really had killed someone with no more emotion than a man would spit. What was McAllister capable of?

McAllister climbed into the river and started wading across, the water waist high. José's first instinct was to run, but his feet wouldn't move, so he just stood there, terrified. Though his throat was tight with fear, a morbid curiosity glued him to the spot.

McAllister made the other bank and climbed out, dripping. He walked about thirty yards, then stopped suddenly and leaned down. Momentarily, he straightened and turned back toward José. In his hand he held a white-tailed jackrabbit by the back legs, and he raised it aloft. His voice floated across the river. "This little man's dead as Custer, boy! Sixty yards—an' right through the head!"

Heart drumming madly, for several seconds José just stood. So certain had he been he had just witnessed a murder, his mind seemed unwilling to relinquish that notion.

He stared at McAllister for a moment longer, and then realization struck him hard. He spun and walked at a fast pace toward camp, his skin tingling and hot. He clenched his jaw and stared straight ahead, seeing nothing but the blurry shape of the wagon sheet fifty yards in front of him. When he reached it and wanted the rifle out of his hands, his first instinct, in his anger, was to throw it to the ground. But he thought better of this, took a deep breath to calm himself, and carefully leaned it against the wagon wheel. Then he turned and started up through the rocks toward the road.

When he reached the road, he followed it up the hill to the railroad tracks. Then he started west, hands in his pockets, staring at the ties as he passed them without really noticing them. He had no interest in anything around him. He only wanted to put some ground between himself and McAllister's black sense of humor.

He had walked only two hundred yards down the tracks when suddenly a hand clutched his shoulder from behind, and he jumped and whirled around, the hand falling away. "What's wrong, boy?" McAllister faced him, smiling with his eyes but not his mouth.

"I don't want to talk to you," cried José angrily, his heart pounding from his fright.

"That any way to talk to a friend?"

"I thought you killed somebody!" José blurted out. "You said you were shooting at a man!"

McAllister chuckled. "All right, loosen up. I'm sorry. I was just havin' fun. Pretendin', yuh know? You ever pretend? I'm still a kid at heart. Why would I wanna kill anybody around here? They're jus' farmers. If I was to kill anybody it'd be one o' them with the gold. Somebody from New York or somewhere."

When José looked at him incredulously, McAllister laughed. "I'm just funnin' again, Lucky. Thought you knew me better. I wouldn't even kill a rich man, just maybe rope 'im an' drag 'im around a bit till he give me some of his gold. Hey. What do you call ten railroad tycoons at the bottom of a river? A good start!" Again he laughed.

José turned around, this time more slowly, and ambled along the tracks. McAllister caught up and walked along silently beside him. They walked half a mile or more while José fought his inner feelings. He wanted to say something, if just to break the silence, but his stubbornness wouldn't let him. He was still angry and fighting to get over his scare.

"You wanna talk, boy?" said McAllister suddenly. His voice had lost its joking tone. José walked a ways farther. "About what?" he asked finally.

"Don't matter to me. But it seems the quiet's gettin' mighty heavy for yuh. If I hurt yer feelin's, I didn't mean to. I was just playin' with yuh."

This was the opening José needed, a way for him to give up his silence without feeling like he'd been first to relent. Knowing McAllister, it was the last chance he would give him. "You scared me," he said reproachfully. "I had no idea there was a rabbit there. I thought we were in trouble again. It made me sick to think you killed somebody."

"Well, I reckon you don't know me as well as I figgered, Lucky. But that's okay. Just believe me now. I wouldn't kill a man in cold blood. I wouldn't even kill a *bad* man from ambush less'n I figgered he'd kill me if I didn't start the shindig.

"I *will* say this. I've killed men before. Some Injuns—an' one greaser that was stealin' my horse. An' I killed a white man, too—a soldier. But he shot me first. It weren't ever fer fun, Lucky. Never. Killin' ain't fun fer nobody, less'n they're sick in the head. You believe in God, it gives you a real empty, sick kind o' feelin' in yer guts the first time. Them other people might be bad, but they're livin' an' breathin' just like you an' me, an' walkin' on their hind paws, thinkin' an' feelin'. As long as you ever live, José, don't ever kill a man if you c'n do somethin' else. It'll stick with you forever, you got any kind o' conscience a-tall. It'll eat on you at night or whenever yer all alone an' settin' quiet.

"You ever kill a man, don't do it 'cause you hate 'im, neither. Do it 'cause if you don't he'll kill you. Or yer wife. Or yer kids. Or anybody else that's innocent. No, José, I'd never kill a man if I had the choice. But if it's them or you I'll be shore ashamed o' you if you git yerself killed, or me, when you coulda stopped it by drawin' down first an' puttin' windows in some other fella's skull."

José listened silently, staring at his feet as he walked.

"Boy," said McAllister. "You watchin' to make sure yer shoes stay tied?"

"What?" José's head jerked up, and then he grinned sheepishly. "I'm just thinkin'."

"'Ponderin's' more like it," McAllister corrected. "If you was thinkin', you'd think to look ahead an' see that train comin' down the tracks at yuh. It's liable to make coyote meat outta you."

José looked, and sure enough, in the distance, an engine was chugging their way, a thick cloud bunching out of its stack and billowing like piles of filthy linen into the sky. They walked off the tracks about fifty yards and watched it come on.

When the engine roared by, the heavy soot from the smokestack tickled their noses, and McAllister spat in disgust. The tarnished main rods cranked the huge steel wheels round and round, making them click loudly along the track—*clickity-clack, clickity-clack, clickity-clack.* Suddenly, a shrill whistle split the air, and the engineer waved at them out his window, smiling broadly. José returned the wave and smile, but McAllister didn't.

José counted thirteen cars behind the engine, and from four of them erupted the mournful bawl of cattle and the acrid stench of dung churned to mire on the wooden floors. He could see shadows and patches of hair through the wooden slats of the cars as the tightly packed cattle stamped their feet, the only movement they were able to make. At last came the red caboose. A middle-aged man in overalls, sporting a bristly handlebar mustache, stood on the rear platform. He smiled when he caught sight of them and waved a greeting. "Beautiful valley here!" he called out above the clacking of the wheels.

McAllister nodded and spoke quietly. "Yeah, it was."

They watched the train out of sight, then on some silent signal started back toward the wagon. It was McAllister who seemed unsociable now, and José glanced over curiously at him now and then. Finally, the silence was too much for him, and this time, his anger now gone, it was he who spoke. "It was a treat to see the train. I really like the sound of the whistle."

McAllister looked at him askance. "It wasn't that much of a treat, Lucky. You didn't know this country the way I did. It used to be wild an' free. Full o' game. These hills around here used to crawl with bighorns, deer, elk, antelope, even some buff, back 'fore my time. There's still deer an' elk, now an' then, but people came along an' wiped out most ever'thin' else, an' that train brought 'em here. I can't stand the sight of a train. An' the worst part about it is the money them railroad boys got. Not the ones you jus' saw. No, they make out okay, but it's them boys back east that make me sick. Ol' Jay Gould an' his bunch o' thievin' cutthroats in New York. They got so much dough it's comin' out their ears. It'd bowl you over to hear the numbers. Jay Gould's got millions. Enough to fill a boxcar an' more. An' here we are, an' we got nothin'. An' we're the ones gettin' scalped by them trains comin' through, destroyin' our land.

"You just look, Lucky. Gould an' all his cronies're sittin' up there in New York in their big, fancy houses, lookin' at this place on a map. An' sure, they ride out here on one o' these damn trains once in a while to see Soda Springs or some such famous place. But they don't care about it like we do. They don't care whose lives they destroy by drivin' these tracks right through our heart. An' I'll tell you, I ain't no killer, but if I ever was, it'd be men o' that brand I'd be killin'. Just the sight o' one o' them damn trains makes my blood go cold." McAllister spat to the side again. "There. I said more to you t'day than any man oughtta say in a week."

José laughed, but it died quickly. It was plain McAllister hadn't meant to elicit laughter. The cynical remarks rang with bitter truth. José had always loved the sound of a train whistle and been fascinated by the sight of the mighty engines, chugging powerfully along like huge bulls, defiant of the world. Yet his mentor had shaken those illusions, and he saw the train and its tracks exposed for what they were to McAllister and his kind: a symbol of the dying of the West.

And yet so many others besides McAllister spoke of the railroad in glowing terms. Even his friend Ben Trombell. He spoke of the railroad as the key to the taming of the land and the growth of a powerful nation. And José guessed that was the whole issue. A few men, like McAllister, wanted the land free, unblemished. They wanted just the way the Indians had kept it. Far greater was the number who wanted it tamed, settled—in their pockets. And this was America. The majority ruled. McAllister and those of his breed would eventually lose the battle, but they would not go down willingly.

This unsettling thought crawled into José's conscience like a colony of termites. It began to eat away at the dreams he had so carefully stored. He had envisioned himself a mountain man, a trapper, a trailblazer. But soon there would be no trails to blaze, no place for a mountain man to roam, no furs to be trapped. Soon, there would be a city in every valley and on top of each hill. It was a lonely realization for a boy who had set his heart on being a man of the wilderness.

"Well, we got things to do, Lucky." McAllister's gravelly voice broke suddenly into José's dire thoughts, and he slapped him on the back. José turned and caught the smile on the man's face, saw it was genuine. His visions of doom had apparently slipped back into the darker recesses of his mind. "Let's get back to the wagon an' line out the rest of the day."

Later, seated beside the fire, they dined on jackrabbit and pinto beans. They sopped up the juice with stale bread and ate happily. They were used to stale bread, and the fresh rabbit added a pleasant change.

After their meal, they went to the river and rinsed the dishes, scouring them clean with handsful of sand and gravel. Then, leaving the pan to dry in the wagon, McAllister turned to José. "Pick up yer rifle, boy, an' let's get to repairin'. I bet one o' them settlers across the river's got a saw we c'd borrow."

José obeyed, and together they crawled aboard the bay and forded the Portneuf on the narrow log bridge they had never had reason to cross until now. They rode on up the hill on the other side and stopped at the first ranch they came to. The main house, like the outbuildings, was of rough, hand-hewn logs, probably snaked out of the canyons behind them. It was a tiny place, but it sported two windows, both with light blue calico curtains. That alone was more luxury than most homesteads could boast of. There were several sheds, one of them large enough for horses. Chickens pecked in the yard and paid them no mind as they walked by, but a long-haired brown and white mutt began to bark at them from just outside the front door and came out to meet them, still barking but wagging its tail.

"Hello the house," McAllister called out. "Anybody home?"

The door creaked open, and a woman stepped into the sunlight, flanked by two small children. "Hello." The woman raised a hand to shade her eyes, even though the sun wasn't in them. "Come on up. Injun won't bite. That's the dog's name—Injun," she explained with a crooked grin.

"Thank yuh, ma'am," said McAllister, pulling off his hat. "We're obliged." He walked closer, and José followed, looking at the dog warily.

The woman was round but robust in appearance—no weakling. Her face was broad, her hands big, and in her bright blue eyes was the determination of pure pioneer stock. She wore a dull blue dress half-hidden by a blood-smeared apron, and lifeless, sandy hair was done up in a bun on top of her head. "Come in, mister, if you don't mind the little ones," she said. "They're trying to be helpful. Sorry about the blood. I just killed a rooster for supper."

McAllister nodded understanding. "Don't worry 'bout the kids, ma'am. I favor young 'uns, even if the feelin' ain't mutual." He and José stepped inside, McAllister ducking his head to get through the doorway.

The floor inside was puncheon, and the furniture, simple as the house, was hand-made of native fir and sturdy as the forest it was cut from. The few luxuries José could see at a glance—besides the wood floor—were a table cloth, real glasses, and silverware with intricate flowers etched into the handles.

"I've seen your camp yonder," said the woman conversationally. "There's Injuns staying with you now, aren't there?"

"Yeah. Friends of mine," replied McAllister. "They're peaceable. Just Shoshones."

She nodded. "Yes, we've seen them before. They never come up here, just keep to themselves. By the way, my name's Clara. Clara Bonn. My husband is Henry. He and the boys are out hunting supper. But I think it's just an excuse to be out of the house." She laughed.

"Well, luck to 'em," McAllister nodded. "Game's scarce hereabouts. Ma'am, my pardner here goes by the name o' Lucky, an' my name's Robert McAllister. Hope yuh don't mind the noise down there. I'm learnin' 'im to shoot a rifle."

Clara Bonn scoffed good-naturedly. "It'd be a sad day without the sound of a shot now and then. Don't worry yourself about it. Would you like to join us for supper this evening? Providing they find something, we'll have fresh meat, cornbread, and mashed spuds with onion gravy. I might even bake up an apple pie if company was about. And I make a good pie." She canted her head and winked at José.

McAllister looked quickly over at José, then back at Clara Bonn. "'Preciate the invite, ma'am. Sounds real good, but I reckon we'll pass this time. Might not seem neighborly to the Injuns, us goin' off thataway."

"I understand. Maybe another time. Is there something else I can do for you?"

"Well, yeah, actually. I was wonderin' if yuh might have a saw. The boy's rifle stock's a mite long, an' I'd like to cut it down. Wouldn't take but a minute."

"Certainly. Follow me."

The woman walked to the doorway and took a step outside. Pointing, she said, "See that little shed there? I think you'll find any tool you need there. Just close up when you're done."

"Thank yuh kindly, ma'am." McAllister clamped his hat back down on his head. "And when my friends leave, if yer offer still stands, I'd shore like to visit again. That apple pie's got my mouth waterin'."

Clara Bonn smiled. "Any time you're hungry, just holler."

"We'll do that, ma'am," McAllister smiled. "An' thanks again."

With a cross-cut saw, they took two inches of walnut stock from the end of the rifle. Then they returned to camp and padded the end of the rough stock with several pieces of heavy buckskin. This they wrapped tightly with wet rawhide to hold it in place. Then McAllister led José once more down to the water's edge. He reinforced his instructions, and this time they protected their ears with mullein leaves. At last, McAllister stood behind José, a reassuring hand on his shoulder, and they stared at the clump of sage the man pointed out.

"That's a rabbit's head, Lucky. An' yer starvin' plumb to death. Ain't et in four days. You got one shot left. An' remember—Lucky don't miss. Ever. They call 'im Lucky, but his real trick is genuine skill. Lucky is the best shot that ever lived."

José gazed at the branch and took a deep breath. Lucky! *That's me,* he thought wryly. Lucky. But this was one shot he had to make. If he didn't make this one, he'd never live it down. And if he made it, he had better never miss again.

Chapter Thirteen

José concentrated on the end of the branch. His heart thudded dully, and the sound was magnified because of the plugs in his ears. To the same level that the sound was magnified, the man's voice was muffled, and it had a soft, hypnotic effect. Soon, all José could see was that naked branch—the rabbit's head. *Lucky doesn't miss,* he said in his head. *Lucky will never, never miss. They don't call him Lucky for nothing.*

The boom of the Remington rolling block broke the stillness of the afternoon, pushing José back slightly like a big but gentle fist. With the padding between the butt and his shoulder it wasn't bad at all. When the smoke drifted away, José searched for the head of his "rabbit". There was no head. It had been totally blown away.

That night Moose Jaw and the other braves returned with four deer, an impressive bag for an area grown scarce in game. They skinned the carcasses and set them to cool near the wagon. Then they all joined around a big fire to roast chunks of venison backstrap and slices of intestine over the searing heat.

While they sat, the Shoshones spoke in their tongue, telling stories and laughing. José wished he could understand and join in. For the first little while, even Moose Jaw and McAllister spoke only in Shoshone. José began to feel like he was alone with a group of strangers, or like he didn't even exist, a figment of his own imagination.

Then Moose Jaw turned suddenly, as if reading his thoughts. "Little-Man-With-Warrior's-Eyes. Your day went well, I am told. Gray Eagle makes you a mighty hunter. What is it we killed today?"

José squinted questioningly at the brave, then glanced over at the wagon and shrugged. "You killed deer. I mean *sogodeheya'a,*" he corrected quickly.

Moose Jaw leaned back and looked him up and down, then smiled, showing his perfect white teeth. "Good, Little Man. Very good. *Sogodeheya'a* is right. White man's 'deer'. You have a strong mind for learning the tongue of the People quick." José lowered his eyes modestly.

"It is too bad, Little Man. The People, they no longer live like before. Our women are far away. Too far to skin *sogodeheya'a* and to do our skins. Now braves must work like women. It is too bad." José let out a laugh, then realized Moose Jaw was serious and quickly clamped his jaw shut. "It is not funny, Little Man. Doing hides, it is important to our way of life. It is important to Gray Eagle. It should also be important to you. Will you do a small thing for us, your friends?"

José looked over at McAllister, who was watching wordlessly. He returned his eyes to Moose Jaw. "Sure, if I can."

"We want to do our hides here, near your camp. Will you help us?"

"Well… sure. Can you show me how?"

Moose Jaw raised his hand and clenched it into a fist, making a satisfied face. "You bet, Little Man. Moose Jaw will help Little Man, then Little Man will help Moose Jaw." He smiled. "Little Man is a good man."

It became a night of story telling. Normally, Moose Jaw told José, stories were reserved only for the snowy months. But because of José, he wanted to make an exception, to let him hear some of the old ways and legends of the People. The braves spoke in Shoshone, then either Moose Jaw or McAllister translated to José. There were stories of the hunt, not only today's but of glorious hunts of the past. There were stories Moose Jaw told to José, stories about the creation of the world with the help of animals such as *ha'nii'i*, Beaver, *tindui*, Otter, and *ba'mus'se*, Muskrat. *Izhape'e*, Coyote, had been created in the beginning as a teacher and a friend of man. Coyote was wise in some ways, yet very foolish in other ways. The People avoided killing Coyote, for they were brothers.

Between McAllister, his teacher, and Moose Jaw, his new friend, José learned much of the Shoshone that night. He was sad to know they spoke mostly of a life that was gone from them forever; white men had claimed their ancestral home.

Two hours after dark, a Shoshone named Rocks-in-the-Stream embarked on a story full of suspense. He spoke of a great battle where Chief Washakie fought the Crow Indians and dealt them a crushing blow. At one point, the Indian stopped and went down to the water to drink. While he was gone, the others were silent. José grew impatient and looked at Moose Jaw. He worked up his courage enough to ask, "Do you know the story? Can you finish it?"

Moose Jaw smiled. "It is not that easy. In tradition of the People, once a person begins a story, he is the one who must finish it. For tonight, this is Rocks-in-the-Stream's story."

Rocks-in-the-Stream returned and went on, and at last his story ended. "The rat's tail fell off." This was the standard ending to every Shoshone story. "The rat's tail fell off," or simply, "the rat's tail." No matter what the subject of the story, it always ended with a rat's tail. Five minutes after Moose Jaw explained it to him, José was still chuckling.

Tongue Eater threw some branches on the dying fire, and soon it blazed back to life. José realized Tongue Eater was staring at him, and for several seconds he met his gaze. But at last he had to look away. It was the first time he had felt fear in this camp in some time. He sensed the husky brave didn't like him, though he didn't know why. But it scared him, wondering if the pock-marked brave would ever lay a hand on him, and if Moose Jaw would stop him, and how. If Moose Jaw didn't, would McAllister? He had little doubt of that answer.

At last, they had gorged themselves with as much bloody venison as they could hold. Two of the Shoshones had already curled up and gone to sleep, just out of the firelight. Fascinated, José still listened to the stories when they came, but talk was growing sparse.

Suddenly, the yap of a coyote cut into a lull in the conversation. It was joined by others until their cries filled the night. From the Bonn homestead, Injun's bark joined the group. Moose Jaw looked at José. "*Izhape'e*, our cousin. That is a good sign, Little Man. Coyote's howl means all is well. Little Man, I want to give you a gift. You grow your hair long, the way a warrior should. But it is not enough." Raising his hands, he unfastened one of two long strips of otter fur from his hair, and he beckoned José closer. Leaning over, he gathered a bunch of José's hair together and wrapped it with the otter fur, tying it there with a buckskin string. "This will bring you good medicine, my little brother. You will see."

In the morning, José awoke to someone shaking him gently, and he looked up into McAllister's face. The sun hadn't topped the mountains yet, but the sky was pale, its light, scattered clouds dyed pink. "Get up, boy. You might wanna see this."

José sat up wordlessly and tugged on his shoes, following McAllister out of the wagon. The Shoshones were speaking quietly. Suddenly, all of them knelt down facing east, and as one they began to sing.

"They do this as often as they can," explained McAllister. "Kind of a religious ritual. They do believe in *Appah*. No doubt about it. When they're done singin', they'll all drink water to purify their bodies, and then they'll go wash in the hot springs. Moose Jaw says we're welcome. Then he'd like to take you somewhere t'day."

José pulled his eyes away from the chanting warriors. "Where?"

"Horse hunting. When they were up in the rimrock yesterday they saw a band of mustangs, next valley over. They got talkin' about it an' thought they'd like to see if they c'n round 'em up. Horses're still good as money to those people."

José had a hard time hiding his excitement. He had seen wild horses in Nevada, the short-backed mustangs with long, flowing manes and tails. They were so spirited, and they moved like the desert wind. If a man was not affected by the sight of a prancing stud standing guard near his harem of mares, he was made of stone. But José had never dreamed he would be able to witness a hunt for the magnificent creatures.

"I'd like to go myself," said McAllister. "But I'll be on foot. You take yer old horse. See what he c'n do." José's heart fell. He didn't know if he wanted to go if McAllister couldn't be there. After a moment's silence, he voiced his thoughts.

McAllister nodded appreciatively. "Thanks, Lucky. But I've been on many a horse hunt. It's yer turn to live." José smiled, and he hurriedly swung his eyes away so McAllister couldn't see his disappointment.

The chanting of the Shoshones ceased abruptly, and José and McAllister walked to the hot springs and shucked their clothes, climbing into the steaming water as the Indians did. Moose Jaw looked over at José and smiled. "Will you come with us? To hunt the horse, as you call it—*bu'ngu*."

"*Bu'ngu?*" José repeated.

"*Bu'ngu.* There are many in this band. Fifteen, maybe twenty. I like the white man's numbers," he said. "Fifteen—you know how an Injun says fifteen? *Semoote-manegitemando'aingend.* White man's way is much faster. Fifteen." José laughed in agreement. He wasn't about to try and repeat that word.

"If you come with me, you will learn much about *bu'ngu,* Little Man. You will learn how to find *bu'ngu,* smell *bu'ngu,* think like *bu'ngu,* talk to *bu'ngu.* You will become *bu'ngu.* We have a saying among our people: a white man will ride the horse until he is tired; an Arapaho Dog-Eater will take him and ride him until *he* thinks he is tired; then a Shoshone will take him and ride to where he wants to go. You remember that. You ride like a Shoshone. You are the horse's master—he is not yours."

Moose Jaw looked over at McAllister. "There is a horse for you, too, my white friend. I would like to see how Gray Eagle rides an Injun horse."

McAllister straightened up in the water. "A horse? How so?"

"Rocks-in-the-Stream. He wishes to go up in the rocks alone today. He saw *doya duku'u* last sun. Mountain lion," he said to José. "He would go and search for this mountain lion and talk to *Da-ma-Appah*, maybe. He leaves you his best horse."

McAllister looked over at the Shoshone, Rocks-in-the-Stream, and by his face José could tell he was moved. He stared at him for several seconds, searching for words, then said something in Shoshone. Rocks-in-the-Stream nodded and smiled, replying in Shoshone. McAllister and the others all laughed.

"If I can't ride an Injun horse, an' I fall off, it's a long walk back, he says," McAllister translated for José. "He obviously ain't seen me ride."

José laughed. Come to think of it, he hadn't seen him ride either, except for his broken-down nag, but knowing McAllister as he felt he did, and considering how he mastered everything else relating to the outdoors, José knew he would be a terrific rider.

After fifteen minutes, José retreated from the water. He still wasn't used to the heat; the coolest of the pools was one hundred and two degrees, McAllister said. He let the cool morning breeze dry him, then put his clothes back on, and by then McAllister and the Indians were starting to climb out, too.

As McAllister dried, he looked over at the Shoshones. Steam rose from their bodies into the cold morning air, making them appear super-heated. McAllister winked at José. "Everyone thinks the steam engine came west with the railroad. Hell, little do they know. If they'd been to these springs they'd know 'Steam Injuns' have been around for hundreds of years."

When Moose Jaw had dressed, he saw José looking at his buckskin leggings. "When the deer skins are done, we will make you Injun clothes, too. I will show you how."

"Okay. I'd like that," José smiled. "What's that around your neck?" he asked. He indicated a small leather bag strung about the Shoshone's neck from a thong.

Moose Jaw fingered the object, his amulet. "This is where I keep my powerful medicine, Little Man."

"What's in it?"

Moose Jaw looked at José solemnly for a moment. "I know you don't know Injun ways, Little Man, so I am not angry. But I must tell you, one does not ask what is in the medicine bag. It is very bad manners. And he who wears it never tells what it carries. If I keep this secret, it keeps me safe, like the skin of the otter I wear in my hair. Today, you wear the otter skin I gave you. You will see I am right."

Taking the advice, José ran back up to the wagon, took out his strip of otter skin, and tied it around a bundle of his long hair. Knowing it was there made him feel more powerful already, and he walked back to the hot springs, his chest held out proudly. McAllister and the Indians came toward him, and he met them halfway.

"We're gonna start them hides out 'fore we go, Lucky," McAllister told him as he drew near. "Come on. We'll show you how." At the fire circle, McAllister demonstrated one Shoshone way of removing hair from the hide. In this instance, ashes wet with warm water were simply rolled up inside the hide, against the hair, and the hides were buried in the ground. Burying them was partly to help loosen the hair, partly to keep them safe from wild animals. The hides would now be left for two or three days and forgotten until it was time to remove the hair and the dark membrane underneath it. Another common method was to tie the hide down in a stream, letting the water swell the pores and work the hair loose.

One further step before making preparations for the horse hunt was to build two large fires, let the flames die down, and then drop the skinned deer heads into the ashes. Here they would stay while the brain was partially cooked, to later be used in the tanning process.

Before departing, Rocks-in-the-Stream took McAllister and José down to see his horse. It was a bay pinto with one blue eye and one brown, a short animal, not quite fifteen hands high. When McAllister and José first came near, the horse was nervous. Most Indian horses were, with white men, and the same was true for the white man's horse approached by an Indian. The odor of their bodies was radically different to the keen nose of a horse.

Between Rocks-in-the-Stream's presence and McAllister's soft, relaxing tone of voice, the horse soon calmed down and stopped sidling. McAllister stepped close and scratched behind its ears, blowing breath from his mouth into its nostrils to accustom it to his scent. He worked around until he could caress its neck, its slightly trembling legs, its short, stout back.

José watched, fascinated. He hoped someday he could win a horse's heart the way McAllister had won the heart of this one. But he had a feeling McAllister was much different than most men in one respect, at least. He was probably more wild mustang than he was man.

The only equipment Rocks-in-the-Stream had for the horse was a blanket and a surcingle with two rawhide stirrups attached, along with a braided rawhide rope he tied to its lower jaw to guide it. But McAllister didn't mind. He said something in Shoshone, and Rocks-in-the-Stream laughed and raised a clenched fist before him as if to wish McAllister good luck.

As McAllister looked into the horse's eyes, he spoke, the tone of his voice still soft.

"Now just take it easy, bronc. Let me give you some advice. You go to buckin' an' break yer leg, I'll have to kill you. You go to buckin' an' break *my* leg…" He paused. "Well, I'll just have to kill you." Without another word, he turned and cheeked the horse and flung himself onto its back.

Chapter Fourteen

The horse sidled several steps, then stopped, peering back, trying to see the unfamiliar rider on its back. But it made no attempt to buck or rear. It just stood warily and waited for a command. José guessed maybe it had understood its rider's advice. McAllister kneed it to a slow walk down toward the river. It moved with a jaunty gait, tossing its head, apparently losing all mistrust of its rider as soon as it started to move. On turning, it walked faster back toward Rocks-in-the-Stream. The wildness was now gone from its eyes.

José could only stare. How graceful this tall, raw-boned man appeared atop the little horse! How perfectly at home, like he and the animal were instantly melded into one. He looked over at Rocks-in-the-Stream. The Indian nodded with satisfaction.

When McAllister stopped the horse before them, the Shoshone said something with a look of admiration. He turned and clapped a hand on José's shoulder and spoke to him, then picked up his rifle, wheeled and headed toward the rimrock at a trot to find his mountain lion.

McAllister leaped down from the horse by José, and José asked, "What did he say?"

The man laughed. "Nothin' important. You ready to go?"

José ignored the question. "What do you mean, 'nothing important'? What did he say?"

McAllister laughed again, and José realized he was embarrassed. "He said to stay with me an' learn, an' someday if you became like me you too would be called a white-skinned Shoshone. His way of a compliment without sayin' it right to me."

José smiled. He was proud. Proud the Shoshones knew this man was his friend.

They followed the river northward up the valley beneath the Portneuf Range. The mountains were heavily timbered above, with large groves of quaking aspens along their flanks that gradually descended into sagebrush and grass. The mountain known as Haystack, the Hogsback, lay long and flat-topped against the horizon, majestic in the early morning sun.

McAllister pointed toward the sagebrush flats sprawling away across the other side of the Portneuf River and the railroad tracks. "Used to be you couldn't ride by here this time o' day without seein' antelope, elk, or deer—maybe all of 'em at once. Bears, too, sometimes. And wolves. But that train yer so proud of come in an' brought its rich swine an' wiped out all the game. You c'n still see their bones bleachin' in the sun where they left the carcasses to rot. Killed the deer an' elk an' antelope an' chased the bears an' wolves into black timber. It's a damn shame."

Moose Jaw was nearby, and he listened and nodded in silent agreement.

José's feelings had been hurt by McAllister's comment about him and the train. He didn't want to make McAllister any madder, but he wanted him to know his mind. "I'm not proud of the train," he said, looking straight ahead. "I didn't know how it was until you told me."

McAllister looked over, and his eyes softened. "Sorry, boy. Didn't mean to growl at you. It's them rich bastards with the guns that won't be still that I'm a-cursin'."

"An animal must never be wasted," said Moose Jaw suddenly. "And I know your friend Gray Eagle will teach you this, too. Kill only what you can eat. Choose the smallest animal you need from the herd. The smaller ones are the tender ones. If you must kill an animal to eat, say a prayer to *Appah*. Offer what is left to the other animals who are your brothers—Bear, Wolf, Coyote, Fox. *Doya duku'u* the lion will not eat. He eats only what he kills himself."

As they rode, McAllister told José stories of the fur trappers who once roamed this fertile valley in search of beaver. They came and trapped, took the beaver, killed off the bison—he called them buffalo—and then disappeared to the four winds. The land had never been the same. Hugh Glass, John Colter, Osborne Russell, Broken Hand Fitzpatrick, Jim Beckworth. They were rugged men with the fierce will to survive out there alone with the Indians and the wild beasts.

"I guess I'd a done the same thing, Lucky," McAllister admitted at last. "Those were shinin' times, as they called 'em, an' it seemed like things'd last ferever. I'd a been right there with them boys. I guess hist'ry'll never change, though. Them that comes along later'll always cuss what them that come before done to their inheritance." He laughed humorlessly, then suddenly pointed overhead, to the north, at a black silhouette that rode the air currents two hundred feet above the sage. "At least we still got the eagle. An' the wild spirit is in 'em. As long as there's an eagle anywhere, the wild spirit lives. And when the last one is shot down, that spirit'll go with 'im. Mark my words, boy. He's the symbol o' freedom."

As the little troop rode, McAllister and Moose Jaw took turns teaching José what they felt were the attributes of a worthy horse. A short back was preferable, both agreed, and large, intelligent eyes. Short, alert ears demonstrated worth, along with barrel bellies, thick shoulders and hindquarters, and a lower leg fairly short in comparison with the rest of the leg.

McAllister liked big horses. They were beautiful to watch, and being seated atop one was like sitting on a throne, looking down on other riders not mounted as high. Yet he agreed with Moose Jaw that many smaller mounts tended to have more staying power. "They got a sayin' down south, Lucky. 'Admire the tall, but saddle the small.' Most Americans tend to think bigger is better, but you been around hosses a while, you'll see what I mean. A lot o' yer smaller mustangs come outta Arabian or Spanish Barb stock. That accounts fer the size an' the stayin' power both. They're a mite flighty sometimes, but an

Arabian'll carry you till hell freezes over—an' a while on the ice."

They had ridden ten miles up the Portneuf by noon, and here they saw their first group of mustangs. The horses spotted them from far away and gave them no chance to come near. From the distance, they watched the stud gather his charges and herd them up toward the hills. José looked anxiously at McAllister. "Do we chase them now?"

McAllister looked over at José. "We ain't gonna chase 'em, Lucky. There's no way we'd catch 'em without grain-feedin' our animals fer a while. Them horses been eatin' the same grub ours have, plus they're not carryin' nobody on their back. No, we'll track 'em a while, find their waterin' spots. But we won't chase 'em. Don't wanna spook 'em worse'n they already are."

Moose Jaw interrupted. "Maybe someone chased this band already. If someone chased them, they will be very watchful. And hard to surprise."

McAllister nodded agreement. "A horse has excellent eyesight, especially a mustang. They spend their whole lives watchin' fer danger. You'll see they stick to the open country, not the trees. That's so they c'n use their eyes. They'll spot you a couple miles off in open country. An' they're jus' too big to hide, so a mustang depends on his legs fer safety. They c'n run like the wind an' keep you in their dust fer days, till most folks'd give up.

"The way to ketch a mustang is strategy. You find where they water, where they like to feed. They're a roamin' bunch, but their whole range usually ain't more'n twenty miles around. An' gen'rally they'll have one or two spots they water. They'll go outta their way by miles jus' to go to their favorite waterin' spots.

"I seen many a way to catch a wild horse. Heard tell o' Injuns an' some Mexicans—whole families of mustangers—that send their little kids alongside a herd on their fastest horse just to jump off onto the back o' the horse they want. Then they'll just ride 'em down. They don't tend to buck when they're already on the run. Others'll run a herd until the colts drop out, then the colts'll follow the riders home. They're pretty trusting. I seen men try to crease a horse, too." McAllister's eyes turned flat and sullen as he said this, and he looked ahead silently.

"Crease 'em?" asked José. "What's that?"

"Shoot 'em," growled McAllister. José realized it was not him McAllister was angry with, but this was another touchy subject, and he didn't know if he wished to hear more. McAllister saved him the trouble of asking. "A man'll try to get up close as he can to a wild horse, then shoot at 'im an' try to crease his spine. You get close enough, it'll stun 'em an' put 'em down long enough to tie their legs an' get set. You get closer, it'll kill 'em. I seen too many a fine mustang die with a bullet through his spine, an' I've run in a few that was healin' from neck wounds. Man starts gettin' fool ideas like that fer ketchin' a horse, he'd best get his knife an' fork out. They're likely to come in more handy than a saddle an' bridle."

José was silent for a moment, contemplating how anyone could be cruel enough to shoot at something as beautiful and free as a wild mustang. He was glad McAllister wasn't that type. "So what way do *you* use to catch horses, Gray?"

"Strategy, like I said. Either put a man on their waterin' spots so they can't drink an' run 'em in relays till yuh wear 'em down, or build secret brush corrals up some canyon or on a waterin' spot an' get a bunch o' boys to haze 'em in. Snarin' on a known trail sometimes works, too, but sometimes it also kills 'em dead. They hang theirselves.

"There's always them that'll rope a wild horse, too. I've done some myself, in my wilder days. But you go plantin' a loop on some studs, you best get ready to shoot 'em or die. When they hit the end o' that rope, they're comin' back with blood in their eye. An' there's many an enemy I'd ruther have than a range stud on the scrap."

They soon reached the spot where the herd had been grazing, and McAllister and the Shoshones made a quick study of the ground from horseback. The sign was marked deeply enough they didn't need to dismount. "They were waterin' over there this mornin'." McAllister pointed toward the river. "See this trail? They use it all the time. Let's go have a look."

The six of them turned along the trail and followed it toward the river. At one point, McAllister stopped beside a pile of horse droppings just off the trail. It was at least three feet high, and José stared in awe, then glanced at McAllister. He wondered how one horse could hold so much before relieving itself, but he had a feeling he'd better not ask that. It didn't matter; McAllister read it in his face. The man laughed and said something to Moose Jaw, and then all of the Shoshones laughed heartily. Helpless, José just looked on.

"It's not what you think, Lucky. Mustangs like to use the same place every time, so it builds up. See how only the droppings on top are fresh? They been workin on this a while." José had to laugh at himself. But he was glad McAllister had explained things to him, or it might have taken him a while to solve the puzzle.

They went to the river bank and let their horses drink. The bank was well-trod by unshod hooves, and McAllister showed José some ways to tell the difference between some of the hooves and so to distinguish the track of individual animals. Walking off a ways from the Shoshones, he pointed to a spot in the dust near a clump of sagebrush.

"See that? That's where the stud relieved himself." When José looked, all he saw was a large indentation in the dust with a sprinkling around it like the spots rain drops make after they dry. "See how there's two hoof prints side by side, an' the puddle's well ahead of 'em?" remarked McAllister. "A mare's spray will be closer to her feet."

They rode on and trailed the herd for several miles. They never saw the big herd again, but once Horse Killer spotted three mustangs alone at the mouth of a canyon. Out of curiosity, they rode toward them, and the horses, though nervous, stayed watching them for a minute or two. They pranced nervously back and forth, tossing their heads and neighing. When they were two hundred yards away, they turned and loped away along the foothills. McAllister sat his horse silently and stared after them. "Three stallions," he told José. "Young ones, prob'ly."

"Don't they have mares?" José asked.

"No, they likely been chased outta the herd by the head stud when they were a year or so old. In the horse world, the strong have many females, an' the weak got none. You'll see three kind o' studs on their own: young, old, an' weak. Ain't got the strength or know-how to hold a herd o' mares."

A brilliant wash of orange, red, and yellow stained the western sky when they found where the mustangs had watered that evening. José had nervously watched the sun fall toward the Portneuf Mountains for an hour or more, and now that it had disappeared, he finally turned to McAllister. "We didn't bring blankets or anything. Are we going to sleep out here?"

McAllister nodded. "Sure, Lucky. We'll just build up a big fire an' hunker down Injun style. Ain't no hostile Injuns around these days. We c'n afford a bonfire."

So they slept there beneath the stars, "back for a mattress and belly for a blanket," as McAllister grinningly remarked. They filled their bellies with roasted deer meat and curled into the sagebrush, and when the fire burned low wolves began to call from the timber below Bonneville Peak. José's skin goose-bumped, but it was not for fear. He looked over at McAllister and smiled happily. He was becoming a man of the wilderness.

They spent the next day studying the wild horses' habits and getting to know their range. They saw them three more times, for it is hard for a herd of mustangs twenty or so strong to hide in rolling country. One of the times, it was up close, and inexplicably the stud let them ride within three hundred yards. But it was plain the big mustang knew who had the upper hand. Some of the mares wanted to make tracks, their young with them, and they moved farther and farther away from the stud. But he stood and watched the riders, his curiosity sparked.

José marveled at the sight of the beast. He had seen mustangs in Nevada, but never so close. This one was a buckskin with black lower legs that turned into zebra stripes at his knees, then faded out above them. His tail, matted around burs and sticks, flowed down almost to the ground, and his mane on one side hid a broad, muscular, gently curved neck. He tossed his head frequently, flinging aside the forelock that hung past the middle of his nose. José knew that stud must be the most beautiful thing in the valley, and though he knew he would never be his, he lost his heart to him that day.

When they returned to their camp at the hot springs, it was with sadness on José's part. He had come to love riding the hills along the Portneuf, watching the horses and the occasional deer and elk. He had learned much of wild horses in three days, and of a way of life coming to a close. But he had also decided he would live this life to its fullest while the wild spirit was still alive.

McAllister himself had said the eagle was the symbol of freedom, and the wild spirit would always exist, as long as there was an eagle alive. Well, wasn't McAllister also called Gray Eagle? And as long as he was around, José's new way of life was secure.

Rocks-in-the-Stream greeted the troop happily on their return. He was busy dehairing one of the hides, so part of his happiness in seeing them probably came from knowing he didn't have to shave all the hides himself, José guessed.

Moose Jaw helped stake the hides out in the sun, then set José to work immediately scraping one of them. After this chore was completed, they opened up the deer skulls and allowed the brains to soften somewhat in a pot of water over a low fire, and then they took time out for dinner. Moose Jaw sat near José and clapped him on the shoulder with a smile. "You'll be a good mountain man soon."

The tanning process took almost three days, and once they began it, very little attention was paid to anything else. They worked the hides mercilessly, stretching them first over the wagon wheels, pulling them and breaking down their fibers, then tugging at them with their hands, and finally with both feet and hands. The brain solution was rubbed deeply into both sides of the hide, then the hides washed again in cold water. The stretching process seemed to go on and on. At the end of three days, José's arms and fingertips ached with the strain, but in his hands he held a perfect brain-tanned buckskin.

"You done good, Lucky," complimented McAllister, admiring the hide. "Three more'll make you an outfit to be proud of." José smiled happily, but it quickly turned to a frown. Three more? He hoped the outfit would last for a long time. After tanning three more hides this way, he didn't think he'd ever want to tan another.

That evening, McAllister and the Shoshones and José lazed about a roaring fire, laughing and telling stories. Tonight, there was very little English spoken, and José didn't care. He was exhausted. He just wanted to sit and let his mind fade quietly away. Away to the timbered Portneuf Range or to the buckskin stallion.

He became aware of someone speaking his name. He looked over to see everyone watching him, and McAllister said his name again. "Moose Jaw wants to tell you somethin', Lucky." José immediately shifted his attention to the big Indian.

"Little-Man-With-Warrior's-Eyes. You are a mountain man. You have shown me. And you are a little Shoshone warrior, too. Your friend, Gray Eagle, he is like a Shoshone brother to us. You are, too. My brothers and I, we have spoken together. We have a gift for you."

Rocks-in-the-Stream stood up with a bundle across his arms and walked over to place it in José's lap. It was the other three deer skins. Tears filled José's eyes, but he didn't say anything. He looked around him at the faces that watched him expectantly, and then he dropped his eyes so they couldn't see his face.

Moose Jaw reached over suddenly and placed his big hand on José's shoulder. "With the morning sun, we will return to our people, Little Man. In two moons, we will come back with our women. We will come to hunt *bu'ngu,* the horse. We would like you to come also. And then you will be dressed as an Injun. Gray Eagle will help make Injun clothes for you to wear."

"I'd like that," José replied. "Thank you for your gift."

Moose Jaw shook his head. "Thanks to you, Little Man. You show there is at least one more good white man. One day you will be a great warrior—and a friend of the People."

The next day, José watched as the Shoshones said their morning prayers and drank their water, and then they all went to soak in the hot pools one last time. Suddenly, the horses began to fidget and neigh, and when José looked over, they were staring toward the east, toward Soda Springs, their ears pricked smartly forward. Everyone turned together and looked toward the road. At first, they saw nothing, but the horses were causing such a stir that they all climbed from the water and pulled their clothes on. Just as José was tying his shoes, he heard McAllister's cautious voice. "There's ten or better. Rest easy, Moose Jaw."

José looked up in time to see a large group of horsemen coming along the road toward them. Several of them carried rifles across their saddles. He looked over to see McAllister buckling his Colt about his hips, and there was a light in his eyes José had come to expect in times of impending trouble. The man still moved in his casual way, but his hand never lifted far from the gun butt, and there was a light spring to his legs. Those legs never seemed to straighten all the way out, but always left a little more room to jump, if need be.

The horsemen left the road and reined in before them, oblivious to the dust they caused to drift across their wet bodies. Two of the men were rough-looking, with coarse beards and dirty slouch hats. They both carried rifles, one a '66 Winchester and one an old Henry, a break in the stock of the latter wrapped with piano wire. The others looked well-off, by their dress. They wore new boots and clean hats, and a number of them had on shooting coats and fine wool pants tucked into their boots. Studying them more closely, José noticed that even the ones who didn't carry a rifle in their hands had one shoved into a saddle scabbard.

McAllister waved the last of the dust away from his face with his left hand as his eyes slowly scanned the group. "Can I help you gents?"

One of the group, a man of about forty-five, with a bushy mustache that grew into his sideburns, swung his eyes from Moose Jaw to let them settle on McAllister. "What are these savages doing here?"

José was watching McAllister when the words came out, and he saw his eyes go flat and hard. "These 'savages', as you call 'em, happen to own the land yer settin' on. An' they're my friends. What's yer business here?"

Again, the man ignored McAllister's query. "This is *not* their land. This is railroad right- of-way. Why aren't they back at Ross Fork, anyway?"

This time it was McAllister's turn to ignore a question. "Why aren't you back at Soda Springs? You come huntin', I expect. But you can't hunt on Shoshone land."

"The hell I can't!" the man retorted. Suddenly, he laughed, and then several of the others joined in. The two rough-looking characters didn't seem to be paying much attention. They were too busy eyeing the camp. "My name's Bulliard. Andrew Bulliard. Who're you, mister?"

McAllister stared at the man for several seconds, then spat. "None o' yer damn business."

Bulliard's eyes narrowed, but he laughed again, humorlessly. "Well, I'm the superintendent of this stretch of the Oregon Short Line Railroad. And I think I'll come back here with the papers to move you all off this piece of ground. How would you like that?"

"An' how'd you like me to jerk you off that fat horse o' yers and tromp you here in front of all yer lady friends."

Now several of the horsemen started to back out of the group and ease up the road the way they had come. They left Bulliard, four men who were obviously his cronies, and the two roughnecks. Bulliard looked around him, and then his eyes settled with a deadly glint on McAllister's face.

"I hope you can back up your talk, Injun lover."

Chapter Fifteen

Bulliard figured his words would be enough. He expected no answer to his challenge. That was plain to José by the look in his eyes, the look that came into them when he stared down the barrel of McAllister's Colt.

José had been watching the interlopers. He hadn't seen McAllister draw the Colt. But it seemed to have appeared like magic in his fist. Now it was leveled at Bulliard's head.

"All right, mister," McAllister said casually. "Now let's find out who can back their talk. The more empty saddles they c'n send back to Jay Gould, the better I'll like it."

Bulliard glared at McAllister, his face slowly going from white to red. "Well, you're not worth getting dirty over, you Injun lover. But you can bet I'll be back. You don't point a gun at Andrew Bulliard and get away with it. And I won't be alone. Mark my words."

McAllister scoffed. "Yer kind never are. Why don't you jus' bring ol' Jay Gould with yuh? I'd love a chance to stomp his worthless hide into the dirt."

Bulliard's grip tightened noticeably on his rifle as he glared at McAllister, then swung his dark eyes across the Shoshones, and finally let his gaze settle on José. "Boy, you'd better find some new company to keep," he snarled. "You won't like what you see if you're around here when I come back. Maybe we'll trim your hair up a little, too."

José's Basque blood was already boiling. He'd had a stomach full of blowhards in the past few months, and being around McAllister and Moose Jaw made him feel braver than he might otherwise have. "You go to hell," he retorted.

Bulliard's face turned bright red, and he whipped his horse around and gouged it with his spurs, making it sidle and then break into a gallop back up the road. The other hunters followed. The two roughnecks lingered a moment, looking about the camp, and José didn't like the gleam in their eyes. Apparently, neither did McAllister.

"You two sons o' bitches throwed in with the wrong crowd," he growled. "Now yuh best strike the same trail yer boss did, or I'm of a mood to empty yer saddles an' take yer hair. Or let the Injuns do it—they're prob'ly better at it. Now ride." The no-nonsense tone of his voice left no room for debate. The two men wheeled their horses and galloped after the rest of the group.

It was a somber camp as the Shoshones prepared their gear to leave. No one spoke. Provisions were quietly wrapped and loaded, and McAllister stood by the wagon staring off the way the hunting troop had departed. There was a glow to his gray eyes that scared José. It was the same look that entered them when he spoke of the railroads and rich men, only magnified several times. José tried not to even look at him. It made him uneasy and sick in the pit of his stomach. But something in that gaze kept drawing José's eyes back to McAllister's face. He feared for the hunters' lives should they return to that part of the country this day or any other.

After the Shoshones had departed, José and McAllister climbed on José's old bay horse and rode across the bridge toward the Bonn farm. The horse walked easily, and José didn't know if it was his imagination or not, but the old fellow seemed to look around him much more than he had of old. He seemed to be more aware of his surroundings, more lively in his gait. Maybe he had regained some of his youth in the time he had spent roaming the hills with the Indian ponies. To José, it felt like a good change.

José sensed the tension had gone out of McAllister's muscles by the time they reached the Bonns' yard. He hopped down, then McAllister did likewise and tied the horse to the shed. "Hello the house," McAllister called out.

A man's voice answered from behind the shed, and soon a short, barrel-chested man in bib overalls walked into sight holding a double-bit axe. He brushed tousled, dark hair from a furrowed forehead and looked from José to McAllister. He didn't smile, but his face was not unfriendly. "Hello. You must be the men from down on the river. I'm Henry Bonn."

McAllister nodded. "Robert McAllister. An' this here's Lucky." José doubted McAllister even remembered his real name. He'd spoken it only once since the day they met, and "Lucky" just seemed natural to him now.

Bonn leaned the axe up against the shed and stepped close to shake hands. He shook José's just like he did McAllister's and spoke to him like he would another man. José was impressed by his firm grip and hard, callused hands.

"Good to know yuh, Lucky. Name like that, yer just what this place needs to hang around a while." He turned to McAllister. "Come set a spell. Clara says I need to learn to rest a bit durin' the day, so you'll be my excuse to sit an' chew the fat."

McAllister nodded. "Told yer wife we'd pay a visit after our friends left."

"The Injuns?" Bonn said. "Yeah, Clara told me." He glanced toward the camp by the river then turned toward the house.

Clara Bonn had come to stand in the front doorway with the two smaller children, and she watched the three till they drew near. "Good to see you again, Mr. McAllister. How are you, Lucky? Won't you come on in and set?"

They all sat down inside, José on the edge of one of the beds, and Clara brought a pitcher of cool water around. They occupied several minutes with small talk before Clara reminded McAllister of her earlier invitation to supper, and he quickly accepted. Then, while she began to prepare the meal, Bonn took José and McAllister on a tour of his homestead.

Bonn was proud of what he had accomplished, and McAllister listened attentively to his plans for the land. As kind as he was it was hard not to be happy for him. And had he been the last of his kind, it wouldn't have mattered. But this was only the beginning.

José knew it, and he knew McAllister did, too. The flood of settlers was just beginning. Idaho was good country, and people were finding that out. Word about things like that spread like wildfire. The frontier was drawing to a close, and McAllister would be caught like a wolf at a turkey shoot. José fancied for a time he could feel a part of McAllister's spirit die. Then he realized it was his own.

Toward mid-afternoon, José heard the dog barking in the yard, and he looked out to see a wagon pull up. He glanced at the driver and for a moment just stared in disbelief. This man was unmistakable and unforgettable. It was Mr. Woodland, from Soda Springs. His chestnut hair shone from beneath the flat gray brim of his hat.

José's eyes pivoted slowly to the two passengers on the seat beside the driver. The one farthest from him was a dark-haired woman. He couldn't have said any more about her, for his eyes didn't linger on her long. They fell almost instantly to the one in the middle, and he felt like he'd been kicked in the stomach. There sat Rebecca Woodland, whose face he could never erase from his mind and whose memory had only recently begun to fade from his dreams.

The girl seemed even more beautiful than before. Maybe it was the afternoon sunlight highlighting her long hair, touching her lips and soft cheeks. Maybe it was the mysterious half-smile, or the way her eyes carefully surveyed the surroundings. He couldn't see those eyes closely, but their deep green color was etched in his memory forever, and again he thought of the harbor where his ship rolled in from South America.

Henry Bonn had stood and walked to the window, and he exclaimed, "Oh, there's a surprise for you. It's the Woodlands."

"Oh, good," Clara beamed. "Thank goodness I made plenty. Those boys of theirs eat like there's no tomorrow!"

When she said that José glanced into the back of the wagon and saw three boys, aged about twelve, seven, and five, and another girl about nine. Two of them had their father's chestnut hair, the girl and the oldest boy had dark hair like their mother.

The Bonns went outside, greeting the Woodlands happily. José looked over at McAllister, who just sat quietly, sipping his glass of water. His face was blank, and he didn't meet José's gaze. José looked back outside, and in spite of himself his eyes fixed on Rebecca Woodland. His heart pounded in his chest, a little too fast and a little too strong. Why did this girl have that power over him? It was the same way he had felt gazing at the buckskin stallion—only different. The horse had made him feel exhilarated; Rebecca Woodland tied his stomach in knots.

"Well, Lucky." McAllister suddenly looked up. "We'd best be sociable."

He stood up and put on his hat and started toward the door, and José's heart leaped into his throat. He ached to see Rebecca closer, but at the same time he wanted to disappear, to not let her see him at all. He hated wondering what she thought of him, knowing he was nothing to her and he would surely make himself look like a fool if he opened his mouth. But like a dumb animal he followed McAllister out the door.

Bonn turned when he heard them come out. "Terrence, Martha, I'd like you to meet some new friends of ours, Robert McAllister and—Lucky, was it?"

José swallowed hard. "Y—Yes, sir," he stammered. His face turned hot, and he felt like a fool. Why didn't he tell them his name before the whole world knew him only as Lucky?

Terrence Woodland spoke in his big, booming voice. "Rebecca and I met the gentlemen in Soda Springs a while back." He touched his hat in greeting. "This is Martha, and you remember Becca. That's Noah, Laban, little Jacob, and Anna," he named off the other children, who had already hopped out of the back of the wagon.

Woodland climbed down and gave Martha and Rebecca a hand off the wagon seat, and they stretched, obviously glad to be off the hard, bouncy seat after the long haul from Soda Springs. Bonn took Woodland's hand and shook heartily. Woodland nodded again wordlessly at McAllister, but neither man offered their hand, and Woodland turned back to Bonn. "Sorry to barge in this way, Henry. If we'd known you had company, we'd a waited. It's the first chance we've had to be out this spring, though. We all had cabin fever."

"Don't you fret about that," replied Bonn. "Always glad to see you folks. The boys'll be back from huntin' shortly. They'll be sorry they weren't here when you got in, though. All they do these days is talk about Rebecca." He turned and gave a wink to the girl, who blushed.

José looked quickly over at Bonn, and his face burned hotter, his heart thudded louder. Then he started wondering about these Bonn boys. What did they look like? How old were they? Did Rebecca Woodland like them? He wondered if they were all of the same religion. That would give them a headstart with the girl. He didn't know why he even thought about it. A girl like that would never notice a Basque boy like him. With that realization, his heart fell.

As if on cue, a call rose from the junipers above the house. José spun and looked to see two boys, aged about seventeen and fifteen, coming from the trees. The older one carried a rifle in one hand and a rabbit in the other. The younger boy carried a rabbit in each hand.

As the boys came closer, the younger one had a big grin on his face, looking from his father to the others, but the older boy appeared serious, and José noticed he studiously avoided looking at Rebecca Woodland.

The older boy, introduced as Jared, was dark of eye and hair, a slender young man with long arms and legs and standing several inches over José's five-foot-five. The younger one, Charlie, was fuller of form, like his parents, and his hair was blond. He laughed a lot and smiled the rest of the time, José noticed, and he was friendly toward José from the beginning, even asking him to share in the honor of cleaning and skinning the rabbits. José gladly accepted, ready to demonstrate his new-found skill.

Jared Bonn skinned his rabbit and gutted it much more quickly than the other two boys, and a little too sloppily, thought José. Then he left without a word to them. Later, José looked toward the house to see him walking beside Rebecca Woodland. Again something sank inside him. His first love affair, imaginary though it was, had just taken a plunge.

Later, while Clara and Martha fried up the rabbits, José walked along the river bank with Charlie Bonn, Noah Woodland trailing along and throwing stones into the river. It had been a long time since José had been around other boys, and it felt strange. He had spent so much time with men lately he didn't feel like he had much in common with Charlie and Noah. Both were younger than he, Charlie by one year and Noah by four, but that shouldn't have made much difference. José guessed he could have relaxed more if not for mooning over Rebecca.

They had walked along the river for three quarters of a mile or more when Noah spoke up, after several minutes of silence. "You known that McAllister fella very long?" he asked José conversationally.

"No. I just met him last April," José admitted.

At this revelation, Noah stepped quickly around in front of the other two and stopped abruptly, darting a glance up toward the house. "Bet I know somethin' you don't."

José looked over at Charlie. Their eyes met, and then both looked at Noah expectantly.

"Promise ta keep a secret?" Noah asked.

José shrugged. "Sure, I guess," he replied, and Charlie concurred.

Noah's eyes darted toward the house again, and then he went on in a lower voice, as if anyone else could hear. "Did you know yer friend's a horse thief? Bet he didn't tell yuh that."

José's pulse immediately quickened, but he put a mask of indifference on his face. "Oh, what are you talking about?"

"Yeah, it's true!" said Noah in an excited tone. "He stole a horse from a fella north of Soda Springs a while back. Becky an' me saw 'im. Well, we didn't see 'im steal the horse, exactly—but we saw 'im on it."

"How do you know it wasn't his?" asked José, feigning ignorance. He had always believed McAllister had done what they accused him of, but he had never dared ask him about it. Now maybe he could get more of the story without McAllister's knowledge.

"There was a bunch of men after 'im, that's why! Me an' Becky were ridin' along the river by town, an' he come along an' ran inta Becky's horse. Knocked her right in the water! Then he grabbed me an' threw me off my horse, 'cause the one he stole was all tuckered out."

José continued to act like he didn't care what Noah said about McAllister. But inside he was scared Noah might turn them in to the law. "Well, why didn't you tell the sheriff, if you're so sure he did it?"

"'Cause he saved Becky's life. She was knocked out cold an' floatin' down the river. He went right in an' saved her when he coulda just left her an' got away. He turned my horse loose anyway. It came back later. An' Becky made me promise never ta tell no grownups it was him. In fact, they caught yer friend, an' Becky had ta go ta town an' see if it was the right fella. She fibbed to 'em an' said it weren't him." Suddenly, a look of worry came into Noah's eyes, and his face paled. "Wait. You— Was that you that was there with him? Becky said there was a kid there."

"Yeah, that was me. But I didn't think he really did what they said."

Noah looked worriedly from one to the other. "You won't tell anybody else, will yuh?"

"I won't tell," said Charlie instantly. "Promise."

José shrugged, glancing up toward the house. He figured it went without saying he wouldn't tell, but he was glad to know at last what had happened and why Rebecca Woodland had set McAllister free when it had been obvious by the look in her eyes she knew him.

"Well, we better get on back," said Charlie suddenly. "Bet supper's on." So they made their way back to the homestead and got there just as the table was being set.

"'Bout time you boys got back," admonished Clara Bonn when she saw them shuffle through the door. "You 'bout missed your supper."

"Sorry, ma'am." Charlie was the only one who spoke.

They took places on the floor, as all chairs were taken, and José glanced surreptitiously toward the table to see Rebecca next to Jared Bonn. He sighed and looked down at his plate.

While they ate, it grew dark, and the grownups kept a lively conversation going. The promised apple pie followed immediately on the heels of supper, and Clara Bonn had had the foresight to make two, so there was plenty to go around. José reveled silently in its flavor.

He didn't hear how the conversation started, but he heard the word "Mormon" mentioned by Clara Bonn, and then turned his ear curiously that way. It turned out all these people were of the Mormon religion, or the "Saints," as they called themselves. McAllister talked with them at length about their beliefs and practices. He seemed genuinely interested, although José couldn't imagine that grubby trapper belonging to any religion. He had to smile at the thought of it. As for himself, he was born a Catholic and would die a Catholic, even though he had attended the Methodist church with Ben Trombell while living in Nevada.

Henry Bonn was seated facing the front wall of the house. Suddenly, he shoved back his chair and jumped up, staring out the window toward the river, a look of consternation on his face. "What's that?" he said.

McAllister caught the look in his eye and stood and spun from the table to look out the window. His eyes widened in surprise, then narrowed dangerously. "Why those bastards! They're burnin' the wagon!"

Sweeping his hat from the floor, McAllister reached the door in two long strides and snatched the Remington rolling block that leaned behind the door. He ran to the horse, and José spilled his pie standing up to go after him. He sprinted but almost didn't make it to the horse before McAllister reined it around toward the river. He caught McAllister's hand and swung on behind him, and they galloped down through the sagebrush, the horse's rough gait jolting José this way and that so it took all the strength in his legs to hold him on.

As they neared the river, the flames from the wagon rose high into the sky, reflecting off the water. José watched in horror as Ben Trombell's sheep wagon was engulfed and destroyed by the crackling, roaring blaze.

McAllister chose the shorter route across the river. Without pause, the horse plunged into the water and started lunging across, and José and McAllister held to the saddle till they reached the other shore, where they leaped down into the shallows.

Clambering up on the bank, José could see riders encircling the flames now, whooping and hollering. In his excitement, he couldn't even count them. They dashed to and fro in the leaping shadows, their horses screaming in terror.

McAllister reached the scene at a sprint, and as a horseman ran by him, not even noticing him in the excitement, he brought him off the horse with an arcing swing of the rifle. The man struck the ground hard, and even in the melee José heard the solid crack of sagebrush branches beneath him. McAllister neared him in a stride and kicked him viciously in the face as he rolled over, then kicked him twice more in the kidneys. The man screamed in pain.

At the scream, José looked around at the other horsemen. There were five more of them, and all of them had turned their heads. Surprise washed quickly over their faces, and then as one they wheeled toward McAllister.

One of them tried to run his horse over McAllister, but the woodsman was too fast. He lunged to the side and then dove out of the way of another horse. Its hooves clipped the ground immediately behind him as he rolled over a shoulder and came up, still holding the rifle.

A third horse appeared behind McAllister. He didn't hear it, and José had no time to warn him. The horse struck him hard and knocked him forward on the rifle. The men fairly flew out of their saddles, and one rushed in and kicked McAllister in the stomach with the flat toe of his boot. McAllister grunted and started to tip to the side, but another boot from that direction caught him, throwing him back toward the first man. A third one landed a foot in the middle of his back before he could make any other move, and he fell on his face again.

José had never done much fighting other than wrestling with his brother and neighbor boys back home. But he knew McAllister would have stood up for him, even at the risk of his own skin, and he could do nothing less for this man who had already saved his life once. Eyes dimmed with fury, José grabbed a big rock off the ground and ran silently at the group of men. Not even conscious of what he was doing, he struck with all his strength the last man who had kicked his friend. The four pound rock, like a prehistoric hammer, took the man across the back of the head, and he went down as José flew over him.

"Get a gun, Willy!" he heard one of the other men yell as he came back up. Before he could say anything else, José threw the rock, and it sank into the man's belly, doubling him over.

Without any time to deliberate, José dove on top of the man, who outweighed him by at least sixty pounds. With sick fear, he felt the man's arms close around him.

Chapter Sixteen

The sound of fighting had resumed behind José, so he knew McAllister was back in the brawl. Someone growled in pain, then screamed as the pain intensified. Something struck against flesh, and the scream turned instantly to a low moan, then was drowned out by louder sounds.

José struggled against the arms encircling him, but their grip only became stronger. His head swelled with pressure. Suddenly, he heard a new voice behind him with a deep-throated growl like a bear. "Get off him, you pack o'—" Immediately on the heel of the words followed a dull *thunk* like a heavy rock hitting the ground, and a man cried out.

The man clutching him abruptly let go, as if realizing he had hold of a rattler, and José rolled away, gasping for breath. The man turned over and leaped to his feet, whirling toward the sounds of fighting.

Head throbbing, José sat up and looked toward the others. His heart leaped. In the dancing firelight he made out the huge, bear-like form of Terrence Woodland, striking out with his fists, throwing challengers this way and that. McAllister was up, too, and slamming one man in the face with his fist over and over until the man went limp and fell at his feet. As another one tried to rise, McAllister caught him in the abdomen with a kick hard enough to lift him from the ground. The man fell and lay writhing, holding his abdomen; he made no further attempt to rise.

The blast of a shotgun crashed in the night, and the fighting ended in an instant. José looked over to see Henry Bonn standing just out of the fire's glow, clutching the scattergun. It was a Remington side-by-side, and his finger hovered near the second trigger.

After a quick glance about, Bonn's look of anger slowly turned to one of wry amusement. "Guess you boys didn't need me at all. Fact is, I guess it was them I saved from a beating."

He looked at the men who lay at McAllister's and Woodland's feet, holding various body parts and moaning quietly. One of them was not so quiet. He cried and held the back of his head with both hands. It was the man José had struck with the rock. He remembered what McAllister had said about killing a man and was relieved to see this one moving. He hadn't meant to kill him, but the blow very easily could have.

José heard commotion and looked up to see the rest of the Bonns and the Woodlands.

They had just crossed over the bridge and stood huddled in a group, lit dimly by the firelight, staring half scared at the roughnecks sprawled around the cluttered campsite.

After a quick but loving survey of her husband, Clara Bonn hustled over to José. "Are you all right, dear? Did they hurt you?"

José hadn't thought about it. He put his hand to the back of his neck and massaged it as he looked down at the rest of his body. "No, I guess not. Just squeezed the breath out of me."

"Oh, you poor dear," said Clara, and before José knew what she was about, she threw her arms around him and gave him a hug. Perhaps worse than the embarrassment, he thought for a moment Clara Bonn was trying to out-squeeze the man who had grabbed him earlier. When she stepped away, he smiled bashfully and prayed she wouldn't hug him again.

He shot a quick glance toward the rest of the family, and his gaze fell as if by magnetism on Rebecca Woodland. She was watching him. Their eyes held for a moment, and then he looked away, feeling the heat rise around his collar.

The fire ebbed, but smoke still rolled away from it in spurts. The wagon wood had been dry and cracked and fed the flames well. Now it lay in a heap of black boards and crackling embers, its wheels leaning into the wreckage with their spokes still aglow. A sick feeling swept over José, and he steeled himself just in time to keep his eyes dry. As much as he would have liked to cry, he couldn't do it in front of these people.

He could never face Ben Trombell again. That was chiseled plainly in stone now. He had not only lost the man's sheep, he had allowed his wagon to be destroyed. The only thing he had left of Ben's was the old bay horse, and Ben had as much as given that to him.

He wandered aimlessly around the camp and started finding scattered gear from the wagon. His heart took hope. The men must have ransacked it before they burned it, and there was no telling what might have survived.

One of the first things he found was the broken Winchester rifle, and he picked it up with a half-hearted smile. Its metal was cold and lifeless, yet reassuring. He suddenly wanted very badly to learn to use a gun well, to protect himself the way Bonn had protected him and McAllister.

He walked around and found other items and became aware that the others were circling the burned wagon and helping him. They started piling odds and ends by the fire hole. A dented pan, a blanket, two spoons, a cup. Then the shotgun McAllister had retrieved from the ground after his near brush with death on Bailey Creek.

"Is this yours?" At the sound of the soft voice, José whirled. Until he looked into her eyes, it didn't register who the voice belonged to. It was Rebecca Woodland, and she stood not three feet from him, dim light reflecting in her green eyes. She was holding a bundle in her outstretched arms, and José recognized the rolled up buckskins.

Tears of happiness at seeing the hides flooded into his eyes, but he fought them back. "Yeah," he said. "I helped tan them. I'm going to make some clothes."

Rebecca smiled and took a step closer, pushing them toward him. He took them, and as he did so he touched her hand. It was cold. When Rebecca started to turn away, José said, "Wait." He knelt and undid the bundle, rolling one hide away from the others. He stood up, holding it. "I tanned this one myself. It's—it's kind of cold out here."

Rebecca hesitated a moment, then smiled again, showing her straight white teeth. She stood still while José wrapped the hide around her shoulders, his hands shaking. "Is your name really 'Lucky'?" she asked.

José dipped his head in embarrassment. "No, that's just a nickname. My real name is José Olano."

Rebecca stood there smiling, then slowly put out her hand. "My name's Rebecca. But sometimes Papa calls me Becca. You can call me that if you'd like."

Heart pounding loudly in his ears, José put out his hand, almost scared, and took hold of Rebecca's. It was very soft, and it amazed him how warm it made his hand and his whole body, in spite of being cold itself. He immediately tried to retract his hand, though not very forcefully. Rebecca held on a moment longer, her grip firm.

José heard Terrence Woodland speaking, his big voice booming in the chilly night. He pulled back his hand and looked over where Woodland, Bonn, and McAllister had the six roughnecks rounded up, all of them standing now, in spite of their injuries.

"I'm a Mormon, men, and I don't hold with killin' folks in cold blood. That's the only reason I don't let Mr. McAllister shuck his knife and give you all an Injun haircut like he wants. But I'll say this: your horses are long since headed back home, an' you'd better follow them if you c'n find the way with your heads bent out of shape. Like I said, I'm a peaceable Mormon, but even we c'n get riled up, and if I see you back here, I'm liable to forget my religion for a day."

"Wait." It was McAllister's voice that broke in. "Where's yer boss—that Bulliard snake?"

One of the men who had been with Bulliard earlier that day glanced quickly at the other one, the man José had struck on back of the head. The second man just shook his head and grimaced in pain. "Ah, Bulliard didn't send us," said the first man. "We come back on our own to git yer outfit, that's all."

"Don't you lie to me, boy," McAllister growled. "I c'n spot a lyin' dog a mile away an' smell 'em, too, an' yer rotten as a dead skunk in a hot breeze. Where's Bulliard? Didn't he wanna spoil his righteous name gettin' caught in this night ride?"

The first man shrugged sullenly, pursing his lips. Angrily, McAllister reached out and stiff-armed him, knocking him backward. "We all know who sent you, no matter how you lie. Do as the gent said an' make some tracks fer home. Come mornin', I shed daylight through the head o' any man o' you within ten miles o' this camp."

After the six of them had limped away, the camp was silent and dark. The only sounds were of the crickets and the popping of coals in the fire. Everyone stood around, at a loss for words, and stared at the wreckage with its dimly flickering flames.

José saw Jared Bonn standing over by his father and Charlie, and Jared's eyes were on him and Rebecca. She suddenly looked over and caught Jared's eye, too, and took a step that way. "I guess I'd better—"

"Wait. Couldn't you stay one more minute?" Embarrassed, José realized he was the one who had spoken. He didn't know why. Well, he did know why, but he didn't know what to say now that she did hesitate. What did a boy like him say to a beauty like Rebecca Woodland?

"I was glad to meet you, Becca," he uttered. "Do you think you'll come back here soon?"

Rebecca shrugged. "I don't know. It's coming on our busiest time of year. We're breaking new ground and clearing trees and—" She stopped suddenly and canted her head a bit to one side. "Where will you go now that you don't have any shelter?"

José shot a glance at the burned-out wagon. "Gray—Mr. McAllister's teaching me to survive in the mountains. I'm getting used to sleeping on the ground."

Rebecca looked down. "Oh. But what will you do when it gets cold? You'll catch your death of pneumonia."

"No," José said, looking down and kicking at the dirt with his toe. "We'll build a lean-to or something."

"Oh," Rebecca said again. "Well, maybe sometime I'll see you in town." She smiled shyly and touched him on the sleeve, then walked off toward her father, looking at the ground.

The pile of gear had ceased to grow now, and everyone stood in silence or talked in subdued tones. McAllister walked over and stopped in front of José, squinting his eyes broodingly toward the wagon. He dabbed at an oozing cut beneath his left eye and wiped the blood on his buckskin pants. "Well, sorry 'bout the wagon, Lucky. I know it meant a lot to yuh. But now you'll get to be a real mountain man, anyway. Hell, they didn't sleep in no wagon. Greenhorn stuff. On the ground, that's where a mountain man sleeps, or maybe up a tree, if it suits 'im an' the bears're thick. I figger we'll head on over to look fer yer mustangs, maybe run in a herd an' sell 'em—make some travelin' dough. Wha' d' yuh think?"

José was silent, and McAllister followed his eyes to Rebecca, who was talking quietly with her father. "Oh-h-h," the man said musingly. "I reckon I know what you think. You gotcherself a case o' the calico fever. Well, a man c'd do a helluva lot worse'n that gal, now. She's a stayer, an' there ain't many stayers that look good, too. You get a grubstake, maybe you oughtta ride back thisaway. But keep in mind, she's a Mormon, an' I get the feelin' they stick t'gether perty tight. She's prob'ly lookin' fer one o' the same—take that Jared kid. So don't be settin' yerself up fer no fall. Let's go ketch us some horses, git you a taste o' real freedom. Then you'll be hooked. You won't be gawkin' at no two-legged chestnut fillies no more."

José smiled and looked back over at Rebecca, then dropped his eyes.

Suddenly, Woodland's booming voice filled the night again, speaking McAllister's name, and he walked closer, his arm around Rebecca's shoulders. He cleared his throat. "Me an' Rebecca were talkin', McAllister, an' she brought up a good point. I'm gettin' ready to clear some land an' do some plantin'. It's a lot of hard work, up where my place sets. Quaking asps an' junipers to knock down and all. Anyway... There's a barn close by where a man an' boy might find sleepin' room. I couldn't pay much, just room an' board an' maybe a couple bits a day, but it's a roof. I'm offerin' you a job there, if you'll take it. Just for a month or so. I c'd probably pay you a couple dollars when you're ready to leave."

José looked quickly up at McAllister. The man didn't even glance his way. "Thanks, Woodland, but I don't think so this time. Me an' the boy were talkin' 'bout goin' after mustangs. We don't need a roof anyway. Makes us nervous as cats in a dog house." McAllister chuckled. "We 'preciate the offer though."

José swallowed hard, his stomach suddenly sick. He didn't know *what* he wanted anymore. He wanted to be an adventurer, sure. But how could he pass up a chance at living on the same place as Rebecca Woodland? Especially when she must want him there, to have brought it up with her father. A man would be a fool to turn it down!

But he wasn't a man, after all. He was only a boy. And when the Woodland wagon rumbled toward the Soda Springs road the next morning Rebecca was on board, and José was not. With knots in his stomach, he watched her chestnut locks fade away up the dusty lane.

José tipped his hat to Jared Bonn, knowing Rebecca was of marrying age and would probably wear his ring before José saw her again. He and Robert McAllister said good bye to the Bonns and to the hot springs, and they walked away leading the bay horse, now loaded down with their worldly possessions.

They located a good campsite at the base of the Portneuf Range, where whispering cottonwoods towered over Pebble Creek. The camp nestled out of sight in the shade, perfumed by sage, cottonwood, and the willows braided maddeningly close together along the water. The creek ran close by the camp, and the water was clear and cold as winter rain.

Their first order was a lean-to, and they built one strong and big enough to shelter them both. They thatched it with several layers of Douglas fir boughs and two inches of mud. Then they stood outside and made a toast with a cup of coffee and dubbed it home. For the next month or two, they would be mustangers, wild and free as the horses they chased.

For the first weeks of their stay, they observed horses now and then, but never did they make an attempt to catch any. José started to wonder if McAllister really wanted to. McAllister kept their time occupied with other aspects of the woodsman's craft, with shooting the Remington, tracking, trapping game, hunting. He taught José to go unseen in the woods, to make himself a part of the landscape, to imagine—and thus make—himself invisible to the beasts of the forest. He taught him about estimating distance, judging wind-drift, accounting for trajectory. He taught him how to reload his own bullets, how to keep his weapons clean and in good repair.

They needed money to carry on their operations, and for McAllister, who expressed regret over the fact, that meant wolf hides. José almost cried the evening McAllister killed the first one. It looked just like a big, friendly dog his family had owned back home in San Sebastián. But the way McAllister shot it José was sure it didn't feel a thing. He watched it drop at the shot, and it never stirred, struck just behind the eye at eighty yards.

Before the week was out they had six of them, and eighteen dollars to spend in Soda Springs. It went to flour, coffee, ammunition for the Colt Peacemaker and the Remington, and two sticks of peppermint they sucked with pleasure. Not long after nightfall, taking turns between the horse and "shank's mare"—their own feet—they were back at camp.

José's wilderness instruction continued, into the edible plants, the medicinal herbs, first aid, and how to bluff a belligerent bear. They spent evenings sewing a suit of buckskin and a pair of moccasins with rawhide soles. Then they would sit in the darkness and José would listen to McAllister's stories and instruction on the ways of the land, the mustangs, the Shoshones, and the rich men of the world who would take everything you owned, given half a chance.

One day McAllister took José out to teach him how to cover his trail. In intricate detail he showed him how to replace overturned rocks in their original position, bleached side up, to straighten a blade of grass or pluck it at its base if it was broken. He showed him how to ride in water and come out unnoticed, how to mask a horse's hoofprints with rawhide shoes.

José followed the instruction with interest, and after several hours of it he built up the courage to ask the question that was on his mind since beginning the instruction. "Won't you be wasting a lot of time doing all this when you could be riding away?"

McAllister nodded knowingly. "Figgered you were thinkin' that. An' I'll tell yuh this way. There's very few men who c'n follow a trail well. But the few who can make everything yuh do to hide yer sign worthwhile. If yuh do it right, they'll be spendin' more time figgerin' out yer trail than yuh will hidin' it. I surely hope you aren't ever on the run, but if yuh are, you'll get to know who's behind yuh, an' it won't take long to figger out if they know trackin'. If they do, it might cost you yer life not hidin' yer trail. Or it may cost them theirs, if they're unlucky enough to catch up to yuh."

José listened silently. He also hoped he never had to run, but if he did he would always remember the teachings of this day.

The month of July quickly passed, and August crawled in lethargically to replace it. José killed his first large animal on August second. He and McAllister were out of camp meat and jerky, so they ventured up Pebble Creek in the dark before dawn, their moccasins making no sound as they picked their way carefully along. José's eyes were accustomed to the darkness now, and he had no qualms about leading the way. When he got to a boulder marking a glade where he had seen deer before, he halted, signaling McAllister to do likewise. Without a sound, they crouched against the trunk of a fir, then waited.

The birds were first to appear. They began to twitter and flit about the trees, seeming not to notice the presence of the humans. The creek gurgled over stones, a hushed, caressing sound, and gray light began to filter across the sky. The stars faded quickly, and three deer appeared like ghosts in the trees across the creek.

Browsing as they went, they picked their way, a doe and two fawns. They flipped their over-sized ears, switched their rope-like tails. José raised the rifle, forcing all emotion from his mind, the way McAllister had taught him. He centered the sights and squeezed the trigger.

At the *boom* of the shot, the doe and one of the fawns started and lunged, bouncing away on stiff legs to disappear into the trees. Where the other fawn had stood, José could only see an indentation in the tall green grass.

They made their way to the spot without speaking. José's heart pounded heavily in his chest. He knew he had taken a life, and it was terrifying yet at the same time exhilarating to realize the power he wielded, as if he were some god of the forest. He had to force himself not to think that way, to be thankful to God for the gift he had offered him.

They found the fawn in the grass, a hole through its forehead. Neither one spoke. McAllister stood close by while José knelt at its side. He placed his hand over its heart and felt the warmth of its skin and said a prayer of thanks. Silently, he apologized to the fawn and to its mother, then thanked them for the gift of this life that would now sustain his and McAllister's.

José had cleaned a deer before. McAllister had killed one and directed him through the process. And he had watched carefully, knowing McAllister didn't like to repeat himself. So José went to work, forcing himself to concentrate, to remember each point McAllister had shown him.

When he was done, he reached into the pile of viscera and cut the liver loose. He glanced over at McAllister. This was the moment the man had long ago told him he one day would have to face. With his knife, he carefully sliced the liver in two pieces, and one of these he handed to McAllister. McAllister looked at him quietly, then took the offering.

"You don't have to do this, Lucky. You've proved yerself a man."

José's only answer was to raise the dripping organ to his mouth.

José's next instruction was with McAllister's revolver. One morning after breakfast, McAllister looked at him and leaned back on his elbows. "You ready to meet a friend o' mine?"

Looking up curiously, José wiped grease on the legs of his buckskins. "A friend?"

"Yeah." The man tapped his holster. "They call 'im Mister Colt."

José laughed. "Mister Colt, huh? Sure, I reckon." Over the past months he had started to pick up some of McAllister's earthy vocabulary.

McAllister stood up, towering over the boy. "Then let's get to it."

They walked through the willows and crossed the creek, eventually entering a meadow bordered by quaking aspen and tangled chokecherry. McAllister slid the Colt from its holster. "This is a whole different game from what yer used to, Lucky. Fer one thing, it'll give you six shots, if you need 'em. But it won't throw 'em as far, an' it won't be near as accurate as yer rifle. If you ever do miss a shot, it'll be with a pistol."

"When I learn to use this, if I get some wolf hides, can I buy me one, too?" asked José. "Nobody'd be likely to come after us then."

McAllister chuckled good-naturedly. "That thinkin' c'n git you killed. Sure, yer more protected, but havin' a gun don't mean much. The problem with guns—or any other weapon—is they don't reserve 'em just fer good men. If you c'n get one, so c'n somebody else that has nothin' in his head but murder.

"Now the first thing yuh need to remember is yuh shoot this like it's a single shot. Don't quit worryin' 'bout takin' yer time just 'cause there's another bullet behind the first. Make every shot count. Most men don't, an' if yuh do, you c'n win. An' the reason I say 'men', Lucky, is that's what this weapon's meant for. Sure, you c'n hunt with it. Yuh seen me kill a deer with it. But you should never have to shoot more than once if yer huntin'. One animal's enough fer anybody, an' one shot should be enough fer any animal, if yuh take 'em in the head.

"But men're different. With them, yuh never know how many'll come lookin' to get killed at once. An' I know I said you'd be a fool to ever kill a man. Don't ferget it. But remember what else I said, too: if he comes lookin' to git killed, that means he's also lookin' to kill. An' if he wants to kill yuh or somebody yuh care about, I'd shorely be ashamed o' you if yuh didn't kill 'im first. Understand?"

José nodded. It scared him, but he understood.

"Now, this gun's made to carry six shells, Lucky. But yuh don't ever carry six unless yer expectin' trouble right now. Otherwise, leave one bullet out from under the hammer. If yuh don't, an' yuh drop yer gun, yer liable to kill yerself, or at least lose a leg or a hand."

McAllister slid the Colt back in its holster and walked toward the aspens, followed by José. Twenty-five yards from the trees, he stopped. "Yuh see that single leaf hangin' out there? The one that don't have no friends left 'cause yuh killed 'em all with yer rifle?"

José laughed. "Yeah."

McAllister suddenly drew the gun while cocking it, held it out at arm's length, and squeezed the trigger. The leaf disappeared, and McAllister turned to José and held the gun out to him, butt first.

"It's just like yer pointin' yer finger, Lucky. Draw an' cock, point an' squeeze. It's just an extension of yer arm. Draw an' cock, point an' squeeze. Cock, point, an' squeeze. But concentrate on yer target, or if it makes yuh more comf'table to use yer sights, startin' out, concentrate on yer front one. Blur everythin' else out. An' keep both eyes open. Never close an eye; it'll throw yuh off."

José took the pistol and turned to face the aspen. He picked a leaf and drew a deep breath. Raising the pistol and holding it out straight, he cocked it and lined the sights on the leaf. He squeezed the trigger, and smoke and thunder filled the air. The leaf shuddered but remained.

McAllister's face was expressionless. "Don't worry. It ain't the exact science a rifle is. Thing is, yuh came close. Yuh moved it with the air. That's more'n good enough to kill a man. An' if the man that's tryin' to kill yuh is any farther than fifty yards, an' yuh ain't got nothin' but a pistol, yuh got no business tryin' a shot anyway. Yer better off hightailin' it.

One more thing: I told yuh to try fer the head if yuh can, but when it comes to a man, yuh shoot fer the chest, fer the biggest place you c'n see. Yuh ain't got time fer finesse. An' shoot 'im two or three times—don't be worryin' 'bout wastin' shells."

José's ears rang, partly from disappointment at missing but mostly from the *boom* of the shot. He plugged his ears with pieces of cloth from his buckskin pouch, then without even looking at McAllister he turned back toward the tree. He raised the pistol and pointed it like a finger, putting the front blade sight between the valley on top of the pistol's frame. He centered the blade at the belly of the leaf, looking at the blade until the leaf became blurred. *Cock, point, squeeze. Cock, point, squeeze.* He repeated the instructions in his mind. *Squeeze.* Again, the pistol's blast shook the clearing, and the leaf disappeared.

Two days later, José was out alone with the Remington rifle. McAllister had told him he had something to do in camp and he might as well go scout for the mustangs, so José took him up on it. He was anxious to get another look at the buckskin stud anyway.

He wandered along the edge of the timber, moving fluidly, the way McAllister had shown him, so as not to draw attention. He kept to the trees, stayed in their shadows, pausing only in their shelter. He scanned the foothills on each side of Pebble Creek, looking for any sign of movement, watching the places in particular that the buckskin seemed to favor. And at one such place he found him.

José counted twenty-two horses in the bunch, all grazing on an open hillside on the other side of the valley. Seven of the mares had foaled successfully that spring, and some of the others had left the herd. Checking the wind, José noted it blew from the southwest. He crossed the creek and climbed the north slope, moving carefully. He was able to work a little northwest of the mustangs without them catching wind of him. At that point, they were yet half a mile away.

Dead Man's Draw came out of the mountains and ran in the direction of the herd, and José started down through its clusters of maple and aspen and made his way closer. When he was nearing the eastern rim of Dead Man's Draw a shrill neigh rent the air, nearly scaring him out of his moccasins. By the sound, he knew the herd, or at least one of its members, was just east of him now, over the rise not a hundred yards away.

His heart pounded furiously. He had never been so near the mustangs, not even with McAllister. Of course, McAllister had never tried to stalk close. He was waiting for something, and he would never tell José what it was. But now José, alone, was practically on top of the wild herd, and the feeling of exhilaration nearly overcame him.

He realized the danger he might be in if the stud decided to fight rather than run. But something in the nature of man addicts him to danger, to the way it makes the blood rage and the ears ring a warning. José felt so alive right then the entire wait had been worth it. Oh, to be an eagle now, as McAllister fantasized, and fly close over the herd! As it was, he was well aware he couldn't get much closer to the horses without them detecting him, if only by sixth sense.

José crawled on his belly through the sagebrush, and his heart jumped when he parted the grass and his eyes fell on a bay mare and her colt. They were only eighty yards off. Moving his eyes to the side, he saw a big, gnarled sagebrush, and he crawled backward and then to the side to get behind it. From there, he sat up and peered between its branches.

There stood the buckskin stud, the master of the harem, the sun shining off his dusty hide. His eyes were bright and roving, scanning the country warily for the slightest sign of danger. A buckskin mare came near him, and he tossed his mane and nodded his head, like they were talking back and forth.

The breeze picked up, lifting his mane and tail, and suddenly he whipped his head to the southwest and pricked his ears forward. He trotted several steps out through the sage, then stopped again, and now José noticed every animal's attention was directed to the southwest.

He tried to see what lay in that direction, but he couldn't let his head get any higher without leaving concealment. Anxiously, he waited, watching the big stud shift back and forth now, tossing his mane and pawing the earth. Some of the mares began to nicker and neigh and move tentatively down the slope toward the valley, only yards away, but the stud turned on them and viciously drove them back, biting their necks and shoving against them with his shoulder. The mares quickly learned the line they couldn't cross, and they stood just the other side of it, neighing and looking up Pebble Creek.

Ten minutes had passed when suddenly the stud raised his head and gave a whistle that split the air. José immediately heard one follow it from far away. He ached with the desire to see what was happening, so he took a chance and rose slowly to look past the herd. There, three hundred yards away up the valley, approached a second band of mustangs, and a big gray led them, performing the same antics as the buckskin!

José ducked down again and waited. He kept half expecting the buckskin to herd his mares away like he always had when approached by man. But instead, the buckskin moved down into the valley, where the ground was somewhat level along Pebble Creek. Here he held his ground, but he didn't advance. The gray was the obvious aggressor.

Curiosity finally overcame José, and he looked out again to see the gray stallion prance forward, tail held out from his body. The buckskin's tail was raised, too, and he began to rush back and forth, almost in a frenzy, whistling shrilly, a sound that must have died only high in the trees. José was transfixed. He intuitively knew a tremendous combat was about to unfold before him, and he wished with all his might he could share this with McAllister.

The gray stallion suddenly stopped his advance, fifty yards from the buckskin. His mares held back, a hundred and fifty yards away, watching. There were about twelve of them in his herd, mostly grays, with a bay and two sorrels mixed in. The gray and the buckskin had both worked themselves into a lather, and they stomped their feet and threw their heads, prancing back and forth, screaming, tails held high.

Suddenly, the stallions trotted out to meet each other, calling out their bloodlust. When only fifteen feet separated them, they reared up on hind legs, as if on some secret signal, and rushed to meet each other, pawing with their forefeet. With their ears laid back and teeth bared, they were a horrible sight. They struck and bit and screamed, and a cloud of dust flew into the air, along with patches of hair.

Even at the distance, José could hear the stallions' teeth click together when they slid off flesh. When they struck out at the same time their hooves crashed like boulders falling against each other. The buckskin threw all his weight into the gray, knocking him off balance. He sought the other horse's jugular with his teeth. The gray whirled away with amazing swiftness. He kicked at the buckskin with both feet, missing only because his speed was equaled by the buckskin.

Blood ran freely now. José could see it on their light coats, even through the cloud of dust. The buckskin's teeth closed on one nostril of the gray. The gray screamed and jerked away, losing flesh in the process. He spun and tried to kick again, missing the buckskin's head only by inches. The buckskin came around and leaped at the gray from the side. He landed half atop his back, staggering him.

The buckskin caught one of the gray's ears in his teeth. When he pulled away, half the ear was gone. The gray countered, but his bite missed the buckskin's jugular. His teeth clashed together with a gut-wrenching sound.

Then it was the buckskin's turn to wheel and strike with his feet. When those iron-like hooves met the gray's ribcage something gave way. The gray screamed, and the buckskin kicked him again, this time in the neck. Then he turned around and ran forward and rammed his entire body against the gray. The gray, visibly shaken, stumbled and nearly went down.

José watched the combat in horror. Tears of tension dimmed his vision, drifting dust stung his nostrils. He stood fully erect now, clutching a sagebrush branch in his left hand and the rifle in his right as if to relinquish his hold meant sure death. He wanted to be away from here, but the fascination of the gory battle glued him in place. His mouth was dry and his knees wobbly as he waited spell-bound for the outcome of the battle.

The buckskin again lunged at the gray. He struck him in the right shoulder, and this time the gray went down. But the buckskin gave no quarter. He rose on his hind legs and drove his clubs against the gray over and over, allowing no chance for him to rise.

At last, between the buckskin's kicks, the gray rolled over onto his legs. The whites of his eyes showed his terror. He lunged to his feet stumblingly, then galloped away toward his mares. Surprisingly enough they still awaited him and departed with him up a south draw, a long cloud of dust finally enveloping them.

The wild-eyed victor pranced back and forth, blowing hard, spraying the sagebrush with blood and mucus and rolling his eyes, tossing his head and screaming out his name. The mares wisely avoided him, waiting for his killing urge to run out. José just stared, standing and not even knowing it. He didn't even care. He not only knew this stallion would never be his, but now he didn't want him. He had seen what he could do to an animal of equal size. What would he do to a hundred and twenty pound boy? You couldn't tame that horse any more than you could an eagle. Or Robert McAllister…

It was a mare that saw José first. He guessed he moved his head, or maybe the wind shifted his long hair, but the mare whipped her head his way, and her eyes nearly bulged out of their sockets. She took one step toward him, then snorted and wheeled to the side, and without another look back she ran down into the valley with the stallion. The stallion looked over, saw the reason for her concern, and though winded, he masterfully herded his harem after the first mare as they thundered down the slope in a swirling cloud of dust and hoof-flung gravel.

At the creek, the stud drove the stragglers hard, and they lunged into the water. On the other side, they turned to give one last, mistrusting glance, then galloped on up the canyon.

Almost physically exhausted just from viewing the combat, José turned numbly and started back down the canyon toward camp. He had crossed the creek and entered a shady patch of firs when he heard the voice behind him.

"Hey, long hair."

José whirled. He came face to face with the man he had struck with the rock the night they burned his wagon. Although the man's lips were smiling, his eyes were full of hate. José started to lift his rifle, then heard the jacking of a Winchester's lever off to the side.

"Better not do that, little boy, or we gonna fry yer brains with our eggs fer supper."

José felt his whole world slip away when he turned. There stood the second man who had come with Andrew Bulliard to the camp on the hot springs, another of those who had helped in burning the wagon. He stood under a big old Douglas fir, holding a Winchester carbine whose barrel was centered on José's torso. And another of the men from the fight stood beside him. He, too, held a rifle.

Robert McAllister always taught José the resourceful man found a way out of every tough situation. And José agreed. But there was only one way out of this.

And that was death.

Chapter Seventeen

José stood silent, his entire body taut. He was helpless. Even *one* grown man was too much for him to handle. Facing three left him in total despair. Fear wasn't an emotion he cared to admit was in him. He wanted to be like Robert McAllister, unafraid, indomitable. But fear charged the pit of his stomach now and flaunted itself in the cold droplets of sweat on his forehead and cheeks. As he stood watching the man in front of him, all sense of time and place deserted him. He was frozen. Only a steady ringing in his ears like the warning chime of the bells of death marred the quiet of the day. Where would help come from now? Would it come at all?

Beside him a stick cracked, and then someone grabbed him by the hair, knocking off his hat. They jerked his head brutally to the side. The rifle was ripped from his grasp, and the harsh, raspy voice of the man before him grated against his eardrums. "All right, now let's see who's got the upper hand. Yuh ain't got yer friends around with their guns to pull yuh out o' this, an' I'm gonna slit yuh from butt to brisket."

José's eyes were rammed shut against the pain that roared in the side of his head. His hair felt like it was being ripped out by the roots. But he forced his eyes open and saw it was the first man talking again, the man he had hit with the rock.

He grabbed José by the throat and bore down savagely. The sneer on his black-whiskered face and his dark, narrowed eyes gave him an evil mask. José stared up at it, his face swelling with blood. Instinctively, he started to bring up his hands. He felt the third man grab his arms from behind and hold them.

The first man relaxed his grip, and José gasped for breath. His throat burned as air surged in. The man struck José brutally across the face, jarring him. José felt no pain, only the shock of the blow and an increased ringing in his ears. The man drew a long-bladed knife from a sheath on his belt. The other man was still holding José by the hair on the left side of his head. Now the first one reached out with his left hand and grabbed the hair on the right side, gripping it and twisting it around his fingers. He brought the knife blade to José's throat until its tip touched his skin. It was cold, very cold, and sent a tingle through his entire body. He felt a wet warm trickle run down his neck and under his shirt collar. Blood or sweat, he didn't know.

José was aware of the pervading stench of body odor. He was conscious of the black eyes staring at him balefully and the hate coursing through the hands that clutched him. But he was beyond fear. He knew by the bloodlust in this man's eyes he would quit nowhere short of murder, and there would be no one to stop him. So death was a certainty. José just wanted it quick. His only other wish was to somehow warn McAllister before they found him, too.

"I was gonna cut yer hair, but it makes too good a handhold," snarled the man in front. "You remember tryin' to kill me with that rock, boy? You hit me hard enough to stove my head in. An' you ain't gettin' another chance. You ever wondered what it's like to suck fer air an' have it come back out yer neck? Well yer about to find out. Let us know how it feels." He licked his lips and smiled. It was the leering grin of a coyote standing over a bleeding lamb.

The sudden bark of a rifle clapped in the dead-still morning like a thunder bolt. José's gaze was pinned to the face of his soon-to-be killer, and he saw his eyes and mouth fly open in sudden, horrible surprise. He gasped and dropped his knife on the ground, clutching his throat.

The hands that held José from behind let go, and he fell backward into the grass. Instinctively, he rolled over and came up on his hands and knees. Frantically he searched for his rifle. He saw the other man's weapon first. It leaned against the tree where he must have set it before grabbing José by the throat. He made the six-foot lunge just as another shot cracked in the trees and someone yelled. He felt his hand close on the barrel of the Winchester as his head struck the tree. The impact flung him to the side.

Dazed, José rolled onto his back. He forced himself to his knees. He knew he must seek shelter. He heard another shot and felt a bullet whip past his ear. It whirred like an angry bee, then smacked solidly into a tree. He whirled to the side.

His head pounded from the collision with the bole of the tree and from having his hair nearly torn from his scalp. He blinked his eyes and tried to clear his vision. When he opened his eyes, they fell upon his savior. Amid the flying shots, José's imagination had drawn up McAllister's face. He felt sure it would be him. But it wasn't. The eyes that met his gaze were those of Tongue Eater, the sullen Shoshone warrior.

Even as José glimpsed the Indian, Tongue Eater fired again, and José heard a man cry out in pain. Another shot followed immediately behind Tongue Eater's. José saw the Indian wince and stagger away from the tree he was hiding behind. Another shot. And another. In horror, José watched Tongue Eater go to his knees.

Whipping his head around, José scanned the woods. His eyes lit on the man who had held his arms. He stood with a mixed look of triumph and relief on his face. Eyes wide and face white, the man jacked another shell into the chamber of his rifle and leveled it at Tongue Eater.

There wasn't time to think, and José didn't need it. Robert McAllister had drilled the required actions into his head time and again. *"Fight for your life. You killed the grizzly; a man's no different if he's after your life. Fight. Defend. Kill."*

José raised the Winchester and jacked in a round. He fired at the forehead of the man who'd chosen to be his enemy. He knew with a grim sureness, with all his being, he had just taken a human life. José Olano had fired a rifle at a target forty feet away. José Olano never missed.

From there on, every movement seemed almost lethargic. José felt himself stand even as he watched the man he had shot pitch backward, involuntarily squeezing his rifle's trigger and shooting a hole in the sky. He seemed to take forever going down, then lit behind a log. José could hear him thrashing in the grass for several seconds, but he averted his attention. He knew his marksmanship. There was no need to pay that man another glance.

Instinctively, José scanned the woods. He saw the first man sitting slumped on the ground, clutching his throat, his face gray. The man raised his eyes, gasping for air. José stared into his eyes, the eyes of death. He looked away to the third man, who lay still in the grass. Tongue Eater's rifle had served him quickly.

At the thought of the Shoshone, José turned and ran to him where he lay on his side, blood trickling from the corner of his mouth. He carried the Winchester with him and turned before crouching to face the dying man across from him. Even as he looked, the man keeled over backward, still clutching his throat. His feet kicked futilely, rustling in the grass as he struggled against death.

José eased Tongue Eater gently onto his back and lifted his head onto his thigh as he sat in the grass beside him. Tongue Eater looked up weakly and smiled. It was the first time José had seen him smile. He said something in Shoshone, and his voice was surprisingly strong. But then he began to cough, flecking his lips and chin with frothy blood, and when he spoke again the strength was gone.

"Little Man—good white man."

Tongue Eater stiffened up like he was trying to rise, then relaxed and was still.

Numbly, José looked back over at the man with the knife. He had ceased to move. He gazed around at the blood in the grass, the still forms of the dead men, the softly rustling leaves. His ears rang from the shots, and the acrid smell of black powder smoke stung his nostrils.

He just sat there in the grass, moving nothing but his head as he stared from Tongue Eater to the other two men in sight. After moments of sudden violence, there is a force that overcomes one not accustomed to it. A kind of quiet shock, perhaps a way of cushioning the mental anguish and letting realization sink in gradually, takes the mind over until the moment one can finally grasp what has taken place. José couldn't move, or didn't want to. He was waiting for something to happen and didn't know what. Maybe he was waiting to wake up from this nightmare.

In the back of his head he could hear the meadowlarks tentatively singing and the gentle sound of the leaves whispering past each other. He was in dappled shade here, but the August sun beat down relentlessly around him, and the grasshoppers rattled their wings in the dry grass.

Little Man—good white man. The last words of Tongue Eater suddenly jumped once more into his mind. Those words were impossible. Tongue Eater didn't speak English! Or so José had believed. Maybe he just didn't like to speak it. Maybe all the Shoshones knew English, just didn't like the feel of it on their tongues. A short burst of laughter escaped José's throat. Who cared? Why did it matter now whether Tongue Eater spoke English or not? He wouldn't speak it again, or Shoshone, either. Not in *this* world. He had gone to the land of *Appah.*

José looked down at the Indian's eyes, dull and clouded, with their ballooned pupils nearly engulfing the irises. Blood had trickled onto José's buckskin pants, and the thought crossed his mind it would always be there, a grim reminder of this day. Lifting the Shoshone's head from his leg, he came to his knees and eased the head down in the grass. Clutching the Winchester tightly, he stood up, staring at the man with the knife, remembering the awful way he had looked as he slowly suffocated. He moved toward him, stopping only when he could look down and see his horror-filled eyes, his mouth open to suck for air.

Next, he went to the second man Tongue Eater had shot. He turned him onto his back, and in his eyes was that same remote, dull stare. And last was the man José had shot. This time he moved more slowly. He advanced, and each step took him closer to the point of no return.

Chapter Eighteen

And then the man lay before him in the grass behind the log, a black, blood-trickling dot above his right eye. His Winchester lay across his chest, its stock clutched tightly in both hands.

Nausea swept over José like a wave, paling his face, and he bent double, retching. Nothing came up, and the sickness remained. He dropped onto his knees, staring at the man he had killed, and began to weep uncontrollably. He sobbed until his breaths came in great gasps and his chest and throat burned like they were on fire. At last, he crumpled and fell over on his side, his energy spent.

The sudden nickering of a horse brought José abruptly erect, and he hugged the Winchester closer to him, eyes scanning the trees and sagebrush. He took to his hands and knees and scrambled into a thicket of serviceberry, then held perfectly still. Barely above the sound of his heart slamming inside his chest, José heard a meadowlark. But there was no other sound. Even the grasshoppers were silent.

And then Robert McAllister's voice, soft and soothing, spoke his name. McAllister had to stand up from where he lay on his belly before José saw him. For several seconds, then, José just remained crouched in the brush, though he knew the man had spotted him.

At last, José stood, the rifle dropping from his weary hands. Tears dimmed his eyes again as he stumbled blindly toward McAllister. When he reached him, he fell against him, clutching him tightly. McAllister raised his arms out to the sides, as if afraid to touch him, and then, hesitantly, brought them down to encircle his shuddering torso. McAllister seemed to relax after a moment, and he squeezed José tightly, and José cried against his shirt.

A minute passed before José heard McAllister's voice, and by then his sobs had ebbed. "It's all right, Lucky. You done lived up to yer name again. Yer all right. Yer all right. Swallow yer tears now, boy. Put the lid on. There's Injuns comin' up, an' they might not understand."

Wiping at his eyes, José looked around, embarrassed. When his vision cleared, his eyes lit upon Moose Jaw and Rocks-in-the-Stream, along with several other Shoshones. There were four other men, a number of boys, three women, and some smaller children. All of them emerged from the trees where they had been hidden. Ashamed they had seen his tears, José turned and walked away. Footsteps followed him, and he assumed it was Robert McAllister until he heard the voice of Moose Jaw.

"To kill a man is not easy, Little Man. I have never had to kill, but I understand. Even a man must cry sometimes. It cleans the spirit."

José listened silently. He already had a deep respect for this red man, but his feelings deepened with those words. If he still had Moose Jaw's respect, then he would make it through.

Moose Jaw put his hand on José's shoulder. "Come." They walked back over where Tongue Eater lay dead. McAllister was crouching over the brave and stood up now. He looked at José and waved a hand sideways at the dead white men.

"All dead, boy. But they needed to die." He reached out and put a finger under José's chin, lifting his head to inspect his throat. "I reckon Tongue Eater got here just in time. Looks like they near had yuh skinned."

Quickly, José put a hand to his throat, and it came away bloody. He remembered the cold feel of the knife blade. Without another word, he started suddenly back toward camp at a fast walk, eyes straight ahead, unseeing.

McAllister caught him before he had made it fifty feet and grabbed him by the arm, turning him around. "Get hold of yerself, Lucky." He looked into José's eyes. "Take some deep breaths. Calm down. We can't go nowhere till we figger what to do with them men."

José looked up at him through blurred eyes. "What *can* we do with them?"

"Well, we either gotta hide 'em or we gotta turn 'em over to the law in Soda Springs an' take our chances. I guess that last ain't even a choice. We better hide 'em."

For a moment, José was stunned to silence. His mind wasn't clear enough to have thought this far ahead. If it had been, he would have automatically assumed he had to turn himself in. You couldn't just hide three bodies! Someone would miss them. They would come looking. Then if they found them, they would ask around and maybe discover José had been involved. They would want him for murder then. No, he had to turn himself in. It was his only chance.

McAllister spat when José voiced this conclusion. "Lucky, I don't know if you understand the whole situation here. You jus' killed a man. And an Injun friend o' yers killed two. *White* men. That ain't gonna wash. They'll end up sendin' the cavalry in here an' wantin' to wipe out the whole Shoshone nation over it, like they about did back in sixty-three. It's always that way. An' who knows where you'll end up? Besides, I'm a wanted man. You go drawin' attention to me, I may end up dead, too. People've been hung fer hoss stealin', boy." It was the first time José had heard McAllister actually admit to having stolen the horse.

"Well, we can't just hide 'em! Somebody will wonder where they went. What if that Bulliard man sent them here? What if he's around here and heard the shots? At least if we go and tell what happened they'll know we tried to be honest. I was protecting my life!"

McAllister sighed and looked away. José waited silently until he looked back at him. "Gray, I killed that man. But I can't go the rest of my life knowing I killed him and just buried him without telling anybody. And I can't always wonder if somebody will come looking for me. *Please.* Let me take 'em back. I'll tell 'em I killed all of 'em so the Indians won't be in trouble."

Abruptly, McAllister turned and walked back over where the Shoshones were gathered, watching him and José. He spoke with Moose Jaw and the others at length, then finally came back to José, a resigned look on his face.

"Yer a good kid, Lucky. I know you wanna do what's right, but I don't wanna lose you. I told you, if you go to the law, you don't know what they'll say. But if you go, you go alone. Give me an' the Injuns a chance to skin out fer Ross Fork. We'll leave Tongue Eater here. Then if you want, go on in to Soda Springs an' tell 'em exactly what happened. But you don't know where I am, an' there weren't no other Injuns here, either. Just you an' Tongue Eater. Understand?"

José nodded numbly. "I understand."

They returned to the site of the shootout and covered Tongue Eater's body with rocks to keep scavengers off. No one spoke during all this time, and at last they turned toward camp.

When they reached the lean-to, McAllister turned to José. He had been carrying a rifle in his hand as they walked. It was on the opposite side from José, and José hadn't been observant enough while they walked to notice it. His mind was elsewhere. Now McAllister lifted it in both hands, holding it out like an offering to José. José stared at it silently, and then his eyes widened. It was the '66 Winchester Ben Trombell had given him. There was rawhide wrapped around the broken stock, sealing it together. He looked up at McAllister questioningly.

"This is yer Yellow Boy. I decided it's about time fer you to take yer own gun back. I glued it with hot pine pitch, then wrapped this rawhide on it, but yuh better wait for it to dry a couple days before yuh use it."

José didn't know what to say. He just wished McAllister had done this sooner, when he could have expressed his gratitude for it properly. With his mind preoccupied, he couldn't respond the way he would have liked. "Thanks, Gray. What about the other one?"

"I'll take it, if that's all right. I'll just build the stock back up to my size."

José nodded and took the Winchester from McAllister's hands, admiring the handiwork.

"Now you remember, it ain't gonna be the rifle that Remington is. Ain't gonna be as accurate or as powerful. Yer gonna have to make mighty sure o' yer shots an' practice a lot fer a week or two till yer used to it. But it'll kill anything from a man to a grizzly if yuh hold it true. Just treat it like I showed yuh, like yuh only got one bullet to yer name. Yuh shouldn't need more than one. Yer a natural."

"Are you leaving now?" asked José.

"Yeah. I reckon me an' the Injuns'll skin over the mountains an' hit the Portneuf ag'in on the other side."

José swallowed hard, his throat tight. He blinked tears away. "Will I see you again?"

McAllister gave a sad smile. "I don't know, kid. Depends on what the law decides, I guess. But yer just about a man growed. Yuh need to make yer decisions the way you see fit. If they believe yuh, they'll let yuh go. Bonn an' Woodland c'n both vouch fer the meanness o' the fellas you an' Tongue Eater killed, so don't ferget to mention them. I think they'd help yuh. If yuh get out, go back to the hot springs, an' then jus' follow the train tracks west. You'll come to a train station called McCammon Junction. Head north from there along the tracks about thirty miles an' you'll come to the Fort Hall agency at Ross Fork. Just ask about Moose Jaw there."

José nodded and dropped his eyes. "Thanks, Gray. Thanks for everything."

McAllister gripped his shoulder. "You were a damn fine pard, Lucky. Good luck to yuh."

José heard hooffalls behind him and turned around. He raised his eyes to meet those of Moose Jaw, who held the lead rope of a stocky red roan stallion. Moose Jaw nodded and gave a little smile. "I bring my friend a gift for hunting *bu'ngu*. Some day, we will ride together again."

With these words, Moose Jaw held the lead rope out to José. Dumbfounded, José reached and took the rope, staring at his Shoshone friend. He stepped forward and hugged the Indian quickly, then stepped back. Moose Jaw smiled and nodded.

"I will ask you to do something for me, too, Little Man."

José looked at him curiously. "Okay."

"I and my friend Rocks-in-the-Stream, we will go and wait at the warm spring. You come and tell us when we can take Tongue Eater to his home. I do not wish him left here."

José smiled, happy to think Moose Jaw would be so near. "I will," he replied.

After José said good bye to the Shoshones and watched them head up the canyon toward Haystack Mountain, he started toward Soda Springs leading the roan stud and his bay horse. McAllister walked beside him for a ways, and both were silent. Finally, McAllister spoke.

"José, I hope yuh learned somethin' from t'day. Yuh can't ever judge anyone an' say you know 'em fer a fact. Remember that. I think we both figgered we knew ol' Tongue Eater perty good, but we didn't know nothin'. We never trusted him, but if it hadn't been fer him, you'd likely be dead now."

McAllister explained how the Shoshones had found his camp and then Tongue Eater, wishing to join José looking for the mustangs, had started out alone to meet his fate.

"I'm not going to ever judge anybody again unless they give me a good reason," José replied. "I didn't know that man at all. He spoke English to me when he was dying. He said 'Little Man, good man.' Did you know he spoke English?"

"I had my suspicions. He caught on to an awful lot o' what we said." McAllister smiled. "All right, Lucky. I hope we cross trails again. Yuh ain't become a mountain man just yet."

José pondered on McAllister's words long after his strides had carried him off toward the timber below the Hogsback—Haystack Mountain. Don't ever judge anyone, he had said. And José guessed that meant for the bad *or* for the good. He realized he didn't know McAllister very well, either. But they had saved each other's lives, and that man of the wilderness would always be his friend.

The roan was a gentle animal, though he still displayed the tools and proud head of a stallion. He and José came in sight of Soda Springs on friendly terms, and José sighed at sight of the buildings sprawled across the sagebrush plain. He wondered what this Mormon settlement would bring him today—jail or freedom.

At the ZCMI store, he slid off the roan and tied both animals to the hitching rail. He stopped for a moment and looked around him at the town, breathing in the odors he had almost forgotten but that now brought back many memories, both good and bad. Baking bread, outhouses, woodsmoke, the scent of new merchandise wafting from inside the store. Here and there on the sagebrush-studded street citizens walked, going about their business, now and then glancing at him and his horses curiously. Their faces were not unfriendly, and some of them even smiled. He wished one of them would be Rebecca Woodland.

Inquiring inside the store, José learned that the sheriff resided in Blackfoot, sixty miles away by the short route. But a deputy by the name of Clint Goss lived in Soda Springs. He was also the owner of Goss' Feed and Supply.

There was a wagon parked along the side of the feed store, two men loading down the two horse rig with sacks of grain. José stood by silently, smelling the musty odor gusting from inside the big open doors of the establishment. Finally, one of the men climbed onto the seat of the rig and pulled away.

José appraised the other one silently. He judged him to be in his early thirties, a man with a good build and easy grace. He seemed to look upon the world around him with an immense sense of self-confidence, the knowing look of a man capable of handling anything that came his way. A man like Robert McAllister. He wore short dark hair and a mustache, and his skin was burned to a deep reddish brown. He was clad in overalls and a blue checkered shirt with its sleeves rolled to the elbow.

José walked up closer, and the man looked him up and down. His cool blue eyes appraised him quietly. "What can I do for you, son?"

"I'm looking for Clint Goss. The man at the grocery store told me he's the deputy here."

The man nodded. "That's right. An' I'm Goss. What can I do for yuh?"

José was surprised. Somehow he had expected a deputy to be a little older. His heart, already rapid, began to hammer mercilessly against the inside of his chest, seeming to cut his breaths short. A cold trickle of sweat ran down the side of his face, and he looked at his feet, then quickly back up. Goss just watched him patiently, half-smiling. But that smile soon faded. "Sir, I have to report four men that've been killed."

Goss straightened up. "What're you talkin' about?"

José swallowed hard. He wished he could be anywhere but here. He almost wished he had gone along with McAllister and hidden the bodies somewhere. "Some men tried to kill me," said José. He didn't know just how to tell the rest, so he stared at Goss like he had lost his tongue.

Clint Goss shot a quick glance around, then skewered him with his eyes. "I reckon you'd best come with me, son, till you can tell me the whole story. Come on into the store."

Once inside the store, away from the view of onlookers, José was able to calm down enough to tell Goss the story. He told it exactly how it happened, even telling how the Shoshones had come to the valley looking for mustangs and Tongue Eater happened upon him. He knew Goss would see the Indians' tracks there anyway, and he didn't want to be caught in a lie. But he didn't tell him he was familiar with the Indians, and he made no mention of McAllister.

By his understanding gaze, Clint Goss seemed to believe the story. In spite of the way things looked for José, he felt Goss was a man he could trust, and he began to breathe easier.

Goss made arrangements to travel to the site of the gunfight to identify the men. He rented a wagon and two big sorrel horses from the local stable, then located two men willing to go with them. He graciously treated José to a meal at the Chinese cafe, and then the cavalcade headed out of town, José and Goss riding in the lead.

Night fell before they reached the battle site, so they spread blankets and slept beneath the stars. It was a fireless camp, for no one had brought along any food but what could be eaten cold. In the morning, they rose early and made it to their destination before ten o'clock. Goss walked over and looked down at the first man Tongue Eater had shot.

"I'll be damned," he said quietly. He glanced up at the others. "That's Lance Germaine."

Another man nodded. "Yeah. And this one's Bill Whiteside. They always were partners."

The third man was standing over the one José had shot. He spoke just loudly enough for José to hear. "Bob Nickels here. Looks like he died fast."

Now that he had returned to the scene, it all came back clearly to José. It made him nauseous to see the bodies. It brought that day's events back too vividly. He wanted desperately to leave, but he had no idea what Goss had decided yet. Maybe he wouldn't get to leave at all, not until Goss carted him away to a cell at the Blackfoot jail.

Clint Goss walked over and stopped by the rock mound. "The Indian?" He looked up at José. José only nodded.

"So you covered him an' not the white men?" one of the others queried.

José met his eyes defiantly. "Of course. He saved my life. The white men tried to kill me."

Goss glanced over at the man and shrugged, his face bland but a smile behind his blue eyes. "I'd've done the same thing, Fred. It's only fitting."

The third man, who stood by Bob Nickels, called Goss' name. "Looks like wolves've been at this one. They ate half his hand."

José looked over quickly. "It was a coyote," he corrected.

"Now how the hell would you know that, boy?" the man retorted.

"I've been looking at the tracks. They're from a big coyote."

Goss watched José appraisingly. "Pretty sure of yourself, aren't you?" He went over and looked at the man's chewed hand, then walked around him in slow circles and finally crouched down by a spot where no grass grew. He studied the ground for a moment, then looked up at the man who had spoken of wolves. "The boy's right, Jeffries. It is a coyote. His track's right here."

The man huffed, face reddening. "Yeah, well…"

Goss stood and walked back over to José. "You didn't move any bodies after this happened?"

"No, sir."

"So walk me through the whole thing again, real slow."

José did so in as exact detail as he could remember. It was sickeningly clear to him, and he knew it always would be. When he finished, he stood silently while Goss walked about the scene one last time, scrutinizing everything carefully. Once, he stopped, leaned down, and came up with the knife Lance Germaine had held to José's throat. There was still blood on its tip. He glanced over ponderingly at José's throat. Finally, he came back to stand in front of José.

"I don't think I'm gonna hold you, son. Everything here fits your story. But I'm just curious. Why didn't the Indians take their dead man with 'em?"

"I told 'em you would have to see the body and they could come back later and get it. I told 'em I'd watch it till they came back. They didn't stay because they thought they'd get in trouble."

Goss shrugged. "Well, I s'pose they have reason to think that. But I don't think any of you did wrong here. These men were always bad cases. They were suspected of killing a couple Chinese miners up at the Carriboo mining camp, but we didn't have enough evidence to hold 'em. Didn't ever seem to work but always had money. A real shiftless group. No, son, I'll buy into your story all the way. You're free to stay and wait for the Injuns to come back if you want. We'll take these three back to town with us. But there is one thing. I'll need you to come into town in the next two or three days and fill out a statement for me to send along to Sheriff Hess, in Blackfoot. I'd appreciate it if you did that."

José nodded. "Sure. I'll try to come soon."

"Good enough," said Goss. "Boys, let's load 'em in the wagon and head back. I got a business to tend to."

They loaded the wagon, and then Goss walked over to José, holding Lance Germaine's rifle. "It was right honest of you to leave the rifles where they lay, son, an' I know them Injuns woulda took 'em if it weren't for you. We'll auction off the other stuff, but you're welcome to this one if you like. I saw yours is in pretty bad shape. Just don't tell anybody where you came by it, all right? But in case anybody really presses the issue, I'll write you out a bill of sale."

"Thanks, mister." José smiled. He took the rifle and looked it up and down. He was still holding it and the signed bill of sale as the cavalcade disappeared from sight.

Standing alone at the edge of the trees, José looked about him at the bloody battleground. Never in his worst nightmares could he have seen himself standing here, a part of this bloodshed. He wanted to cry over the loss of his innocence, but there were no tears left inside him. He knew the world was a better place without the three thugs in it, but he wished he had been somewhere far away when they met their end.

He looked down at the rifle in his hands. It was a '66 Winchester, like his, and in much better shape. But he knew he couldn't keep it. As long as he owned it, it would bring back bad memories, for it was the rifle he had used to take the life of Bob Nickels.

When he came in sight of the hot springs late that afternoon a small tepee stood there on the grass, a dirty canvas one, its top three feet blackened by soot. No one was in sight, but as he rode up to the camp the voice of Moose Jaw hailed him from the river.

Moose Jaw and Rocks-in-the-Stream, both naked, came from the river and fastened their breech clouts around their waists. Other than their moccasins, that was the only clothing they put on. They walked up the slope to José, and Moose Jaw embraced him quickly, then pushed him away, holding him by the upper arms. "Little Man, you are free?"

"Yes. And Tongue Eater is still there where we covered him."

"How did you like your present?"

José smiled. "We became quick friends. He's a very good horse. *Bu'ngu,* I mean." On a sudden impulse, José pulled away from Moose Jaw. "Wait here. I also have a gift for my friend." José hurried to the bay horse and drew Lance Germaine's rifle from his pack. He came back and held it out to Moose Jaw. "This is for you. And always keep this with it." He handed him the bill of sale.

Moose Jaw was very pleased with the gift. "It is a good trade," he said.

They all slept in the tepee that night, and in the morning they traveled together back up the Portneuf to retrieve Tongue Eater's body. On returning to camp, they began quickly to break down the tepee, and José did all he could to help. He was anxious to be on his way back to see McAllister at Ross Fork.

They were just finishing up preparations to take to the road when a movement in the corner of José's eye drew his attention. He turned to see two horses coming along the lane above them, from the direction of Soda Springs. He soon recognized the broad frame of Terrence Woodland on one horse, and Rebecca sat the one beside him. They were alone this time.

José waved excitedly, happy at the unforeseen fortune of seeing Rebecca again. The horses paused at the bridge, and José could see Rebecca speaking to her father. At last, they turned back and came toward him. They left the road and drew up in a cloud of dust. "Hello, son," boomed Woodland. "We thought you'd be gone from here by now."

José shrugged. "I just came back a couple of hours ago."

The Woodlands were both silent for a moment, conspicuously so, and finally Woodland spoke again. "I heard you had some trouble." José's heart jumped. He had hoped they wouldn't know and feared what they would think of him now. His only response was a nod.

Woodland glanced over at Rebecca, then back at José. "Well, bad things sometimes happen, son. God doesn't intend folks to stand an' let other folks kill them."

José met Woodland's gaze, and a slow, grateful smile came to his lips. "Thank you, sir." Tears suddenly dimmed his vision.

"I'm glad you weren't hurt."

José's eyes leaped to Rebecca, who had spoken. His smile broadened. "Thanks."

"Well, we came up to see if we could hire one of the Bonn boys to work on the place with us for a spell," volunteered Woodland. "Guess we better get up there. Good to see you again." Rebecca just smiled at him.

They wheeled their horses about and headed back up the road, their horses' hooves making hollow clopping sounds as they crossed the plank bridge. A sick feeling in his stomach, José watched the horses head up the slope and disappear behind the cotton-woods along the river. Rebecca kept looking back until they were out of sight. *Of course one of the Bonn boys will accept,* José thought with a heavy heart. Sadly, he turned away.

"Are you ready?" Moose Jaw asked.

José looked at the Shoshone. "Yeah. Well…" He paused, glancing toward the Bonn house. "I'm going to catch up with you. I want to say good bye to the hot springs. And I also have to go back to town and write down my side of the story for the sheriff," he said as an afterthought.

Moose Jaw smiled knowingly. "Okay. You say good bye to the hot springs. And the little girl with red hair. We must take our friend to be buried. We will wait for you at the agency."

After Moose Jaw and Rocks-In-The-Stream had departed, José sat on the river bank. He broke off blades of grass and aimlessly flung them into the current, watching them rush away downstream. He didn't know exactly why he stayed here instead of starting back for Soda Springs. Perhaps to get another chance to talk to Rebecca Woodland. He knew with a sinking heart this would be his last chance to talk to her, too, for once Jared Bonn found a place on that farm he would soon find one in her heart. It was obvious there was already something between them.

And maybe that was part of the plan, after all. Maybe Woodland was trying to find a son-in-law. And why not? Jared Bonn was a tall lad, and strong. A good-looking boy, too, and clean-cut like most of the Mormons José had seen. José could cut his hair, too, but that wouldn't change the fact he was a foreigner—to the Woodlands' country and to their religion. There was no reason in the world such a girl as Rebecca Woodland should choose a drifting Catholic like José Olano. José knew it, and it saddened him, but it was the way of the world. He just had to have one last glimpse of her and hope it would endure the rest of his life.

It was two hours before the horses crossed back over the bridge, and José searched for Jared Bonn but didn't see him. His spirits started to rise, but then he told himself

Jared would probably catch up to them later.

José peered toward the horses, hoping to see Rebecca's eyes in the shadows of her bonnet. A lonely feeling tightened his throat. "Good bye, Becca Woodland," he whispered.

Chapter Nineteen

To José's surprise, the riders turned off and came toward where his horses were tied to the sagebrush. Springing from his seat, he walked quickly back up the grade and stood by the horses. He was nonchalantly petting the roan as the Woodlands stopped before him. He looked over like he had hardly noticed their approach. His eyes went immediately to Rebecca, who was saying something to her father. She stopped speaking and looked over to meet his eyes.

"Brother Bonn needed his boys too bad to let one go," Woodland said. "They fed us mighty good, though. Listen, son—José, wasn't it? We could always use a hand. Unless you're still plannin' to go hunt wild horses, we could use a boy like you on the place. 'Course I'd have to expect you to go to church with us on Sundays. You'd be like one of the family. If you're interested, come along. If you're a good enough worker, I'll even pay you three dollars a month for the time you put in. Sister Woodland's a mighty fine cook. Right up th're with Sister Bonn, I daresay. An' you've tasted *her* vittles. What do you think?"

José was bombarded with a world of different feelings all at once. His loyalty lay with Robert McAllister, who still had many things to teach him about being a woodsman. He had no desire to be a farmer—none at all. He wanted to be free like the eagle, the wolf, the mustang. But something else had him roped and tied. He guessed maybe it was the calico fever of which McAllister had spoken once before. He didn't know what he really wanted, but he did know Rebecca Woodland was headed east, and Robert McAllister was nowhere near to talk him out of following her.

"I'd like to work for you, sir," said José with a smile. He was afraid to look, but out of the corner of his eye he thought he saw Rebecca Woodland smile, too.

When they rode into Soda Springs, José pulled over at Clint Goss' farm supply store, and the Woodlands stayed outside with the horses. Deputy Goss raised his eyes from some paperwork to look at José as he walked through the front door. "Good to see you, José," he nodded. "Some men wouldn't've come back."

José shrugged. "I gave you my word."

Goss nodded again, then waved toward a chair on the other side of the table he used for a desk. "Well, have a seat there. I'll get you some paper and a pen."

While José wrote, Goss patiently helped him outline the important events of his story, then had him sign his name at the bottom. He looked over the paper with approval. "You write good, kid. Real good."

"Thanks," José said quietly. He stood and picked up his hat. "Did you need anything else from me?"

"Nope. You're free to go. But I want you to know somethin'. You're all right. You're a man of your word. You ever find yourself in need of help, you come look up Clint Goss. I'll see what I c'n do for yuh."

José smiled shyly. "Thank you, sir." He turned and walked outside and climbed back onto the roan stallion. Woodland and Rebecca mounted also and turned up the street, José riding along quietly beside and leading the bay horse.

Many thoughts coursed through his mind now—confusing thoughts. Happiness and excitement were at the fore, he had to admit. He was riding beside Rebecca Woodland to a farm he supposed he would soon call home. And what boy his age wouldn't be pleased with that? Being beside Rebecca, that is. But at the same time he felt unfaithful to McAllister and wondered if his decision to come here would hurt that man who had become his best friend. McAllister expected him to arrive at Ross Fork soon, yet here he was some sixty miles away, and he as yet had no idea José wouldn't be showing up. Would he wonder what had happened? Would he come looking for José, thinking him hurt or lost? He guessed he should have sent word, but he didn't know how. Maybe by telegraph, but he didn't have any money, and he didn't dare ask Woodland to spare any of his. So he would fret and wonder until finally his thoughts of Robert McAllister faded away, forced into dormancy by other, more immediate ones.

At the crossroads east of Soda Springs they passed a sign that pointed them left to the mining town of Carriboo, right toward Georgetown, Bennington, Paris, and Montpelier. They took the right fork, to the southeast. It carried them into rolling sagebrush country bordered by fir-tipped mountains on the east and west with aspen and low-lying brush along the foothills.

Evening started to settle, the deep blue washed from the sky, and cool breezes swept in from the southwest as the sun slipped behind the Bear River Mountains. Wildflowers dotted the sagebrush, speckling the valley floor in brilliant hues, and the last of the meadowlarks sang long-windedly from the sage. A white-tailed jackrabbit jumped from the roadside and leaped away through the brush, causing the horses to shy nervously. José watched till it disappeared, and then his eyes resumed admiring the view of the higher eastern mountains, still lit brightly by the sun.

A couple miles after leaving Soda Springs they turned northeast off the freight road and onto a narrow, rutted lane just wide enough for the passage of a single wagon. Woodland made a waving motion with his hand. "The homestead's not far ahead now. Those three canyons you can see are three branches of Sulphur Springs Canyon. The place is just this side."

The road wound along through the sagebrush and occasional isolated stands of quaking aspen toward a broken range of mountains heaped around the three ragged canyons of which Woodland spoke. A strong smell of sulphur soon drifted to José on the breeze. His nose tickling, he looked over at Rebecca and caught her watching him, stifling a giggle.

"That's the sulphur ponds," the girl explained, glancing over at her father. When José looked at Woodland, he just pointed off to the north. There several pools of standing mineral water bubbled and gurgled from the earth like giant witches' cauldrons. They gave off a strong smell, yet not an unpleasant one, when taken in small doses.

To the right, a creek bed meandered through tall grass that crowded out the sagebrush. Here, several head of Jersey cattle moved off the road as they passed, bawling after them. As they went on, they passed the first signs of moisture in the creek bed. More cattle stirred in the cattails and willows waving in the marshy area where the creek's waters seeped into the earth.

Topping a rise, José caught his breath. A small scattering of buildings lay ahead, a large barn, several sheds, and a log house with smoke creeping out of its chimney into the sky, the smoke stream outlined starkly by broken timber in the canyon behind it. A light shining through the two front windows of the house cast its inviting glow across the sage, and José smiled at the quiet beauty of the scene, the towering mountains, shaggy with pointed beards of trees, and the yellow roses that grew wild along the left side of the lane. If it was like this all the time, thought José, it was no wonder these people liked it here.

As soon as they stopped in the yard, Woodland put his new hand to work. He instructed José to unharness the horses and brush them down, then turn them loose to pasture with a generous supply of oats. They didn't need to be watered, for here at the mouth of the canyon the creek ran full to its brim.

Woodland turned to his daughter. "Becca, go up to the house and see if your Mama needs any help. I'll go see the chickens are settled in for the night."

Rebecca shot a glance at José, then looked at Woodland. "I'll go up in a minute, Papa. I'd better stay and show José where everything is first."

Woodland turned quickly, his bright eyes lighting on Rebecca's face. "Now, Rebecca, you heard..." He looked over at José, back at his daughter, then chuckled. "Oh, all right," he relented. "Go help José." He walked away toward the chicken coop, shaking his head.

Rebecca lit a kerosene lantern, and José unharnessed the horses by himself and hung the sweaty tack where Rebecca instructed him to. Then, when he picked up a curry comb to brush one horse down, Rebecca found another brush and started to run it over the second horse's withers. José sensed her behind him and stopped working to turn and look at her. He thought of asking her not to help so she wouldn't get them both in trouble, but he didn't dare. He didn't want to hurt her feelings, and besides, he liked her near him.

"I thought your father was going to whip you when you didn't do what he said," he spoke suddenly as he worked.

Rebecca glanced over, but he had looked away. She ran the brush down her horse's thick, muscular neck. "Oh, Papa's like this horse. He's big and tough-looking, but he's just a sweetie at heart. Don't let him fool you."

José laughed. "He's big and tough-looking, that's for sure."

Rebecca didn't talk again for a while, and although José ached for something to say, just so he could hear her voice when she answered him, everything he thought of sounded foolish. He worked quickly brushing the horse, wishing it was more in his nature to work slowly so he would have more time with Rebecca. Then he went to the oat barrel and filled two nose bags full, hanging them over the big horses' heads. Last of all, he went to his own animals.

Rebecca watched him move around the horses and talk softly to them. Her lips looked like she was about to smile, but she just watched him in the lantern light, her eyes shining softly.

"You really like horses, don't you?" she said.

Surprised at the sudden voice, José looked over. "Sure, I love 'em. Yours are sure pretty."

Rebecca giggled. "Oh, they're just old plow horses. They're not *that* pretty. Not like this roan. And not like the one your friend had the first time I saw him. That horse was beautiful!"

For a moment, José only stared, his lips parted. "I thought—" He stopped himself abruptly. There was no point going on. He knew McAllister was the thief they had accused him of being in town, and he knew Rebecca knew it.

Rebecca eyed him knowingly, faint humor in her eyes. "You thought what? I know your friend stole that horse, but he saved my life, too. I couldn't let them punish him, especially when he didn't even get away with the horse."

José looked away quickly. He hated the subject of that stolen horse. He wished McAllister hadn't taken it, even though it was that theft which had led to their union. Because of that twist of fate, he guessed it wasn't all bad, but he hated to think the man he looked up to would steal someone else's horse.

José patted the horse's neck and looked over at the girl. As he had sensed, her eyes were fixed searchingly on his face. They gazed with an intense light, and he tried desperately to look into them, but it didn't last. His eyes dropped quickly, and he struggled for something to say.

Hearing the rustle of Rebecca's skirt, José looked up in time to see her reach out gingerly and take hold of his fingers. A pulse of heat ran up his arm and into his entire body, making his heart jump. "Come on," Rebecca said. "I'll show you where we keep the hay."

José gulped. The hay? He had heard enough jokes about what boys and girls used hay for to make him blush. Quickly, he tugged his hand away before she could tighten her grip. The girl's smile faded, but she said again, "Come on. Come with me."

There was just enough magic in that voice, in those eyes, and in those soft, parted lips to render José defenseless, and when Rebecca started up the ladder into the loft, he followed her, aware of the heat rising around his collar. At the top of the ladder, she waited for José to make it up, then held out her hand. He took it hesitantly and used her weight to balance him as he climbed the rest of the way into the loft.

Turning, she motioned broadly with her hand. "That's our third harvest this year," she smiled. "Daddy and I put it up here by ourselves—with a *little* help from my brother."

José breathed deeply of the dry grass smell, a little *too* deeply, for he sneezed soon after, then again. "Bless you," Rebecca giggled. "Come on. Sit down."

Saying this, she plopped down in the hay and scooted forward till her feet dangled over the edge of the loft. Hesitantly, José followed suit, leaving plenty of space between them. Rebecca sighed, putting her hands in her lap and looking around her at the shadowy rafters. Just enough light shone up from the lantern below for José to tell when she looked over at him.

"Isn't it wonderful up here? I love the smell of the horses and the straw and hay. You can smell the oats, too, if you try hard enough. And the leather. I like to come up here sometimes just to sit and think. This is my own little hideaway. Do you have a place you go to be alone?"

José shrugged, then shook his head. "Not really. Just anywhere in the mountains."

"I love the mountains, too," Rebecca beamed, and he caught her smile in the darkness. "They're so pretty when the snow's melting off and everything's turning green. Some people are afraid of the mountains. Mama thinks they're pretty, but she doesn't like to go to them. She's scared of bears, I think. You'd think with Papa around she'd be used to bears." She laughed.

José had to laugh, too, considering the comparison. But in the back of his mind he didn't laugh. He was ashamed to admit he was just as scared of bears as Mrs. Woodland. Probably more so. Just the thought of them horrified him, and sometimes he wondered how he even went back to the mountains like he did. He knew if everything else there didn't please him so he would probably find another place to roam. In spite of his dreams, he didn't know if he could ever face a bear again.

"You're not scared of bears, are you?" José regretted saying that as soon as the words left his mouth. According to unwritten principles of conversation, it was likely sooner or later the question would be put back to him.

Rebecca sighed. "Oh, I guess sort of. They're so big! But I won't ever let being scared of them make me leave the mountains. You just don't take chances with bears—that's what Papa says." She paused, looked down at the floor, then back at José. "Are you scared of them?"

José's heart dropped. He had called that one right. But since Rebecca had admitted she herself was frightened of bears, it shouldn't have been hard for him to concur. Still, he was a boy, and boys' minds don't work the way girls' minds do. In a boy's philosophy, to admit fear of anything is to forfeit all chance of winning a girl's respect. He wondered what Clint Goss would say about this "man of his word" now. "No, I'm not scared of them. They're more afraid of us than we are of them. That's what Robert McAllister told me."

Instantly, a feeling of self-loathing filled the pit of José's stomach. He had told a lie to this girl after her barely revealing her feelings to him. It wasn't right. He had to tell her. But how? He would have to admit he had lied. How could he admit that?

"Rebecca!"

Terrence Woodland's call came from the direction of the house, and José looked quickly that way. "That's your father. We'd better go."

"Oh, let's stay and talk some more," Rebecca countered. "He won't hurt you."

"Rebecca, get up to the house. Dinner's on. An' bring José with you."

Without hesitation, José started to get up, and Rebecca put her hand on his. Instinctively, he jerked his hand away, losing his balance in the process. He started to tip backward, and with a squeal Rebecca reached out and grabbed him by the hand just in time to keep him from falling out of the loft. As soon as he was planted securely on the boards once more, Rebecca put her hand to her mouth, then started laughing. It was obvious she didn't want to, but laughter sometimes has a mind of its own.

In shame, José dove for the ladder and started down it, descending so quickly he almost fell when still four rungs from the floor. He managed to catch himself and climbed the rest of the way down more carefully. He started to move toward the door, then stopped abruptly. He had to brush the hay off his clothes first. He wouldn't last long on this place if they saw hay on the seat of his pants when he was supposed to be out taking care of horses.

By the time he was satisfied all the hay was brushed away, Rebecca had come down to stand beside him. She held the lantern and looked bashfully at the floor. Finally, she looked up at him. "I'm sorry for laughing. It wasn't funny. Come on, let's go see what Mama has for supper."

Without another glance at him, she turned and strode out the door and toward the house, swishing her skirts vigorously to dislodge the hay. She opened the cabin door as they reached it, then stood out of the way for José to go in. Well, he might have lied to her, but he hadn't lost *all* chivalry, and stubbornly he took the door from her and nodded for her to go in first. She hesitated, but then, with a smile trying to turn up the corners of her mouth, she walked on in.

"Well, good evening, young man," Martha Woodland smiled from her station at the cookstove. "Terrence tells me you've come to stay for a while. That's very nice. Won't you take your hat off and sit down?"

Embarrassed at needing to be reminded, José jerked his hat off, his tousled black hair falling down around his face so he had to brush it back behind his ears. He glanced quickly about the room, noticing the four children were already seated at the table, and Woodland sat on a bed that was covered with a patchwork quilt, honing a long-bladed hunting knife.

The big homesteader made an ominous picture there in the dim light of the kerosene lamps. His chestnut locks hung down to his collar, his heavy beard brushed his neckline, and his deep eyes looked at José with a glare that would scare flies off a sheep carcass. Did he somehow know where José and Rebecca had been?

Woodland's deep voice broke the uncomfortable silence as he nodded toward the table. "Go ahead and have a seat, son. We won't bite."

"Come sit by me," twelve-year-old Noah said quickly. "I'll protect you from Becky."

"Oh, stop calling me that," Rebecca reprimanded. "You know I don't like that name."

Noah rolled his eyes and looked over at José. "She's just tryin' to act like a grown up. *Rebecca.*" He exaggerated the name with a stilted tone. "Rebecca, Rebecca. She's too old to be Becky anymore like she always was."

"Oh, hush," Rebecca said. "Just be quiet... *Noey.*"

"Hey—" Noah began.

"All right, now you both be still," Martha cut in. "We have company. You can at least *try* to act civilized."

José was soon reminded strongly that none of the Woodland children was very shy, for he was set upon with a string of chatter that seemed never-ending, going into and beyond supper. Finally, Woodland's voice boomed over the din made by the children. "Okay, young'uns. Kerosene's runnin' low. You'd best be findin' a place to lay down for the night before the bears come out." He wiped milk from his beard with the back of his hand. "'Specially you, Noah. You gotta go out in the mornin' an' show our new hand about milkin' a cow."

José sighed. He guessed he had his work cut out for him here. He already knew how to milk a cow, from back home, but he wondered what other toil would be heaped upon him.

In the next three weeks, José found his chores more numerous than they had been even back home in San Sebastián. His new boss drove him harshly, he thought sometimes, but he was a hard worker, and he never let on when he was tired. He couldn't let Rebecca think him a weakling. But when evening came, it was never long from the time his head hit the pillow until he snored peacefully away.

The Woodlands' wasn't a large house, built purposely small to keep it warm in the winter, but the same principle kept it warm in the summer—very warm, and stuffy, too. José had to share a large bed with Noah, Laban, and Jacob. The Woodland boys were all accustomed to that, but he was used to sleeping beneath the stars, being able to toss, turn, or do somersaults if he wanted to. He could hardly stand the feeling of being cramped up with three growing boys. So most nights he found his way outside, laying his bed out in the barn or in the grass beside it, depending on what the sky looked like.

The girls of the Woodland clan were more fortunate. There were only the two of them, and since Woodland had made their bed large in anticipation of other daughters, they had plenty of room. So Rebecca was able to go unnoticed the night she crept from the bed and came outside under a bright full moon to find José.

The young woman was normally light on her feet, and tonight even more so, but José had lived with Robert McAllister too long to be easily crept up on. He had made his bed in an inconspicuous spot at the side of the wagon, between it and the barn, where it was not readily visible. When he first sensed someone near, he rolled out of his loose bedding and crept to the tailgate of the wagon. He heard the footsteps in the grass and guessed them to be Rebecca's. He crouched lower and waited.

Soon, her shadow appeared in the moonlight, her eyes searching along the wall of the barn. They stopped when she spotted his blankets, and with the lithe movement of a mink, he tiptoed along the side of the wagon. "Up late, aren't you?"

Rebecca's hand shot to her mouth and she whirled, stifling a scream. José stood just behind her at the end of the wagon. "Oh, you—"

José laughed. "Well, what are you sneaking up on me for?"

Rebecca sighed, putting a hand to her throat. "Oh, I couldn't sleep. Anna's restless. I think she plans to kick me to death!"

José laughed. "Well, in that great big bed of yours, you should be able to get away without getting up."

Rebecca shrugged. "I guess so. But I wanted to take a walk anyway. It's hot in there."

José's muscles ached from a day chopping tree roots, trying to loosen stumps from their stubborn grip on the earth and rocks. But as always sight of Rebecca brought his senses to life. He was still scared of her, but he had learned to hide it better in the three weeks since he had come to stay here. He had learned she wasn't untouchable, as he had once thought. He had never tried to test the theory, but by the way she was always trying to take him by the hand to show him things, he was pretty sure she wouldn't mind if he decided one day to take hers.

José didn't know what to think of Rebecca anymore. She frightened him, yes, but more every day she seemed like a friend to him, someone he could confide in. She was the only one in the neighborhood close to his age, and after talking to her a few times he had learned that sometimes age is more a common ground than gender. Oh, Noah was all right, but he had some growing up yet to do, and he didn't display the deep love of nature that Rebecca did. She and José understood each other, and a feeling had grown between them that neither one could explain.

So when she invited José to walk along the creek with her, he accepted gladly. He wouldn't have wanted her walking alone. He picked up his Winchester, which he always kept nearby, and they strolled off through the sparse sagebrush of the yard.

It was easy to feel special walking beside this girl. She never tried to cut José down, even when sometimes they didn't agree on something. Her words toward him were always soft and encouraging, and a smile from her could brighten an otherwise dispiriting day. José had heard others speak of the phenomenon of falling in love, and inside him he knew. He was falling—falling like a stone in a whirlpool without any bottom.

They walked along the softly gurgling creek, over stones, among aspens whose leaves fluttered in the dark. They said little as they walked, just listened to coyotes bark in the foothills and once the faraway cry of a lone wolf. Another time they startled some animal that had come to drink from the stream. After several seconds listening to it bound away, José whispered his conclusion to Rebecca that it was a mule deer. Rebecca smiled. She had come to believe anything he proclaimed about the natural world. He was usually proven right in the end.

They turned around at a silent signal and walked back along the grassy bank. Suddenly, José started as he felt her hand touch his. He pulled away for a second, then realized he didn't want to anymore, and he slipped his hand over hers. They walked that way back to the house.

In the morning, Terrence Woodland found José currying his roan stallion in the corral. The cow was already milked, the pigs fed, as well as the horses, the chickens and geese. Woodland walked right up to José, towering over him, and came to a stop.

"Hold out your hands, José." José looked up at him. He couldn't read what was on his mind, but he hesitated, half worried. "Go on, hold out your hands." Wondering if there were some unknown way for Woodland to tell José had held his daughter's hand just by looking at his, José haltingly held them out, palms down.

"Well, turn 'em over. It's the palms I want to see." Starting to worry now, José obeyed, looking at his palms, then back up at Woodland. The big man grunted and shook his head, reaching out to take hold of both José's hands. Pulling them toward him, he peered at them closer, then grunted again. "José, you beat all. I've had you here what, four weeks now?"

"No, sir—three."

"Hah, that's right! Three weeks you've been on this place, an' I've seen you do a mountain of work most full-grown men wouldn't do in five weeks." José caught a glow of respect in Woodland's eyes. "Look at those hands, boy. Just look at 'em. You're workin' yourself to a frazzle. It looks like they've been bleedin', an' you already have calluses half an inch high."

Woodland was exaggerating, but José beamed with pride thinking he had noticed those calluses. He was right proud of them himself. He realized suddenly Rebecca must have felt the calluses when she held his hand last night. She must have told Woodland about them.

"I don't know where you learned to work, José, but I'm gonna have to hold you up a mite. Don't want you killin' yourself on account o' me. So listen. It's Saturday today, an' tomorrow's Sunday. I want you to take a rest for two days. In fact, we're so far ahead o' where I figured we'd be, thanks to you, I think I might get Martha to make us a picnic, an' we'll go over to the river."

José grinned broadly. "Thank you, sir. I'd like that."

"Well, come on, then. Let's go talk Martha int' fixin' up some cookies or somethin'."

Woodland put his big hand on José's shoulder, the way José had seen him do with his own children, and they started toward the house. They had gone only ten yards when Woodland suddenly swore and pointed. "There goes that mangy coyote that's been killin' the chickens!"

José looked, and his woodsman's eye instantly picked up the coyote, covered almost to its neck by sagebrush and skulking away fifty yards off.

"I'll get that varmint," Woodland said angrily, and he ran toward the house.

Meanwhile, José ran back to the barn and pulled out his Winchester, jacking a round into the chamber, then letting the hammer down. He had put fifty rounds through the rifle since coming here. He knew where to hold to hit a target. They both came back to the yard at the same time, and José, out of deference for the older man, held his fire. He had nothing to prove.

Woodland raised the rifle to his shoulder just as the coyote stopped, now about one hundred yards away. It turned and looked straight at them as if defying them to touch it at that range. Slowly, Woodland squeezed the trigger, and the weapon boomed. The coyote took off at a dead run through the brush, its head the only part of it in constant view. Woodland swore again. "Well, he's home free now."

José stared at the running coyote. He took a deep breath and judged the distance. One hundred thirty yards now, still running straight away. It bounced up and down in the sagebrush, now revealing its shoulders and tail, now only its head. With another deep breath, he raised the Winchester to his shoulder and drew back the hammer. He aimed at the tiny, camouflaged form, now one hundred and sixty yards away. Then he squeezed the trigger. The coyote did a cartwheel, its back legs appearing from the brush and going up and over its head, and then it disappeared from sight.

Clamping his mouth shut, Woodland stared blankly at the place he had last seen the wild dog. He gaped, then looked over at José. "Boy, if you just killed that dog, that was the best shootin' I have ever seen!"

José blushed. "Well, it wasn't that far."

"Not that far!" Woodland boomed. "Had to be a hundred an' eighty yards, I'd guess. If he's dead, I'll swear you been taught by Buffalo Bill himself."

José just looked down, embarrassed. "Maybe he just hunkered down out there. I prob'ly missed." But he knew the coyote was dead, and the way Woodland was carrying on about it he almost didn't want him to go see it. But they did.

They found the coyote atop a clump of sagebrush, draped like a rag, its tongue lolling out. The bullet had gone through the back of its skull. Without a word, Woodland grabbed the coyote by the tail and started back toward the house, his strides so long José had to run to keep up. As Woodland strode, a big grin started and grew within his beard until he could barely contain it. Thirty yards from the house he bellowed, "Martha! Martha, come here! You gotta see this!"

Martha came out drying her hands on a dish towel. The children came from all points of the yard, trying to see what the excitement was about. "What are you yellin'—" Martha stopped, looking down at the coyote. "Heavens, Terrence. Is that the one that's been killing the chickens?"

"Sure enough, Martha," Woodland affirmed. "But that's not the thing. I took a shot at him when he was standin' still at a hundred yards. When he took off runnin', José up and kills him at one hundred and fifty-five yards. One hundred and fifty-five yards, Martha, an' runnin' dead away! I paced it off myself. We got us a sharpshooter here. Or else that nickname o' his is really true. Lucky, I'll say!"

Woodland turned to José, still holding the coyote by the tail and shaking it vigorously. "José, you gotta stay here till November, at least. We gotta put you in the turkey shoot they have in town. There ain't a man in the valley can shoot like you just did."

By now, all the children, including Rebecca, were gathered around, and José's face was so hot he had to loosen his collar. Woodland was making way too big a fuss of this one shot, making it so he really had something to live up to. He didn't like that at all. He would rather go unnoticed and now almost regretted making the shot, though he guessed a chicken-killing coyote had to be taken care of if he was to earn his keep here. Anyway, if it made Woodland feel generous enough to invite him to stay clear until November, maybe he could live with the embarrassment of all the attention.

Woodland didn't stop talking about José's shot the rest of the day, through the three mile trip to the Bear River for the picnic, all through the meal, and even after, as he pulled out his fishing pole and line. José was relieved when Rebecca and Noah invited him to go walk along the river with them.

They walked in the knee-high grass, José carrying his rifle as he always did in bear country. The Bear River hadn't come by its name on accident, either. According to Robert McAllister, grizzly bears were as thick as fish in the ocean here twenty years ago, and even now they were not an uncommon sight. But being with Rebecca Woodland made him lose all fear, or at least forget to think about bears, or other frightening things.

They came to a wide, deep spot in the river, and suddenly Noah started slipping out of his shirt, then pulled off his pants, down to his long underwear. "I'm goin' swimmin'," he announced. He plopped down, tugged off his shoes, then jumped up and ran for the river. "Come on," he shouted. Then he was in mid-air, and a great splash marked the spot where he met the water.

The other children had followed along, and they were quick to go after Noah. Laban stripped down unabashedly and dove in, but Anna hid herself from José's view behind some bushes to take off her clothes, and moments later he heard her hit the water, too.

Laughing, José and Rebecca ran to the edge of the river, where a bend in its normally shallow course created an eddy and a swimming hole apparently well known to the Woodlands.

"Let's get in, José. Come on." Rebecca motioned for him to follow her.

José gulped. He hadn't expected to do anything but watch.

Noah called out from the water. "Come on, José! If yer scared, just leave yer pants on. Becky won't see nothin'."

"Oh, be quiet," Rebecca yelled, blushing. She turned back to José. "Come on. It'll be fun."

"Ah, I'll wait a minute," José replied. "You go on."

"Okay. You're missing out." With that, Rebecca ran to the bushes where Anna had undressed, and in just a moment she stepped out and dove, her white underclothing flashing in the sunlight.

Embarrassed, José looked away. What would her parents say when they found out she was sporting her unmentionables in front of a boy? Then he thought about the cool, refreshing water and the fun they all were having, and he unbuttoned his shirt and started to pull it off. But he stopped himself quickly. He wasn't like other people now. Ugly scars marred his back, and he didn't want anyone to see them, especially Rebecca. He pulled the shirt back on and was tucking it in when Rebecca called out from the water.

"I thought you changed your mind!"

Embarrassed and half angry, he yelled back, "Well, I changed it again!"

Rebecca clamped her mouth shut, her smile vanishing. José regretted his harsh voice when he caught the wounded look in her eyes.

"What's the matter, you scared? Can't yuh swim?" Noah taunted.

"You shut up, Noah," Rebecca turned on him almost viciously. "Can't you see he doesn't want to?"

Confused, Noah looked back and forth from Rebecca to José. "Sorry. I was just kiddin' around." He backstroked out farther into the current, tilting his head back and looking up at the clouds.

José looked over at Rebecca, wanting to apologize. She was still watching him, searching his face, and under her stare he turned and walked away.

Noah, Laban, and Anna enjoyed their swim, splashing each other and laughing. Jacob stayed on the grassy bank, trying to catch frogs. But Rebecca swam silently, staying away from the other children, and later, as José sat with his back to the river, watching the mountains, he heard her walking toward him through the grass. Her hand touched his shoulder as she stopped beside him, and she squeezed. "It's okay if you can't swim. I don't mind."

She came around and sat down cross-legged in the grass before him, her dress wet where water was soaking through from her underclothes. She ran her fingers through her long hair like a comb, tilting her head to one side to let the water drip off as she watched his eyes.

"I can swim," José said at last. "It's not that."

Rebecca nodded and gazed at him for a moment longer before looking down. The question was there in her eyes, but she didn't ask. He knew she would wait until he volunteered, and this time he didn't intend to.

After a few more minutes of silence, Rebecca got up and wandered along the river bank, picking a flower here and there as she went, sniffing at each of them, regardless of whether or not they were fragrant. When she was out of sight, José stood and picked up his Winchester, following her at a distance so she wouldn't know he was keeping an eye on her.

He hadn't walked more than a hundred yards after her, at a stroll, when he heard her scream, a sound full of terror. She screamed again, and then he heard the noise that made his blood run cold. The unforgettable bawling roar of a grizzly!

Horrified but wanting to protect Rebecca, he started forward. But something grasped him, something so powerful he couldn't move. Glued to his tracks, he stared toward the sound of her screams. They intensified with each one, and by their sound she was running toward him. Suddenly, he caught movement in the streamside willows, a bending of the branches that marked something large moving fast.

Rebecca screamed again, but José stood frozen, his knuckles turning white as his fingers closed around the stock of the Winchester. Then again came the roar of the bear.

Chapter Twenty

"José! Help me! *Help me!*"

The sound of his name pulled José from his trance as Rebecca broke from the willows. He saw the horror in her wide eyes, her open mouth. Her bodice was torn by the clutching willows and dogwood, and there was a rip in her skirt. She ran toward José.

Pivoting his eyes back to the thrashing trees, José was just in time to see a two- or three-year-old grizzly charge into sight. "Shoot, José! *Shoot it!*" screamed Rebecca.

But José couldn't move. Sheer horror held him in place as if his feet were nailed to the ground. Her breath ragged, Rebecca stopped, staring at him with wide eyes. When she looked back at the bear, it was only forty feet away. Desperately, she jumped over the river bank into the water. The bear halted suddenly, standing half up on its hind legs. Its eyes snapping back and forth in confusion, it looked over the bank at the water, sniffing the air.

The blood drained from José's face as he stared at the bear. Rebecca looked from the bear to José. She stood in the middle of the slow moving river now, in a spot where it was only a little over two feet deep. The bear could easily reach her there.

The grizzly turned from the river bank and started in a slow, swinging gait toward José, its nose testing the air. José didn't move. It came on, now fifty yards away. José took a clumsy step toward the river, forcing his legs to work, and the bear suddenly stopped. It reared up on its hind legs, sticking its nose in the air and snorting loudly. It looked back at Rebecca, then for no apparent reason dropped to all fours, turned, and ambled off to the bushes. José stared as the bushes parted and the tan rump disappeared from sight.

His dropped to his knees, staring numbly after the bear. His heart slammed against the wall of his chest, and he felt a tear roll out the corner of his eye. His senses came back slowly. Conscience-stricken, he glanced over at Rebecca. She stood in the water with her hands to her mouth, staring at the trees where the bear had disappeared.

What had he done? How could he have been such a coward? He had dared fight grown men—twice now, facing possible death each time. But when confronted by the bear, he had lost all his nerve. He had left Rebecca defenseless, and she had run so hard to reach him, thinking he would save her. A wave of sickness washed over him, then nested in the pit of his stomach. He felt suddenly very weak, and very cold. How could Rebecca ever forgive the cowardly way he had stood and watched her look death in the face, never once lifting a hand to help her? She couldn't. He would never again be more than a coward to her.

He wanted to run, to go away somewhere. He wished he could escape facing the rest of the Woodland family, admitting he had left their loved one to face the bear alone. But most of all he hated to think how Rebecca's eyes would look at him from this hour forth—reproachfully, sick with herself for trusting him to help her. He wanted to die.

José was staring at the trees, wondering why the bear had gone and if it would be back, when he became aware of a soft swishing at the bank of the river. He looked over in time to see Rebecca climbing out, wet and bedraggled, her hair a mess from the branches that had raked through it as she ran. He stared at her, but she looked past him. When she came near, she just continued slowly along the bank, staring straight ahead. Her face held no expression.

Stumbling to his feet with the help of the rifle as a crutch, José walked off through the sage, away from the whispering sound of the river. A rattlesnake startled him, setting up a whir at the base of a gnarled sage. He glanced at the snake, then continued on. He could hear its buzz for half a minute after he went by.

He crawled up on a little ridge of black lava on the other side of the road, plopping down on it with his lower legs hanging over the edge, the rifle across his thighs. He stared around him numbly, his heart heavy. He knew he could never regain Rebecca's confidence, and in silence he cursed himself vehemently and wished the bear had torn him in two for his cowardice. Right now he would even trade death by the bear for the chance to go back again and stand up to it in front of Rebecca. At least he would have died a hero, and he didn't think he would have minded dying too badly with her kneeling over him and crying.

But no, he was stuck in this life, knowing he was a coward, knowing Rebecca knew it, too. That was a fate worse than the most horrible death. José hung his head and wept bitterly.

It was a silent ride back to the homestead. The only sounds were the clopping of the horses' hooves, the rumbling metal tires, and the jingle of trace chains. José sat at the rear of the wagon, facing backwards, staring blindly at the dust that billowed up behind them and trying not to cough when it got into his throat. He could feel the grit on his teeth and tongue. He clutched the rifle in his hands so tightly his fingers turned numb.

It seemed like an eternity before they at last pulled into the yard, and everyone climbed out. Even young Jacob had sensed the grimness of the mood, and he got out of the wagon bed slowly and ambled toward the house, kicking at dirt with his bare feet.

"How're you folks t'day?" At the sudden voice, José's heart jumped, his eyes widened. "How yuh been, Lucky?"

José whirled about, half falling off the wagon bed. Robert McAllister stood at the corner of the barn. When José didn't reply for several seconds, Martha Woodland spoke for him. "It's good to see you, Mr. McAllister. How'd you find the place?"

McAllister chuckled. "Oh, it took a while. But I had some help."

Woodland cocked his head. "Oh? How's that?"

"The Bonn boys—Jared and Charlie. I was up to their cabin askin' about José, an' they tol' me where he went. They was wantin' to make a trip up this way anyhow, so I trailed along."

Martha glanced quickly about the yard. "Oh, did they leave already? Rebecca will be disappointed." She glanced quickly over at Rebecca, whose eyes were downcast.

"No, they're up in the mountains above yer place there. They wanted to go huntin' while we waited for yuh to come back. They been gone two or three hours."

Woodland had walked over and stood beside Martha as they talked. Now he reached out his big hand. McAllister looked down at it, then back up at Woodland. Hesitantly, he took the hand and shook.

"Well, come on in the house," Woodland invited. "We've ate, but there's leftovers in the picnic basket. Beef steak, coleslaw, an' apple cobbler. Come on in an' set a spell."

While the Woodlands had McAllister engaged in conversation, José hurriedly made his departure toward the barn with the team, avoiding looking toward McAllister so he wouldn't have to meet his eyes. He was still ashamed he had deserted him, and now he was sick inside at the thought of him finding out about the incident with the bear. After releasing the horses to pasture, he found refuge inside the barn, up in the loft in the mound of hay. He lay there on his back, staring blindly at the ceiling as tears streaked down his cheeks into his ears and hair.

He had lain there half an hour, and now his tears were dry. But he hadn't moved. He still lay on his back staring at the ceiling, salt marks on the sides of his face. Suddenly, he heard the creaking noise of someone stepping onto the ladder, and he hurriedly pushed himself into a sitting position. To his surprise, it was Martha Woodland's face that appeared over the edge of the loft. "Hi," she said simply, and climbed up the rest of the way, standing with her hands on her hips and looking around at the hay.

She was a handsome woman, her dark hair tinged with red, her eyes soft and understanding. Those eyes lit upon José's face, and he tried to meet them but couldn't. He just stared at the floor, knowing she was watching him and wishing he could disappear. "Do you want to talk? I'd like to listen," she said softly.

José glanced quickly up, then back down at his moccasins. He just shrugged in response. At her own invitation, Martha sat down three feet away. Her eyes roamed about the rafters, and she breathed deeply of the barn scents. She picked up a piece of hay and began breaking off pieces, letting each one drop as she did. She didn't look at José when she started to speak. "I'm very happy you came to stay with us, José. You have brought a new warmth into our lives. And I want you to know you can stay as long as you like."

How can she say that? thought José. *After what I've done?* But he said nothing.

"Your friend Mr. McAllister has come to take you away with him, you know." This time José looked up quickly. When their eyes met, he looked back down. Then he raised his eyes again, wanting to ask if they had told McAllister about the bear. His mouth opened, but the words wouldn't form, and he dropped his eyes.

"He doesn't know anything, José," Martha offered understandingly. "He has no idea why you didn't come in to see him. If anyone tells him, that's your place." José sighed gratefully. He wished he could thank this kind woman, but his tongue wouldn't work.

Martha scooted over closer and put a hand on his knee. "I know you don't believe this, but I know just how you feel. I'm scared to death of bears. I had a close call when I was young, and I never got over it. But everyone has told me, and down deep I know. That bear didn't want to kill me. If it wanted to, it could have. Nobody can outrun a bear. Do you think Rebecca could? I don't. As scary as that bear was, he was only having fun, José. He could have done whatever he wanted. And if you had shot at him, it might have made him angry enough to really want to hurt you. You did the right thing."

José swallowed a heavy lump in his throat and looked up at Martha through bleary eyes. Still, no words would come.

Martha took her hand from his knee and put a finger under his chin, holding up his head so he couldn't lower it again. "José, you have done some brave, distressing things that would terrify some older men. You aren't a coward. But you're still just a boy! Don't give up on yourself. A bear is a scary thing for anyone. They're powerful, and they can be vicious. You stood your ground, and that's what counts."

"But I didn't want to! I couldn't move!" José blurted out. "If I could have moved, I would have run."

"But you didn't," Martha said firmly. "Your heart knew what to do, and it made you stay. You stood your ground, and that bear respected you. He left because you didn't run from him. Don't you see?"

Suddenly, José practically threw himself against Martha, putting his arms around her and squeezing. She came to her knees, to be closer to him, and hugged him tight. She patted his back and smiled to herself. "It's okay, José. Everything will be all right. Don't worry anymore."

José couldn't believe the kindness and understanding of this woman, the closest thing he had known to a mother since leaving the old country. He loved her very much, but in his heart he knew his stay here had come to an end. Her words were a comfort, for certain, and probably they had some truth, but the fact was, he had wanted to kill that bear and couldn't raise his rifle. Now he could never stand to stay here knowing what Rebecca must think of him. Robert McAllister had come to take him away, and with him he would go.

Finally, Martha took him by the shoulders, holding him away from her. "Don't you think you should come say hello to your friend?"

José nodded, and together they stood up and descended the ladder. As he walked toward the house, his heart was heavy. He wanted to talk to McAllister, but Rebecca and her father would be in the house, too. After his act of cowardice, he didn't think he could face them.

The heavy door creaked open under Martha's hand, and José followed her inside. McAllister walked over and clapped José on the shoulder, then held out his hand to shake, which José did. "Yer lookin' good, Lucky. They must be workin' you like a horse. I swear yer fillin' out since I last saw you."

Embarrassed, José looked at the floor. "Mrs. Woodland's a good cook."

McAllister and Martha Woodland laughed. "Well, that'll do it," said McAllister. "An' I agree. She shore makes a fine apple cobbler."

Martha was watching José sympathetically, and suddenly she spoke. "Well, Terrence. Children. I think José and Mr. McAllister would like a few minutes alone. Let's go feed the pigs."

Woodland nodded understanding, and they herded the children out the door. José didn't dare look at Rebecca as she left.

When they were gone, and the door was shut, José couldn't bring himself to look at McAllister. But as always his friend came to his rescue. "I've known since I got here somethin' was wrong, Lucky. The missus takin' ever'one out is a sure enough sign I called it right. So go on. You c'n tell me. What's happened?"

Haltingly, José told McAllister the entire story, emphasizing his cowardice repeatedly throughout the recital. McAllister listened silently. When José finished, he placed a broad hand on his shoulder.

"Well, you listen to me, Lucky. I've done wasted a lotta time on yuh if yer a coward, an' I say yuh ain't. I've seen yuh tackle a man twice yer size to help me out of a bind, an' yuh kilt a man right out to fight fer Tongue Eater. You ain't no coward. At least yuh didn't run, an' that most likely saved yer bacon. Bears like a runnin' target.

"Yuh got a scared spot in yer guts fer the griz, Lucky, I'll admit that right out. But bein' scared don't make yuh no coward. Hell, boy, yuh fought a bear hand to hand, a damn big bear, an' he ripped yuh to shreds. Now who wouldn't be scared o' bears after that? But you'll have yer chance again. You'll face another bear. I guarantee it. An' the next time the story'll come out a heap diff'rent. Mark my words. I c'n see it in yer eyes. I've thought the same way, times past. You'd ruther die next time than have folks think yuh was a coward. Next time it'll be the bear that's on the run, or he'll be dead at yer feet. Yer one o' the best shots I've ever seen, boy, an' I've seen a-plenty. Yer a natural—I heard about the coyote this mornin'. Next bear that comes after you's gonna have two-hunnerd grains o' lead twixt his eyes."

Suddenly, they heard a commotion in the yard and a new voice, and they stepped out to see what it was all about. It was the Bonn boys, leading their horses into the yard, and there was blood on both their hands and clothes, and a smudge on Jared's cheek. Charlie was grinning from ear to ear, and Jared walked with his shoulders square.

Charlie's was the voice they had heard from the house, and he was talking excitedly. "He's the biggest bear I ever seen. Jared got 'im! Killed 'im dead with four shots. Dead as c'n be. You oughtta see 'im. He's huge!"

When Charlie spotted José, he practically ran over, yanking his horse behind. "Hey! You should see the bear Jared killed. A big grizzly. Right up the canyon there. Wanna come back up to fetch it? Brother Woodland's fetchin' his wagon an' the big horses. Heck, it's right on the trail up there. Big as a barn!"

"No thanks. I gotta get my stuff ready to go." José turned abruptly and walked to the barn, feeling sick inside. Now Rebecca would really have reason to despise him. Here was her old boyfriend, bringing in a bear right after José's show of cowardice. The timing couldn't have been worse. But he wouldn't be here to see it. He was leaving as soon as he could saddle his horse.

As José drew the roan's cinch tight, he heard the wagon rumble out of the yard, heading toward the mountains. He tried to will away the sound and make his hands move faster. He packed his meager belongings on the old bay and led him and the roan stud into the yard.

Martha walked over, looking at him knowingly. "I was afraid you'd go. José, you know you're welcome here. I told you that. But if you feel you have to go, I won't ask you to stay. Terrence and the boys will be sorry you left without saying good bye, though."

"Sorry," replied José. "I didn't think they were going up the canyon so soon."

"Well, you're always welcome—you know that. So come back and say hello sometime." Martha took José in her arms once more and hugged him tightly, then turned him loose. "You take care of yourself now."

"I will." He looked at little Anna, who stood beside her mother. "Now, you be good, Anna," he admonished.

Anna grinned. "I will. Bye, José."

Involuntarily, José's eyes swept the yard. He thought Rebecca had probably gone up the canyon with her father and the Bonns, but he found he was wrong. She was standing next to McAllister, watching him. Before he could say anything, she looked away. José turned back to Martha, his throat tight. "Please tell her good bye for me, ma'am," he said quietly.

Martha looked from her daughter to José, her eyes misted over. "Okay." She mouthed the word. "Good bye, José." She started to raise her hand, then dropped it, and José climbed onto his roan and rode away at a lope leading the bay, not waiting for McAllister.

When he had ridden out three hundred yards, those in the yard watching him go, McAllister turned to Rebecca and Martha, who had both walked over near him. "There's somethin' you folks need to know before I go. Somethin' I reckon José never told you, an' I shore wish he would've, 'cause I know he's feelin' mighty bad right now. That boy was perty near killed by a grizzly last April. I found him in the woods, near dead, an' nursed him back to health. An' he was a sorry sight. Busted leg. Busted arm. Ripped all up. So if you wonder why he froze up on the river t'day, there's yer answer. He's got a lot to get over."

Upon hearing these words, Rebecca whipped her eyes from McAllister's face. Tears had suddenly welled up in them. She ran a few steps after José. Her voice weak, she called out to him, but he had already disappeared over the rise in the lane. He couldn't have heard her, and only Martha was there to comfort her.

José slowed back down to a walk after a couple of miles and heard a horse coming behind him. Looking back, he recognized McAllister and stopped long enough for him to catch up.

McAllister was riding a beautiful blood bay gelding with three white stockings, a large white splash on its left hip, and a blaze that ran crookedly down its nose in the shape of a crude question mark. He saw José admiring it as he drew in beside him. "Like 'im? I traded Moose Jaw for 'im. I give 'im that shotgun the fella over on Bailey Creek tried to kill me with."

That revelation disappointed José a little. He had admired the shotgun himself and hoped to use it one day. But he forced a smile anyway. "Well, it looks like a good horse. Got a good chest and legs. Got a lot of bottom, I bet."

McAllister chuckled. "You learn good, Lucky."

They rode for a while in silence, trotting to cover miles. They soon came to Soda Springs, and McAllister slowed to a walk, José following his cue. A big, black engine stood puffing at the train station, a line of cars behind it, and José scowled at the smoke piling into the sky. McAllister's dislike of the railroad had started to rub off on him. He looked over at his friend to catch his reaction. McAllister's mouth made a sullen slash across his face. His eyes stared at the locomotive and the twelve cars and caboose lined up behind it.

"I'd like to take out one o' them things someday," McAllister said suddenly. "Blow up a bridge or somethin' an' just watch it fall in the river. They've done 'bout killed off all the game in this country, an' they're fixin' to finish the rest." He looked over at José. "Remember that fella Bulliard, the one claimed he was some kind o' superintendent? He's back up on the Portneuf, up where Tongue Eater got killed. The Injuns an' me, that's where we're camped. We heard some shootin' one day, then later on found four dead mustangs. I figger Bulliard an' his boys were target practicin'. Worthless trash. Why is it a man gits a little gold in his belt an' then thinks he owns the world? Lucky, I'm tellin' yuh, I think we oughtta go rob a train or somethin'. Git some o' the money back they been stealin' from this country since the track come through."

José met McAllister's eyes quickly, hoping to find that old joking light in them. But it wasn't there. "You're serious about that, aren't you?"

"Dead right I am. We oughtta make us a plan, just you an' me. Get 'em where it hurts."

José shook his head and looked down at his saddle horn. "I don't want to, Gray. I don't like 'em either, but I don't want to rob anybody. It's just not right."

"What the hell're you talkin' about? Not right! Is it right what they're doin' to this country?" McAllister retorted angrily. After a moment of silence, he spoke again, more softly. "Sorry, kid. Guess I'm just worked up. I don't wanna drag you inta nothin'. But it's mighty temptin' sometimes."

They had ridden into the main part of town as they talked, and McAllister glanced over as they passed the bank. "Now there's the place a man c'd hurt the railroad—an' *all* them folks with the gold. If we was gonna do somethin', that'd be the place, no doubt. That'd be the place. Well, Lucky, let's ferget about that. You wanna go ketch some mustangs?"

"Sure," José responded excitedly. "When?"

"Right away. We got that buckskin stud an' his bunch 'bout nailed down. We're settin' up to head 'em in. That's why I fetched yuh. Figgered yuh'd wanna be there."

José smiled. That would be a dream come true. "Well, let's go!"

They arrived at the camp on Pebble Creek an hour after sunset, saving time by taking a shortcut trail along Fish Creek, a mountainous path the freight road had to skirt because of its steep grade. José caught the strong scent of cottonwood smoke, then saw the firelight through the trees and the dim glow on the sides of tepees and wall tents. Soon, he heard Shoshone voices, and a group of dogs started barking and ran out to give them a dubious welcome.

Wearily, they climbed off their horses. McAllister kicked at a dog that got too near, and it slunk off growling with its tail between its legs. The others kept their distance.

Moose Jaw and some of the others came out to meet them. When the big brave saw José, he strode quickly to him and shook his hand heartily. "It gladdens my heart to see you, Little Man," he smiled. "Come and sit at my fire. Tell us where you have been."

The reunion party lasted several hours into the night, and José was able to forget about Rebecca Woodland for a time. It was good to have her buried deep in his heart so he could relax again. Thoughts of her since the bear incident that afternoon were just too heavy.

But when the feasting was done, the fires burned low, and most of the Shoshones had gone to bed, the dark memories once more crowded in—not of only today's incident, but of the bear attack on Bailey Creek. That struggle was just as clear in his mind as when it happened, and it drew his stomach into knots, made him almost physically sick. He could still smell the fetid breath, see those yellow teeth, those black gums, feel those awful claws raking down his back and the hot saliva on his neck.

José came to a conclusion right then. If ever he was faced with a shot at a bear again, he would take it. He had to prove to the world, but most of all to himself, that he was a man to ride the river with. A man full grown. An *hombre*. Never again would he quake in the face of danger, but would bury his fears deep inside.

The moon was full. It shone down and lit the canyon, turning the softly fluttering aspen leaves to silver. It reflected off the waters of Pebble Creek, in this spot where they ran slow, it made ghoulish forms of the junipers and glanced across the big, round boulders that looked like gigantic muffins, deceptively soft-looking there in the semi-darkness.

A day had passed since José returned to be with McAllister and the Shoshones—a day of preparation. José crouched in the sagebrush, and his heart thudded in his chest. He strained his ears into the night, but past the crickets, the aspen leaves, and the gurgling creek he heard nothing. Somewhere in the trees around him and across the stream waited others, all quiet like him, watchful, their ears keened to the night. The little people, *Nenembi'i*, and the red-haired cannibals he guessed were forgotten tonight. There were more urgent things afoot.

They had spent the day touching up breaks in a brushed-over pole corral that surrounded this place in the creek. The Shoshones had used this spot in the past, a favorite place for herds of mustangs coming to water at night. Moose Jaw himself had captured two herds here. The corral was a common sight to the horses who came here on the well-trod trail, and they paid it no attention. But tonight would be the test, for now it was tainted by the scent of man.

McAllister, José, and the Shoshones had gone to bathe in the Portneuf River for an hour after working on the corral. Then they had gone into the sagebrush, smearing themselves liberally with sage, dirt, wild mint. Anything to cover their human odor. Now they shivered in the dark, dressed only in their breech clouts and moccasins, their other clothes left in camp.

McAllister, Moose Jaw, and two other braves were off in the dark, somewhere along the horse trail. They expected the horses to balk when they caught human scent, and they would drive them the rest of the way into the corral, if all went as planned.

Fortunately, the night winds were still. Any human scent not masked by the sage and mint hopefully would just linger in the air and not send its warning to the stud.

The stud. José sat and dreamed of the buckskin stallion he hadn't seen in some time. What a handsome devil! He hoped the Indians and McAllister would let him have that horse. He thought he could tame him. McAllister had told him a horse that old couldn't be controlled, but he would show him. He would show them all.

He thought of how he had last seen the wild horse, of how fierce he had looked and of the fear he had sent coursing through his body. But how easily that was forgotten. Like Rebecca, the horse still haunted his dreams.

Inexplicably, the hair began to prickle at the back of José's neck, and he glanced about. He couldn't see anything, but there was something on the air. A tension. The feeling something was about to happen.

And then a faint whistle drifted to him, and he held his breath to listen closer. Over the crickets he couldn't hear anything else. He released his breath and waited, heard a distant stirring along the trail. The stirring grew louder, becoming a faint rumble—the rumble of hooves. Again he held his breath, and suddenly the sounds ceased. Even the sound of the crickets died down, or at least it did in his head.

The horses had stopped. Wary as they were, they wouldn't just come to water without making certain there was no danger. They always waited.

Presently, the rumble began again, and José's heart began to beat faster. His breaths were more shallow. The goose bumps stood out on his arms and legs as he crouched, waiting to spring, to run for the bars of the corral and close the mustangs in.

Like a ghost, the frosty form of the lead mare appeared in the trail, out of the gloom, and then she stopped. She turned her head in all directions, lifted her nose, tested the air. She stepped off the trail, revealing shadows of some of the horses behind her, and José's heart jumped. Had she winded them?

The old mare pranced around the others, causing them to crowd up in the trail, all of them snorting, stomping, tossing their heads. Then suddenly she took to the trail again, and this time she led the others on in, right past José, only twenty yards away. With his heart in his throat, José watched the last of the herd, the big buckskin, trail up to the creek, into the arms of the corral.

Then he was up and running quietly, trying to stay to the edge of the brush. The horses were making so much noise they didn't hear him. Their hooves clattered on the rocks of the creek bed, they snorted and sucked in the water.

Other forms materialized from the gloom—dark-bodied Shoshones, also running noiselessly, and as they reached the corral bars, some of the horses caught their scent and spotted them. The Shoshones sent up a blood-curdling yell, turning the mares and the stud as they lunged for the opening. José slid a bar across, leaning out from it to pass a young Indian taking a lower bar in the opposite direction.

The stud led his mares in another run on the quickly disappearing opening, but again the screams of the Shoshones turned him about. And then the sounds of other horses surged around them, and José looked up to see McAllister wheeling his horse in a circle. "We got 'em now, Lucky! We got 'em now!"

The mustangs worked themselves into a frenzy, throwing themselves into the sides of the corral, snorting and screaming in terror at the man scent that surrounded them. They splashed back and forth through the creek, testing every side of the enclosure, but it held them tight.

Finally, when the men backed away into the darkness, the horses started milling. Now and then, José could hear one slam into a corral pole, but by the sounds they had no luck. And at last the night was still, disrupted only by the occasional snort or whinny. The crickets chirped, and a breeze swayed the aspen branches, making their leaves tremble in the night chill.

When morning came, the horses had calmed down. The hunters climbed from their beds of grass and moved toward the corral, talking quietly. Those who had horses saddled them again and cinched down tight, ready in case any break was made in the corral.

The buckskin stud was wild-eyed, and he snorted at the scent of the men who approached. He began to prance about, eyeing the sides of the corral closely. He made a couple of circles as José watched in awe, and several times he turned his head to stare intently at one point on the far side of the corral, a spot that led up the south canyon.

"Watch the stud!" McAllister warned suddenly. The alarm in his voice quickened José's pulse. "Watch 'im—he's gonna break!" Even as he spoke, the stud made a prancing run and leaped into the air. He crashed halfway across the top pole of the corral, grunting as the dust from his hide swirled around. He pawed and fought and groped at the corral with his back feet, suddenly finding a purchase, and just as he was about to go over, the pole broke under his weight.

The stud toppled over the low place, his hind feet going high into the air. He pawed to catch his balance but his front feet lit in a pile of rocks and he lurched over on his side with a frightened groan. Scrambling in the rocks, he pawed his way to his feet as the riders raced to reach the other side of the corral, and then he was up and away.

In the excitement, José couldn't see it all through the cloud of dust, but he saw the stud run and then go down. He saw him struggle to rise, try to run, and fall to his knees again. And then the riders were around him.

Chapter Twenty-One

Winded, the stud lunged to his feet one more time. He stood with lowered head, sucking air in great gasps, staring in fear at the riders who blocked his escape. Dust rose around him in a high, choking cloud as he whirled around stumblingly on three feet, holding his right front hoof off the ground. His frenzied eyes jumped this way and that, searching for an opening, but there was none.

José ran close, his heart in his throat, and through the ring of whooping, waving riders he glimpsed the great piece of horseflesh. And in that glance he knew the buckskin stud had seen his final sunrise. He had seen a horse with a broken leg once back in the old country, when a cousin of his tried to chase down a rabbit across one of their fields and the horse stepped into a hole. The stud's leg had the same grotesque, twisted shape as his cousin's horse, and José knew he would never run the hills again.

Even in the instant of this soul-numbing realization, the report of the pistol shocked him. His eyes were glued to the stallion, and he flinched when the explosion hammered his ears. When he looked at the stallion again he was stumbling, lurching sideways. He fell heavily onto his side, and a billow of powdery dust *whooshed* into the air, drifting lazily toward McAllister and the Shoshones, who started to back away.

The other Indians gathered around now, eyes wide, staring at the fallen monarch. There was no sound except the shuffling of hooves and the solemn drum of the heartbeat in José's head. At last, one weak, grunting sigh escaped the stallion's throat, and the muscles there and along his ribs trembled slightly. One of the wild band in the corral whinnied, and other calls followed, but none of the horse hunters looked that way. All eyes remained pinned to the silent, twitching form of the great brute before them.

José felt his knees weaken as something inside him died, and he looked up to see McAllister slowly holster his Colt while staring blankly at the horse. So it was McAllister who had pulled the trigger! He should have guessed. Of all the injustices José could imagine, this was the worst. The mustang was like a brother to McAllister. They shared the same land, the same love of freedom, the same urge to be ever on the move.

A man should never be forced to kill his friend.

With their master gone, the mares and young became almost docile, willing to join with the tame animals of the Shoshones—all except the old lead mare, who proved to be a belligerent matron with no young one at her side. She wanted to lead the other wild ones away, and she gave nothing but problems from the start, so they drove her from the herd. Three times they chased her off, and the last time Moose Jaw told José they would have to kill her if she returned.

The last time they sent her running, the Shoshones had been rough and loud enough that she must have sensed her cause was hopeless, and she didn't return. But for a long time, she stood on a sage-covered bluff five hundred yards away and screamed to the wild ones. Some of them called back, some nickered, but down here in the valley there was good water and an abundance of lush grass. The mares were all hobbled anyway, and none of them made any move to go.

Later, the campfires crackled and the smell of roasting horse flesh filled the air. McAllister guarded his silence, watching the Shoshones move silently about him. Concerned, José regarded his mentor. He had known McAllister long and intimately enough now that he felt he could read his deepest feelings. They had both lost a friend today, in the wild stud. Because of their actions, he had been taken out of the world, and it was a sad day for them both.

José scooted over closer to McAllister. He looked up at him and tried to read behind his veiled eyes. "I'm sorry you had to kill the stallion," he said suddenly.

As if deaf to José's words, McAllister continued to stare into the night for several seconds. Finally, he looked over at José with a sad smile. "I know it. Me too."

José peered at him but didn't speak.

"I would've turned him free if he'd just waited," McAllister went on gruffly. "I know you wanted him, but he was meant to be free—to stay out here and breed more of his kind. You can't keep 'em captive when they're like the buckskin. They're too old an' set in their ways. If he hadn't broke his leg an' we hadn't turned 'im loose he'd a just willed hisself to the grave. I c'd see it in his eyes. He was too much the leader to belong to any man. You couldn't a made a decent mount outta him in a lifetime o' tryin'. I'm cursin' myself for my part in this whole nightmare. An' I'll say one thing: I'm done with mustangin'. My heart ain't in it no more."

A thought came suddenly out of nowhere and struck José like lightning. He sat silent for a moment, too surprised at the revelation to voice it. When he did find his tongue, he decided not to say what had whispered itself to him. In McAllister's eyes, he and the buckskin were the same. He knew you couldn't tame the stud because you couldn't tame McAllister. And in the horse's passing McAllister saw his own. With a heaviness in his heart, José sadly bowed his head.

And then José thought back on the killing of the stallion, and an ironic realization struck him. Through the fog of his emotions, he realized McAllister was the only one who could have done the killing and simply been playing a part with Nature. If a mustang was in distress and bound for certain death, best it be brought by a friend—one who loved him. The stallion's brother watched over him, and he had made certain he suffered very little. With a calm certainty and a steady hand, the brother of the mustang had sent him on to a kingdom with no more strife.

Camp had returned to normal the following day, with the Shoshones rising early for their morning rituals, then sitting to a filling breakfast of cornmeal gruel, ash bread, and horse meat. After breakfast, everyone bustled about picking up camp, even the men, anxious to head back to the agency with their newly acquired herd.

Moose Jaw and his family had invited José and McAllister to stay with them over the winter, and McAllister had accepted. So they, too, packed their meager belongings and prepared for the fifty mile trip.

Riding along with the travois, the going was slow, so José ran the bay pack horse in with the rest of the bunch, and he and McAllister left the troop to cross the Portneuf and pass the time of day with Henry and Clara Bonn.

Henry was working his field when he saw them coming, and he came to the house, where Clara was baking bread. Sweat beaded her forehead and ran down her temples from working over the stove, and the neckline of her bodice was soaked. When she saw the visitors coming, she pushed the damp strands of hair off her forehead and smiled her welcoming smile. "Why hello! I'm glad you stopped. Dinner will be ready soon."

"We'd be obliged, ma'am," replied McAllister, pulling off his hat.

José followed suit, then stepped into the cabin, which although shaded was almost super-heated by the stove. It had been a few days since he'd seen the inside of a house, and he didn't like it. It was much too stuffy, the air too close. Clara saw him and McAllister tugging at their shirts uncomfortably. "Why don't we all go sit under the awning in back? It's much cooler back there, with a fine breeze blowing."

They did so, and a short time later were joined by the Bonn children. Right away, José noticed a change in Charlie. He didn't smile gaily, as he usually did, and he wasn't full of talk. When his eyes met José's, he didn't like what he saw there. Charlie stared him down a couple of times, and he looked away, uninterested in a contest of wills. He guessed Charlie and Jared had heard about the bear and were angry with him. If they were, that was their problem. He would probably not see them or Rebecca again. Or at least telling himself that made him feel better.

When they had eaten and were preparing to go, McAllister and José stood in the yard with the Bonns, holding their horses' reins. McAllister spoke with Henry and Clara, while José hung off to one side, Jared and Charlie nearby.

Charlie edged steadily nearer to José. Finally, he leaned close, and his eyes were hard. "You sure 'bout turned Rebecca against us. An' you some long-haired Nancy-boy," he jeered.

Nancy-boy was a term applied back then to one presumed to be effeminate. The term was lost on José, however. Through grammar books and expert tutelage, he had mastered the proper English language, but living under the roof of sheepman Ben Trombell had given him little chance to pick up colloquialisms. He only knew by the tone of voice it wasn't good. And he was surprised when Jared spoke up for him.

"Leave 'im alone, Charlie. He's headin' out anyway."

"It's a good thing," sneered the younger brother. "I guess I better tell you, Nancy-boy—Jared's savin' up his money, an' he's gonna ask Becca Woodland to marry him. So don't bother ever goin' around there anymore."

José stared silently at Charlie, this time stubbornly holding his gaze. His ire built like a thunderhead in his chest, and if it hadn't been for his respect for Henry and Clara Bonn he'd have punched Charlie in the mouth right then. It was obvious Charlie wanted a scrap. But if what he said was true, if Jared was planning to seek Rebecca's hand, he reckoned there was no more reason to think of her. Surely she wouldn't turn down a farmer's son. And a Mormon one, to boot.

But whether there was reason or not, Rebecca Woodland filled José's thoughts when they rode away and crossed the river, breaking into a long lope to catch up to the Shoshones. How could he have let Rebecca down? How could he have let her go? There would never be another girl like Rebecca Woodland.

The next crossroads was McCammon Junction, where the Oregon Short Line crossed paths with the Utah and Northern and turned north toward Pocatello Junction and Ross Fork. Here a grand hotel was nearing completion, and a sign in front said it would be called Harkness House. It was a two story affair and sported twenty-one sleeping rooms, eleven general purpose rooms, an office, a dining room, a parlor, and a huge kitchen. A porch extended its entire length, and in close walking distance a livery stable would furnish horses and rigs for the hotel guests and surrounding community. H.O. Harkness, owner of the establishment, had just opened stage service to the south. He was a successful horse and cattle breeder, an influential man in that part of the country and wealthy, as testified to by the construction underway.

McAllister related all this to José as they passed, and José stared at the place in awe. It was a castle by his standards. But he didn't say anything about its impressive size or architecture. He had seen McAllister when the assets of the rich became the topic of conversation. It was best to avoid the subject. Instead, he looked around at the burgeoning settlement. "Looks like they're fixing to grow."

He judged by McAllister's sullen return glance he hadn't picked his words carefully enough. He should have said nothing at all. His need to remark about everything had to change. When it came to some subjects, nothing could be said to lift his friend's mood.

Not long after, José discerned a faint cloud of dust ahead, and he turned to see if McAllister was watching it. Of course, that should have been a forgone conclusion. José saw very little McAllister didn't spot first. His companion watched the dust silently, nudging his bay into a little longer lope. A few minutes later, José made out the forms of the Shoshones through the dust. He wondered how long ago McAllister had known it was them.

They were in broken country now, where the Portneuf Range reared up on the east and black basalt cliffs made a vertical wall above the Portneuf on their left. The black rock rose for twenty feet, then seemed to level out flat, and slabs of its broken columns had fallen away from the main wall, crumbled, and littered the ground below.

At one point, in the shade of some towering cottonwoods, McAllister drew his horse in, and José pulled up beside him. A canyon here snaked up toward Haystack Mountain, red maple and yellow aspen bristling along its sides, and a creek rambled down over polished stones. McAllister drew a lung-filling breath and stared about him.

"Now that's a piece of country, Lucky. Robbers Roost Canyon. Some fellas supposedly robbed a stagecoach back in the sixties an' buried the loot up here somewhere. Just look at that! Listen to them leaves talkin' to yuh. Even with the train runnin' so close, this is a place I wouldn't mind stayin', if I had to settle anywhere. Good thing I don't." He winked at José, who smiled.

On McAllister's suggestion, they stopped in the shade of the trees and climbed down, loosening their cinches to air the horses' backs. They sat in the grass, watching grasshoppers leap back and forth on spring-loaded legs. As one of them passed, McAllister's hand darted out and caught it in mid-air. He winked again at José, then opened his hand and let it flutter away, its wings clicking angrily.

After a strip or two of jerky and a swallow from their canteens, they tightened their cinches, mounted, and started again after the Indians. Long after they had passed, the memory of that quiet, peaceful setting lingered in José's mind. He, too, would have liked to stay there, and unlike Robert McAllister, someday he *did* hope to settle down. Unfortunately, that little parcel of land was smack-dab in the middle of the Fort Hall Indian Reservation.

They wound through this constricted, grassy canyon, then left it and turned sharply west at the old Blackrock station. Here, they stopped to survey a grassy area just past the stage station. Ultimately, they decided to camp here, and sometime in the night, as José lay staring at the stars, the lonesome, high-pitched whine of a train broke the utter peacefulness. He frowned; as much as he didn't want to be, he found himself touched inexplicably by that lonesome moan. He guessed he just wasn't the wilderness man McAllister was.

In the morning, they ate a leisurely breakfast, then loaded up and pointed north once more. Tall, rounded hills flanked them on the right, looking almost soft at a glance, like huge, slumbering sheep, covered only with sagebrush, shrubs, and tall yellow grass. On the west, it seemed barren, like nothing could survive there, but he had seen worse in Nevada. Here, the only trees were junipers and maples that grew sparsely in the draws, the only places José guessed they could find enough moisture to survive.

Another half hour of weary plodding with the travois-slowed Shoshones brought them into a gap with steep-sided, juniper-covered slopes on the right and sage hills on the left that reared steeply out of the ground and into the sky, defying the adventurous to take to the precarious game trails that laced together the ragged fabric of their flanks. McAllister called this Portneuf Gap. Almost another half hour brought them in sight of the scattered railroad stop of Pocatello Junction.

In 1883, Pocatello Junction boasted scarcely more than a hundred and fifty inhabitants. A ramshackle collection of tents and shacks housed most of its citizens, the railroaders who called Pocatello Junction home. The motley troop passed a deserted train depot, only a shack itself, near Billy Barnhart's restaurant at the edge of town. And farther up the line, along the railroad right-of-way, sprawled other railroad buildings, these of newer and more permanent construction: the huge engine house, repair shop, section house, and sand house. The railroad buildings were painted a deep brick red.

The Utah and Northern tracks and those of the Oregon Short Line paralleled each other, then separated at a huge, round water tank. Rising up on the other side of the water tank, seeming to gloat in its opulence, was Keeney House, the brand new hotel and railroad depot, opened July twenty-fourth of that year.

Keeney House was the largest building José had seen since leaving Nevada, all of forty feet deep and one hundred forty long, and two stories high. Its grandeur was overwhelming. José counted thirteen tall second floor windows at the front of the building alone, and gawked at the awning that went all the way around the structure.

The Shoshones had seen the hotel before, and they didn't seem impressed. In fact, most of them stared straight ahead as they drew abreast of it, making an effort to avoid looking at it. José guessed they were saddened at what their homeland had turned into. But as for José, he had to see the inside of this place, and he turned excitedly to McAllister.

"Can we go in? Just for a minute?"

McAllister sighed, looking over. Moose Jaw was just passing them, and he stopped, too. José caught his knowing glance. "You want to see white man's big mistake?" He smiled.

McAllister spoke to Moose Jaw in Shoshone, and the big Indian laughed. They turned their eyes simultaneously to José, and McAllister spoke. "I won't hold you back, Lucky. You ain't seen the elephant yet. An' I'll even go along with yer curiosity fer fifteen minutes or so. But after that, if you wanna snoop around, yer on yer own. I'm sick to my guts o' seein' what the rich men an' the railroad've done to this land."

Though McAllister had a way of dousing enthusiasm, José still wanted to see the inside of the place, so he steered his roan toward the south end of it, where there was room to tie the horses. Moose Jaw and McAllister went with him.

There were no steps to the porch, which lay flat on the ground. They walked right in through the front door, greeted on their right by a spacious dining room. They made a quick tour of the rest of the structure. The furnishings in the dining room, two large waiting rooms, and even the offices dazzled José with their elegance. Even a simple country boy knew none of these things came cheap. The carved rugs, the oak and mahogany tables and chairs, the huge windows, the silver brocade sofas, all was of the highest quality, somehow very out-of-place in what seemed little more than a stop-off on the way to more important settlements. Jay Gould and his railroad cronies seemed to foresee a great future for Pocatello Junction.

When no one was looking, they crept down to explore the spacious cellar. Here they found refrigerators and crates of supplies, mountains of stores José couldn't imagine that town using up in a year.

Just as they came back up the stairs and topped out on the landing, three men in business suits on their way up to the second floor almost crashed into them. José's heart jumped. One of the men was Andrew Bulliard!

Bulliard seemed just as shocked as José, and he stopped dead in his tracks when he recognized them. McAllister just stared, his eyes narrowing. The other two men looked indignantly from Bulliard to José and his friends. Something obvious had crossed the space between them—an ill wind. It was plain Bulliard knew José and the others.

Yet even though he was the superintendent, supposedly a most important man, Bulliard seemed too surprised to say a word. So one of the others, a short, balding man, took the lead. "And just what do you think you were doing down there?"

"Lookin' about," McAllister replied coldly. "Just lookin'."

José caught the caution that washed across the man's face when he looked into McAllister's eyes, but he had spoken and obviously felt pressed to go on. "Well—" he started.

Suddenly finding his tongue, Bulliard snapped, "Call some of the men from out back. I'll have them thrown out of this town!"

McAllister had been waiting for the right moment. Before either of the other men could move, he sprang forward, clutching Bulliard by the lapels of his jacket. When he yanked, Bulliard came forward on his tiptoes, staring into McAllister's iron eyes.

"Don't do anything, Moose Jaw," McAllister growled out the corner of his mouth. They both knew it would be unhealthy for the Indian—and the rest of his tribe—if he became involved. In the West, little incidents became mammoth where Indians were concerned.

McAllister kept staring straight into the now frightened eyes of Andrew Bulliard and didn't seem to notice when Moose Jaw leaped after the other two quickly departing men, both frail compared to him, and grasped them around the napes of their necks. "You stay here," ordered Moose Jaw calmly, as if they had any choice. Neither of them wore a weapon of any kind in sight and even together they stood no chance against the giant Shoshone.

McAllister shoved Bulliard forward roughly until he slammed up against the wall, then drove his elbows into his body as he kept a hold on his suit coat. Bulliard's face had turned an ash-gray now, and his mouth hung open under his drooping handle-bar mustache. A gurgle rose from his throat, as if he were trying to speak, but no words came forth. McAllister drove against him harder, and when he spoke it was directly into Bulliard's face, only inches away.

"I'm fixin' to gut you like a goose, Mister *Super*intendent."

Bulliard gasped. "You can't—"

McAllister pressed even harder, his voice turning to a snarl. "I can't what? Looks like I c'n do as I please. I like this boy I'm with, mister, an' I don't wanna see him get mixed up in a killin', or I'd cut you from bow to stern. Now—" He jerked him forward and slammed him back harshly into the wall. "I've had enough o' yore mouth, an' I've had enough o' seein' yer ugly face around. If you wanna be livin' an' breathin' t'morrow, it'd be against yer better judgment to set one foot outside this door till you know I'm long gone. You understand me?" He tightened his grip still more, breathing into Bulliard's ashen face.

When Bulliard paused, McAllister let go of one lapel and reared back his fist. "Yes, I understand!" Bulliard burst out. "I understand!"

Still clutching Bulliard's lapel and glaring into his eyes, McAllister spoke to José. "You had enough o' this damn fancy hotel now, boy? Or you wanna stick around fer more?"

"I've had enough," José blurted. "Let's go." He was paralyzed by the thought Robert McAllister would snap Bulliard's neck. He had the feeling he could do it, too—just like a twig.

"All right. Bulliard? The next time I see you killin' game of any kind on reservation land, or horses, I won't call no Injun agent, an' I won't call no soldiers. It'll jus' be you an' me. An' I'll fix yer wagon fer good—savvy?"

Bulliard only nodded, and suddenly McAllister yanked him away from the wall, whirled with him, and before anyone knew what was happening he shoved him at the open doorway to the cellar. Bulliard stumbled backward, trying to regain his balance, and caught himself on the door frame just before he would have tumbled down the steep stairs.

At McAllister's cue, Moose Jaw let go of the other two, and the three of them backed slowly out the front door, watching Bulliard and his partners for any sudden move.

Outside, they leaped into their saddles, and José laid his heels to the roan. But he quickly realized McAllister wasn't pushing his bay the way he would have liked to see him do, and Moose Jaw hung back with McAllister. They came on at a healthy trot, but not the gallop José ached to put the roan into and which the horses also seemed inclined to. The animals seemed to sense the tension and the urgent need to leave the town behind.

José knew their rate of travel out of Pocatello Junction was strictly due to McAllister's stubborn pride. His friend refused to let the railroad he hated see him run.

Behind them an army of voices rose from the porch of Keeney House and the street in front. José glanced back to see five or six men run into the street, common laborers, from what he could see at a quick glimpse. Another glance showed Bulliard and his colleagues standing under the awning of the hotel. Bulliard was waving his fist angrily and yelling something José couldn't hear above the pounding of hooves on the hard-packed clay.

At last they were too far away to hear the commotion at Keeney House, and José's last glance revealed only the tiny, toy-like forms of the men before it. Following the Oregon Short Line tracks, they trotted past the last of the shacks and the huge engine house of the Utah and Northern, a few hundred yards to the east. Then they rode back into the sagebrush and yellow grass, the only reminder of civilization the telegraph poles and wires and ribbons of track that crawled on north before them, finally fading into the horizon.

Before they had traveled three miles, they heard the shrill whine of a steam whistle from Pocatello's direction, and turning they saw an engine approaching, its huge black cloud billowing into the sky and trailing out behind it. With a disgusted snarl, McAllister slowed and eased off into the sagebrush a hundred yards, José and Moose Jaw following. They pulled up and sat the saddle watching the approach of the black iron monster.

When it drew abreast of them, it was obvious the engineer had seen them, for he gave a shrill blast with the whistle, then shook his fist out the window threateningly. McAllister just laughed, saying quietly, "Yeah, why not come over here an' try me, big man?"

José laughed nervously. He hoped McAllister's temper and hatred of the railroad didn't cause him to run and attack the whole train.

At last the red caboose rocked by, and the brakeman just looked at them malevolently, then turned inside to be out of their view. McAllister started his horse with a nudge of his knees, and they moved on at a lope, the train becoming smaller and smaller, seeming to sink into the rail bed as it rolled on.

It was José who spotted the eagle.

The dark, golden-headed bird lay in the grass, its eyes wide with terror, staring at the passing horsemen with its mouth wide and its sharp tongue poised halfway between the roof of its mouth and its lower jaw. One of its wings was spread out to the side, its feathers separated and clearly defined against the yellow grass. The other wing was crumpled underneath it.

"Gray!" José cried out as what he had seen registered on his senses. "Gray, I think there's an eagle hurt back there."

McAllister pulled back hard on the reins, bringing the bay hop-walking to a stop, and Moose Jaw circled and came back around. McAllister turned to José. "You sure? Where?"

José pointed. "Right in there. It looked like its wing was broken."

Whipping around, McAllister guided his horse back along the tracks, then suddenly stopped, and José drew in beside him. The golden eagle's deep yellow eyes stared at them in terror. Seeing they had spotted it, it shuffled its good wing, trying to get away, but it was only able to make a quarter turn in the other direction before coming up against sagebrush. It wriggled back around to face them, leaning back and ferociously opening its mouth to bear its tongue.

"Damnit," McAllister spat, turning to stare after the train, now only a tiny black dot where the twin ribbons of track converged. "Train hit it. See the rabbit?" He pointed to a lifeless jackrabbit half concealed in the grass. "Musta been liftin' off the tracks an' just didn't have enough momentum to get outta the way fer the extra weight."

"What're you going to do?" asked José. "You won't just leave it here, will you?"

McAllister glanced over quickly at him. "Hell, no. It'd be coyote supper t'night. Nothin' against coyotes, Lucky, but this is a golden eagle. They don't deserve to die that way."

He swung a leg over the cantle and dropped to the ground. He kept a large, white-speckled blue bandana about his neck, and he pulled it off now and stood looking thoughtfully at the eagle. Its sharp yellow eyes watched him alertly, full of terror at its inability to fly.

McAllister spoke softly, the way José had heard him speak to horses. The voice that could be so dark and callused became almost a purr, touched by a crooning quality. He took several steps closer, and the only movement the eagle made was rearing back its head to keep its eyes on him. Finally, it flapped its good wing, trying to rise, but came to rest again, its sharp-taloned feet now sticking out in front of it.

"I won't hurt you, friend. I won't hurt you," McAllister soothed. "We're brothers."

He continued to close in, his eyes glued to the bird's feet so it wouldn't feel the threat of eye contact. Then suddenly he opened the bandanna, and holding onto only two corners of it he let it sail out, catching air beneath it. The eagle tried to dodge, but the scarf settled over it, and its movement ceased. The man walked around behind it, and the cloth moved as the bird followed the sound of rustling in the grass.

"Make some noise, Lucky," McAllister ordered. "Talk loud to me."

José started jabbering, talking about the train and the eagle. He knew McAllister was only trying to cover his movements. The man reached out, and very gently his brown hands pushed down on the bandanna, effectively pinning the good wing to keep it from any further movement, and also pressing those sharp-taloned feet to the ground. He began to work his hands carefully, his fingers deftly bringing in the wing and taking up the legs of the magnificent bird, folding them against its breast. It moved its head back and forth, but without being able to see anything it made no quick or violent movements.

To José, the whole act was like magic. A wild bird, recently soaring the skies, now crippled but still surely capable of delivering great pain and bodily damage, apparently had been completely tamed by McAllister's soft voice and smooth manner. He assumed it was because of the cloth covering its head, but his romantic side preferred to believe the bird had fallen under the influence of McAllister's animal magnetism.

After tying a more permanent covering over the eagle's head, McAllister nestled it as comfortably as he could in his saddlebag, only its head protruding. They started off again at a slow walk, and they held that walk the rest of the way to the Fort Hall Agency at Ross Fork.

The Fort Hall area had been a hub of activity for many years. Travelers along the Oregon Trail had stopped here to restock supplies. Mountain men and Indians of different tribes had halted to rendezvous with friends, to trade and rest. Trails went in most every direction out of Fort Hall like the spokes of a wheel.

After finding the wounded eagle, McAllister had drawn into himself, and by the surly set of his face he was in no mood to make conversation. Consequently, José ended up riding beside Moose Jaw for the remainder of the trip. He scanned the hills about them, and the endless, undulating sagebrush plain. It was a country where a roving man could ride forever.

"What do you want to do with your life?" Moose Jaw queried suddenly as they rode.

José looked up at the big man, pondering for a moment. "I'd like to be a mountain man. I'd like to be free, like your people."

Moose Jaw smilingly shook his head. "You are wrong about us, Little Man. Look—" He pointed out a tiny cabin out in the sage with a lonely, tattered tepee beside it. "This is the way the People live now. We are not free. The white man controls us. We eat only when they want us to. We name our children as they want us to. Our children are punished if they speak their own tongue. They must dress a certain way, and we must, too, if we want to be favored in the white man's eyes. Even to do our sacred ceremonies and dances we must hide. To do them with the knowledge of the soldiers is to ask for trouble, and we are not strong enough anymore to fight. The spirits of the People are broken. No, Little Man. You and Gray Eagle are the free men. Never wish yourself to be an Injun."

With a sudden feeling of despair building in his stomach, José stammered, "But— What about the horse hunting? And the deer? I thought you were free to do as you wanted."

Moose Jaw chuckled, but there was a distant sadness in his eyes. "No, my friend. If the white men knew what we had been doing, we would be chastised. But a man must sometimes take his chances. Sometimes we must pretend we are free to make our hearts feel better."

José didn't reply. He only nodded and looked with new understanding at the little cabins and forlorn tepees they passed. The Shoshone life was truly gone.

As they drew nearer the agency, José watched crews of Indians digging large canals, and others farming or herding cattle. These Indians were dressed like white men— the same pants, shirts, vests, and boots. Their hats often differed, in their hugeness. Almost invariably they had a high, round crown and a perfectly flat brim. But even these Indians retained some symbol of their heritage. Often, they still wore their hair long and in braids. Some of them wore beaded gauntlets or hatbands.

Moose Jaw nodded at the men they passed, even waved at some. But he wasn't overly friendly to any, and the feeling seemed mutual. "Progressives", he called them. They worked like women because the white man didn't like to see Indians idle. They were the Indians who had accepted white man's ways. Those like Tongue Eater, who had never been taken in by so-called civilization, were referred to by the Indian agents as "non-progressives." Or, in layman's terms, "blanket asses," "prairie niggers," or simply "reds." Moose Jaw laughed as he repeated these names. He admitted, with some embarrassment, he wasn't really either one. He had once tried to adopt white man's ways, as attested by his grasp of English. He had even earned the white man's coveted "certificate of competency." That's what they gave a red man who essentially became white. But he had gone back to the old ways, angering those in charge of the agency. They claimed he had gone "back to the blanket." But damnit, that was where he belonged!

"They made me put my hands on a bow and arrows and shoot my 'last' arrow," Moose Jaw said with a grunt. "It was a foolish ceremony. They took my hands and placed them on a plow handle. Then I was a progressive. They gave me a buckboard, because I was a 'good Injun'. I had studied English, and I could speak it better than anyone in my class. Better than anyone in the classes before mine, too. That's what they told me. Maybe to flatter me. But I didn't listen long. I saw how they treated the progressives—like little children. I decided to go back to my old ways."

Soon, ahead on a completely treeless plain, José glimpsed the buildings of Ross Fork. One long, impressive granite block building was flanked on the south side by numerous tepees and wall tents, and a mass of people moved around here. As they drew near, the Indians stood aimlessly, watching them. Most of the men, as those José had already seen, were dressed identically to white men. Some of them sat on broken-down horses, some stood with buckboards nearby. The women dressed in hightop moccasins and one-piece calico cloth or two-piece elk hide dresses, and many had Hudson Bay blankets and Scottish plaid blankets wrapped about them. Dark-skinned, hungry-eyed children watched the procession curiously as it passed, and the usual concourse of dogs trotted annoyingly out to bay their greetings.

"Ration days," Moose Jaw mused. "Little Man, this is what the People have come to. Groveling. You don't see us in groups like this, except once a month, when it is time to pass out the scraps to us poor redskins." He chuckled, but there was regret in his clouded eyes.

The headquarters of the Fort Hall Agency was white man's message to the Indians that they were here to stay. For this reason, several of the buildings were constructed of granite—some of them imposing structures, like the ration house where the tepees and wall tents clustered. Moose Jaw pointed out each building as they neared them, and some bore self-explanatory signs. OFFICE FORT HALL INDIAN AGENCY; GOVT. TRADING POST. The latter title was sprawled across the front of a large clapboard building butted up against the old log trader's post. To its north was the trader's house, a nice dwelling itself.

To the west of the tracks, across from the trading post, stood the railroad depot, painted the dark brindle common to most railroad buildings along the line. Many Indians sat in the shade of the buildings, some whittling or tinkering with beads and leather, some just staring blankly while they awaited tomorrow—ration day. Occasionally, one of them smiled and waved a greeting when they recognized Moose Jaw and the other Shoshones.

They rode past the agency, then turned abruptly west. On the other side of the railroad depot was a huge slaughterhouse surrounded by corrals. Today, bawling cattle filled the corrals to overflowing. Tomorrow, they would be dead. The Indian agents would dole them out, and the Shoshones and Bannocks, in turn, would chase them one by one across the sagebrush and shoot them down in a pathetic imitation of the buffalo hunts of yesteryear.

"I guess that gives some of the People a good feeling—it brings them back to the earlier times," said Moose Jaw. "To me, it is all very sad."

The big Indian pointed out one door on the side of the slaughterhouse where they would push gut piles outside as they did the butchering. Outside, the Indians would fight over the intestines. They considered them a delicacy.

They crossed a stream, and then later a scattering of tepees and wall tents came into view on the horizon. José was anxious to see a real Indian encampment, and he stood up in his stirrups, gazing at the cone-shaped forms pointing toward the sky. The tepees were of canvas, not buffalo hide, as in pre-Anglo days. They were tattered and worn out, patched in many places, and their tops were blackened by the smoke of many fires.

As they rode closer, emaciated dogs came out, growling and barking in mock ferociousness at their comrades who accompanied the cavalcade. Several Indians stepped out of the tepees and tents, gazing at the two white newcomers. A good-natured banter went back and forth between several chubby young women as they pointed at José and McAllister and laughed. Young children ran alongside the horses, staring open-mouthed. But the looks in the eyes of some of the men chilled José to the bone. Their hatred was unveiled, and he was glad to be riding beside Moose Jaw.

"These are my people," said Moose Jaw. "They are the 'prairie niggers' you white people talk about. They are mostly the people you whites call Bannocks. The non-progressives. You see? They come to camp on my land instead of going to the agency with the rest of those old women. They hold onto the old ways."

"But a lot of them are dressed in white man's clothes," José argued.

"Yes. They dress that way to pick up rations. Sometimes it is good to let the white men think your skin is paling. But these are the true People here, and Bannocks."

On the farthest side of the camp, near a water course heavily overgrown with reeds and willows, sat a tiny log cabin, chinked with mud between the logs. Moose Jaw stopped here and indicated it with a wave of his hand. "This is my house. They made me build it when they allotted me this piece of land. But I do not stay there. It's too cold! And we have a saying among us. When the People were allowed to live in their round houses, they lived; when they were made to live in square houses, they died."

So they put up the old tepee, and they stayed in it that night. Moose Jaw fed them well. His wife, Slim Willow, a Bannock, moved shyly around them and hardly spoke at all, but she was gracious and willing to please. She filled them with her best fare and gave them a buffalo robe to use for their bed. It was too hot to sleep underneath it, but the robe made a mattress to keep them away from the hard ground. It was obviously very old, worn through in many places, but according to Moose Jaw it was one of the best ones in camp. Many people now slept on the bare ground or on mats of grass or cattails. It was a time of great hardship and poverty for the Fort Hall bands.

The Shoshone couple's two children, six-year-old son Weaving Blue Rags and three-year-old daughter, Eats Grass, sat on a rolled-up blanket against the far side of the tepee from José. They stared at McAllister's bristly jaw, their big eyes like bits of bright obsidian, shining from copper-colored faces.

In the center of the tepee, surrounded by a circle of rocks, a sagebrush fire crackled quietly. Its flames lit the tepee's occupants and made faint, eery shadows dance around the walls, and its gray smoke spiraled toward the ceiling and out the smoke hole into the star-filled sky.

In a manner of silent prayer, McAllister and Moose Jaw passed a long pipe back and forth, smoking kinnikinnick, a mixture of "Ree Twist" tobacco from the trading post and the inner bark of red willow or bear berry. José sat silent, sleep tugging at his eyelids. He fought to stay awake, but the smoke and the droning voices of McAllister and Moose Jaw, speaking the Shoshone tongue, slowly hypnotized him.

Then Rebecca Woodland climbed into his ponderings, and soon he was fully awake.

Her memory danced there like an apparition, taunting him, seeming to call him back to her. That was foolish, he knew. She would be Mrs. Jared Bonn before long. But still he couldn't erase those chestnut locks, those soft cheeks and sea-green eyes. He couldn't erase those parted pink lips from before his vision nor strip the musical song of her laughter from his ears. He wished silently he had never met her, but still he knew that meeting had enriched his life.

Finally, the warmth, the smoke, and the strangeness of a new place drove José outside. He walked out by the horses and in the darkness searched among their moonlit forms. The roan stud nickered at him but made no move to come near.

José's thoughts drifted far away to the old country, to the waters of the bay that lapped up against the rocky shore and sent their salty mist into his hair. The water was so blue, and the ships so bright against it. He could picture the fishermen throwing their nets far out into the water. He thought of what was left of his family there in San Sebastián, his sisters, uncles, aunts, and cousins. Did they still get together every week to dance and sing, to play *pelota*, eat *chorizos* and smoked fish and bread pudding? Did they ever think of little José and wandering Alfredo? A whole world separated them now, and he knew he would never see them or San Sebastián or the Bay of Biscay again. Even if he did, they wouldn't know him, for he had changed. If only he could be there just one last time. He had never meant to go away for good. But now he could never live there again. Wild America had forever captured his soul.

But Alfredo was still in Nevada, as far as he knew, still working for Ben Trombell. He hadn't thought of Alfredo in weeks, and the realization stunned him. They had once been so close, but now they lived in two different worlds. Still, he wished he could see Alfredo, could converse with him in the Basque language, feel its beautiful syllables roll once more across his tongue. He wanted to embrace his brother and relate to him his many adventures of the past five months. But he had no way to reach him, and the distance between them was immense.

José drifted off to sleep that night with alternating visions of Alfredo, Rebecca, and his homeland meandering in a dreamy medley through his mind.

He awoke in the morning to a startlingly familiar voice. He sat up, half-believing it was another dream. His heart began to pound. He looked around and rubbed his eyes. Everyone else was already out of the tepee. He heard Robert McAllister speaking, and then again that familiar voice, a voice he thought had been swallowed up forever by the past.

Chapter Twenty-Two

José's heart raced. Why had that person come here? Was it something to do with the incident in Pocatello? Was he involved with the law? Had he come to bring José, McAllister, and Moose Jaw to justice? The thought was only fleeting, for José knew that couldn't be true. The only reason he could imagine this person coming here was to visit a friend.

The kindly eyes of Ben Trombell flashed into his thoughts now, looking down upon him with a soft twinkle. It was a vision of comfort, not one causing horrible guilt, as he had so often imagined. Could it be his old boss had forgiven him?

José let those hopeful thoughts creep into his consciousness, but he couldn't make himself believe they were true. He had lost an entire flock of sheep—deserted any that might have survived attack by the bear and the wolves. He hadn't even made the attempt to find them. How could Ben Trombell forgive him for that? He didn't know the value of those sheep, but he guessed it must be tremendous for Trombell to have made such a move to Idaho because of them. It wasn't something to be shrugged off.

Outside, the voices stilled, and for a moment José only heard the pound of his heart. Then suddenly the tepee's flap was pushed to one side, and the bright light of early morning flooded across that close space and blinded him for a moment. When a shadow shielded him from the light, he opened his eyes.

His friend Ben Trombell looked down at him.

Neither one spoke for several moments. They stared into each other's eyes, and there was no need for words. All José's fears had been for nothing, he knew of a sudden, for in Trombell's eyes there was no malice, only an almost overwhelming joy at the sight of him.

Ben Trombell was a man of fifty-five years, his hair mostly gray now where it showed from under a sweat-stained white hat. His eyes were a soft brown, filled with a glow of affection, and lines creased his leathery face. His sudden smile revealed a perfect row of upper teeth, false ones, José had learned. But they looked good.

Trombell started to nod slowly, his eyes fixed on José's and glistening softly. He seemed about to burst with emotion, but still he didn't speak. He didn't say one word until José laid back his blanket to rise.

"José," Trombell said then, so soft it was almost a whisper. "José, my boy. Where have you been?"

José pushed to his feet hesitantly, but then he rushed forward, falling against Trombell with a bear hug full of pent-up emotion from the past months away from his old friend. Trombell clutched him to his chest, and neither one spoke. The tepee door had slipped shut again, and they stood in the gloom and hugged each other tight.

Finally, Trombell took José by the shoulders and held him at arm's length. "José Olano, you don't know what it does for me to see you. I thought I'd lost you forever, son. What in the world happened? Why didn't you come to me?"

José swallowed hard, choking back his tears. "I'm sorry, Ben. I— I lost all your flock. I thought you'd hate me. I wanted to come, but…" He stopped, not knowing how to go on.

"I heard about the bear, son. I heard about your friend Mr. McAllister, the Indians, and a lot of other things since I saw you last. Some friends of mine from Soda Springs tell me you stayed with them a while. That's how I finally found you."

The Woodlands!

"You're friends with the Woodland family?" asked José incredulously.

"Well, sure."

"Then why didn't I ever see you when I stayed with them?"

"Well, I'm a busy man, José. I live ten miles from the Woodlands, you know. Besides, you weren't with them very long, and while you were I was on a little trip. Do you want to know where?" José nodded. "Went down to Nevada, I did. Back to the house. I had to check on the other flocks and see how everyone was. Oh, and I brought something back for you, too. Do you want to see it?"

"Sure," José said hesitantly.

"All right," replied Trombell with a big grin. Letting go of José's shoulders, he threw his arm around him and led him back out the tepee door into the bright sunlight. It took José's eyes a moment to adjust. When they did they came to focus on his brother, Alfredo.

Alfredo didn't give him even a moment to react. He sprang forward and threw his arms around him, laughing, slapping him on the back almost fiercely. "Little brother!" he kept saying over and over, in the Basque tongue. "My little brother, José. You're alive! You're alive!"

Alfredo stepped back and looked at José just long enough for them to see the tears in each other's eyes, and then they embraced again, not caring what anyone thought of their display of affection. There were two Olanos in all of North America, as far as they knew, and the two were reunited. That was all the cause they needed for celebration.

And the celebration went on throughout that day, then into the night. There was much to talk about, and José's tales held Trombell and his brother spell-bound. He told them both in English and in Basque, and it was a joy to feel the native language on his tongue again. He hadn't had cause to speak it in months.

Trombell had a flock of three thousand sheep not far from Soda Springs now, with two Mexican herders and their gang of dogs watching them, and now his brother Alfredo. But he made it plain there was still one job open.

"You're welcome back any time, José. I know you've been feeling guilty about the sheep you lost, but we got most of them back. In your condition there wasn't much you could do anyway, except come and tell me. But I can see why you didn't dare. Anyway, that's all behind us, my boy. I'd like to have you back any time you want to come. What would you like to do?"

José was silent for a few moments, and some of the excitement drained out of the day. As much as he liked Ben Trombell and would enjoy working beside his brother with the flocks, he didn't know if he could relinquish his free life just yet. He was enjoying the wandering ways of a woodsman too much, and he didn't want to let Robert McAllister go when there was still so much he could learn from him. His thoughts must have shown in his eyes, because something in Ben Trombell's face seemed to fall, and he placed an understanding hand on his knee and squeezed.

"Like I said, son, you're welcome back any time you want. I'm not asking you to make a decision this fast. I know you have some new friends here, and you're living an exciting way of life. But when you're ready, we'll be in Soda Springs. Just come into town and ask for me, and there'll be a place for you. I promise that will never change."

José smiled gratefully but didn't trust his voice to speak.

José and McAllister accompanied Ben and Alfredo to the train station in Ross Fork the next morning, and there was little talk between them. José thought glumly of their imminent separation and wished there were another way.

While they waited for the train, Ben Trombell took José off to one side. "There's something I'd like to ask you about, son. It's kind of a personal thing, but it might be important to you. Did you ever have any feelings for the Woodland girl, Rebecca?"

José swallowed, and his eyes darted away. He wanted to hide his feelings, to protect his dignity, but he knew he might as well tell the truth. Ben always seemed to know anyway. "Yeah, I reckon I did," he admitted shyly. "But it doesn't matter now, not after that day with the bear." He had related the entire story to Ben and Alfredo the night before, knowing they, of all people, would understand.

"Well, that's all I wanted to know," replied Trombell. "Son, she knows about the bear up on Bailey Creek. She found out after you left. And while I was there all she could talk about was you. I think you ought to go back and see her."

José pondered the words silently for a moment, then said, "But what about Jared Bonn?"

"As far as I can see, there isn't anybody else. Rebecca isn't spoken for. But as pretty as she is, I don't think that will last too long. If you ever had any feelings for her, I don't think I'd neglect them for very long. You might regret it the rest of your life."

His mind racing, José nodded numbly. There was nothing he wanted more out of life, he guessed, than Rebecca Woodland forever at his side. He supposed he could admit that now, after what Ben told him. He simply found it unbelievable she could forgive him his cowardice. But unless he could show he was not a coward, and then forgive himself, he still didn't know if he could ever face her again.

"Remember, José, true love has only so much patience before it dies. It needs to be nurtured like a lamb. So just don't make any decisions you'll regret."

"Thanks, Ben." José wanted to say more, but the lump in his throat wouldn't let him.

At last the train whistle blew in the distant north, and ten minutes later it chugged up to the station, releasing a gush of steam out its side as if from gills. With one last embrace, Ben Trombell and Alfredo climbed on board, and ten minutes later the train lurched off toward Soda Springs. José stood beside McAllister and watched them go, waving sadly. It was a shame he couldn't live in two worlds, but for now this was where he wanted to be, not stuck on some hill watching sheep, or even cattle. He liked the life of a mountain man. There was only one thing that would ever draw him away from it, and that one thing gripped his heart stronger than ever. It had green eyes and chestnut hair.

Nothing more was heard that autumn and winter of the incident at Keeney House. José and McAllister lived quietly with Moose Jaw's family, and when they needed supplies they went to the trading post in Ross Fork, or farther north to Blackfoot. Fortunately, the town wasn't very far, so they didn't have to go to Pocatello Junction for anything and wouldn't chance running into Superintendent Bulliard again. José sensed McAllister only stayed out of Pocatello because of him. He had a strong feeling he would have gone in and challenged Bulliard outright if José weren't around to suffer the consequences.

José continued to learn the ways of the outdoors through the tutelage of Moose Jaw and McAllister. Some of the older Shoshones, both men and women, also took him under their wing and unofficially adopted him into their tribe. A wrinkled man of untold age named Wind-Wandering-Through-The-Grass taught him what plants he could eat, expounding on what McAllister had already shown him. He also taught him the medicinal plants and their uses and preparations, and it was he who showed him how to worship the Shoshone god, *Appah*. He taught him about the sweat house and recited many legends from the beginning of the world, concerning Coyote and the other animals. They called these "coyote tales", he said, and they were to be told only in the winter months. Each of them ended with the common line, "The rat's tail fell off."

Moose Jaw taught him the tribal dances, and his wife, Slim Willow, revealed her own secrets about tanning and working skins in the painstaking manner of a Shoshone wife. Rocks-in-the-Stream demonstrated the patient way a warrior waited for his quarry, making sure his position was one of comfort, then sitting perfectly still for hours, even as long as a day, waiting on a deer trail, a rabbit path, or by a beaver dam for the desired prey to relax enough to show itself. It was a little easier for Rocks-in-the-Stream to sit quietly than for José. Like all the Shoshones, he had spent his infancy unmoving in a cradle board.

McAllister, when he wasn't busy trying to win the friendship of the eagle he'd given the name "Golden," continued José's lessons in marksmanship, and some days they competed. Often, the scoreboard was equal. For fun one night, McAllister passed on his scant knowledge of the art of quick-drawing and how to twirl a Colt on his finger, throw it into the air, and catch it again.

"I ain't much of a hand at the game, Lucky," McAllister openly admitted. "It's a tinhorn's sport, fer nothin' more'n fun. I only learned what I did from show-offs I knew in my army days. They used to have a lot o' time on their hands, now an' again. You got anythin' better to do, best you do it an' leave the tricks to the circus."

José nodded attentively as McAllister spoke. When the man finished, he asked, "But what about the quick-draw part? That'd be worth knowing, wouldn't it?"

McAllister shrugged. "Reckon there's times it c'd come in handy, but like I said, it all takes time. I ain't a fast draw. That's one thing I never took the time to learn. Just didn't seem too important to me. Bein' able to shoot straight's what I cared about. I ain't no gunman an' never had no call to be."

José swallowed, wondering if he dared ask what was on his mind. When he looked up at McAllister, the man was watching him closely, and one corner of his mouth lifted in a knowing smile. "Go ahead an' ask it, Lucky."

José laughed sheepishly. "Is there any way I might use your pistol now an' then to practice drawin'? Just for fun?"

McAllister nodded, the humor still in his eyes. "I reckon so, as long as you promise to unload it before you do. That a deal?"

José nodded, and McAllister pulled the pistol and handed it to him butt first. "You wanna waste yer time, ther's no time like the present. Get to it."

So was born José's new pastime. And as he had told McAllister, he never intended it for anything but fun. Well, almost. Actually, there was a minor reason he hardly admitted even to himself. All the things he knew how to do, no matter who had taught them to him—except reading and writing, of course—McAllister could do better than he could. Just once, he wanted to master something McAllister wasn't very good at, and maybe that way win respect from him. He knew he could be fast. He wanted to show McAllister he could learn something on his own, something others couldn't do nearly as well. So there was a drive in him from the beginning, and every night he tried to spend at least an hour with McAllister's Colt.

After some weeks and more hours than he could ever count, José was able to draw and point the Colt so fast it was difficult for the eye to follow. He could do it with both hands, the left only a little slower than the right. Then McAllister started letting him load the weapon, and he proved his speed didn't hurt his marksmanship at all. Almost unfailingly, he managed to put two or three holes in a chest-sized target at twenty-five yards in a two second time span from the moment he touched his holster.

Then one afternoon he reached his desired end.

McAllister and some of the Shoshones had gathered to watch him practice down on the bank of the river, quick-drawing on small sticks some of the Shoshone boys threw in for him. Out of ten sticks, he only missed one, and that by a fraction of an inch. The Shoshones watched in awe, and their admiration was plain. But as always McAllister kept a mask on his face, observing impassively.

When the final stick came floating down, José drew in a blur and struck the eight-inch mark once, kicking it up out of the river, then hit it again the instant it landed. The second bullet snapped it in two, and without even hesitating José fired twice, striking both pieces of the stick and catapulting them into the air. With glowing pride, he turned to McAllister.

McAllister was nodding slowly, watching José. A smile parted his lips, and his nod turned to a sideways shake of the head. "Lucky, I've seen many a man do what he called a quick-draw, an' some of 'em 've been mighty fast. But I never seen a man who could draw as fast as you an' hit the mark most every time. You've beat me all to hell when it comes to usin' that Colt."

For a moment, there was silence. José stared at McAllister, his jaw slack. Never had he expected anything more than a mere compliment. A compliment wasn't out of character for McAllister, even if it wasn't always deserved. But he had never admitted to being bested at anything. Probably because he never had. It sent chills up José's spine to hear the admission now, and he swelled with pride. To beat McAllister at any game, to José, was to take a giant step into manhood, and he knew this day would forever shine in his memory.

Pistol practice remained only a small part of José Olano's daily training. The rest of his time he spent stalking, hunting, and tracking. As the snow piled higher, he also whiled many days away trapping along the Snake River and Spring Creek. And on the days he rode the roan, he didn't simply ride. He tried always to apply what McAllister and Moose Jaw and Rocks-in-the-Stream had taught him about horses until he and the roan became one. It took no more than a nudge of the knees to get the roan to move forward, another nudge with one knee or the other and leaning slightly in the desired direction to get him to turn left or right. He was a "damn good *bu'ngu*," as Moose Jaw put it one day, and they were a good team.

From the trapping operation, José put quite a few dollars aside as winter went on and February blew briskly into March. On the third of March, he and McAllister went north to the freighting center of Blackfoot to buy José a revolver. Frozen mud rutted the streets, and every exhaled breath left gusts of silvery frost hanging in the air. Great piles of brown, grit-blown snow lined the edge of each boardwalk and the side of every building.

They tied their horses in front of the hardware store and tried to kick the mud off their boots on the edge of the porch. But there was just as much mud inside, it seemed, as there was out. The store reeked of leather and new wood and smoke from the cherry-red Franklin stove in the center of the floor. There were long counters down either side of the store, and they walked up to the left one, where the clerk, a man with thinning red hair and pale, profusely freckled skin, looked up from a ledger.

McAllister had coached José extensively in the art of bargaining with businessmen. He had drilled him on guarding a stern composure, keeping his wits about him, and countering every move if he thought he had good reason. Inside, José's heart pounded with excitement. This was a new game to him, for he'd always been shy around strangers. But he felt ready to dicker, and more ready to have his way and show this clerk he was a man to reckon with.

"What can I do for you, sir?" The red-haired man automatically looked at McAllister as if José weren't even there.

McAllister returned a bland glance and shrugged, jerking a thumb toward José. "I'm with my pard—just taggin' along. You'll have to talk to him."

Taken by surprise, the clerk raised his eyebrows, then shifted his attention to José. "Well, then. What can I do for *you*?"

"I'd like to look at some guns."

"You're referring to revolvers, I presume?"

José made a puzzled face, looking over at McAllister, then back to the clerk. "I said guns, yes. Not rifles." He was a little surprised a Westerner had to verify that by "guns" he meant pistols. That was about all he'd ever heard a revolver called, outside of books.

Disapproval washed fleetingly over the man's face at José's reply, but he hid it with a condescending smile. "Well, then. What type of *gun* do you like? A .45, maybe? That's the most powerful revolver—*gun*—they make."

"No, sir, I'd like to look at Frontier Colts only. One of these days I'll be sharin' the cartridges with a Winchester. Show me only what you have with a barrel five and a half inches or less." "Frontier" was the Colt company's official designation for their revolver chambered for the .44 centerfire cartridge. The .44-40 remained, however, a Peacemaker, and as such the most popular handgun in the West.

From Colt's brochure and a Meacham Arms Company catalog procured at the trading post, José had memorized every last bit of information about Samuel Colt's pistols. He had learned all possible variations of the gun they called the Peacemaker, and he was proud to display this knowledge.

Reaching below the counter, the clerk laid three pistols on its plank top. The first was the sheriff's—or storekeeper's—version with mother-of-pearl grips and nickel plating. The sheriff's model was known for its snub-nosed barrel and lack of the customary housing which hugged the barrel and contained the ejector rod and spring. The second pistol had a four and a half inch barrel and bright blue finish, with checkered black rubber grips bearing a freedom eagle and the Colt insignia. The last was the five and a half inch variety, this one blued and boasting carved walnut grips of a deep red hue and a barrel, frame, and cylinder extensively and tastefully engraved with a floral design corresponding to that on the grips.

The clerk had taken a hands-off attitude, perhaps convinced José knew something about what he wanted. José was proud of the part he was playing and continued to play it to the hilt. His rejection of the sheriff's model was instant and final. "Put that one back. I'd be spotted a mile away." McAllister smiled, seeing José had heeded his preaching about shiny weapons.

José picked up the other two pistols, one in each hand, and hefted them. McAllister's, the one he was used to, had a five and a half inch barrel, so José was more comfortable with that weight. He permitted himself a little showing off, twirling the two simultaneously, and saw the shorter-barreled version was easier to maneuver. But that was of little consequence—he didn't plan on using the pistol for juggling.

From his reading, he knew the engraved model generally ran two dollars and fifty cents more, but he liked the way the engraving broke up the metallic glare, and it was a beautiful piece, a weapon any man should be proud to own. Besides, he had been able to put a little extra aside, and this was where he meant it to go. He handed the other pistol across to the clerk butt first with the casual smoothness of one who'd been using guns all his life. "How much for this one?" he queried.

The clerk narrowed his eyes in thought. "I can let you have it for seventeen-fifty."

José quickly thought back over the prices he had memorized. "What do you mean you can 'let me have it' for that? That's standard price. And I'll need all the reloading tools, too. The reloader, bullet mold, and charge cup. How much for all of it?"

The clerk, still blushing at José's straight-forward accusation, cleared his throat. "The set of tools is normally four dollars by itself. I'll give you all of it for twenty dollars."

"Well, you just reached my limit. Twenty is all I have to spend," José replied. "But that creates a slight problem: I'll need two boxes of shells, too."

The clerk looked over sharply at McAllister, then returned his gaze to José. "All right, young man. Twenty dollars, and I'll throw in *one* box of shells."

José canted his head to the side. "I need two boxes—one for practice."

"Well, you can't expect—" the clerk started exasperatedly. "Boy, a box of .44's runs a dollar and fifty cents. Those shells don't grow on trees."

José sighed. "Well, then, let's do this: you throw in one box of cartridges, a can of powder, and a pound cake of lead."

The clerk thought for a moment, running his tongue along the inside of his lower lip. At last, without a word, he emitted an annoyed sigh and pulled out the Colt's wooden case, sliding it across to José. He then selected a box of .44 shells, a half pound can of powder, and a lead cake from the shelf behind him and placed them one by one beside the case. "There's an extra cylinder and cleaning tools in the case," he said. "And please don't tell anyone what kind of deal I gave you. A man has to have some margin of profit."

"Thanks, mister," replied José, pulling a sack of coins from inside his shirt. From it he counted out a gold eagle, a half eagle, and five silver dollars. The sack still jingled as he returned it to his shirt.

The clerk, his neck reddening, sputtered, "Excuse me, young man, but when I made you the bargain you said you only had twenty dollars. What's in the pouch?"

"I never said I only had twenty dollars. I only said twenty was all I had to spend. The rest is savings." With that, he picked up his purchases, turned and stepped outside, McAllister close behind him.

When he turned around, McAllister was smiling. "Now that weren't so hard, was it?"

José wiped his forehead with his sleeve and sighed. "It wasn't all that easy, either."

McAllister laughed. "Well, I'm tryin' to teach yuh to survive, kid. That means in town, too. Remember, that's where the really dangerous animals live. An' I won't be around ferever. I guess I better quit callin' you kid," the man said suddenly. "Yer sixteen goin' quick on seventeen now, ain't yuh? Yer the age of a man, an' you act like one, too. You done good in there, Lucky."

José turned seventeen years old on the fifteenth of March, and they celebrated his birthday and the arrival of spring with foot and horse races, shooting competitions, wrestling matches, and gambling. It was ration days, and the Shoshones killed a fat steer and cut it into roasts. At night they sat around a bonfire gorging themselves, laughing, and telling stories. It would be the last of their story telling until the following winter.

And the rat's tail fell off.

March and a cool, rainy April slipped gently by, summoning May, with its warmth and green grass. Then spring turned into summer, with June bringing two weeks of soft, steady rain. Little by little, the last of the snow disappeared from Mount Putnam, the bald-topped mountain to the east. By the end of June, grass was rank from heavy rains, and when the days turned hot it yellowed quickly. After the common afternoon lightning storms of July and August, from time to time José sat at the tepee and watched great blue-gray clouds of smoke billow into the distant sky, where sagebrush and grass fires rolled unchecked by man out on the Great Desert. Out there, the only landmarks were the snow-capped mountain ranges that shouldered into the far horizon and the buttes—the monolith of Big Southern Butte and its twin sisters, rising like colossal camels' humps from the sagebrush and black lava plains.

José had gained two inches in height in the time since he met Robert McAllister. He stood five feet and seven inches tall, probably as tall as he would ever grow. But lean muscle had been packed onto his shoulders, chest, and back, and his arms and forearms were hard and defined from working heavy hides into leather—a task which he continued alongside the Shoshone women, even when ridiculed by the men. Because he didn't shirk manual labor he was able to wrestle many of the Indian boys his age at least to a draw, if not to total defeat. And that was no small chore, for there were some giants among them. José's ace-in-the-hole was a grim determination that he would not be bested in front of McAllister.

McAllister had worked many hours with Golden, who had become his pet, and through the kindness of time her wing had healed, allowing her to soar the skies. But she never left him for long. He gave the bird her chances every day, but always she came back before the sun set.

McAllister had begun by letting Golden land on a stout branch he held in his hands. He had to first build a trust for the bird, knowing an eagle could snap the bones of a man's forearm. In northern Europe, they used the big birds to hunt wolves, although only one in a great number of them could be trained for this dangerous sport. The eagle would land on a running wolf's rump, and when it turned its head to defend itself the bird would clamp one foot over the wolf's mouth to keep it from biting. The final blow was dealt with the other foot, whose talons sank through the wolf's chest, piercing its heart.

But in spite of this daunting knowledge, McAllister later fashioned himself a heavy leather cuff. He would call Golden to him with a whistle while she was soaring, and she would come back and land on his forearm with a great *whoosh* and settling of her wings. Her alert eyes would flash about her, and she would look down at McAllister expectantly and take the mouse or furred piece of rabbit he offered her.

The golden eagle was McAllister's pride and joy, and in his friend's eyes José perceived the light of a whole man, a man who rose each morning to a pleasureful existence. Through Golden, he lived his dreams of flying, and many times José had watched McAllister and sensed him willing himself spiritually into the soaring bird. Those were some of their happiest days.

One day José asked McAllister if he was ever afraid Golden would just fly off and never return. The man looked thoughtful for a time, watching the great bird circle and swing, and then he looked down at José.

"They say the only true way to know if somethin's yers is to set it free. If it comes back, it's yers, if it don't, it wasn't meant to be. That's if an eagle really ever belongs to anybody."

That night, José pondered those words as he stared at the stars. Would McAllister ever try to set *him* free? He never spoke of it aloud, but there was a restlessness growing inside José that he couldn't explain.

September came and neared its end, and one evening McAllister took José down by the waters of the Snake when the sun was going down. It had been cloudy and cool that day, and the sun's last rays lit the sky gloriously before evening's purple shadows would come to wash them away. They painted the clouds golden and threw an orange carpet across Mount Putnam. A chilly breeze lifting off the river and the sage added a perfect accent to the waning day.

McAllister gazed out across the water at the brilliant clouds, and in his eyes was a peaceful glow like the soft, faded blue of the sky behind the clouds. "Lucky, you done growed into a man. You turned seventeen what, last March? An' by the way you've handled yerself, you been a man long before that. You c'n go in the mountains or woods anywhere you want, or even in town, an' yer a man to be reckoned with. A man to ride the river with. That's a far piece from the ripped-up kid I found layin' in the woods up Bailey Creek.

"I 'bout taught you all I know, Lucky. If you wanna keep it, you'll spend the rest o' yer days workin' at it, an' you'll live in a wild place like this. But I heard yuh talkin' to Moose Jaw the other day 'bout that chestnut-headed gal, an' I've seen a homesick look in yer eyes fer a while. There's only one thing I want outta you before I turn yuh loose to go back to yer people or come on with me to other places."

At that moment, Golden emitted a shrill cry from her perch on the dead branch of a cottonwood tree by the river, and goose bumps rose on José's skin. It was a lonesome sound that hovered hauntingly in the air, its spirit there long after its eery echo died.

"You remember that little canyon we saw outside o' McCammon Junction, way back when we were comin' here? Robbers Roost?" José recalled it vividly and said so. "Well, that's halfway to yer Rebecca Woodland, an' I'd like you to go there with me. There's one more test I'd like to see yuh pass 'fore I feel good about settin' yuh free. We'll head that way in the mornin'.'"

Again a strange chill rose up inside José, and it wasn't from the wind. He gazed at Golden's untamed, almost glowing eyes and at the yellow clouds. A lump came into his throat. McAllister was right, as he always seemed to be. José was ready to move on, and he couldn't explain why, even to himself. The only thoughts he could pinpoint were of Ben Trombell, Alfredo, and of course Rebecca Woodland, who was never far away from his heart anymore.

"All right, Gray. I'll trail along with yuh." He smiled to himself at his manner of speech. In spite of Trombell's careful instruction in English grammar, McAllister had finally rubbed off on him for good.

"I'll give you one bullet a day."

A cold evening wind bled down from the top of Robbers Roost Canyon, flickering the flames of the juniper fire and making them dance and whisper. McAllister's gravelly voice was the only other sound there at the mouth of the canyon. José Olano huddled a little closer to the fire and listened intently to what his friend had in store for him.

"One bullet is all you'll need, if you do things the way I've showed yuh. Now, this is a test of survival, an' it's gonna take all I've taught you about shootin', an' stalkin', an' trackin'.'"

José nodded. So far, nothing McAllister had said worried him.

"I'll pick out a diff'rent animal every day, an' I want yuh to bring it back to me. Or at least some sign you really killed it. In camp, I'll tell yuh what animal to bring back the next day. That'll give yuh one night to think on how to hunt it down. An' don't shoot anything but what I send yuh after, or you fail the test. I will allow yuh one thing, Lucky. If yuh don't get the animal I sent yuh after the first day, you c'n stay out another day, or however long it takes. But don't be eatin' plants an' such. Yer stomach's gotta depend only on that one critter to eat. That's the most important part. We both know you c'd survive on plants, but that ain't part o' the test. Yuh have to be able to force yerself to go hungry long enough to find one partic'lar critter."

José nodded slowly. "Okay. So what animal do I have to bring back tomorrow?"

McAllister rubbed his jaw, where he was just letting beard grow back after shaving it off for the summer. He held up a .44 rimfire cartridge between his thumb and forefinger and looked into José's eyes, his face perfectly serious.

"Tomorrow I want you to bring me a mouse."

Chapter Twenty-Three

Like a prone statue José Olano lay, moving only his eyes.

Stretched out in the grass and sagebrush, he didn't even budge when ants scurried across him or when an occasional fly landed on him to rub its front feet together and tongue his salty skin. He breathed slowly, with great control, and made no sound in doing it. These were the things Rocks-in-the-Stream had taught him, the fine points of self-control that had netted him close-up glimpses at many species of wildlife. In front of him was a mouse hole, and his hand, stained green by the sagebrush leaves he used to mask his scent, half-encircled the hole, waiting.

He had studied Robert McAllister's plan until late into the night, examining it from every angle. The whole thing, he had decided, was a carefully devised scheme. McAllister had put many hours into perfecting it. He had always been meticulous in how he taught anything to José. There was no reason for him to change now.

Given this, José knew he also had to be meticulous in how he looked at this final test. It was in this manner he reached some conclusions. First and foremost, he knew deep inside that on the ninth night when his teacher revealed to him the tenth animal he was to bring in it would be a grizzly bear. There was no question in his mind. There were ten animals, and the first was a mouse. To start with such a small animal, McAllister obviously intended to build up. And José recalled him making the promise he would one day face another grizzly. So this was not just an educated guess, it was a fact. And he must prepare himself—mentally and in other ways.

Secondly, McAllister had told him he had ten animals to kill with ten bullets, yet he had never said how many bullets he could use for each animal. On this account, it *was* an educated guess, but he had a feeling McAllister was testing his ingenuity. He wanted to see if José was smart enough to figure out the scheme of things in advance and prepare for it. That meant using other means to capture the smaller of the animals, thus saving his bullets for the last.

He was an excellent shot. He wouldn't have said that to anyone but himself because it sounded like a boast, but there was no point ignoring the fact. He could kill a grizzly with one well-placed shot from his Winchester, but he didn't want to be forced to. He wanted an edge, just on the off chance he had a misfire or some such accident. The more cartridges he could put aside, the better he would feel.

So here he was, day number one. It was early in the morning, and he already had his first prey pinpointed. He had seen a mouse go into this hole, and he figured sooner or later either it or another one would come out the same hole. And why waste a bullet? Where does one shoot a mouse with a .44, anyway? His sage-scented hand was camouflaged with grass, and when the rodent appeared it would be taken totally by surprise, the life squeezed out of it, and there would be his first day's meal. He was half-tempted to forego the "pleasure," but he wasn't above trying anything once. He could always spit it out if it was that bad.

He waited, and an hour passed with still no sign of life other than the insects that used his body for a runway or a tongue-sharpener. Suddenly, his keen ears picked out a faint rustling in the grass five or six feet away from him. He wondered if the mouse had somehow discovered his presence and gone out another hole. Still he didn't move. Impatience couldn't play a part in this "man and mouse game." He never shifted his eyes from his hand.

When the mouse shot out of the hole it was with such swiftness his hand didn't have time to close before it was gone. But reflexes closed his hand, and as it closed he saw the dark blur his fingers surrounded. His first thought was one of elation. Although he had missed the first mouse, there had been another behind it, and by sheer luck he had captured it instead!

Then, from inside the hole, he heard a muffled buzz as he started to sit up, and as he pulled back with the hand that held his trophy, it refused to come, and an inch of the dirt around the hole came instead. Several things struck his mind at once in the split second that followed. First, he had the strange sensation against the palm of his hand and his fingers that this wasn't the furry, soft little body he expected it to be. Secondly, it was mighty hard to pick it up, as if it were tied to the ground. And third, when it did at last come out, it kept on coming, and its dry gray scales dully reflected the morning sun.

With a startled cry, José opened his hand and fell back, and the rattlesnake, just as surprised as he was, sat still for a moment, looking about as if trying to gather its wits. It must have thought the mother of all mice had been waiting outside that hole. But suddenly its head sucked back down the mouse hole as if someone had jerked its tail from the other side, and José could hear its muffled rattle nonstop until he gathered himself up and moved away, his knees weak and heart racing.

Catching a mouse wasn't as easy as he'd anticipated.

But the next time his patience paid off, and although more leery now of what might be coming out the hole, he reacted quickly when the moment arrived. At four o'clock that afternoon, he plopped the little gray and white body of the deer mouse on the ground at McAllister's feet.

McAllister looked up from stroking Golden's neck. He looked at José appraisingly but didn't say anything about the obvious fact José hadn't used his bullet on the rodent. He switched his eyes to the eagle. "What do you say, Golden? Is that a nice present Lucky brought yuh?" Golden cocked her head, and her eyes held an almost frightening intensity. She made no move until McAllister picked up the mouse and threw it out three feet in front of her. Then she hopped over to it in her ungainly manner, her wings flapping slightly, and picked it up in her beak. She blinked once as it went down.

McAllister grinned and looked back at José. He nodded, then looked away and didn't look back as he spoke. "Don't give someone else a chance to eat food you killed fer yerself." José just smiled and waited. "Well, you got three more hours before dark, Lucky. Go out an' find a place somewhere to talk to yer spirits. You won't eat t'day, so you'll need to save strength fer yer hunt t'morrow." Without another word, McAllister reached down and picked up a twig, which he started breaking into tiny pieces and dropping on the ground.

José turned around wordlessly and walked off up the canyon.

The next day he killed a rabbit, not with the numerous deadfalls and snares he set but with a well-placed rock in the head. Then the following day it was a skunk, and it died quickly once lured to the deadfall fifty yards outside its hole by a rabbit's leg that had cured in the sun for a day. Fortunately, he wasn't too hungry that day, for though the taste wasn't as horrible as he'd expected, it was hard to get past the lingering acidic odor on his hands.

The fourth day he shot a sage grouse—McAllister called it a sage hen—out of the air. He couldn't help being proud of that shot.

That evening, they ate well. Golden enjoyed the meal, too. She ate hers covered with feathers, the roughage which raptors need to live. McAllister picked a leg bone clean with his teeth, then tossed it out toward the edge of camp. "Good meat, Lucky. Now tomorrow, I thought about sendin' yuh after a porky—porkypine, that is. But I decided against it. A porkypine is one o' the few animals a man who's lost in the woods an' maybe hurt can kill without much trouble, an' I'd like to see 'em left alone to breed. The one you kill t'day may be the one that woulda saved yer life t'morrow. So I decided on a chuck instead. Let's get a good fat juicy one, all right?"

José nodded but didn't say anything. Tomorrow would be a day of rest for him, for he knew right where to get a marmot within an hour after sunrise. The broken lava country where he had killed the sage grouse fairly crawled with the chubby rodents.

Sure enough, the next morning at eight-thirty he stalked and killed a young, healthy marmot with a rock. Then he found a shady spot deep in the lavas where it was moist and cool enough to grow ferns and went to sleep. He dreamed, and when his dreams were pleasant they found him with Rebecca Woodland. When they weren't, grizzly bears rampaged through them gnashing their teeth.

The marmot tasted good after a day with no food. McAllister roasted it in the coals with the hide still on, Indian style. José found most of its meat on its legs, a little on its back. He was surprised at how little there was to eat on the rest of its body. For all its plump appearance, it was mostly hair, skin, and fat around its middle.

The next evening's feisty badger died angry, like most badgers do, and it took half an hour to skin it. Its hide was practically glued to its body with a thick, yellow layer of fat. The next day he killed a coyote and had to use another of his precious shells. But he had only used two, one on the coyote and one on the sage grouse, and he figured if he couldn't kill a bear with the six bullets he would have saved by then he shouldn't be out here.

Back in camp, José was leery of dining on the coyote. The Shoshones were scornful of the Arapaho tribe, whom they called Dog-eaters, and their opinion of those who ate any type of dog had begun to rub off on him. But when he saw the relish with which McAllister tackled his piece of backstrap, he swallowed his pride and started to eat. It wasn't like any meat he had ever tasted, but it would keep a man alive. That was the best he could say.

When José set off from camp well before dawn the next morning it was with jubilation. He was after a deer today, his favorite animal to hunt. It wasn't so much the kill itself, but the search for the game he relished, pitting his hunting skills against a worthy prey.

It was still early in the day when he passed up three big bucks, their huge antlers fully matured and hanging with the last tiny scraps of velvet. He watched them browse along the southern exposure of the canyon, through the maples and sage, then make their way up along the ridge, keeping off the skyline. When last he saw them, they faded like shadows into the cool firs above him.

The deer he killed was a fawn, and that was by his own choice. He passed up two yearling two-point bucks and three does in the same herd, then killed the smallest of them. It had the least chance of making it through the coming winter, and McAllister and the Shoshones had taught him not to waste.

He threw the fawn over his shoulders, took all four legs in one hand, and hiked back down to camp carrying his rifle in the other hand. Robert McAllister nodded with satisfaction when he saw the animal's size. He had taught José well how to choose.

Meat was meat, and all of it nourished, but José was glad to fork the fresh venison into his mouth that night. Its juices seeped down his throat, its wild-flavored goodness filled his stomach, and he ate until he was ready to burst. As he became full, his mind wandered, and he found himself pondering with curiosity what McAllister might send him after tomorrow. He was more certain than ever the last day's animal would be a grizzly bear, of which he had seen two at a distance in the last seven days. But he had always sort of figured the deer would come right before it, for size had generally augmented each day. By the time McAllister decided to break his silence, José fairly ached with curiosity.

McAllister wiped grease off his mouth and leaned back on his bedroll, studying José's face. José watched him, half-amused at the entertainment he seemed to be enjoying at his expense. "You ready fer a little fun?" McAllister asked suddenly.

José shrugged. "I've been havin' fun every day. What's next?"

"I'd like to see you pack a moose down outta there. An' be ready, 'cause they're in a fightin' mood. It's matin' season."

José's initial reaction was one of excitement, but after they had crawled into their blankets and he lay looking up at the stars his heart fell a little. McAllister had never been one to waste meat, and he guessed scavengers would pick up what was left, but it seemed a waste to kill such a big animal just to prove a point. He lay pondering that thought a long time, wondering how he would pull the trigger. Moose acted so stupid it hardly seemed sporting to shoot one. Maybe he should make a real challenge out of it and jump on one's back, then strangle it to death. He pictured that in his mind, then laughed quietly to himself. It wasn't a pretty sight.

As he lay there, a shooting star whizzed past, seeming to spear right through the mountain rather than behind it. To his amazement, another followed soon after, in almost the exact same spot. Both were brilliant, as bright as any he remembered ever seeing, and for a long time he lay and contemplated them. Was there some meaning there? Had God decided to send him some type of sign to guide him on his way? He had seldom seen two stars fall within such a short span of time, and never two that bright and traveling the same way. He was a Catholic, but he had found a lot of truth in Shoshone beliefs. He decided to follow his instincts and go in the direction indicated by the travel of the stars.

Again, he set out long before dawn the next morning, for he had never seen a moose moving around very long into the day. And even as big and dark as they were, they had a way of disappearing like ghosts into the shadowy woods. Instead of heading up the canyon, he cut over the steep side of the ridge, onto a long sagebrush flat, and into the next drainage, then into the next. He alternately climbed and scanned the canyon across from him, and as the sun crept over the mountains his carefully searching eyes stopped on a thicket of serviceberry and stunted aspen and buckbrush. There, camouflaged in the purple-gray branches, were the ears of a moose.

He sat silent for a long time, staring as the rest of a head with little eyes and a big, bulbous nose materialized in the brush. The head finally moved, the mouth opening as it dropped and coming up with long stalks of grass protruding from its lips. As he watched, another mysteriously appeared, a large bull with a spreading rack of antlers probably wider than four feet. The two beasts moved slowly, their long, gangly legs lifting them over the brush like stilts. They came up out of the thicket and moved toward the top of the ridge, and although he knew it would cost him time José didn't fire. He soon saw a young, awkward-looking calf follow them out and up on top of the hill, where all three stood silhouetted against the pale sky.

Overhead, a red-tailed hawk screamed, and seconds later its mate mimicked it. José gave them his attention for a moment, and when he looked back, the moose were slipping out of sight over the ridge.

Moving swiftly but silently, he trotted the rest of the way down the sagebrush-covered hill, then up the other steeper, aspen- and brush-covered south side. On nearing the top, he slowed to a snail's pace, reaching the summit on hands and knees. He crawled through the sagebrush until the ground beneath him tilted off steeply into the next canyon.

A steep slope greeted him, on his side, and a gentler one on the other, tangled heavily with maple and dotted with juniper. The maples were bright red, made more brilliant against the backdrop of sagebrush and dark junipers, and José stared in awe. A dry creekbed wound down the middle of the canyon past the junipers and red dogwood that lined its banks, and to his far right appeared a wide spot in the canyon, a perfect place, he thought, to set up a camp. Or even build a house. He wished McAllister were there to see it.

Wrenching his eyes from the beauty of the scene, he looked down the ridge where the three moose were making their careful way. The bull moved ahead of the other two, obviously aware he had few rivals. He didn't scan the country like a deer or a predator would, just ambled along, looking occasionally at the trees in the bottom of the canyon for which he was bound.

Out of the corner of his eye, José saw a mouse run across the grass and dive into a hole. For a moment, he contemplated shooting it and taking it back to McAllister. He would hand it to him and laugh at the look on his face when José told him he didn't realize he said *"moose."* He would have done just that, too, but he had already decided to go through with shooting a moose. It would not only feed a few scavengers, but he knew from sightings and from droppings and tracks there was a bear nearby, and the rotting moose carcass would draw it in.

He was watching the moose, trying to decide which one to shoot, when he again caught movement out of the corner of his eye. Moving only his eyes, he looked across the canyon toward the motion, and he spotted another moose, a younger bull, moving slowly toward the first three, watching them intently. He was still four hundred yards away.

There was very little cover on this side, so José moved slowly. He worked his way down until he was only two hundred yards from the trio, and when they stopped, he lay still. Glancing up the south ridge, he couldn't see the younger bull, but he could hear him coming. He was breaking bushes and coming at a long walk, oblivious to what got in his way. He stopped, and José heard him grunt in the trees, then slash branches with his antlers. The big bull was starting to take notice now, but if there was reason to be worried he wasn't intelligent enough to be. The look in his eyes said he was ready for any challenger and would take them head-on.

The young bull began to move again, and soon he appeared from the trees, staring toward the other three with no idea José was anywhere near. José noticed then he had a misshapen antler. It bent down uncomfortably close to his eye and still hung with the dead, black velvet he had worn off the rest of his rack. It wasn't a big thing, and maybe didn't even bother the young bull, but it was enough for José to make his decision. Both bulls appeared healthy, but the one with the bad antler was the one he would take.

Only one hundred yards separated him from the small bull, two hundred from the big one. He leaned forward and rested his elbows on his knees. He leveled the barrel of the rifle at the great, awkward head, at the place where his brain would be, and squeezed the trigger. In the narrow canyon, the blast of the shot seemed extraordinarily loud, and José was curious to see how the big bull reacted. But he had to make sure of his shot, so he watched the younger bull while his legs folded under him and he fell on his chin, then rolled onto his side.

Whipping his head, José saw the big bull and the other two standing perfectly still, watching where the young bull had been. They didn't know what they had heard! José crouched back down as the bull trotted up near the smaller bull. It wasn't until he was near that he stopped, stuck his nose into the air, then suddenly whirled and trotted away, his clumsy-looking legs carrying him with amazing speed.

José watched the three moose all the way up through the trees until they disappeared over the next ridge. Then he turned to the chore at hand. It was a struggle, but he managed to eviscerate the moose, then severed its head and neck from its shoulders. Leaving these lying on the ground, he reached up inside it and cut loose the tenderloins and laid them beside the head. Next, he propped the body up as best he could on piled sagebrush to keep it cool, put the cuts of meat in his pack, shouldered the great head, and started back toward camp.

He hadn't gone far before the heavy load started to tell on him. He wasn't holding his rifle; it was slung by a strap around his neck. But even with both his hands to hold the head it was driving him to the ground. It and the cuts of meat must have weighed ninety pounds or more. But he had set out to pack it, and he refused to quit. He had the remainder of the day, and he wouldn't have it rest on his conscience that he'd given up.

He was laboring along, head bowed beneath the load. He had crossed into the next drainage, with only a mile or so yet to go, when he saw the track. It was a bear, and brazen as can be it had walked right through the sagebrush, headed down in the direction of the railroad tracks. And it was not just a bear. By the length of its claws and of the paw itself, it was a grizzly, and a good-sized one.

The load atop his shoulders seemed to lighten considerably, or else he just forgot to worry about it. Goose bumps raised on his skin, and his heart started to pound faster than his exertion could account for. With new vigor, he started up the next slope through the heavy sage.

It was four o'clock in the afternoon when he reached camp. His rush of energy hadn't been enough to keep him going at the speed he had assumed, and even with his awareness of the nearby bear, he slowed and plodded on, frequently checking his backtrail. McAllister was hanging strips of venison on sagebrush branches to dry when José walked into camp, and he didn't even turn around. That was his subtle way of showing he had heard José coming and knew who approached.

"Is this proof enough I got one?" José gasped.

When he threw the head down on a bush, it made a loud thump and crash, and McAllister turned around with a questioning look. His eyes sought out and found the moose rack protruding from the bush, and he just shook his head. "I'll be... Yer unbelievable, you know that? Were you already lucky, or did namin' you that make you that way?"

José's only answer was to flop down on the grass and close his eyes.

"Yer a hell of a man, Lucky," he heard McAllister say. "It's too bad we can't eat horns. We'd both be stuffed t'night."

In the back of his consciousness, José caught McAllister's sarcasm, teasing him about bringing back the head instead of meat. But he was too tired to care. He was snoring within moments.

Four hours later, José's own snoring woke him up. He lay still for several seconds, staring up at the star-sprinkled sky and feeling the ache in his legs and back. Finally, the smell of sage smoke and roasting meat registered on his senses, and his eyes started to open a little more. He forced himself to sit up and looked over at the orange flames of the fire that crackled and popped and sent sparks into the dark. McAllister leaned over the fire, prodding some large object in the coals with a stick. This made a profusion of sparks dance up and sail away.

Gathering his strength, José pushed to his feet and walked over to the fire, squatting down across from McAllister. The man looked at him appraisingly. "How yuh feel? You were sawin' some logs, I'll say."

José laughed. He glanced around him quickly, then asked, "You gonna cook the tenderloin I brought?"

"Oh, that? I already ate it. But I got somethin' better in store fer you."

Quick anger rose up inside José when he realized McAllister wasn't joking. There had been enough of the tenderloin to satisfy four men. But McAllister always had eaten like a bear. His anger subsided as he watched his friend spear the large hunk of what he assumed to be neck meat and drag it out of the coals. Its aroma filled the air, and his stomach began to complain.

"My stomach thinks my throat's been cut," said José, borrowing the phrase from McAllister.

McAllister laughed. "Well, yuh won't regret the wait."

Even as he spoke, he began to carve at the hunk of meat, and José watched him curiously. He had never seen meat cooked just lying in the coals that way, and it seemed a waste to have to cut off the burned outer layer just to get to what wasn't burned on the inside.

José closed his eyes for a few moments while McAllister finished shaving off the hard rind from the meat. Minutes later, McAllister nudged him, and José opened his eyes to see him holding a plate out to him. The plate contained two long strips of meat. Without a word, José picked up one of the strips and tried to gnaw off a piece, finding it shot heavily with gristle. He looked up at McAllister with disgust. But what he did chew away and swallow was delicious, maybe in part because of his gnawing hunger, and even though it tasted different from deer he made no comment about it. There would be time enough for talk when his belly was full.

As he finished the plate, he looked up expectantly, and McAllister filled his plate again. This time there was no gristle, only solid, red meat, and the flavor was perfect. He began to slow down about halfway through the plate. At last, he sat back and forced down the last few pieces, refusing a third helping.

"Well wha' do yuh think? Yuh like it?" queried McAllister.

"Yeah," José replied, wiping his mouth with a sleeve. "The second plate had a lot less gristle, but the first plate had good flavor."

McAllister shrugged. "That's because the second plate was the tenderloins; you didn't think I'd really eat all of 'em, did you? That first plate was nose."

"*What?*" José exclaimed, straightening up.

"Nose meat. I took the whole nose an' threw it in the coals, hair an' all. The hair burned off, an that stuff I was cuttin' off was the hide. Perty good, wasn't it?"

José just shook his head. As much as he hated to admit it, it really was good. But a *nose?* What a way to wake up of an evening. "Any more surprises up yer sleeve?" José asked jokingly.

"Well, I don't know. 'Pends what yuh call a surprise." McAllister looked at him blandly, then dropped his eyes to stir the coals and plop a couple of large sagebrush branches onto them.

"Huh!" José exclaimed. "'Bout anything you do anymore's a surprise. I hate to think what else you'll make me eat before yer done."

McAllister cleared his throat and spat into the dark. His face was serious when he looked back at José, and the firelight cast an eerie glow across it, shadowing his eyes from below.

"You've hit yer last night, Lucky—if yer name runs true. By this time t'morrow, you'll be free to choose yer way, an' nobody c'n ever say I didn't give it all I got to teach yuh to live off the land."

José listened quietly, meeting his gaze. "You've taught me more'n I ever thought I c'd learn in a lifetime, Gray. I'll always remember that." His mind raced ahead, knowing what McAllister would soon reveal, that the last animal he had to slay was a grizzly bear. And he was at a point now he had no doubt about the outcome of that duel. He could shoot a pine cone from the crotch of a tree at a hundred yards, and when McAllister gave him his last cartridge he would have six to put his grizzly down. Knowing first-hand the lethal fury of a grizzly even mortally wounded, he didn't think he'd want to face one with one shell, but with six he was confident.

Just at that moment Golden hopped closer, and McAllister threw another piece of hairy raw meat in front of her. She picked it up and threw back her head so it fell into her mouth, then blinked once as she swallowed it, like she always did.

McAllister absently wiped the blade of his knife on the leg of his buckskin pants, then spat again. "Well, pard, I reckon yer ready fer yer final test. But before I tell yuh what yer after, ther's one thing. You should have saved up nine empty shells since the beginning o' this whole thing. I'd like 'em back now."

Chapter Twenty-Four

A stick popped in the fire as if to emphasize McAllister's ominous statement, sending a large coal arcing out to land in the dirt two feet away. José stared at McAllister, whose eyes gazed back mildly. It wasn't that José was trying to stare his old friend down; his suddenly shocked mind just riveted his eyes in place.

After the exploding coal, there was no sound in the night but the far-off gurgle of Robbers Roost Creek, the crickets' endless chirping, and the whisper of aspen leaves. José's mind began to whirl. He wondered what to do. He couldn't give up those shells—he had to have them, if just for peace of mind. Why not tell McAllister he had thrown them away after firing? That thought was discarded almost as quickly as it came. McAllister had drilled it into him to save every shell he ever fired, for reloading purposes. And even though the Winchester Model 66 took a rimfire shell, which he couldn't reload, McAllister had convinced him to save these, too, to keep him in the habit for when he bought his new '73. He knew José wouldn't throw them away now. That left only one recourse. He would refuse to go after the bear. Yet even that he couldn't do. If he didn't hunt the bear, he could never call himself a man.

"I've got to keep 'em, Gray. Why do you need 'em back?"

"Question is, why do *you* need 'em? They're all empty—aren't they?"

José shrugged. He wasn't going to lie. "No, they aren't. I have five full ones."

McAllister narrowed his eyes, running his tongue along the inside of his lower lip thoughtfully. "Five shells, huh?" Suddenly he laughed, the corners of his eyes wrinkling up with pleasure. "I wondered if you'd tell me. I kind o' figgered it out when you kept bringin' in them little critters all butchered already, like you were tryin' to hide somethin'. I never did see a bullet hole till you brung in the sage hen."

José shrugged sheepishly. "I thought you were testin' me to see if I'd really shoot animals I c'd get another way."

"Yer sharp, but this test is straight down the line. I'm mighty glad to see yer usin' yer head, but when I said one bullet a piece, I meant it. You know better than to have to shoot twice at somethin'. *Any*thing."

José nodded and looked at the ground. "I know. But…"

"But what? There ain't no buts about it. Hand me over them shells—four of 'em, anyway." McAllister held out his hand.

With a plummeting heart, José reached into his pouch, dug around a moment, then pulled out his hand and dropped four shells into McAllister's outstretched palm. When he looked down into the bag again, he saw the lone remaining rifle shell, and when he moved its dim reflection disappeared, then reappeared, as if it had winked. José swallowed hard.

Frost was heavy on the sagebrush as José moved up the ridge, and now and then a pebble cracked sharply as it broke from the frozen soil. José moved like a hunter, forced by his inner self to see this quest through to its bloody outcome, in spite of the odds. But he didn't know if he felt like a hunter, or like the hunted.

He peered around him at the cold hard world of the pre-dawn, seeing the forms of sagebrush and trees begin to materialize from the dark hills around him and the narrow draw below. He didn't feel the cold. His heart pounded swiftly enough so that his blood kept him warm. But each breath drifted visibly into the air before him, silvery in the halflight, seeming tangible and solid like something he could reach out and catch.

Nearing the crest of the ridge that dropped down into the canyon where he had left the moose carcass, José dropped to his stomach in the frosty grass. He crawled noiselessly, using his elbows to drag himself forward. The silence was eery. The dim light molded bizarre shapes of the bushes, the rocks, the trees. Each one became a grizzly bear or some other-worldly creature with an image too horrible to describe. They crouched, leering and evil, watching silently as the young Basque man cowered by.

When José knew he was close enough to see the moose when light increased, he stopped, staring intently into the dark toward that place. At times, he thought he could see the dark form below, but the vision would fade, and there would only be the gloomy shadows. He closed his eyes, resting them for half a minute, then looked again. At the distant spot where the moose lay, only vague, formless shadows gathered to taunt him.

Time seemed to stand still. A breeze picked up, rattling up the slope at him. For that he was thankful. McAllister had told him bear's eyes are no better than man's, but their sense of smell is incredibly well-honed, and if the wind had started to blow downslope, the bear would be long gone. Or, worse yet, he would come this way to confront whatever man was waiting to steal the food he had found.

And then daylight began to creep up from the lower hills and make its way toward Haystack Mountain—the Hogsback—and José's carefully searching gaze pinpointed the moose, hidden in the brush. It hadn't been moved.

Mixed emotions washed through him. The bear hadn't come here in the night. Now he had no idea where it had gone, without finding and following the tracks of yesterday. But he felt no particular urge to do that. Truth was, he would just as soon have walked back to McAllister and told him the game was done. But his pride wouldn't let him do that. He would never give McAllister reason to say he had quit. And more importantly, if he didn't confront that bear now, knowing it couldn't be too far away, he might never overcome his fear. Thoughts of grizzlies would slowly eat away at him each time he ventured into the wild country, and finally he would just go insane. No, there was no option. He must meet this challenge head-on. He must prove there was nothing in the wilderness he couldn't master.

Later in the day, the bear had still not shown. With one last careful look around, José rubbed his hands and face heavily with sagebrush, and smeared his buckskins, too. He crept carefully down into the canyon and went to the moose carcass, where he skinned back part of one side, cut off several large chunks of hump meat, and went back up the hill.

But this time he only went halfway, about two hundred yards from where the moose lay. Here was an outcropping of broken limestone jutting out of the hillside and surrounded by yellow grass. The rock itself was rotted to the point that large chunks of it sloughed away, creating a small slide on the downhill side.

Avoiding the rock slide, José gathered armsful of the dead grass and lay them on the ground where the rock created an overhang, a spot that would break up his silhouette and shelter him from any sun or buffeting winds or rain the rest of the day might bring. He nestled into the grass, sitting Indian-style with his rifle cradled across his knees, and he tried not to contemplate the lonely shell in the rifle's chamber.

When he got hungry, he gnawed on the cold, raw moose meat. The flavor wasn't bad. After raw deer liver, skunk, and some of the other "delicacies" he'd enjoyed as a student of Robert McAllister's, little affected him unfavorably. He'd even dug into a dead log once, like a bear, and eaten the big white grubs, the size of the tip of his pinkie, he found snuggled up there. So he swallowed the moose meat raw, took sips from his canteen now and then, and waited in patient silence.

It shaped up to be a bitter cold night on the side of the canyon. He waited for sight of a bear. He *wanted* to see one now. But none ever showed—only two drifting coyotes that had wandered close until they caught the man scent, then drifted warily to a safe distance to watch. And the magpies and huge, black ravens. They had kept him company most of the day, hovering around the carcass and eating eagerly, their raucous calls echoing back and forth across the canyon, signaling all their friends and relatives.

As the sun dove into the sea of mountains in the west, cold shadows swept over him, and immediately he began to shiver. He ached for his blankets or for a heavier coat. He wished he had skinned out the moose and carried the hide up here to shelter him. It wouldn't have been a bad idea, but he wondered if the bear wouldn't smell the hide and stop here first on its way down to its free meal. He shivered, this time not entirely from the cold.

Rising after dark, he pulled more grass and some sagebrush, then lay down on his bed of grass in the little shelter and covered himself with grass and brush. He didn't sleep much, if any at all, but at least he could feel his extremities every time he tried. He snuggled back into his bed and tried to will the cold away. A couple of times he even thought it worked, but the chattering of his teeth made him think different.

He was up long before dawn, sitting with the rifle on his knees and watching the silent canyon below. All he could see was the thin, light ribbon of the game trail that meandered up the center of the canyon, fifty feet from the creek bed. The rest was a black abyss.

The sun rose achingly slow, but when its yellow light splashed across the hill José threw caution to the wind and crawled out into it, disrupting his silhouette as best he could with dead sagebrush branches. He soaked in the warm rays, almost searing after the cold he had endured. He let them seep into his body, dry the dew from his buckskins, put the feeling back into the tips of his ears that, even though covered by hair, felt frozen clear through.

In spite of his gnawing hunger, he dozed and was only vaguely aware of the throaty ravens' cries, the never-ending *maggie, maggie,* of the magpies as they called in their kin, then fought them for the best pick of the carcass.

The warmer the sun grew, the more sleepy José became, until finally he just fell over on his side and slept, even his dreams of charging grizzlies failing to wake him up. When he did finally sit up and rub the sleep out of his eyes, the sun was about as high as it would get. The two coyotes had returned, and they circled the carcass warily, then sat for a long time, watching.

Toward two or three in the afternoon, José caught movement farther up the canyon and turned his head to watch a lone gray wolf padding silently along the game trail, his nose testing the air. He paused when near the carcass, and his laid-back ears gave away the fact he had caught the human scent nearby. But he didn't wait long before going in to the carcass and scattering the scavenging birds with a toothy snarl and a raised-hackle charge. The birds lifted off, crying angrily at the disturbance, then landed in nearby trees, watching the wolf tear at the red flesh as they screeched boisterously back and forth.

José watched about as long as he could keep his eyes open, then let himself doze again. It was close to five o'clock, and already the cold was dropping down like a blanket. He made up his mind right then he was going to go down and take a piece of that moose's hide before he spent another night on the hill. But not until he took advantage of the last of the sinking sun's rays and caught some more sleep.

His dreams were very real. As they had been for months, they were filled with grizzly bears, helpless wrestling matches where he struggled under close to half a ton of stinking fur and felt hot, putrid breath on his face. He could never win these battles. Usually, he couldn't move, or when he could it was at such a ridiculously slow pace he couldn't save himself if he tried. He seemed to be struggling in a barrel of sand, a heavy weight upon him that forced the air from his lungs and left him gasping.

He moaned helplessly when the huge bruin charged him with a roar. He heard magpies and ravens object noisily. Another roar, and it seemed so real. He rolled, trying to fight the giant beast he struggled with, that slapped him around like a toy. He knew this was a dream, yet when the bear growled again it was too lifelike, so real he had to leave this dream. He struggled, trying to rise from his sleep, knowing he must succeed if he were to escape the claws and fangs that reached for him with rabid insistence.

His eyes came open like they were loaded with springs, and he lay staring at a sunset-streaked sky, feeling the cold air that eddied around him. Evening had come at last, and filling the sky were orange and yellow and pink clouds whose intensity promised to grow only more spectacular in the next several minutes.

And then he heard the roar again, just like in his dream, and he jolted upright, his eyes wide with terror. There, near the dead moose, a large silver-backed grizzly made another charge at the birds that flocked around it. The magpies and ravens scattered before it, while others flitted back down behind, seeming to taunt the bear purposely. It whirled, roared, and chased them away again, then stood with one paw on the moose's chest, bloody pink saliva falling in large drops from its lips as it swung its head about, daring any of the birds to approach again. The coyotes stood prudently fifty yards away, watching the proceedings. They had probably already filled their own bellies and were only curious now. The wolf was nowhere in sight.

José sat frozen, his rifle gripped tightly in his right hand, his left supporting him against the ground. He stared in awe at the powerful beast. How had he come so silently, carrying all that great bulk? Was he even real, or a dream? Goose bumps covered José's skin under his buckskins.

Help me, God, he prayed. *Help me move!* He was glued in place, just like he had been on the river bank with Rebecca Woodland. He was helpless. Something seemed to be grasping him by the skin of his cheeks, pulling it tight toward the back of his head. His fingers turned white on the ground and around the rifle barrel.

He tried to move. He prayed silently to God, to *Appah,* to the sun, to anyone, any powerful being believed in by any tribe of man who might pull him from his trance, give him the strength at least to run away. He had to leave here if he couldn't find the courage to face this bear. He couldn't just stay here through the night. The grizzly would surely scent him before it was through, and judging by its awesome size and temper it would probably come to investigate. It was unlikely this monster was intimidated by man.

Just when the situation seemed most desperate, a face appeared before José, a calm face with strong, rugged features, and eyes the color of worn gunmetal. The vision was silent. It just looked at him knowingly, then at last raised a hand and gave him a half-salute and a nod. Then it was gone, and Rebecca Woodland's face appeared to take its place. There was no expression, just a quiet, sober look in the sea-green eyes.

José closed his eyes and shook the vision from his brain, and when he looked up, there was the bear. Although two hundred yards away, it appeared to be right before him, and for a moment he thought it was watching him. But it quickly flung its head the other direction, eyeing the birds and coyotes warningly.

José was carried. He never could explain it any other way. By his instincts, his tortured soul, or God—who knew? But something carried him down that slope, walking slowly, not even trying to hide. When he reached the trail, he was only sixty yards from the bear, and he knew it had seen him when its eyes left the birds and came to rest upon him with an intense glow, a glow that came only partially from the orange-dyed clouds overhead.

His heart must have been pounding. His vision should have been blurred. He might have been shaking like the maple leaves in the evening breeze. But if any of this were true, José didn't know it. He was aware only of the cold metal of the rifle in his hands and the wild-eyed silver-backed grizzly that glared at him.

There was no sound, at least none José could hear, until slowly he became aware of the hoarse, hollow, half-growling sound that was the bear breathing in and out. Or maybe it was his own breathing.

No longer did the scent of fear fill the air. José was calm, unlike he should have been. Unlike even McAllister would have been, in the same position. McAllister had told him there were three extremely dangerous situations to get into with bears. One was if the bear was wounded. Two was standing between a mother and its young. Three was the foolish act of approaching a bear guarding a food supply it might dine on for two or more days, if it could keep intruders away.

And here was José, with one shell in the chamber of his Winchester.

He had no idea how long he stood there, the silence complete except for the breathing of the bear. He observed its great sides heaving in and out with each breath. He saw the orange light fade from its eyes as the clouds slowly grayed. Not knowing he was about to speak, the sound of his own voice startled him. "I'm a fool for standin' here, bear. You could be on me in three seconds. But yer a fool, too. I'm José Olano. They call me Lucky. An' I got a bullet in this rifle with yer picture printed on its nose. They say José Olano doesn't miss. I guess now we'll find out."

As he raised the rifle and centered the sights on the bear's left eye, the bear came half up on its hind feet, dropped down, then came all the way up, staring at him more curiously than threateningly, he thought. His finger tightened on the trigger as the bear dropped to all fours again, moving its head back and forth as if shaking it. José stopped squeezing, and his finger relaxed. He let out a sigh, then breathed in deeply.

"Yer a mighty big boy, bear," he said at last. "An' you got a big dinner ahead of you. So get to eatin'. I could kill you, but... I already killed my bear."

Holding his rifle at the ready, he backed slowly down the trail, and the bear stayed in its tracks, watching, sniffing the air. It made no attempt to advance.

McAllister watched as José piled sagebrush onto the dying coals and shoved a nest of dry grass underneath it. The flames leaped up, lighting their faces. It was ten o'clock, and McAllister had been nearly asleep, but his instincts told him when José was near. Now he just looked at him silently, knowing by the self-confident look in José's eyes that he had found his grizzly.

At last, José jacked the lever of his Winchester, and the cartridge flew out and landed near the fire, its brass shining brightly in the orange light. McAllister glanced down at it, seeing the lead still protruding from it, then looked back up blandly at José, who still didn't speak. "I c'n see by yer eyes yuh found yer griz. Don't tell me you killed 'im with yer bare hands."

José laughed. "I already killed my griz—on Bailey Creek." With that, he turned and went to his bedroll, and without even undressing he climbed into it. He was snoring within seconds.

In the morning, José awoke to the smell of bacon frying, and he rolled over and rubbed his eyes. When he opened them, he saw McAllister squatted near him, staring across the camp. McAllister motioned with his hand in the direction he was looking. "Friend of yers?"

Curiously, José let his eyes follow the invisible line made by McAllister's. They stopped two hundred yards away, on the form of the grizzly from the day before. José started, his eyes opening wider. Then he took a deep breath and climbed out of the blankets, walking to the far side of camp. Soon, he heard and felt McAllister walk up and stop beside him. José turned and looked at him, observing his half-hidden smile. "In fact, that is a friend of mine."

The bear stood up on its hind legs and sniffed the air, then at last dropped to all fours. He turned and lumbered on up the draw, ignoring the two men who watched him, and disappeared in the gray bushes. McAllister clapped José on the shoulder and grinned, and together they walked back to camp. Something unspoken had passed between the two men and the bear, and nothing needed to be said.

There was a chill in the air by the time afternoon arrived, and even though only scattered, wispy clouds cluttered the sky, the rapid drop in temperature threatened rain, maybe even snow. José and McAllister were sitting in camp, enjoying each other's company silently, and the horses grazed peacefully nearby. Golden sat in her perch in the top of an aspen and preened her wings.

A rifle cracked harsh and hollowly in the silence of the quickly graying day. It startled McAllister and José. They whirled about, coming to their feet in surprise. For a moment, they were uncertain where the shot had come from. But it had whirred very close to camp, for they had heard it clipping tree branches as it went.

The second shot came from the north, and with a sickening *thud* it struck its mark. José and McAllister turned. Numbly, they stared as Golden plunged from the tree in a shower of feathers and thumped lifelessly to the ground. Uncharacteristically throwing all caution to the wind, McAllister ran to the base of the tree while José dove for his rifle. He picked it up and jacked a shell into the chamber, waiting to see if whoever had fired the shot would come to pick up their trophy. Whoever it was, José couldn't see them, and chances were good they had been so far down in the draw when they saw the eagle in the tree they didn't even know there was a camp nearby. José prayed that was the case, at least. Otherwise, there was about to be a killing, if McAllister had his way. Maybe there would be anyway.

José turned to see McAllister sitting on the ground, holding the eagle in both hands, stroking its lifeless breast. He quickly averted his gaze, and at that moment the first of the hunters stepped into sight.

There, like a never-ending curse, stood the railroad superintendent, Andrew Bulliard.

Too fast to know what was happening, José heard a strangled curse and turned as McAllister charged past him. Andrew Bulliard was taken just as much by surprise as

José, and he stared in shock until the butt of McAllister's rifle caught him squarely in the teeth.

McAllister's momentum carried him right over the top of him, and Bulliard landed on his back on the ground. McAllister's movements were a blur as he came back around, catching Bulliard as he rose to his knees, and kicked him high in the chest, then swung the rifle again and struck him alongside the head with its stock.

So violent and uncontrolled was McAllister's reaction it scared José. Then he saw four other men come huffing up to the top of the hill, all of them armed with rifles, and for a moment he thought he would have to kill again. Most of these hunters were city men, dressed in fancy hunting clothes, wool pants and jackets with shooting patches on the shoulders. But although they might not have been the hardened woodsman McAllister was, they were just as capable of killing, and that fact glowed blatantly in their eyes.

Carrying the rifle, and with the Colt tucked behind his belt, José strode forward, hoping he wouldn't have to resort to gunplay to bring the scuffle to an end. He reached McAllister before the others and grabbed him by the shoulder, yelling out his name. Such was McAllister's fury, he didn't even seem to hear him, and he lashed out at whatever had touched his shoulder. José dodged the blow, dropping his rifle as he lunged out of the way.

As he whirled back, he heard the sickening *thud* of metal against bone as one of the men yelled out a curse and slammed the metal butt plate of his rifle into the back of McAllister's head. McAllister stumbled forward, trying to turn around, but the blow had taken his equilibrium away. He fell to the side, catching himself with one hand.

The same man, using his rifle like a shovel, sank it into McAllister's stomach, tearing the wind from his throat, and through the excitement in his head José could hear one of the other men yelling at the top of his voice.

"Kill 'im! Kill the son of a bitch! Shoot him, Johnson, or I will. He's gonna get back up! Shoot 'im now!"

The man was almost frenzied, but José could tell by a glance at him he didn't have the nerve to carry out his own commands. Yet his words finally sank into Johnson's head, for when José looked at the man who was being addressed, he saw with a falling heart the subtle change in his eyes, the look of a man who is agitated enough and has heard something in the back of his head just enough to suddenly believe it his only course of action.

With a sudden sucking in of breath, José's right hand drove for the pistol in his belt.

Chapter Twenty-Five

McAllister knelt half-conscious on the ground, retching. Johnson started to draw back the hammer of his rifle, its bore aimed at McAllister's head. The popping report of the Colt .44 whipped all their heads about, and the slug broke Johnson's arm before he could even draw his hammer all the way back. With a cry of pain, he hurled the rifle from him, clawing at his arm with his left hand.

Like a cornered animal, José pivoted the gun barrel toward the other three men, and they froze, motionless as carved Indians. One of them, reading José's mind, opened his fingers slowly and let his rifle drop to the ground at his feet.

José swiveled his eyes on the man who had done all the yelling. The man's face was pale. His mouth worked silently, as if praying, and he took a step backward, still clutching his rifle tightly but seeming unaware of its presence. The second man who still held onto his weapon just stared at José with his mouth open. His eyes strayed toward the Colt but nev 'r looked directly at it as if for fear it would go off.

"Drop the rifles," José barked. No one seemed to notice the tremble in his voice, or if they did it didn't matter. The two rifles fell to the gravel, the awful grating sound of rock against fine metal having no visible effect on their owners.

Bulliard lay on his side on the ground, and José dared a glance at him. He was alive; that was apparent from the way his sides heaved in and out with breath, but he made no other sound than wheezing through blood and broken teeth. His hands were clutched tightly to his face.

Johnson had dropped to his knees and was whimpering quietly, staring at José. It disgusted him to hear a grown man make such noises. "Now back on down the hill," he spoke again. "Go get yer horses and bring one back up here fer Bulliard. You go, too," he ordered Johnson. "Maybe that'll work some of the fight out of yuh." The words came from José's mouth like they weren't even his, and he realized it was because for the moment they weren't. He had willed himself into the mind of McAllister, knowing that was the only way his nerves would survive this confrontation.

There was no more fight on the railroad men's part, and they left their guns lying where they fell. José wondered if they wouldn't just leave Bulliard here. If they did, he would probably die, for a storm was coming on, and José certainly didn't intend to look after him. The world would have been better off without him anyway. On that score he had to agree with McAllister. If it hadn't been for the fact it would make McAllister once more a killer, he would have wished death on Bulliard himself. As it was, the railroad man's face and body had already suffered punishment enough for that day's sins, if a man could pay for the death of an eagle.

When the men were gone, José rushed to McAllister and helped him up. He was still retching, hanging onto his stomach, and two thin trails of blood ran down the back of his head where the rifle had struck him. José wrapped his head as best he could, then helped him sit back down as he hurriedly broke camp. He wanted to be gone before the men came back for Bulliard.

Loading everything he could on the bay horse, José threw a tarp over the gear and tied it down with a diamond hitch—a formidable chore for a man to do alone. Then he saddled his roan and McAllister's blood bay, and it took all his strength to help the big man onto his horse. For good measure he lashed his hands to the saddle horn. He doubted he would stay on if left to his own strength, for not much of that appeared to remain.

As José mounted the roan and took the lead rope of the bay, McAllister's mount fell naturally in behind them, and they started up the draw. Huge black clouds were quickly closing on them from the south when they made the crest of Haystack Mountain two hours later, and the smell of rain was strong on the wind. The summer-dried grass waved back and forth, pitching and rolling in time with the gusts of cool air that swatted at it like an angry giant's hands.

Haystack Mountain, appearing flat and wide from either side, was deceiving, José learned, for in some places on top it was only two or three feet wide. Thus the nickname, Hogsback. Here, the cold wind buffeted them, nearly blowing José's hat away before he tightened down his braided hat strings. So José, having no idea where he was headed except in the general direction of Soda Springs, rode down the western slope, out of limber pine and rock outcrops into a landscape made up largely of shortgrass interrupted by heavy stands of subalpine and Douglas fir. The wind diminished in the timber, but the going was slow and difficult through the deadfall and undergrowth, and José prayed they cleared it by the time the sun went down.

With a brilliant flash that seemed to scorch the tops of the trees, lightning branched crookedly across the sky. Immediately, thunder bellowed like a cannon, then rumbled so nearby it sounded like a hundred washtubs first falling, then being dragged across the rocks until it rolled away into the distance. Then the rain came down.

The sky was black and sullen, the rain shaking loose in metallic gray sheets that drenched the valley and mountaintops. Now and then lightning played across the horizon, then sent its grumblings José's way, and he pulled his hat lower over his eyes and pressed on, riding through stretches of fir, then aspen or sagebrush. He didn't feel "lucky" now; his position on top of the world with the rare autumn lightning was not to be envied.

Hours passed, and José wiped wearily at the rain that pelted the side of his face. They had ridden out of the heavy timber half an hour earlier, just in time, he saw, for day to lose the battle to the storm. Even as he rode the dark closed in, earlier than normal, but in spite of it José rode on, eyes casting cautiously through the sheets of driving rain for any sign of trouble.

They splashed across the Portneuf sometime after dark, and José said a silent prayer of thanks for the good sense of the horses beneath them, for they never balked when the cold water rushed up to their stomachs. They turned south along the railroad tracks, and then half an hour or so later drew near to the hot springs where the Portneuf made its sharp bend west. José paused near the hot springs, thinking of how good that warm water would feel against his skin now. He and McAllister and the horses were about as wet as they could get, and the sleet that now pelted them threatened to turn to snow if the temperature dropped any further.

Hoping the snow did come, to hide sign of his and McAllister's passage, José walked the horses across the bridge, the hollow clopping sounds of their hooves almost drowned in the howling storm. Minutes later they pulled up in the yard of the Bonn homestead. With unreal abruptness, the sleet subsided, and an uncommonly bright moon lanced its rays through a window in the clouds.

In the morning, José rolled over and blinked against a bright light. A sliver of it burst through a crack around the door of the dank shed where he and McAllister had spent the night. He looked over at McAllister, who lay against the wall, covered with a damp blanket. He had to watch for a second or two before the man's chest expanded with breath, and at the faint movement he sighed with relief. Leaving McAllister asleep, he stumbled outside, shivering in the chill air. A fresh new light blanketed the grass, the trees, and the muddy, furrowed fields. He stood and soaked in the beauty around him, the fresh blue sky and shimmering yellow and green leaves of the cottonwoods along the river. He wished the beauty could last.

Trying to press his tousled hair down with a tongue-wetted hand, José stuck his hat down low over his eyes and started toward the Bonns' cabin. He knocked on the door, and it was quickly opened by Clara Bonn.

"Good morning, José," she said with a smile, brushing flour off her shirt sleeve as the little ones crowded up behind her to get a look at him. "I'm working on some biscuits, if you'd like to come in. Henry and the boys are out hunting."

"Thank you, ma'am. I'd like to just get some grub into my friend, if you'd let me buy somethin' offa you. Maybe some soup or somethin'. I don't want any charity," José said flatly.

Clara handed him a stern glare. "Now there's no need for you to say that. I have never offered charity, José. You know that. I will expect the same from you one day when I visit you at *your* house. But I won't take money from you."

"All right," José laughed, shamed by her blunt refusal. "But you'd best promise to stop by my place someday. I'm beholden to yuh."

Clara gave him soup and soda crackers, and he took them over to the shed, thinking the smell of the soup might wake McAllister. He was surprised to see him already awake, sitting quietly against the wall. His eyes swung to the door and riveted there until José blocked the sunshine, and then their gazes locked.

For a moment, neither one spoke. McAllister hadn't said a word since yesterday's incident. He had been conscious all the long trip to the homestead, but he hadn't been in a talking mood, and it seemed to take all his strength to grit his teeth and hang on to the saddle horn. Now, the black look of his face told José his words weren't long in coming.

"Well, they done rolled the ball," he growled suddenly, pushing to his feet and almost at the same time tearing the bandages off his head, dropping them carelessly to the floor. His blood-stained hair fell forward, hanging in his eyes until he swept it back, his fingers breaking through the tangles.

José stared silently, waiting for McAllister to continue. His fingers were tight on the rim of the soup bowl, and he didn't even notice his left hand crushing the brittle crackers.

"They're gonna pay fer this, boy. I ain't lettin' it lie. There's only so far a man c'n be pushed by them rich sons o' bitches, an' I been shoved to the edge."

McAllister paused, staring at José expectantly, as if awaiting a response. His gray eyes had changed, as if darkened by storm clouds, and his mouth was drawn in a thin, bitter line.

José shrugged and set the bowl and crackers down on a shelf. "I don't know what you want me to say."

Irritated, McAllister waved a hand as if to brush José away. "Ah hell, you wouldn't. Well, I'm goin' after them railroad boys. You comin' with me, or ain't yuh?"

José's face remained calm, for he wasn't surprised. He had expected this, knowing how McAllister already felt about the wealthy, the railroad, and Andrew Bulliard, and knowing how he had loved his pet eagle. It had been laid out there plain between them now.

"I think you oughtta wait," José replied simply, his voice emotionless. "You already took care of Bulliard anyway."

"Wait fer what?"

"To see if a posse comes after yuh. I don't know, but you might've killed Bulliard—stove in his head."

McAllister looked at him sharply, then his eyes narrowed and became ugly. "Then he went too easy."

José shrugged. "Whether he's dead or not, we'd better get to somebody we c'n trust an' hole up. That rain last night hid our trail, but it's only a matter of time before someone runs into us. This country's pretty small, when it comes to findin' folks who kill important people. You told me that yerself."

McAllister grunted and turned away. José shifted his feet nervously. His friend was on the verge of doing something horrible. The only question was, what would it be?

Suddenly, McAllister whirled back, his eyes almost glowingly intense. "If yer right about Bulliard, then I ain't got no regrets, except his life wasn't an even trade fer that bird. But I guess yer right about holin' up. We better skin south fer a while an' see what comes along on the wind. Let's head up Dempsey Creek, here. I know some places we c'n hide."

José's mind worked swiftly, feeling the pressure of McAllister's eyes on him. "That won't work, Gray. We gotta be where we c'n find out if Bulliard's dead. Who'll bring word to us up Dempsey Creek? A bird?"

McAllister's eyes narrowed again, and the burning look he sliced José with sent a shiver along his spine. "All right, then what's *yer* idea?"

"We go over to the Woodlands' place." McAllister immediately shook his head and started to open his mouth to speak. "Now hold it," José said, raising his hands to halt McAllister's words. "You c'n trust the Woodlands. Rebecca already saved yer skin once. They'll let us know if Bulliard died. Hell, they were here the night we fought with Bulliard's men. They know what he's like. It was self defense." He knew it really wasn't self defense, but it sounded like a convincing argument.

McAllister's face relaxed a little. "Ah, hell, Lucky. I know yuh miss that red-haired gal. That's the main reason yuh wanna go there—that's plain. But if Bulliard dies, they'll put out a reward fer his killer, an' I don't trust many people when money comes inta play. Yer about the only one. You an' maybe the Shoshones.

"But I'll tell yuh what. Let's head over there. We'll take the long way over the mountains. I'll find me a spot to hole up in the trees, an' you c'n go on down to yer people. When yuh get word about Bulliard, just come after me. We c'n make our plans when we know if he's alive."

José breathed a quiet sigh of relief, knowing he had won a round. At least maybe they would be safe for a while now. But the thought of what McAllister had in mind still scared him. If it was murder, he wanted no part of it. Even robbery, of the railroad or whatever it might be. José wasn't a killer or a thief, and he swore to himself he wouldn't be dragged into this affair any deeper than he already was. But if he could get McAllister away from here, and back up in the hills for a while, maybe his friend would have time to think, to come to his senses. Maybe José wouldn't have to turn him down when he came asking for a partner in crime.

McAllister downed the soup and started on the crackers as he and José stepped outside. They hadn't discussed just what the Bonns knew about the incident with Bulliard, but McAllister must have assumed José had told them all of it, because he wanted to saddle up and ride out without saying good bye. José refused, and his mind would not be changed, so while McAllister went to saddle the horses José walked to the house to see Clara Bonn for what he felt deep inside would be the last time.

Clara said good bye with a bearhug, patting José's back with three sound slaps. "You take care now, José." She looked curiously toward McAllister but made no mention of his aloofness.

José looked at Clara for a long moment, first trying to decide if he should ask her what was on his mind, then trying to untie his tongue. He just had to know. "Mrs. Bonn," he began. "Last time I was here Charlie told me Jared was gonna ask Rebecca Woodland to get married. Do you mind if I ask why he didn't?"

Clara smiled knowingly, folding her hands in front of her. "Well, dear, Jared *did* ask Rebecca to marry him. She didn't exactly say no, but she wanted to wait." Clara glanced around her as if making sure none of her family could hear her, then went on. "Rebecca is a lovely girl. A beautiful young woman. And very intelligent, too. I would be proud to have her as a daughter-in-law. And I love Jared with all my heart, and I feel for him, too. Young love is hard, as you must know, too. But Jared can't have what isn't his, and I don't think Rebecca ever will be. It's hard to say *what* Rebecca wants. But Sister Woodland has told me Rebecca speaks of you often. Nothing serious, mind you," she said with kind warning. "Don't be too anxious. But I would talk to Rebecca, if you have feelings for her. Nobody can tell you what to do, but they say some people are destined for each other. Don't ever let anyone say I stood in the way of destiny, even if I do still think Jared and Rebecca would make a lovely young couple. You're a fine looking young man yourself, José, and Rebecca is long since of marrying age, as far as I'm concerned."

Trying to keep his countenance calm, José listened silently to Clara, while his heart nearly beat him to death from inside. Thoughts he hadn't even dared hope for welled up inside him and threatened to burst out on his face, and he was afraid it already showed in his eyes. "Thanks. Thanks for everything, ma'am," he said simply. He turned and saw McAllister standing with the horses, looking studiously toward the north to avoid meeting Clara's gaze. "It looks like Gray's ready. I better go."

Clara smiled warmly, reached out and squeezed his hand. "All right, young man. You take care of yourself. Come back and visit if you can."

José turned away and strode to McAllister, taking his horse's reins and swinging up without a word. He and McAllister rode out of the yard, and Clara Bonn watched them until they disappeared over the sagebrush heading up Dempsey Creek.

Two days later, José dropped out of the Bear River Mountains and walked the horses across the three foot-deep Bear River, his heart lightening with each step, carrying him closer to the Woodland homestead. McAllister had remained behind in a stand of Douglas fir on top of a nameless ridge in the mountains. It was a secluded spot, with a spring nearby and plenty of graze for his horse. It was unlikely any searching posse would find him hiding there.

With the familiar mountains looming ever nearer, José turned into the lane that led to the Woodland place, and he could scarcely quell his excitement when the acrid smell of the sulphur springs drifted to his nose. The ranch buildings appeared two miles later, when he came over the rise, and the familiar Jersey cattle looked up from grazing to watch him pass.

When he neared the house, he caught sight of little Jacob running for the front door. At least he guessed it to be Jacob, though he appeared to have grown. He would be about seven years old now.

After Jacob went inside, the door soon reopened, and Martha Woodland stepped onto the threshold, holding the door with her right hand, supporting herself against the door frame with her left. Suddenly, she stepped away from the cabin, leaving the door open, and ran out toward him, holding her dress up out of the dirt. A radiant smile lit her face and set her eyes aglow. She came to a stop at the side of José's horse when he drew up and smiled broadly down at her.

Without a word, José leaped out of the saddle, and they threw their arms around each other, both laughing. Finally, Martha leaned away, still smiling. "Let me look at you. My, how you've grown! But still the same pretty black hair." She ruffled his curls playfully.

José blushed, glancing about the yard. Martha caught the look in his eyes and smiled knowingly. "Terrence is dragging firewood out of the canyon, and he took everyone with him but Jacob." She turned and patted the boy, who had just come up beside her, on the head. "He stayed to protect me."

José laughed. "You should feel perty safe then. How are yuh, Jacob?"

"Fine," the boy said with a bashful shrug. "Could you call me Jake now? Pa says I'm growin' up."

"Sure, Jake." He reached out and tousled his hair.

Martha offered to help him put up the horses, and the three of them went to the barn and curried and fed them, turning them loose in the corral. When they had finished, they started out the big barn door and saw Terrence Woodland approaching with the team. Engrossed in his work, he didn't notice them standing there until he had drawn the team to a halt in front of the wood pile and leaned against it, wiping the sweat from his face. The horses stood with sides heaving, lather oozing out from under their harnesses. Three twenty-foot logs stretched out behind them with a chain connecting them to the harness.

Surprise leaped into Woodland's green eyes when he caught the three of them watching him. It took him a moment to recognize José, but then his ground-eating strides carried him to them in seconds. "José!" he thundered. "How are yuh, boy? What brings you back this way?" He didn't wait for an answer but clasped José by both shoulders and looked down at him. He still towered over him by a good ten inches.

José gazed up, smiling. As best he could, he tried to answer the questions Woodland fired at him. Afterward, they all walked to the water pot while Woodland poured cool water over his head and neck, shaking his head like a bear and splashing droplets everywhere.

José was looking expectantly over the way Woodland had come, wondering where Rebecca was. He ached to see her face, to see how she had changed in the thirteen months since he had left her. They hadn't parted very happily, and if not for Ben Trombell's and Clara Bonn's kindly advice he would have been filled with dread at the thought of her seeing him. In truth, he probably wouldn't even be here. But those two seemed to think she had forgiven him for any cowardice he had shown, and now, after facing down the bear, his own conscience felt ready for a reunion. But as always there was that faint inkling of a doubt down deep in his heart. He even nourished it, he decided. He had to keep the doubt there so his disappointment wouldn't be too harsh if he found out he really meant nothing to the girl.

Woodland looked at José, then over at Martha with a knowing wink. "I reckon there's someone else you'd rather see than us, José."

José blushed and dropped his eyes quickly, feeling the heat in his face. "Well, no, I was just lookin'," he said. "Wonderin' if the rest of the family was comin' along."

"Well, sure, son. I understand." Woodland's deep-throated laughter rumbled like thunder, and José had to smile. He had missed that sound. Woodland wasn't a light-hearted man, so when he laughed it seemed special, and it eased the minds of everyone around, knowing this hulk of a man was in a laughing mood.

"I'll tell you what, José. I got another load or so of logs to haul out of the canyon. I'll let you drive the team on up there, and we'll just surprise old Becc— I mean we'll just surprise the kids. I was gonna grab a biscuit or somethin', but I got a feelin' we're in for a big feast tonight." He winked again at Martha. "So I think I'll just save my appetite. Don't know about you."

"Oh, sure," said José nonchalantly. "I c'n wait." In truth, his stomach was grumbling with hunger, for he hadn't eaten all day. But he had something more important on his mind right now.

Heading the team up the road, with Woodland and Jacob walking beside him, José's mind raced ahead. What would Rebecca look like now? And more importantly, what would she act like? Would they still be able to talk openly like they used to? Would she have that twinkle in her eyes when she laughed? The thought of it made his stomach queasy. Would her hair hang long, or would it be drawn back in a bun to keep it out of her way while she worked? How old was Rebecca, sixteen now? Maybe seventeen. He didn't know if she'd ever told him her birthday, and if she had he couldn't remember it now.

All around them in the canyon, aspen and maple leaves fluttered in the breeze. Some of the aspens were still green, but a good share of their leaves had turned to gold, and most of the maples were brilliant red. The wash of all the colors together was a sight to behold, and the mixture of their scents, together with that of mahogany, was milder but more fragrant than any rose. And more genuine, he thought.

The creek running over the rocks gave a welcoming chuckle and a warm hello. All this José took in with his heart in his throat. The only thing that would make it better would be Rebecca smiling at him the way she used to, and the touch of her hand on his.

They must have heard Woodland and José coming, for when José first saw Rebecca, Anna, and Laban they were walking down the skid trail to meet them. José was blocked a little by the big horses, and with Woodland walking beside him he was dwarfed. To anyone more than a few yards away, it probably looked like Woodland was driving the team, especially to someone who expected him to be. Woodland had an unwitting way of making everyone around him seem inconspicuous, even non-existent.

So when Rebecca got close, and her eyes caught the form of the person beside her father, she faltered in her stride. Taken by surprise, it took her a moment, but it was obvious when the look in her eyes changed from one of confusion to one of recognition. Her mouth popped open, and she brought her hand half up to it, then froze.

The other two children noticed him seconds later, but it was Anna who recovered first. "José!" she squealed excitedly.

José gave Anna a self-conscious smile, feeling Rebecca's eyes on him. "Hi, Anna. Hi, Laban." He thought Rebecca's name and meant to speak it, but it caught in his throat, and he just stared at her like a dumb kid. He didn't realize she was staring at him much the same way, searching his eyes.

José suddenly realized Anna had him around the waist, hugging him, and he gave her a squeeze, then punched Laban lightly in the shoulder as he walked over. "How are yuh, Laban? Boy, yer gettin' big." He hoped his voice sounded lighter than it felt. He ached to say something to Rebecca, but he couldn't get his voice to work when he looked at her. And she hadn't moved, either. She still stood exactly where she had stopped at the sight of him.

It was Woodland who broke the silence between them. "Well, come on, you two. Ain't seen each other in over a year an' all you c'n do is stand an' gawk. At least say hi."

José blushed, feeling foolish. He forced a smile, knowing it was a sorry effort. It wasn't until he saw the smile start and grow on Rebecca's face that his own lips seemed to melt, and every emotion he felt for this girl sprang forth in a grin that spread from ear to ear. "Hi, Rebecca."

"Hi, José." Rebecca was moving forward even as she replied, her hands drawn up in tight little fists. She walked as if it took every bit of effort she could muster not to lunge into his arms. Her face, beautiful beyond belief in the afternoon light, strained not to laugh, or cry, or succumb to whatever incredible feeling lit her eyes like polished jade as it struggled to burst forth.

Rebecca came to an abrupt halt three feet from José, just out of his reach. Anna and Laban wisely backed away, giving their older sister space. Rebecca seemed stuck to her tracks, and suddenly José became aware she was shaking. He saw the quiver in the sleeves of her blouse, the movement of her throat as she swallowed. And then without warning she threw herself into his arms, hugging him around the neck. When José realized what had happened, he encircled her back with his arms, hugging her so tightly he was afraid he would break her ribs. He just hoped she would tell him before that happened, because he didn't want to let go of his own accord. He didn't care if Woodland was right there watching. He didn't care about the other children. He only knew his dreams of the past year were answered while he held this girl—this young woman—tight, and all the nightmares vanished like storm clouds dissolved by the sun.

Just then José heard the voice of Noah Woodland, deepened a little since he'd seen him last. He had just walked out of the trees. "Looks like Becky c'n quit pinin' away. She's got just what she wants."

Martha Woodland spread a table fit for royalty that evening, serving José's favorite dishes, including large sausages smothered in chili sauce. These reminded him of the *chorizos* his mother used to make. They ate venison steaks, cooked rare and smothered in gravy, with potatoes, onions, carrots, turnips, and squash—autumn's bounty. Last of all she brought out the pumpkin pies José suspected he'd been smelling, topped off with real cream. When the evening finally began to ebb, the young Basque had no doubt he was more than welcome in this house. He was like the prodigal son returned home.

While they ate, he told them all about the events of the past year, of the mustangs, the Indian reservation, the railroad, the fine hotels he had seen, McAllister's eagle, and of course his final test. His eleven day examination culminating in his facing the grizzly bear, then walking away. He told that story with unhidden pride. When he was done, Rebecca's and Martha's eyes were both filled with tears, and he caught Anna rubbing the goose bumps off her arms.

All good things must end, and when it had been dark for an hour or two and the wicks were burning low in the two chimney lamps, Woodland decided it was time for bed. After he had shooed the younger children off, including Noah, he turned to Rebecca and José, who both had their eyes lowered, hoping somehow they wouldn't be noticed.

"That goes for you, too, Becca. It's been a long day, and it'll be just as long tomorrow."

Rebecca swallowed, visibly disappointed. She shot a glance over at José, then looked up pleadingly at her father. "Can't we just stay up a little longer? We're not children, you know."

Woodland grunted. "I'm painful aware of that, sis. But you need your sleep, same as the rest of us. Besides, you know how Mama feels about young folks like you bein' alone together at night. An' you both know it ain't smart. Anyway, the Lord says we should bed down early so we c'n get up early. I tend to agree."

Several moments of silence passed, while José summoned his courage. He had to have more time before the lights went out. He had to tell Woodland, Rebecca—someone—about his friend hiding in the hills. He had to tell them about the eagle being killed and Bulliard possibly being dead, too. The longer he let it go, the harder it would be. And if any danger was to come to this house because of José leading a posse here, he wanted the Woodlands to be facing it with their eyes open. The time to explain was now, not when guns were pointed at the house.

"Sir? I have to talk to yuh about somethin'. I have somethin' that needs sayin' tonight. It can't wait any longer."

Woodland watched him quietly, judging him. José met his gaze with a steady one of his own, not challenging, but straightforward. "Well, say your piece, son."

José cleared his throat. "Well, sir, I'd kinda like to say it to Becca first. I have to see what she thinks. I promise I won't lay a hand on her," he added quickly.

Woodland stared at José, and then his face relaxed. "All right. You ain't of our religion, José, but I trust you as much as any Saint I ever met. Go on an' tell her outside. But don't be long. I'm needin' my sleep, too."

José smiled gratefully and turned his head to look at Rebecca, whose eyes were full of bewilderment. They rose together and went outside. José walked beside her and stopped in the middle of the yard. When she stopped and looked up questioningly at him, reaching for his hand, he jerked his away. He looked at her apologetically. "I promised I wouldn't touch you."

Rebecca just stared for a moment, then smiled. "You're right. I forgot. Can I say something before you start?" She didn't await a reply. "That's why I like you so much,

José. Your honesty makes me happy. And I know Papa and Mama respect you, too."

Embarrassed, José looked down. "Thanks. That's just the way I was raised."

There was silence then for half a minute while José struggled with a way to begin. Finally, Rebecca reached out and put her finger under his chin. When he started to pull away, she said, "I didn't promise not to touch *you*. Now what did you want to say? Just say it."

José smiled. McAllister had drilled into his mind the evils of "beating around the bush," or "going the long way around the barn," as he put it. And with the encouragement from Rebecca, he told her in detail what had occurred the day after he faced the grizzly.

When he had finished, Rebecca assured him it would be best to tell her father and mother, so they called Woodland and Martha out, and José repeated everything once more. His last words were the only sound for another half a minute. José looked from Rebecca, to Martha, to Woodland, trying to read in their faces how they were taking the story, trying to guess what they would have to say. Martha's brow was knitted with worry, but her husband's face was an inscrutable mask.

Finally, Woodland cleared his throat ominously. "Well, José, it doesn't look good. You know, whether this fella Bulliard dies or not, they'll likely be lookin' for your friend. That's an aggravated battery charge. It's a felony. You know what that means?"

José swallowed. "Yeah, I reckon. Ben Trombell taught me some about laws."

"Oh, that's right. The English teacher took you in." He chuckled. "That Ben's a good man. Well, anyway, you're lookin' at a felony, son. That's prison time if he gets caught an' convicted. An' he could hang if Bulliard dies."

"Honey," Martha said emphatically.

Woodland looked at her. "I'm just tellin' it straight, dear. José's a man, an' he has a right to know. No sense runnin' around with blinders on."

The big man turned back to José, and he didn't speak for several moments. When he did it was with a gravity that made José's soul throb, knowing what was to follow. "I reckon you know what else I have to say, son. They'll be wantin' you for aggravated battery, too. Maybe even attempted murder. You shot a man. An' you c'n bet them fellas'll have a different story worked up than the one you told. All folks ain't as honest as you an' me."

José sighed heavily, looking over at Rebecca. His stomach felt like it had five pounds of mud in the pit of it. His eyes were dull. What would become of him? He had fired his pistol at Johnson only to protect McAllister from sure death. Would they send him to prison for that? Would he not get his chance to stay with Rebecca after all? The thought made him want to cry. And what about McAllister? It was plain their days together had come to an end. McAllister might as well drift on, as he was inclined to anyway. Maybe he could head into Wyoming, like he had once talked about. Just change his identity and disappear. It was the only hope he had.

As for José, was there *any* hope? Would he, too, have to leave Idaho Territory, drift to some other place, and leave all thoughts of Rebecca Woodland far behind? Now that he had made it back to her, and she had *accepted* him back, he wasn't sure he *could* leave. He wasn't sure it wasn't better to face a court of law than to leave this young woman again.

And then a thought came to José, a desperate thought. The realization that there was one man who might help him—Deputy Clint Goss. He remembered the Soda Springs lawman telling him to come to him if he ever needed help. He didn't know what, if anything, Goss could do for him now, but he had to get to him with his own side of the story before it was too late.

Robert McAllister sat silently and listened to José. His face seemed to lighten a little when José first started talking and told him Andrew Bulliard had survived. And with bandages still wrapped around his head he was back to work at the railroad station, though word was he had put in for a transfer. But for no outwardly obvious reason, McAllister's face suddenly blackened again, and his eyes grew dark like thunderheads.

"So he kills Golden an' then jus' goes about his business," McAllister growled angrily. "Where the hell's the justice? An' what about the fella you shot? You hear anything 'bout him?"

José went on to tell how the four men with Bulliard had all disappeared from the country two days after the incident, headed back east without pressing charges. José and McAllister conjectured the men thought McAllister might die after his beating and they hadn't wanted to stay in the neighborhood for questioning. It was Deputy Clint Goss who had related developments to José. José had gone to him to turn himself in, and Goss had admitted already knowing the story. There would be no action against José. And as for McAllister, Bulliard had pressed no charges either. He seemed to want out of the country, too.

After spending the night with McAllister in the trees, José rose early and prepared to head back to the Woodlands'. He hadn't told McAllister his plans yet, and it wasn't until he was throwing on his saddlebags he realized McAllister knew.

"Why don't you hang on with me, Lucky?"

The words took José by surprise. He turned about to see McAllister watching him, nursing a cup of coffee in his hands. "They did us both wrong. Not just me. Golden was yer eagle, too. She was the symbol o' freedom, remember? Yers an' mine both. They killed 'er. They killed 'er like they been killin' everything. Like they been killin' every*one* that has any wild spirit in 'em. They're tryin' to drive us down to the dust, Lucky. You an' me. They're stretchin' them damn iron ribbons over this country, runnin' their trains in places they weren't never meant to go. Just take a look around. I've showed yuh.

"Come on. Let's hit 'em where it hurts. Let's take their money an' run an' don't look back. We c'n hit that train station an' get inta Oregon or Washington before they know what happened. Hell, maybe even Canada. I hear they still got virgin timber up there you couldn't ride through in a year. Elk an' deer an' moose—an' sheep. Goats so white it makes yer eyes hurt. That's the place fer you an' me. Wha' d' yuh say? Come with me. It'll be the first an' only time we steal. We'll hit 'em hard, take what they got, an' live off it an' the land. They're fixin' to kill us, Lucky," he said, driving his right fist into the palm of his left hand. "You saw that fer yerself. They're either gonna shoot us outright or drive us inta the ground an' snuff out our will to live. You gotta make yer stand now."

When McAllister's speech ended, José looked out over the canyon. As fate would have it, an eagle soared there, its wings spread wide, its tail tilting just slightly to turn it this way or that as it glided across the air currents. Holding his reply, he motioned toward the eagle with his chin, and McAllister turned and saw it.

A faraway look engulfed his eyes, and he rubbed a hand absently down his bearded cheek. "There she is, Lucky. The symbol o' freedom."

José sighed again. McAllister had said he had to make his stand, and he was about to. But he wouldn't make the choice McAllister hoped for. The lawlessness had to end somewhere, even if it meant an end to his freedom, in a sense. Running from the law wasn't freedom anyway. Sooner or later, they always caught up to you. There were too many people who trusted José Olano. Ben Trombell, Alfredo, Clint Goss, and most importantly, Rebecca Woodland and her family. He wasn't going to destroy that trust. And he wasn't going to destroy any chance he might have to win Rebecca Woodland's hand. She meant the world to him. To join McAllister now meant to lose her forever.

"I am takin' a stand, Gray. Just like you said." He looked gravely into the older man's eyes. "You've taught me well. I ain't as good as you, but I know enough to get by. You've been my friend, an' I'll never forget it. An' you saved my life, in more ways than one."

McAllister shrugged that off, a dullness coming into his eyes as he came to understand the answer José was building toward. "We've saved each other's lives more than once, Lucky."

José nodded. "Yeah. An' I won't forget it. But I can't go stealin'. It just ain't in me. If I could stop you by askin', I would."

"No point askin'."

"I said I'm not," José retorted, half-angry. "I just hope you don't get yerself killed."

"Hell, what's it to you?" McAllister's voice turned suddenly cold, icy like the light in his eyes. "I taught you what you wanted outta me. Now you c'n just leave. You got what you want waitin' back at that cabin. Well, go on then. Get the hell outta here an' don't come back. I don't need you around no more. I always said I work better alone."

Numbly, José stared at the bigger man, an empty feeling in the pit of his stomach. He had to leave. He had to ride away while he still had control of his emotions. He turned around and walked briskly to his roan. His eyes were blurred, but he found the reins, then the stirrup, and swung into the saddle. His heart ached inside him. His eyes burned. He had never thought it would end this way. Robert McAllister had been his best friend, and in one bitter moment he threw it all away. All the months of friendship, of constant companionship, of the teaching-learning partnership.

A hot tear trickled down José's cheek, and he swiftly brushed its trail away, hoping McAllister wasn't watching. He wanted to see his friend one last time, but he wouldn't let him see him crying. He turned and rode into the bottom of the canyon.

McAllister stood silently on the slope of the canyon, outlined against the dark trees behind him. He watched José Olano's roan stud pick its way down through the shale and brush. His heart throbbed. Why had he spoken that way to Lucky? Sure, his feelings were hurt he wouldn't go with him, but the kid had to choose his own way. It was one of the most important things he had drilled into him. *You stubborn bastard*, he said to himself. *Why?*

Yell after him, he thought suddenly. *Say something. Wave. Let him know you're not angry. Let him know you're still his friend.* But he couldn't let José see Robert McAllister grovel. He was a man—he wouldn't apologize. It was a sign of weakness.

And then José was gone, down into the heavy brush and rock in the bottom of the canyon, and McAllister could no longer see him. "Lord, what did I do?" he said aloud. "God forgive me." He looked longingly one last time down the silent canyon, then saw the shadow of the eagle glide by on the slope.

"Good bye, Lucky. So long, my friend."

Chapter Twenty-Six

It was evening, and purple shadows gathered about the Woodlands' yard like pools of mist as José and Rebecca sat on the bench at the front of the cabin and watched the panorama of the Bear River Mountains, a wash of orange and pink clouds spilled out behind them.

A rider appeared past the thicket of aspens in the crest of the lane. José knew from the white hat and the slouched, easy way he sat the saddle it was Ben Trombell. His friend drew up in the yard and saw José and Rebecca watching him. He climbed down stiffly and turned his eyes to them, and a great sadness shone in them like the fading day. "Hello, Rebecca. Hello, son. Is your friend anywhere around?" He looked unwaveringly now at José.

José stood up uncertainly. "My friend? You mean Gray?"

"Yes, that's what you called him. Mr. McAllister. Is he here?"

José shook his head, dread creeping up inside him. "No. He didn't come back with me."

Trombell sighed, and his face visibly lightened. "That's too bad. I just wanted to say hello. Does he still ride that blood bay horse with a white marking on its left hip and a blaze that looks like a question mark?"

"Sure, last I saw him he did."

Trombell nodded musingly, stepping right up to José. "Well, how've you been, anyway?" He smiled, throwing his arm around José's shoulders. "Where's everyone else?"

Taking a curious moment to study his friend's face, José nodded toward the house. "I've been fine, and everyone else is inside, there. Gettin' ready for supper. Why don't you come on in?" He led the way into the house, wondering at Trombell's odd behavior. Something was wrong, and he was afraid he knew what it was.

Later, after supper was over, Ben Trombell leaned back in his chair and said conversationally to Terrence Woodland, "You probably didn't hear that someone robbed the Oregon Short Line depot in Pocatello."

José's heart leaped, and he stared at Trombell. His eyes shifted fleetingly to Rebecca before he dropped them to his plate.

"No, I didn't hear that," Woodland replied. "When did it happen?"

"Oh, just a couple of days ago."

José waited breathlessly after Woodland's next question. "Anybody hurt?"

Trombell glanced at José, then quickly away. "No, fortunately. But they got away with close to a thousand dollars."

"Who did it, do they know?"

Trombell shrugged. "If they do, they're not saying. They don't even know how many were in on it. There's a posse out searching, but there isn't much sign left to follow, they say."

José stared at his plate until the two men's voices turned to a low, dull hum. He felt the heat in his face and perspiration break out along his sides. Trombell must suspect McAllister had committed the robbery, or why had he asked about him? Had he thought José was in on it? It seemed that way, but that was just speculation on José's part.

So his friend had gone through with his plans. Whether anyone else knew it or not, José had no doubt. McAllister was not a man who did things brashly, without contemplation. He had said he would rob the railroad, and he had, even though it took him two weeks to get the job done. José found himself saying a silent prayer of thanks no one had been hurt.

He stood out in the yard long after Ben Trombell had gone to sleep in the barn. He wore a linen duster over a wool vest against the night's cold and stared unblinking at the brilliant stars overhead. The Big Dipper told him it was near midnight now. Somewhere in the aspens a great-horned owl hooted, and instinctively he almost answered it, like he would have in his carefree days with McAllister. But he found he didn't have the heart.

Hearing the door open behind him, he stiffened, but he didn't turn around. Although he strained his ears, he couldn't make out the sound of footfalls, so he guessed it wasn't Woodland. He became suddenly aware of a presence beside him, and his sixth sense told him who it was. He glanced sideways to find Rebecca standing there. Her arms were folded against the cold, and she gazed across the yard with a faraway look in her eyes. He knew when she felt his eyes upon her, for a subtle change came over her face. She blinked, a prolonged action, and turned her head simultaneously. When she opened her eyes they rested on José's, black and shadowed in the starlight. She held her strong chin up and met his gaze steadily, and then at last she unfolded her arms and stepped into his, holding him tightly. There was no talking, no more movement, no sound. Just two young people in love with an understanding between them that needed no words.

At last, when Rebecca relaxed, José thought she meant to pull away, and he dropped his hands from her back. She took his fingers, and as her eyes gazed searchingly into his she leaned gradually forward until her face was so near it started to blur. Her lips pressed to his hesitantly, and the heat of them meeting made his scalp tingle.

He had never been kissed before, except in a motherly way by Mrs. Woodland or his own mother. Certainly never like this. Two warm hands slipped inside his duster and vest, pressing tightly against his shoulder blades as their lips met with soft fire and his mind whirled dizzily. It was a warm kiss, intimate yet not sensual in nature, and though it awakened desires in José that startled him he was not aroused beyond control. If there was one thing he had learned from the Shoshones, it was self-control, and a deep feeling of respect for his religion. That flowed naturally over to a respect for Rebecca's religion, and neither hers nor his allowed for intimate relations outside the bonds of marriage.

Anyway, José believed anything he wanted from Rebecca Woodland would in time be his. One day her name would no longer be Woodland.

When Rebecca leaned her head back to look at him, José was startled by the discovery that her beauty had grown in his eyes, due solely to the power of that kiss. His heart beat wildly, and the palms of his hands were wet with perspiration.

Rebecca looked down, her hands still resting on his shoulder blades. She raised her eyes again and met his with a frank gaze. "It was your friend who robbed the depot, wasn't it?"

José nodded sadly. "Yeah, I reckon it was. He wanted me to go with him."

Rebecca swallowed. "I'm glad you didn't. I want you to stay here with us."

"I'll stay as long as you want me to," José promised, and felt her lean against him again with a sigh. In silence, he stared past her hair across the starlit yard.

The crisp crackling sound of his axe striking a log and splitting it lengthwise rang in the early morning stillness and faded into the trees. The scent of fresh-cut fir filled the air. Around him birds were singing, most of them in the trees, some in the yard. Robins and chickadees with their feathers all puffed up against the chill put forth their bright music: *Pretty bird, pretty bird, pretty bird.* And *chickadee-dee-dee-dee.* Their gladness filled the air.

Blue smoke puffed from the house's rock chimney in short spurts, rising cloud-like into the air to evaporate and leave no sign of its passing. A lamp glowed through the side window of the house; there, bacon and eggs would soon be frying, for Martha Woodland, too, was awake.

McAllister came silently into the yard, but José felt his presence, and a chill came over him as he sank the double-bit axe one more time into the chopping block. He cupped his hands together and blew into them, trying to ease the chill, and turned cautiously to see his old friend watching him from the side of the barn.

A smile creased McAllister's whiskered face when he knew he'd been caught, and he stood away from the wall and walked forward, casting a wary glance toward the quiet house. He stepped close, his moccasins making no sound, and stopped three feet away from José.

José was silent. He was glad to see his friend, happy to see him smiling. But why was he here? To persuade him to go away? He didn't want to go through that scene again.

"Hi, Lucky. Yer lookin' fit as a fiddle."

José laughed. "An' you look good as a guitar."

McAllister's eyes lit up, and he chuckled. "I figgered you'd forgot."

"I reckon not. What're you doin' here, Gray? They're out lookin' for you."

McAllister cleared his throat and swung his eyes toward the house. "You heard, huh?" José didn't reply, but the look in his eyes said enough. "Well, they ain't lookin' fer me anyhow. They don't know who done that job. I wore my bandanna over my face."

Clearing his throat, José motioned toward the house. "I bet breakfast'll be ready soon. Wanna stay a while?"

McAllister's eyes swung to the house, and he paused. José was sure he would turn down his offer, but to his surprise he said yes. "I'm a sucker fer that woman's cookin'," he said. "If they welcome me too, then sure, I'll stay a while."

Just then, Ben Trombell stepped from the barn, his hat back on his head. He rubbed his eyes and stopped three yards out from the door. As his gaze settled on McAllister the pleasantness faded from his face.

"Morning, Mr. McAllister." The man's voice was cool. "What brings you over this way?"

"Hello, Trombell. Just come to visit José a while," McAllister replied casually. José watched him, saw his eyes carefully scan Trombell's clothing. José knew he was looking for a weapon. But Trombell didn't carry any sidearm, just an occasional rifle on his saddle.

Trombell slid a warning glance toward José, then returned his eyes to McAllister. "Well, let's go on inside then."

They stepped into the cabin, and talk that was already low sort of died away when Martha, Rebecca, Anna, and Noah saw McAllister standing with José and Trombell. Finally, Martha found her tongue. "Why hello, Mr. McAllister. You're up and about bright and early."

McAllister shrugged. "Yes ma'am. I was just passin' by on my way to Wyomin'. Thought I'd stop an' see José."

"Oh. Well, won't you sit to breakfast with us? There's plenty of eggs for everyone."

"Don't mind if I do." McAllister pulled his hat off courteously, letting his hair fall across his forehead, then brushing it aside. He took the place Martha offered him at the plank table.

José and Trombell sat down, too, and José looked over at the kitchen counter in time to see Rebecca standing there staring at him. There was undisguised pleading in the girl's eyes, and her fingers were wrapped tightly around the handle of a spatula. José gave her a small smile and a wink. *Don't worry, girl,* he wished he could say. *I won't be leaving you again unless they drag me away.*

At that moment, the door swung open, and Laban and Jacob hurried inside, followed shortly by big Terrence Woodland. José realized almost immediately that Woodland didn't yet suspect McAllister of the robbery of the depot. He would never have let him stay if he had.

"Why, good mornin', Mr. McAllister." He nodded but didn't smile. "Sorry to hear about your eagle."

José caught McAllister's look, one of appreciation. Woodland had picked the right words to make himself a friend. "Well, it's over," McAllister replied simply. "I wish it coulda been diff'rent. That was a fine bird."

"So I hear. So I hear." Woodland nodded solemnly. "And I reckon the Good Lord has a place for her. I believe he takes care of those that need it."

Inside, José laughed at that ironic statement. If that were true, McAllister would surely be taken care of, he thought. But maybe not in the same way as Golden would be.

Breakfast wasn't even over when there came a knock on the door. Surprised, everyone looked up, and Woodland pushed back his chair and stood. "It sure is a day for comp'ny," he said, going to the door and swinging it open.

"Good mornin', Charlie," Woodland's voice boomed. "You musta rode all night to get here this time o' day. What brings you by?"

Although José couldn't see past Woodland and the door, it was Charlie Bonn's voice, a little deeper than he remembered it, that replied. "Oh, I didn't ride far. I was in town with friends last night. I just came by to see José. I heard he was visitin'."

José was surprised. Last time he had seen Charlie Bonn, they weren't on friendly terms. He recalled Charlie being downright unfriendly, in fact. Was he here to apologize, after all this time?

"José?" Woodland spoke. "You got a visitor."

"Yes sir." As José stood up, his eyes passed by Rebecca, then swung back again to her. She was watching him, warning in her eyes. Apparently she had caught wind of Charlie's feelings for him. Now he knew nothing had changed.

Although Charlie's was the same face José remembered, it was harder now, blockier, and his eyes had a narrowness José didn't recall. He had grown an inch or two since José had seen him, and packed some meat on his shoulders and neck. Charlie smiled at José, but it wasn't the same old carefree smile. "Howdy, José. Long time, no see. Sorry folks," the young man said. "Could you excuse me an' José for just a minute?"

Wordlessly, José stepped past Charlie into the yard, wondering if he had come here to fight him. If so, Charlie was in for a beating. José's training at the hands of the Shoshones and McAllister would not be for nothing.

Charlie Bonn didn't speak for several moments. He just walked out toward the corrals, José in step beside him but five feet away. José prepared himself mentally for a fight but held his tongue, and when Charlie leaned up against the top bar of the corral he turned to face him, resting one hand on the corral rail.

"Yer friend McAllister still ride that blood bay with a question mark on its face?" queried Charlie suddenly, looking out across the corral at José's horses.

"I reckon he does," José replied. "What of it?"

Charlie's face hardened, and all pretense of friendliness had vanished when he slowly turned his head and met José's eyes. "Then I reckon I got you by the short hairs, Nancy boy."

José's eyes hardened. "Say yer piece, Charlie. Lay it on the line."

Charlie grinned humorlessly, showing a broken front tooth he hadn't had last time José saw him. "All right—*Nancy boy*. I'll say what I came for. I told you once, Rebecca Woodland's gonna marry my brother. An' I told you not to come around no more. Or did you forget?"

"I didn't forget a thing, Charlie. But Rebecca ain't marryin' Jared, and both of us know it. What'd you really come here for? Chew it finer. You come here lookin' for a fight? Is that it?"

Charlie laughed out loud, his eyes hard. "Fight you? Hell, Nancy boy. You got a damn fine handle growin' outta your head. All I'd have to do is grab that an' go to town. No, I didn't come to fight. There's no sport in fightin' the likes of you. I just came to tell you, if you want yer friend to live, you best be hightailin' it away from Rebecca, an' I mean today."

"Or what?" José retorted.

"Or I'll go back inta Soda Springs an' give Deputy Goss some interesting information. Seems a man ridin' a blood bay with three white stockings, a white splash on its left hip, and a marking down its face like a question mark was the man they suspect of robbin' the train depot in Pocatello Junction."

The sickness welled up in José's stomach. McAllister was had now. If he didn't ride out, Charlie would have the law out here. There was no doubt about it. And even if he did ride out, they could have wanted posters out on McAllister from the information Charlie could provide them.

José's mind whirled with shock. McAllister had been too good to him, given him too much. Saved his life, even. And although the thought of leaving Rebecca Woodland tore him apart inside, he couldn't let Charlie go through with his plan if there was anything he could do to help it. He would have to leave with McAllister.

Of course, if Charlie wanted to he could always turn his information over to the law anyway. But José hoped Charlie was smart enough to know if he did that he could easily come back here after Rebecca. Charlie wouldn't dare take that chance and miss out on the sister-in-law he was so dead-set on winning. Unless she was married to Jared before José could return.

"I'll ride out," José said. "But if I hear you ever said a word to the law, I'll come back. And I'll kill you, Charlie. I'll kill you deader than hell."

Charlie turned and faced José. "You ain't seen the day you c'n whip me, Nancy boy."

José's fist was a blur. He fought the way McAllister had taught him—to win. And he gave no warnings. His hard knuckles contacted Charlie's chin like a hammer blow, and the younger boy went down hard on his backside, his eyes wide with surprise.

José had learned to judge an opponent's intentions by fighting the Shoshones and Bannocks at Fort Hall, and it was plain when Charlie started to his feet that the fight wasn't over. With all his vigor, José kicked sideways, knocking Charlie's feet out from under him before he could even come fully erect. Charlie went down hard again, and José followed the first kick with one to the stomach that sprawled Charlie over on his face. He lay there coughing and sputtering in the dust of the yard. When he attempted to rise, he kicked him again.

Now the fight was over.

José stood by while Charlie struggled to his feet, planted his hat on his head, and walked over to his horse. He climbed up without looking back at José and turned toward Soda Springs.

When Charlie rode off at a lope, José trotted to the house. He tried to calm himself down before he opened the front door, and then he looked in at McAllister. "Gray, c'n I see you?"

McAllister left the remains of his breakfast and stepped outside, following José in brisk strides toward the barn. At the corner of the barn, José whirled around, and after a quick glance toward the house he looked up at McAllister. "Charlie knows about the depot, Gray. If I don't leave Rebecca alone he says he'll turn you in. We gotta get outta here now. We gotta ride to Wyomin'."

A wild look bounded into McAllister's eyes as they swept the yard and came back to rest on José. "Then we best ride now, Lucky. Wyomin' border ain't far."

José saw a light in his friend's eyes he hadn't seen in a while, like he was happy to have his riding partner back. For all his talk of riding alone, José knew Gray had missed him, and it made him feel good. But he had to battle back his tears at the thought of leaving Rebecca. This time it would probably be forever, because as Clara Bonn had said, she was past marrying age, and if it wasn't Jared Bonn it would be someone else before too long. José tried desperately to force those green eyes out of his mind, but they kept coming back, haunting him.

Gritting his teeth, José stepped toward the barn beside McAllister. Suddenly, the cabin door creaked open and then shut, and José turned to see Rebecca standing there. Their eyes met, and again he felt her kiss. His eyes burned, his vision blurred.

McAllister had also turned at the sound of the door, and he looked at Rebecca and thought back to this pretty little girl sitting on his horse after he saved her from drowning in the river. He recalled her gazing solemnly into his eyes. He paused and stared at José for a moment, and a look of resignation suddenly washed across his face as he saw José wipe at his eyes and turn away from the girl. He grabbed José by the shoulder and turned him so that they faced each other.

"Lucky, you ain't goin' with me. I ain't costin' you yer whole future. I want yuh to know I didn't mean what I said to yuh back there at the cave. I just felt like my last friend was desertin' me." He looked away, embarrassed.

Jose nodded and smiled, wiping at his eyes again and choking down a lump in his throat. He was kind of glad McAllister hadn't actually voiced the word "sorry." That was a life-long code the man couldn't break now. "I know you didn't mean it, Gray." He could see McAllister had made up his mind, that even if he wanted to go with him now he wouldn't let him. He was willing to take the chance of sacrificing his own freedom for Jose's happiness. Jose ached suddenly to embrace his old friend. He longed to be close to him one last time. But somehow he thought McAllister wouldn't understand. The last time Jose had hugged him, the day Tongue Eater died, he'd been just a boy. And McAllister had seemed almost scared to respond. He wasn't the touching kind. Did men hug men anyway? Jose wasn't quite sure, so he just held out his hand.

McAllister looked at the outstretched hand with a puzzled glance. At last, he looked back up at Jose's face, and he took the hand and shook it, holding on for an extended time like he didn't want to let go. He started to step forward, then stopped himself, lowered his eyes and chuckled. Still holding Jose's hand, McAllister reached up and gave his shoulder a squeeze.

"Reckon I knew you couldn't go with me. But I had to see."

McAllister let go of Jose's hand and dropped his own, staring out across the yard with a faraway look, the look Jose had caught a time or two in Golden's eyes. A haunted, lonely look. Was that the look of freedom? No, McAllister had entered the realm of those who go bad. For him there would be no more freedom. He was destined always to run. McAllister swung his eyes back to Jose's face. They stared at each other, and the older man swallowed a couple of times before he settled the hat on his head and smiled crookedly.

"You take care of that chestnut filly. An' keep yer nose to the wind. You've become a man to ride the river with. Take care . . . Jose." It was the first time he had spoken Jose's real name since the day they met.

With these words, Robert McAllister started to turn. He looked up the road, then turned back and surprised Jose by holding out his hand again. Automatically, Jose took the hand, his eyes turning misty. He ached with longing for his friend to hold him close. Instead, McAllister just watched him sadly. But instead of dropping his hand, he raised his other to cradle Jose's between his two rough ones. He dropped his hands suddenly and took a small step back, as if to go. Then he raised both hands and clasped Jose's shoulders, searching his eyes.

"Well, I oughtta go. You take care, Jose." He stepped closer and moved his right hand in nearer to Jose's neck, giving a little squeeze.

"Goodbye, Gray," Jose choked out, not knowing how to tell his friend how much he cared for him.

"Don't say that, Lucky," McAllister reprimanded softly. "The Shoshones don't ever say goodbye, except to their dead. When they part, they say, *un-boin-na-he.* I'll see you later."

Jose smiled and raised his hand to rest it on the solid muscle of McAllister's arm. Tears spilled out of both of his eyes at once to roll down his cheeks. "Un-boin-na-he, Gray."

As if scalded, McAllister dropped his hand. In a broken voice, he said, "Un-boin-na-he." He did a sudden turn and walked across the dusty yard, disappearing into a grove of aspens at the base of the foothills. In minutes, he reappeared atop a nondescript dark bay horse, and a smile broke through Jose's tears. McAllister was wise to the end; he had known the blood bay paint would mark him wherever he went. The one he rode now resembled a million others. McAllister kicked the horse in the ribs and loped out toward the main road, a long funnel of white dust rising up behind.

Near the crest of the road, he slowed down and nearly came to a stop. He started to turn around, then lowered his head and straightened back up in the saddle, disappearing over the rise.

Even as strong as McAllister was, he couldn't look back at Jose.

Part Three
The Last Eagle

Chapter Twenty-Seven

The grass waved long and green, for it was spring. So the calendar said, anyway. But the wilting temperatures of that June 2, 1902 contradicted the calendar's claims, and as far as José Olano was concerned, it was summer that once more seared the range.

José lay on his side in the grass, resting his head on the palm of his hand under the shade of a lone juniper. His dark eyes drifted lazily from the clouds that seemed glued in place to the sagebrush hills, to the Hereford cattle that lazed in small groups, silently chewing their cuds while they waited for the day's heat to subside. Behind him loomed the timbered mountains, and below lay the land of rank grass they called Marsh Valley, with Marsh and Goodenough Creeks winding down its middle to their junction. Beyond that was a low jumble of black lava overgrown with juniper and sagebrush that stretched for a mile or so to the town of McCammon. All this he could see from his grassy perch on the bench.

Several yards away from José, a young sorrel mare named Duster cropped grass contentedly. She wore a saddle with tapaderos on its stirrups to ward the brush away from his boots and a yellow slicker tied behind the cantle in case of some wandering thunderstorm, always possible on these afternoons of high temperatures and tall, billowing clouds.

The years had whipped and burned and pounded José into leather like his friend, Robert McAllister. His face was deeply tanned by the battering sun, his lithe body hardened from years in the saddle. Crows' feet surrounded his eyes, which had retained the glittering, dark sense of mystery from his youth. Was it humor shining in those deep-set eyes? Was it anger? Or just the mischievousness of a carefree cowpoke? Well, not quite carefree. Now he was a man with ties.

He wore his black hair long, curling several inches below his collar, and a mustache of impressive proportions drooped to the clean, solid line of his jawbone. His receding hairline was concealed by a broad-brimmed Stetson, the type folks had taken five or six years ago to calling a "cowboy hat". His Justins, too, the so-called "cowboy boots," were of the typical style of the range rider of the day, their heels high and angled at the back, their toes pointed to slip easily into a stirrup, their tops cut in V shape to better facilitate movement.

He wore tan canvas trousers and a white cotton pullover shirt with navy blue stripes. And there on his hip the old Colt Peacemaker nestled in its battered holster. The scratches and nicks in the holster and the worn-away bluing of the backstrap and exposed frame told of the hard use they had seen in the brush country and of the hundreds of rounds that had exploded from the chambers over the years. José laughed to think how the Peacemaker's status had changed since he bought this one back in eighty-four. Originally priced at seventeen dollars, he could buy one brand new eighteen years later in any store for fifteen. Their standing had been taken down a notch by more advanced models, the automatic and double action Colts, to name just two. But the Peacemaker fit José's hand like it was made for it, and he would never change his preference.

A shadow passed close by, and when José looked up his eyes lit upon the dark-feathered underbody of a golden eagle. It soared a hundred feet over his head, its tail and wings tipping slightly. Its mate appeared in the distance, just a tiny black line in the sky, wavering in the sun's glare. Eventually, the first bird disappeared, and the second replaced it, its route more direct as it moved after its mate. José watched until it disappeared behind him, and then his mind drifted off to another era…

Nearly eighteen years had gone by since he last glimpsed Robert McAllister loping up the lane that led away from the Woodland homestead. But he still thought of him often, of his wry sense of humor, of his casual confidence about everything he did, of the way he sat a saddle, tall and invincible. And of the ease with which he fired a rifle and never missed. Oh, what had become of the years? And what had become of the Basque boy camped on Bailey Creek?

José was thirty-five years old now, and for one who had never gone off to a foreign war, he had seen more of the world and done more than most his age, especially for a time when the train was still the fastest mode of travel. He had lived in Spain, South America, Nevada, and Idaho. He had killed a grizzly bear at point blank range, trailed a cougar across a battered, snowy shale slide to its lair in the cliffs, ridden—or *tried* to ride—most every bad bronc these Idaho hills could produce, roped and branded more cattle than he could ever count. He had survived in the wilderness, all on his own. He had faced down another grizzly bear and walked away. He had killed a man to protect a friend, had to shoot another for the same reason, and both of those incidents still haunted him some nights in his sleep, leaving him sweating and crying in anguish. And—most importantly, in his mind—he had won the heart of a beautiful chestnut-haired lady, and they were raising three children that filled their lives with love.

He was foreman on the ranch of Ben Trombell now, in charge of all the hands and of the process of raising fat, healthy beef cattle. His brother, Alfredo, watched over the flocks of sheep and oversaw the other Basque herders who worked for Ben. Unlike the early 1880's, Basques were no longer scarce. They had swarmed into Idaho in the last few years, most of them bound for Boise, now known as the Basque capitol of the United States. But many had drifted to other parts of the state, like Pocatello, following the flocks of sheep that invaded the range.

Trombell himself was an old man now, in his seventies, and rare was the time he set foot away from his house. He trusted José completely, and both knew that trust would not go unrewarded. José, against his will, often thought about what lay ahead of him and Ben Trombell. The man's health was failing, his heart giving him problems, and it was a sure bet he wasn't long for this earth. That realization made José ache deep inside.

José supposed Ben would probably leave him and Alfredo the ranch when he was gone, for the old rancher had no one else. His family was long since dead of cholera. The thought of all that land in José's possession was almost overwhelming. It was the silver lining in the cloud of Ben's approaching death, he guessed. But some recent developments in this part of the country had José's mind drifting elsewhere in the last few weeks, to another piece of land.

In February of 1898, four hundred and eighteen thousand acres of the Fort Hall Reservation had been ceded to the federal government, including all reservation lands south of the town of Pocatello. And now, four years later, the government was ready to disperse it. They had chosen an utterly democratic method to do so. It consisted of opening the gates, just like in olden days, and letting the white man swarm over those ceded lands, find his piece of heaven, and stake his claim. An old-fashioned land rush, just like in Oklahoma. Once the land had been claimed, the privilege had to be paid for, at anywhere from a dollar and twenty-five cents to ten dollars an acre, depending on its location.

Still, it was a cheap price, to José's way of thinking, because right in the middle of that freed reservation land sat the little creek he longed to own, with Haystack Mountain's flat-topped bulk looming over it. Robbers Roost and all the land surrounding it would go into the pot that sold at the cheapest price, a dollar twenty-five an acre. To José it was a beautiful dream. But he dared not let the dream go too far.

Anyway, he hated the thought that white men would own all that land now. He had seen what white men could do to wild country, and it made his heart grow cold. It sickened him to think he was part of it.

José sat up and scratched the back of his neck, flicking an ant off his shirt with a fingertip. He looked out across the green expanse called Marsh Valley, where Trombell's spread seemed to stretch forever. He could see Haystack Mountain and Bonneville and Snow Peaks on the northeastern horizon, and the friendly buildings of McCammon closer in. A crooked black line sifting across the skyline told him a train was stopped at the depot.

The land in Marsh Valley was cut into squares, some of them green with alfalfa now, some still in the original sage and native grasses. Fences surrounded the ranges that once were free. He pondered them regretfully. The scourge called barbed wire— "bobwire," by Westerners—ran in every direction to the horizon. José looked down at an ugly scar across the back of his hand, a "gift" from a fence he had been repairing two years earlier. It had ended up costing him more to repair himself than the fence. He cursed the bloody string bitterly and knew Robert McAllister would, too, if he was still alive. The fences marked the death of his beloved freedom.

Where was McAllister now, anyway? *Was* he still alive? Was he in a prison somewhere? Was he on the run for some crime, hiding like a harried wolf out in some dank cave? Or did his bones bleach white among the sage or on some dried-up creekbank?

José guessed he would never know. But never would his mind stop wondering. McAllister had affected his life forever, and good or bad he was still beside him in nearly every move he made.

Picking a canteen up off the ground, José took a long swallow and thumped the cork back in before standing and dusting off his trousers. He walked stiffly to the sorrel and slung the canteen across the saddle horn, then took the bridle from where it rested on his slicker and slipped it back over the horse's head. She took the bit without a fight. After all, she had been trained by the best.

He rode the hills for the rest of the day, checking fence and daydreaming, and it was evening when he rode into the ranch yard. The wind sighed warmly and stirred the scent of sage and juniper, blending them with the smell of dust kicked up by his horse. Brilliant pink clouds hovered over Scout Mountain and Old Tom, and over the Portneuf Range, creating soft shadows in their canyons and in the timber below the white escarpments of Harkness Canyon.

The ranch was no small affair, for Ben Trombell had always been a man of some means. Trombell's own house was small but showy, with a white picket fence surrounding it and a stone path leading up to the front door. Flowers lined both sides of the path, blooming brightly under constant care, and an American flag hung languidly from its fifteen foot pole in the yard. A single light shone from the window of the sitting room, and José looked at it pensively, wondering after his old friend as Duster slowed to a stop.

The Olano house was much larger than Ben's, but like Ben's it was constructed solidly of lodgepole pine logs shipped in to McCammon on the train from west of Rexburg. Flowered yellow curtains in both front windows gave the house a feminine touch José enjoyed coming back to, and their sidewalk was also lined with the flowers Ben insisted on. They were the only pastime of his twilight years.

The rest of the ranch consisted of a two story barn with a hay loft and stalls for several horses, two tack sheds, three corrals, and an outhouse fifty yards to the east of the Olano house.

Two boys, one about thirteen, the other eleven, ran from the house as he drew up at the barn. The thirteen-year-old had black hair like his father's, only shorter, and his eyes were dark as the midnight sky. The younger boy had the red hair and green eyes of his mother, and both of them bore broad smiles that warmed José's heart.

The boys' names were Robert and Ben, after Robert McAllister and Ben Trombell, the two men José respected most in the whole world, outside of his brother, Alfredo, whose name he had never liked. He jumped from the saddle and smiled as they stopped before him.

"Hi, boys. Kinda anxious to see me, aren't you?"

The boys looked at each other, then back at him, and he knew there was something afoot from the mischievous look in their eyes. "Ma said to come out an' take care of Duster for you, that's all," replied Robert quickly. "She said to send you on in."

José grinned again, turning his eyes to slits under his wilting hat brim. "Well, I won't argue that. Go ahead." He handed the reins to Robert and cuffed him lightly on the shoulder as he went past, headed for the barn. Then he walked on to the house, his curiosity sparked.

The skills of a tracker don't come easily, but once learned they become deeply ingrained, like remembering one's name. Reading sign in the dust comes as naturally to a tracker as a traveler reading the name of the next town on a crossroads marker. So as José neared the house his eyes swept the ground before him, almost without his thinking about it, and before he reached the front door a mark there in the dirt drew him up fast.

It was a track, the track of a large man, and though it had no sharp heel as a boot or shoe would leave it had no toe marks of a barefoot man, either. Looking closer, he assured himself of what he had supposed, that these tracks were made by a man in moccasins. José knew few men who wore moccasins anymore. Could it be an Indian, or...

José straightened up. He didn't move forward. He couldn't quite force himself to step out of his tracks. A strange feeling had welled up inside him, one he couldn't explain. His hair prickled on the back of his neck and rose on his hands as he looked from the tracks up to the door, where they led. There was a presence in the air, the sixth sense sensation a well-tuned hunter gets when near something unknown—his quarry or someone who is on his own trail. With a deep breath, he walked up to the door and pushed it open quickly, making his entrance as sudden as he could.

There was silence in the room as Rebecca Olano looked up from where she was slicing a pie on the kitchen table, their seven-year-old daughter, Lauris, sitting beside her. Rebecca's face had matured, and the indistinct lines about her eyes bespoke the hard life of a rural Idaho homemaker. But she was as beautiful as ever, even more so, and José's heart caught as he looked into her eyes. It always did, and he guessed it always would.

Lauris had brought her hand to her mouth in surprise as the door swung open, and involuntarily her eyes moved away from José, just for a brief moment, then lit again on his face. She was a lovely child, her hair red like her mother's, her eyes dark like her father's. But unlike her father's they were easy to read, and the message in them spilled across the room. There was no further question in José's mind who the visitor in his house was, and that man now stood behind the door, to his right. This he surmised by following the flicker of his daughter's gaze.

The visitor seemed to read José's thoughts, just like long ago. He stepped around from behind the door, his moccasins making no sound on the braided rug. José only knew where he was first by instinct, then by seeing him from the corner of his eye. He stopped beside José, and José slowly turned his head.

His eyes came to rest on those of the wanderer, the outlaw, Robert McAllister.

There was a long moment of silence in the room, a moment when Rebecca and Lauris looked expectantly back and forth from José to McAllister. McAllister watched José, a sparkle in his eyes, but his lips made a thin, impassive line, and José just stared in shock, unable to make his throat voice any words.

The years had changed McAllister, and they had not been kind. The lines that only creased his face while he was in his late thirties now tracked across it jaggedly like deep canyons, around his eyes, his mouth, across the wind-whipped, dark skin of his forehead. His hair, still kept above his collar, but now shaggy and unkempt, had mostly turned to gray, and his hairline had receded by a healthy inch. The whiskers on his cheeks were silver in color, bristly like wheat stubble, and they partially hid a long, jagged scar that ran from his left ear almost to his chin. His hands still appeared powerful, yet age spots marred them, and they were battered and cracked. The small finger of his left hand was missing, giving the hand a misshapen, grotesque appearance. He was no longer ramrod-straight through the spine, and slighter of body—still big-boned, but lean and haggard through the chest and shoulders.

José let his eyes pass over his old friend, across his moccasins and buckskin pants to his gray cotton shirt, patched and dirty, and his wool vest, from one pocket of which dangled the tag from a sack of Bull Durham tobacco. He held a battered, sweat-stained hat in one hand, and on his right hip José was half surprised to find the old Peacemaker he had learned to shoot with replaced by one of the new Colt Lightnings. He was somehow saddened to see the old gun gone, but it didn't surprise him. A man on the run must often have to leave things behind.

The beginning of a grin touched McAllister's whiskered face, then grew until the lines outside his mouth were crevices. The chapping of his lips showed plainly as his smile grew, and his gray eyes sparkled happily. That was one thing which hadn't changed. His eyes. Still expressive, still full of life, they shone like beacons, assuring José he had been missed.

"Howdy, Lucky. The years been kind to yuh."

In spite of himself, José's vision blurred, hearing the way the voice had changed, had grown scratchy and hoarse, another sign of his aging. Or maybe it was just full of trail dust. He wished he could tell McAllister the years had been kind to him, too, but he knew he wouldn't believe him.

José expelled a long-held gust of breath and stepped forward, almost stumbling. McAllister extended his hand to shake as José came close, but José didn't even see it. With a laugh, he took his friend in a bear hug, slapping him on the back. McAllister quickly followed suit and threw his arms around his friend, and then they abruptly pulled apart, grinning broadly.

Eyes moist, José glanced over at Rebecca and Lauris, then looked back quickly at McAllister, still unable to speak. All he could do was shake his head. Then he cleared his throat and dropped his eyes. He swallowed and looked back into McAllister's aged face. Was that what freedom looked like, after all those years?

"I don't know what to say, Gray," José uttered at last. "It's so good to see you again. I was just thinkin' about you while I was out ridin' today."

Rebecca laughed, looking lovingly at her husband before she spoke. "He thinks about you *every* day, Mr. McAllister. We speak of you often."

Embarrassed, McAllister lowered his head. He looked over warmly at Rebecca, then back at José, swallowing. "Well, kid, let's go outside an' ketch up. I'm feelin' cramped in here."

When José glanced over at Rebecca, she just smiled and threw her hands out in front of her, palms up, like she was feeding chickens. "Go ahead, José. You won't be any good in here for a while. I can see that's a fact."

José grinned and threw an arm around McAllister's shoulders, steering him back outside. They walked off by the barn and leaned up against it to silently watch the gray sky fade into night. Neither one spoke for several minutes. They just kept looking over at each other, and then one or the other would shake his head, and they would chuckle. Finally, McAllister spoke.

"I come here fer a partic'lar reason, Lucky. I heard about yer land run."

José took a deep breath, then let it out. "Well?"

"Well, there's a pretty piece o' land I'd like us both to share. I don't need to say more."

José gazed at him searchingly, then allowed himself a half smile. "You're serious, aren't you? You wanna run for Robbers Roost?"

McAllister nodded. "Half fer me an' half fer you."

"You're tellin' me the man of the woods is thinkin' about settlin' down?"

A deep-throated laugh rumbled from McAllister's throat. "Well... I guess I don't really aim to settle down *all* the way. But it'd be a place to light, when I get the urge. You ain't the kind that would need help to handle both claims, I hear."

José straightened up. "Hear from who?"

"Hell, Lucky, I don't think I c'd ask anybody in McCammon or Pocatello 'bout José Olano without they tell me he's a good friend o' theirs an' what a hard worker he is. Yer a popular fella—with the women, too. You must be popular, to be able to keep a long head of hair like that in this day an' age."

José blushed. "Oh, cut it out."

"It's true. I spent a few hours down at Harkness House buyin' drinks an' listenin' to stories 'bout José Olano, the hero of Bannock County. They tell me they bring the worst broncs to you. An' that you win every turkey shoot they hold. They also tell me you've tracked down an outlaw or two fer the sheriff an' that they used you to find three boys after they got lost in a bad storm two years ago. But most importantly, they say that fer a Basco yer all right, an' that yer gonna go places. High places. Now that's the kinda man I'd like to have watchin' over my spread."

Embarrassed by all the praise, José just stood shaking his head. When McAllister stopped talking, he looked up at him, into eyes that were only dark shadows now in the twilight. "I was thinkin' about that canyon just today, Gray. An' I was thinkin' about you. But I never figgered you'd come back here. I didn't think you'd dare, but I reckon they've forgot all about you by now down at the sheriff's office. What's it been, seventeen years now?"

"Eighteen, Lucky. Eighteen long years this fall. An' I didn't find a real friend in all that time. Truth is, I won't need yuh lookin' after my land. I come back here to stay. I'm done driftin' around, runnin' inta fences ever' time I blink. I'm fifty-five years old, an' I'm too tired fer any more runnin'. I come back here ta die in peace."

A cool breeze swept into the yard and a cold emptiness filled José's chest. He looked quickly away from his friend and stared into the gloom. A great-horned owl hooted from the back of the barn, and it was a lonely, hollow sound in the summer evening. José couldn't find words for several minutes, and if he had been able to he couldn't have spoken them.

Suddenly, McAllister slapped his arm lightly with the back of his hand. "Wha' d' ya say, Lucky? With yer luck, we should be able to slip right inta that canyon an' stake our claim without so much as an argument from the coyotes. Let's go pards again."

José thought for a moment, but he wasn't wondering whether or not he'd do it. He was thinking about how it would be, back beside his old friend again. As far as doing the run, he had already wanted to, and now he had double the reason. McAllister had voiced what he himself had thought. He was too old to be on the run. He was an old man, far older than his years.

"You still on the run, Gray?" José queried suddenly. "Is the law after you?"

McAllister laughed quickly, almost too quickly, and José shuddered, already knowing the truth. "Hell, kid. I told you I'm done runnin'."

On the evening of June 16, José and McAllister rode into Pocatello, the hooves of their horses making muffled thumping sounds in the heavy dust. The railroad town was growing up. Harboring a permanent population of over four thousand now, there were over a hundred businesses there, a couple of banks, and a newspaper—the Pocatello Tribune. Most of the businesses, including a seemingly over-balanced faction of saloons, were along First Street, formerly Front Street, on the east side of the tracks.

Pocatello even had its own volunteer fire department, which consisted of forty-five volunteers and fifteen Oregon Short Line members. They had two hose carts, one hook and ladder truck, a chemical engine—which was too heavy to use—and sixteen hundred and fifty feet of hose. They had an alarm box system, too, and twenty-eight fire plugs. The problem was, the town was growing so quickly they needed more.

West of the railroad tracks, the streets running north and south had been named after United States Presidents, beginning with Harrison, and the west and east running streets had just the past year taken on the names of famous explorers and soldiers like Lewis and Clark, Custer and Carson. Where sagebrush, boulders, and grass had once covered the plain, leafy shade trees now lined the streets of Pocatello, and many of the yards were carpeted in grass.

Yes, Pocatello had changed. It was no longer the rough community of the eighties, known as the last frontier town. It had a school, churches, women's clubs, a theater; it had culture. There were families here, farmers and ranchers and merchants who had come with the sure knowledge this was where they wanted to live out their lives. José watched McAllister's reaction to the town as he took him on a tour of the dusty streets. All his friend could do was gaze about and shake his head, and his eyes seemed to glaze over with a sick helplessness.

McAllister never spoke, just listened to José's occasional commentary. When at last they reached the northern limits of town, the older man reined his big dun gelding around and sat facing the city, gazing at the many lights of the gas lamps that began to glow as shadows took in the streets.

"This valley used to be full o' deer, Lucky. An' elk, an' bighorns, an' antelope. Not too long back, either. An' the buffalo." A faraway look seeped into his eyes as he said that, and he repeated the word in a throaty whisper. "Buffalo." He swung his eyes about the town, a dazed look on his face, and turned at last to José, his face settling into hard lines. "But there's one place that won't be made into a city. You an' me'll see to that. Robbers Roost will stay the way it is."

José nodded. "You bet. We'll do our best."

McAllister's face suddenly brightened, and he looked over at José. "What say we go on over to First Street and find us some saloon? I'll buy you a drink."

Warily, José shrugged. He didn't want to bring his friend's mood back down by refusing. But on the other hand, he wondered if liquor under his belt wouldn't kick his mood in the belly anyway.

"I'll go with you," he agreed at last. "But I don't wanna drink. I'm not a drinker."

McAllister chuckled. "Yeah, I guess you ain't changed."

As they rode back toward the business district, José glanced about at the crowded streets. Word had spread far of the land rush, and he guessed two or three thousand people had come to town to take their places in the race. Trains had been dropping off passengers all week, and wagon loads of land-hungry farmers had rumbled in from every point. They came from Butte and Boise, Cheyenne and Salt Lake City, some even as far as Alaska, he'd heard it said. Prospectors looking for mines, cowpunchers looking for a chance to grab a ranch of their own before they got too old and the cheap land was gone. There were lawyers come to mediate affairs and pull in their own fortunes with their wits, and other aimless souls looking for the sheer adventure of what could be the last land run in the United States.

There was not a room to be had in the hotels or boarding houses of Pocatello, not a rig or a horse to be rented. Even the sorriest nags, unless lame, stood near one camp or another or in the livery stables, rented and ready to give their all, running for some promising piece of land. The horses and mules ate well that night. Those who owned or rented them gave them nosebags full of good grain in hopes it would boost their energy enough to carry them through.

Eager tension was in the air as the shadows spread. For every star that ignited in the velvet sky it seemed a campfire in some Pocatello sandlot leaped to life. Men talked excitedly of the land they would claim. Since no one was supposed to be allowed on the reservation land before noon the following day, many of them spoke with suspicious familiarity, too—not just those who had taken advantage of the reservation lands for years, but strangers to the country. Farmers' children watched and listened, wide-eyed, while their mothers caught the excitement, and the hopes and fears for tomorrow shone in their eyes.

These were desperate people, but their spirits were high. Although many of them were failures in other places, other boomtowns, other states, each of them believed this was their big chance. They knew they would be among the lucky few to claim a choice piece of land, to finally gain something they had always hungered for but never had the capital to obtain.

When José and McAllister reached First Street, it was aswarm with people, Pocatello citizens and newcomers alike. The saloons wouldn't open tomorrow, upon orders of Police Chief Barnett McGarvey. *Sober* land seekers were trouble enough. So tonight those who were drinkers would fill their bellies and charge the air with merriment, killing their tension, their nervousness about what tomorrow might bring.

After putting up their horses temporarily in the nearest livery stable, José and McAllister started up the street through the crowd. Several people called out José's name as he passed, and he turned and tried to wave and smile as the crowd hurried them on. McAllister laughed and slapped José on the back. "You've made quite a name fer yerself, I tell yuh! Maybe we oughtta run you fer mayor."

José laughed back and allowed McAllister to steer him into one of the saloons, where a tinny piano banged away to the tune of "A Hot Time in the Old Town." They pushed their way up to the bar, and McAllister ordered himself a drink of whisky. "Sure you don't want anything?" he asked José above the din. "I'm buyin'. T'night an' ev'ry night!"

José shrugged, then turned to the bartender, who appeared about to go to another customer, depending upon José's reply. "Ah, sure. I'll take a root beer. A big one."

The bartender complied with a grin. "Good move, José. There'll be enough trouble tonight with sober men, I figger."

José nodded agreement and drank deeply from the root beer mug pushed his way. He turned and saw McAllister watching him with a bemused look in his eyes. "Ah, the teetotaler. That's okay, Lucky. You'll prob'ly outlive us all. You never did like the hard stuff, as I recall."

José laughed. "Good thing, too. I've helped bury a few men who did like it."

McAllister raised his glass in agreement. "So have I, Lucky. An' I've come near buryin' myself a time or two, because of it. I—"

Someone jostled McAllister, spilling some of his whisky on the bar, and he turned and eyed the man angrily. "Watch yerself, buster. I just paid fifty cents fer this."

The stranger was a stocky man with a heavy black beard and powerful-looking hands lined with veins. Scars littered his knuckles. He had a blocky brow and deep-set eyes, and a hard, cruel mouth. When he realized McAllister was speaking to him, he pushed a sweat-stained derby back on his head with a knuckle, stepping back from McAllister a bit. By the odor of whisky on his breath, he had been celebrating for a while.

"If you can't stand t' lose a little, this ain't the place t' be, old man," the stranger said belligerently. "Now get outta my way."

There were explosives inside McAllister tonight. José had already seen them in his eyes and hoped others would, too. But the stranger was too drunk to notice and probably wouldn't have cared anyway. McAllister's response was quick and certain, and José saw in the blur of movement his friend had lost none of his speed. His left hand flicked out, splashing the remains of his glass of liquor into the black-haired one's face, and as the stranger staggered back, McAllister followed him and laid a right fist across his cheek that sent him stumbling back into the surprised crowd.

Someone yelled, and José saw a stranger dodge out of the way. Then the black-haired man was coming back, and before he could swing either of the fists he had raised, McAllister kicked between them, catching him in the solar plexus and sending him retching. McAllister followed the kick with several more blows with his fists, and all the other man could do was helplessly try to protect his face with his hands.

José was surprised to see the fight hadn't yet spread. He guessed maybe this big-mouthed fellow just didn't have any friends. But even so, a good fight usually carried over into others, so he watched the crowd warily, ready to step in if the need arose.

Then the stranger was on the ground, and McAllister mercilessly kicked him in the side of the head, sent him rolling. The crowd was backed up, packed into the rest of the room to leave a clearing fifteen feet around for the brawlers. Except there was only one brawler now. The black-haired stranger was unconscious on the floor, his face smeared with blood.

Jumping forward, José yelled out McAllister's name, then touched his shoulder. He ducked as his friend came around, expecting him to swing. McAllister's hands were still at the ready, but he instantly recognized José and dropped them to his sides.

"Come on, Gray. Let's go find some place to sleep. This ain't no place to be tonight."

For a moment, McAllister just stared at him, wild-eyed. Then gradually his breathing slowed down, and he ran a hand across his mouth, bunching his jaw muscles. "All right. Let's get the horses outta the stable."

José gave a sigh of relief and glanced at the crowd of onlookers to see if they approved. Several of them were acquaintances of his. One of them nodded and raised his drink in salute. "We'll drink t' yer friend, Olano. That big feller's been shovin' his weight around all night."

When several other men drank to the toast, McAllister raised his hand to them in a half salute and pushed through the crowd toward the door. José turned to the bartender. "Sorry about that, Fred. My friend's a little tense with all the people stirrin' about. Can I give you some money to buy new sawdust for the floor or somethin'? I feel bad about leavin' you with this mess."

"Don't worry about it, José. I saw how it started. Like they said, that feller's been achin' fer a beatin'. I'd probably pay yer friend fer the service if I made better money here."

José smiled, still embarrassed, and gulped down the remainder of his root beer, letting out a belch. He wiped his mouth with a sleeve. "Thanks, Fred." With that, he turned and strode after McAllister, several patrons patting him on the back as he passed. He guessed he really did have a lot of friends in this town, and it made him feel good. He couldn't go very far in Bannock County without finding a friend, and he had to ride all day to come upon someone who openly showed dislike for him. Rebecca always said he had a way of winning people over, and as much as it embarrassed him to admit it, he guessed she was right.

When he cleared the doorway of the saloon, he turned his head to the left and right, looking for McAllister. He spotted him next door, standing in front of a hardware store, looking in the window. José started forward, then stopped. McAllister seemed to be gazing intently at something in the store, but its windows were dark. He had his hand raised to his head, fingering his hair, and the gas lamp at the front of the saloon lit the side of his face just enough for José to see the silver of his sideburn where his fingers touched it.

Old man. That was what the black-haired stranger had called his friend. Old man. It struck José suddenly how much it must bother his friend that the words really fit him. It was his hair he was looking at, in the reflection of the hardware store window, and maybe those lines on his face. It was the name the stranger had called his friend, not the rest of the exchange, that had set him off so violently. *Old man.* His best friend had ridden away eighteen years ago and come back an old man, ready to die and wanting to do it on his own piece of ground.

McAllister, suddenly feeling eyes on him, turned toward José. When their eyes met, his tension faded, and he turned toward the livery stable. "Let's get outta town, Lucky. I can't take the air here no more."

They spoke no more as their horses carried them up the crowded street to Center Street, thence toward the west side of town. The town hung thick with woodsmoke, mingled now and then with the scent of cigar and pipe smoke. Dust, too, drifted everywhere and settled in sheets on everything in sight. Vacant lots were no longer vacant tonight, and within them weary strangers laughed and dreamed, their eyes bright. Campfires crackled in the night and children fell asleep, in spite of every attempt to fight it. Banjos, fiddles, guitars, and mouth organs chimed their lively tunes into the sky: "Oh, Susanna," "On the Banks of the Wabash, Far Away," "The Sidewalks of New York," "Grandfather's Clock." José was a music lover, and he picked up on each tune as they passed and found himself humming along. His favorite was "Good bye, Old Paint." Trace chains jingled as wagons passed, and saddles creaked in time with hooffalls as dusty riders wove among the crowd. Pocatello was on the eve of its greatest adventure.

Picking their way among the thoroughfares, José and McAllister found a way out of the valley by going west up Clark Street. The road made a sharp bend and slanted upward to the flat, sagebrush-covered area they called the West Bench. The dark silhouette of Kinport Peak loomed above them.

There were other campers here. They passed them as they rode, looking for a suitable spot to lay out their bedrolls; but the din was not so great up here, although that from below still carried to them like the strains of some bizarre carnival. They climbed down at the edge of the bench overlooking the town and picketed their horses and fed them an extra bait of grain. Then they sat down, chewing on jerked venison and looking out over the firelit city.

Yes, José had a lot of friends, he thought suddenly. A lot of friends he could never thank enough for what they would do for him tomorrow. They would sacrifice any chance they might have had at gaining land for themselves in the great run…

There were some glaring problems with the whole reservation run process. The biggest was the fact that many white settlers had already made their homes on reservation lands without permission, and their homes would be up for grabs with the rest. Of course, for the land-hungry, that wasn't *their* problem, for *they* had waited for the government to make it legal.

The big problem for the runners was the fact that the United States land office was in the town of Blackfoot, twenty-four miles north of Pocatello. And after the runners posted their Notice of Possession, they had to travel all the way into Blackfoot in order to have the privilege of filing on that land and paying for it.

Another problem was the same as that with every old time land run. The sooners. These greedy souls would sneak onto the reservation in the night, perhaps had already done so. Then they would wait for daybreak and try to beat the honest men to the choicest pieces of land. Of course there were guards to drive them off the reservation. They were forbidden to enter Indian land before noon. But there were only thirty-five Indian police to guard four hundred eighteen thousand acres of land—six hundred fifty square miles! Thirty-five mounted Indians guarding a hundred miles of reservation boundary. Many a man, unsure of his chances at getting land legally, would be willing to risk getting caught with those odds.

As for the trip back to Blackfoot after the run, there was a special train that would leave McCammon at one-thirty in the afternoon, an hour and a half after the run began. The train would travel to Pocatello, stop two minutes, then head on for Blackfoot before three o'clock. But thanks to McAllister José wouldn't be on the train.

McAllister was a man of big dreams and strong convictions. He hated the railroad with an immeasurable passion. He hated the rails, the iron engines with their cowcatchers, their black clouds of choking smoke. He hated the railroad men, too. And he didn't want to have anything to do with the whole entity.

That was where José came into play. He was young. He was light. He was the best horseman around this country, some said. With his skill and luck he could ride all the way to Blackfoot and beat the train. He could be the first in line at the land office. He smiled, thinking back on the day they planned it all out. All they had to do was set up a relay of horses between McCammon and Blackfoot, with some of José's many friends to hold the horses until he arrived. And the question of horses was really no question at all. José not only worked for a rancher who raised admirable Tennessee Walkers and had three thoroughbreds on his ranch, but he was friends with Henry Harkness. To anyone who lived in southeast Idaho, that was a name to be reckoned with. Harkness was the owner and builder of Harkness House and of a vast spread at McCammon that was home to some of the finest horses in the country. He had seen to it that José had all the horses he needed.

José broke a tiny branch off a clump of sagebrush and crushed the leaves between his fingers, sniffing the pungent odor with pleasure. He smiled to himself as he listened to the strains of "The Zebra Dun" from a nearby camp. Between him and McAllister, they had formed the perfect plan. At noon tomorrow, there would be fifteen friends holding fifteen horses for José, at intervals along the road from McCammon to Blackfoot.

And with constantly fresh horses, he could beat that train. Those horses could do it, at eighteen or twenty miles an hour. He *had* to beat the train. He had to do it for McAllister. The irony of it all was McAllister wouldn't be beside him. Because of his size and his aging bones, when the train departed for Blackfoot on the morrow, he would have to swallow his last ounce of pride.

McAllister would be on that train.

Chapter Twenty-Eight

The yellow sun pounded down on Pocatello and on all the feverish souls inhabiting the Gate City the morning of June seventeenth. An excitement coursed through the veins of the landrunners that even the pall of choking dust couldn't smother. Now and then a whirlwind spun angrily through the streets, pelting hapless passersby with gravel and grit, and each time they cursed but just as soon forgot. The Gate City's greatest day loomed at hand, and more important things governed their thoughts.

José and McAllister rode up Center Street and over the wooden bridge, staring at the camps along the Portneuf. Most of the menfolk had vacated them, leaving only women and children with dust- and sweat-streaked faces. Many of the children were barefoot, and patches marred the knees and seats of their pants—sometimes patches on top of previous patches. Some were shirtless, their skin burned dark as an Indian's. Many sat under makeshift canvas shelters, fanning themselves, watching men ride by. José wondered what hopes and fears must fill these people's hearts. For some, their livelihood depended on what this day would bring.

They rode to the old Keeney House, now called Pocatello House, and found it almost deserted. The rockers on its porch were empty, a forgotten newspaper here and there, loose pages rattling in the wind. McAllister went inside and bought a ticket on the special train that would take him from McCammon to Blackfoot later that day. When he came back outside, a lost look washed fleetingly across his face, then disappeared behind a mask of anger.

He looked over at José as he swung into his saddle. "I swore I'd never pay the railroad a penny. Now I'm too old to have a choice." He laughed, but not out of happiness. The sound bespoke bitter darkness from a man of passionate hate.

The farther south they rode the more crowded the streets became, the more abustle with activity. Groups of men gathered everywhere, some in quiet conference, some trading bawdy jokes to hide their tension. They studied documents, maps, made quick sketches for one another in the dusty streets, then swept them away with the soles of their boots, as if anyone seeing them would know what they meant or even care.

Men would gallop in on horses, go into some establishment, then come back out to ride off again. Some of the finest horses José had seen in one place gathered here—along with some of the worst he could imagine. Only the very lame would escape the saddle today.

As for José and McAllister, both rode Thoroughbreds, José's a gray stud, and McAllister's a dark bay gelding. Both had been chosen not only for their capacity for an initial burst of speed, but for their ability and drive to keep it up over considerable distances. Neither one paled in comparison to any other horse José had seen, and he could thank the horse sense of his friend Ben Trombell for that.

José's horse pranced beneath him, absorbing the morning's excitement from José and from the other horses and the landrunners around them. He rolled his eyes warily, looking this way and that, certainly wondering about all the commotion. In spite of the heat, José felt the horse's sides quiver beneath the stirrup leathers.

José glanced over at McAllister. Uncharacteristically, the older man's eyes were fixed straight ahead, not scanning the town in the wary manner for which José knew the man. His jaw muscles were bunched, his brows lowered, his left hand unconsciously gripping his thigh. José stopped thinking of his own desires long enough to look into his old friend's heart, and he felt for him. He knew how much this land meant to him. José wanted it, too—wanted it so bad it caused a burning in his guts when he thought of it. But he made up his mind right then. If he were to win even a part of Robbers Roost, and for some reason McAllister fell out of the race, he would let McAllister have his part. Someday he knew it would come back to him anyway.

At the Pocatello assay office, McAllister suddenly drew his horse to a stop and climbed down, so José followed suit. There was no particular reason to stop here, except it just seemed the place to be. People crowded around the building, going in and out, faces anxious. In light of the fact no one was to have entered the reservation, a lot of fresh ore certainly found its way to the assay office this fine morning, José mused.

Across from the assay office stood a group of Mormon farmers in grim conference. At least José assumed them to be Mormons by their characteristic beards, conservative clothes, and work-hardened hands. They always seemed to be the most determined workers around, excepting, perhaps, the Chinese.

Children wove in and out through the crowd with their dogs, running, skipping, playing tag—whatever children do when excited. José didn't remember much of that stage of his life. Women stood in groups, or now and then with their menfolk, looking around anxiously, asking pointless questions, biting their lips, wringing their hands. Others of the female persuasion, dubbed tomboys, were set to ride in the big run. José had heard of several and seen some of them, the brazen, hard-eyed women in baggy jeans and loose shirts, with battered slouch hats on their heads. Some of them were daughters of men too old to run, some were wives of men who hoped for an extra claim or were too heavy or crippled to stand a decent chance. But some were widows or had never been married, and they were interested in finding a place of their own.

At that moment, José looked down the street and saw two of these female runners. One was dressed in the customary baggy pants, a pistol strapped to her waist. The other wore a blouse and skirt, and her face, though grim now, was pretty, her eyes like dark, glittering jewels that danced in the sunlight. He smiled as his eyes took in the braided quirt coiled in her little fist.

As the pair walked by, they happened to glance over at José, and he smiled again and touched his hat brim in greeting. "Good mornin', ladies. Good luck to you."

The one in the skirt returned his nod. "Thanks. You too. It's a good day for it."

That was all she said, and then she walked on, sure and smooth in her strides, her form diminutive but full of energy. José smiled. He honestly hoped she would get her piece of land.

Three young men nearby told José they had just come in from Thunder Mountain—"Thunder," they called it in Idaho. There they had failed, but here they would win. Their spokesman was a friendly man, but not garrulous, in his mid-twenties with dark hair, sun-burned skin, and a quick wit and dry humor. He shook José's hand with a firm, strong grip and introduced himself as Ned Ballister. Then he and his comrades strode along their way.

One old man stood alone, a dusty, sweat-stained hat guarding eyes of cornflower blue. The skin of his face mimicked the cracked surface of the desert, burned red from the sun, and a long, stringy white beard hung from his cheeks and neck, stirring in the hot morning wind. He wore a checkered red shirt and threadbare jeans, and the heels were nearly gone from his boots.

It was the old man's eyes that kept drawing José's attention. They held a haunted look, a yearning look, and they swept the hills with a dream thinly cached beneath their surface. The old man probably stood on the brink of his final gamble. With a sigh, José swung his eyes away.

Someone said there had been a shooting on the reservation. Folks had spoken for days, even weeks, of how the sooners would bring trouble. Had one of them challenged the Indian police? Had someone died? But soon further word came there had been no shooting after all, just a rumor torched off by bored tongues and ears hearing imagined words.

Still, José remained wary, for today he counted more pistols under coattails than he had seen in years. Although accustomed to having his at his side, he generally didn't wear it into town. Not even today. McAllister, on the other hand, had a gunbelt strapped about his hips. His Colt was in plain sight, and his gnarled brown hand never strayed far from it.

For several minutes, a one-legged cowboy named McLaughlin paraded the street, leaping around with his crutch beneath his arm. He swore he could ride as well with one leg as most men could with two. And here and there José saw the four cowboys, Cottrell, Marley, Neeser, and Hillman, all of whom had made plain their challenge against the eight car train that would make its run for the Blackfoot land office that afternoon. They were not the only ones, just the most outspoken. And they were younger than José, which worried him. But he didn't believe they were after the same spot of land he and McAllister wanted.

The most verbal of the cowboys, and the most flamboyant, was Will Hillman. Little Will Hillman. He dressed light that day, no gun in sight. His hat snugged low over his ears, its string already done up under his chin, and to his legs and arms he had attached long streamers of red and green ribbon so folks would know who he was. They would cheer him as he beat the train to Blackfoot, a fifty mile ride from where he intended to stake his claim. And even if they didn't cheer him, it mattered little. He would have his land.

Then José noticed a quiet element there in the crowd—the red man. The Shoshones and Bannocks walked, stood, or sat in silence, forgotten by the crowd. One of them rode a pinto pony up the street, his face dignified, gazing about him with eyes that saw but didn't understand this need of the white man for land to call his own. This Indian, a Shoshone, wore a broad brimmed "Boss of the Plains" Stetson, blue jeans, a striped shirt and yellow bandanna, with small-roweled spurs jingling quietly at his heel. He was dressed as a white man except for his beaded hatband, but by the look in his eyes he would never be white. And José was glad for that.

Even women represented the Indian element today, and they, unlike the man José had watched, still dressed in native fashion, carrying Hudson Bay blankets, wearing embroidered floral shawls with hand-tied fringes, loose skirts, and high-topped moccasins. Some of them carried papooses on their backs, and they walked down the center of the street as if afraid to touch the white man's buildings nesting in the midst of their fathers' land.

The streets began to thin out as if cleared by an awesome wind, carrying everyone in its path toward the south. José and McAllister went with the crowd, leading their horses, enjoying being on their feet for the last few minutes. Stores began to close. The saloons were silent, shutters drawn. They passed the lumberyards, passed the brewery, its roof crowded with anxious spectators. They rode by the cemetery and reached the reservation line near the big brickyard. For hundreds of yards either way swarmed the people, horses, wagons, buggies, even an occasional bicycle.

Spectators climbed the butte on the east, called Red Hill by some, killing rattlesnakes as they went. Others crawled up on top of the Oregon Short Line freight cars or roofs of nearby city buildings. Still more climbed the distant West Bench—the shore of ancient Lake Bonneville.

In front of the runners stretched miles of gray sagebrush, made grayer by the dust driven thickly upon it, waiting to be stirred to life once more by thousands of churning legs and wheels.

A skinny fellow in a black suit ran out onto the reservation ground with a camera on his shoulder, then quickly turned toward the runners and ducked beneath the black hood of his camera. The uproar was so great from the miners and cowboys, yelling at him for entering the reservation before noon, that he ran back into the crowd without getting his photograph, thinking the threats were serious.

José listened to several men jeering at some Indians who stood watching the show. They yelled insults and meaningless threats, and José had to shake his head. One would have thought the white man would thank the red for his land. Instead, they only made fun of him. He swallowed, looking away—embarrassed by his own people. They would never know the dignity of the Shoshone as José had.

José dug into his vest pocket and pulled out a heavy brass pocket watch. It was ten minutes to noon, if the big black hands were right. He looked over at McAllister, who was peering at the watch too, and then their eyes met.

"That thing keep good time?" McAllister hollered over the hum of the crowd.

José shrugged. "I guess we'll find out. Think we'll be able to hear the whistle?"

McAllister nodded, glancing around at the feverish crowd. "We'll hear it. Just get set."

They checked their cinches, secured their bridles, their hats. José pulled out his Notice of Discovery, his Notice of Entry, his Homestead Notice, thumbed through them nervously. He knew little about legal matters, but he knew he had to hang onto these papers at all costs. He tucked them back into his money belt, patting it three times for good measure.

They climbed up on their horses, as everyone else was doing, then worked to hold them in check. Farmers boarded their wagons, men with sleeve garters hugging their calves readied their bicycles, checking tires and moving parts. Ridiculous, José thought, for a man on a bicycle to think he could beat the fastest horses in Idaho, especially on the unimproved roads of the day. When a road in 1902 was referred to as "unimproved," it was no joke.

From atop his prancing gray, José spotted the dark-haired girl in the skirt. She was seated atop a black horse of Arabian descent, and it danced around with its tail held up and its head proud and little ears erect. The girl and the horse made a pretty picture. José looked around and saw no man that appeared to be with the girl, and he wondered if she was alone. He thought of Rebecca, waiting for him back at the ranch. He was glad she wasn't here, readying to ride, to put her life on the line like this girl. He looked forward to her greeting him in the yard that night when he finally made it home.

The three young miners sat in a buckboard on the left, Ballister holding the reins, one friend beside him, and the third behind, holding onto the back of the seat. They didn't speak to each other. Their eyes were glued straight ahead.

And there, seemingly lost in the dust, sat the old man with the haunted blue eyes. A chill passed over José, and he quickly glanced away, his eyes lighting on McAllister. Someday he might be that haunted old man, if they didn't win this race.

Shuffling around the way they were, José wondered if the horses wouldn't use up their energy before the whistle even blew. He tried to calm the big stud down, but it couldn't be done. He champed at the bit, foam starting to form at the corners of his mouth. He tossed his head and blew forcefully through his nostrils, eyes flashing wildly about. They were back a ways from the front of the line, but José had faith this big gray would quickly pick his way to the fore.

José's heart slammed inside his chest. Sweat soaked his armpits, beaded his face. He thought of looking at his watch, then thought better of it. His eyes darted about the crowd, up Red Hill, at the trees that shaded the grassy cemetery. They swung over the mountains to the south, to the west, to the dusty sagebrush that seemed to stretch into eternity, and far beyond which he had to ride.

Then suddenly the roundhouse whistle began to moan. Even at that distance he could hear its pathetic onset. Soon it was a wail rising above the din of voices and rattling chains.

And they were off.

Cowboys spurred their horses with devil-may-care foolishness from the beginning. Miners whipped and slashed their reins and cursed the way miners must do to keep their sanity. The line held straight for a time, a huge cloud of dust billowing up behind them. José lost sight of the dark-haired girl, of Ballister and his friends, of the old man. Beneath him, the gray's hooves pounded furiously, in time with McAllister's, beside him.

Soon, José and McAllister were in the lead, along with a handful of others. Dust rose in a roiling mass, filling the valley from Red Hill to the West Bench, turning the land into a boiling gray sea, where only dark forms trailing away in the haze could be seen from town. The sound of thousands of hooves, of rumbling wagon wheels, was awesome to hear. It filled the valley, shook the earth to its core. Voices could be heard in the melee, triumphant voices, desperate voices, voices already filled with the pain of defeat or the ecstasy of anticipated success.

Far to the rear, two white-topped wagons reeled along, their tarp covers whipping in the wind. The drivers' faces were grim, and they leaned forward, lashing their horses furiously, yelling obscenities. Several bicyclists peddled madly, their legs almost a blur, but already they lagged hopelessly behind.

Still running together, José and McAllister rode through the Portneuf Gap, their horses heaving with the exertion of the run. There were only thirty or forty horses still up with them. Some of the runners began to pull off after they left the gap, racing for spots of good ground along the river course. But José, McAllister, and many others bore on, bringing their mounts to a more manageable trot now that the initial surge was over. They stood in the stirrups, bent slightly forward at the waist to let their legs take the strain and not their backs and rumps. They rode past Blackrock Station, past the spot where they would soon be building the settlement called Inkom. They were in the narrow valley of the black rocks, the sheer lava cliffs on the right of them with masses of jumbled, shattered boulders piled up below.

Running, running, running. Trotting, clopping, jolting like their teeth would come loose. The horses were lathered. José had tried to keep his gray back with McAllister's bay, but the bay was tiring more swiftly under the bigger man's weight. José pulled ahead, not wanting to leave his friend but needing to win that land for him if he could. Sweating, aching, face still stinging from bits of gravel sent flying at him by churning hooves, José drove on, settled into the rocking of the saddle. There weren't many riders with them now. Most of them had pulled off to claim land or gone on past them. But José wouldn't pull off. He had Robbers Roost in his head, and there was no other reason to make this run. He wiped the sweat from his eyes, wiped his hand on his trousers, chanced a look behind him.

McAllister came on doggedly, valiantly. His jaw was set, his eyes straight ahead. His hat was jammed low on his forehead, tied down tightly at the chin. When at last José drew up at Robbers Roost Creek, he realized with elation no one else stopped there. The others trotted grimly by. In spite of his fatigue, José yelled triumphantly, sure of his claim to the land. But he didn't want to claim it without McAllister by his side, now that he knew they could both make it.

McAllister came alongside him just as he started the gray moving again, and as he passed José saw the corners of his mouth lift in a smile. That made José smile, too, and let out another whoop of joy. They rode on together, side by side, and when José looked at his friend his smile was wide, and his hat sailed back on its string, letting his gray hair fly with the wind.

José was still looking at McAllister, his heart full of gladness, when his friend's smile disappeared as if slapped off his face by a giant hand. A wild look leaped into McAllister's eyes, and José whipped his head about to look in front of them, where McAllister's eyes were fixed.

It was as if a world full of beauty had suddenly burned to the ground, as if someone had ripped the heart out of José's chest and thrown it beneath the horses' hooves.

Both horses ground to a halt in a cloud of dust. There before them, standing next to his claim notice tacked to a cottonwood tree, a skinny, whiskered man smiled up at them, a Remington double-barrel shotgun clutched loosely in front of him. The man wasn't even breathing hard, and the bay horse tied to a tree near him hadn't broken a sweat.

For a month or more, José had listened to stories of sooners, stories of honest men cheated effectively out of precious ground they had run their hearts out for. He hadn't *dis*believed the tales, but he had never related them to himself. Those things only happened to others, and the lucky ones sat around later and shook their heads, observing as how that was too bad to happen to such a nice fellow. But it couldn't happen to José.

"Mornin', fellers." The man's smile broadened, but there was unmistakable warning in his eyes and in the shotgun across his legs. "This spot's taken," he said.

Numbly, José looked past the man. "What about farther up?"

"It's took, too. Some of my friends got up there ahead o' me. We got some good horses, you c'n bet."

José swallowed, wiping absently at his mouth. "I thought I was in front. Where's the horse you rode here?"

The man just jerked his thumb toward his saddled horse, his eyes hardening noticeably but the smile still frozen on his lips. "You blind? It's right there."

"Hell, mister! He ain't even breathin' hard," José retorted.

The man's smile slowly disappeared. Warning filled his pale eyes. His lips twitched before he spoke. "So what of it, greaser? You callin' me a liar?"

The heat had started to rise into José's face, and words began to form on his lips, when the sharp crack of a .45 stunned him, made his head whip to the side. The Colt Lightning bucked again, hammering against McAllister's palm, and José looked at him in horror and disbelief.

José whirled back to the sooner as his horse shied warily away from McAllister. The man had dropped his shotgun and was looking back and forth from McAllister to José, his eyes shocked. Both of his hands tightly gripped his stomach, and blood started to trickle between his fingers. Then the gun cracked again. José didn't see where the bullet connected, but he knew it did, for it was Robert McAllister who held the gun, and he didn't know how to miss. The man's eyes rolled back in his head, and he slumped over on his side, crushing his hat into the grass.

McAllister turned and barked at José, "Now git that paper off the tree an' post yers up there! This is *our* land!"

Unable to speak, José turned, McAllister's words not even registering on him. His mouth hung open, and he stared at McAllister while trying to hold the gray in check.

"Hey!"

At the sound of the voice, José turned in the saddle in time to hear the report of a rifle from up the canyon and hear the bullet whiz past. With an oath, he reined the gray down-canyon and rolled spurs across its ribs. In a moment, he realized McAllister wasn't following, and he stopped and turned to see what was the matter.

Three men had run into sight up the creek, all of them brandishing rifles. One of them was heavy-set, well over two hundred pounds, and further proof these men were sooners; a man that size could never have beaten them here on horseback. Shots whined past McAllister's and José's horses, startling them. They fought to keep them under control. José looked at the dead man, then back at the three with the rifles. He and McAllister stood no chance.

With a curse, José yelled at McAllister. "Let's go!" Then he turned and cantered down through the rocks toward the freight road.

Clamping his jaw grimly, McAllister reined the horse about and rode down the canyon, his back a broad target for two hundred yards. As if he had lost all sense, he made no attempt to hurry. Other shots rang out and flew past him, but none connected. He slowed down even more. Before McAllister rode out of the mouth of the canyon and back onto the road, he paused. He sat his horse for a long, breathless moment, his back to the sooners. He stared straight ahead, his face emotionless. When there were no more shots, he lowered his head. "Lousy sooners can't even shoot," he said quietly, and rode on to catch José.

José had turned south at the mouth of the canyon, knowing McCammon was not far away and he might have to go there for help. Hearing the shots, he sat the gray and waited anxiously for McAllister to show. He was about to turn and run when his friend appeared and trotted down onto the road. McAllister put his heels to the horse's sides and rode up to José in a swirl of dust.

"They stoled our land. Stoled it right from under us," McAllister spoke, then studied José's eyes, searching for a reaction.

José just stared back, unbelieving. It had seemed so easy for McAllister to kill. How many other times had he killed since they had parted ways? A tight, nauseating hand clutched his stomach, wrenched and wrung it until the bile seemed to rise in his throat.

"You just killed a man," he said helplessly. "Shot him down like a dog."

"He weren't as good as a dog. He needed killin'. He'd a killed you if he had the chance, if it would git 'im that piece o' land. He stoled it—flat out stoled it."

"You can't just kill a man! You can't shoot people down like animals!"

McAllister hawked and spat, ignoring José's admonition. "I'll have to run, kid," he said huskily. "I didn't count on bein' seen by them others up the canyon. But yer still free. They got nothin' on you. You still got half a chance. Remember that spot o' land a couple canyons south, where yuh faced down the griz? You said you saw a place that'd be perfect fer a house. Well, run for it! Don't look back. You got fifteen men waitin' for yuh to pick up horses on the way to Blackfoot. Don't let 'em down. Don't let *me* down. You c'n do it. You c'n make that run!"

"What about you?"

"I got a run of a diff'rent kind, Lucky. I'm runnin' fer my life now. I'll let Trombell's horse go when I'm safe."

McAllister stuck out his weathered hand, and José shook it hesitantly, his mind churning. Then they spurred their horses together, headed for Wagner Canyon. When they reached its mouth, they turned up it together. But when José stopped to post his notice, McAllister continued on, heading for Haystack Mountain. When José saw his back disappear up the canyon at last, he turned and threw himself onto his horse, heading for the main road.

He blocked the killing from his mind, hid it, disguised it, channeled his fearful energy into a desire to win a race. He wiped out memory of McAllister, of his wild eyes as he leveled the Colt .45. He drove his horse relentlessly until he came upon Les Muldoon, a cowboy friend who held his first relief horse half a mile north. With the flourish of a Pony Express rider, he leaped from the saddle of the gray and mounted a sorrel, and he was off again, running for all he was worth. Pushing this horse like he had never pushed one before.

Three miles farther, he made the change for a bay with four white stockings, and this quarter horse had a sprint that took his breath away. He drove it, whipping it with the long ends of his reins, yelling wildly, letting his mind go blank. He knew only the challenge of the race, no longer the horror of killing. The wind slapped at his hair, throwing his hat about on its string. He rode and rode until his sides ached, his back cringed, his rump cried against the pounding.

His third mount, another bay, carried him past Blackrock Station, the train's first stop. He hardly even gave the little depot a glance as he tore away valiantly, long hair streaming in the wind. The horse didn't have the initial speed of the last one, but this one kept up a good pace for an incredible time.

José was flying, free like an eagle, squinting his eyes against the wind, the dust, the sweat, seeing the shapes of the rocks and mountains ahead of him, of the occasional horses and wagons he passed. He picked up a buckskin and drove on through the afternoon, the sun throbbing down on him mercilessly.

Up ahead, he saw two more horses, both running toward Pocatello, and soon he recognized the dark-haired woman and her companion. They were riding the same jaded horses, and José flew past them in a cloud of dust, waving back at them. He hoped they would make the train at Pocatello. If they didn't, they wouldn't make the land office at all, not if they tried to ride those same horses all the way.

On and on and on he went, his body aching for a rest. The miles seemed endless, but he had to force himself not to think about it. He rode into Pocatello and out the other side with a crowd cheering him. He rode through the sage, the saddle pounding him, his head pounding him, his heart pounding in his chest. And soon he heard a faint noise behind him, and he chanced a backward glance. A rider coming near!

He spurred onward, pushing for his next horse, yelling at this one to encourage it, knowing it was just about winded. Then ahead of him, through the sweat and dust in his eyes, he saw the shadowy shapes of a man and horse at the side of the road. No, two of them. The other one must belong to the rider behind him. He had to make sure every time he came upon a horse that it was one meant for him, for the other riders also had mounts staked along the way.

This time he traded his horse for a strawberry roan, and he feared right away they had put his lesser horses in the middle of the relay. The roan was a good horse, but it didn't have the bottom to run all out for three miles, not the way José wanted to push it. And this time it didn't take long for the other rider to close on him.

With a sideways glance, José saw the green and red streamers, the sweaty little man on the giraffe-legged bay, and he recognized Will Hillman. The little cowboy gave him a yell and a smile and wave as he pulled beyond him. José's heart fell, but he didn't let up. He was behind, but not by far, and besides, he might get to watch the ride of the decade. If he didn't beat the train, this wiry little man just might.

They were five miles from Blackfoot when José heard the train whistle. It was a long, sharp whine rising up out of the sage, spitefully warning José and Hillman it was on its way. Somewhere ahead waited one more horse, José knew. He prayed they had given him a good one.

And the train closed in.

Chapter Twenty-Nine

José knew Will Hillman heard the train too, for he began to kick his horse even more brutally, to lash more wildly with the reins. His yells rose up to José through the choking thick cloud of white dust, through the sweat that puddled in his ears, over the pounding of his own horse's hooves. Will Hillman was desperate, more desperate than he. He had bragged up this wild ride for weeks now. He had put his name on the line, his very reputation. He just *had* to beat that train, or he could never hold his head up again.

The sagebrush flew by, giving up its coat of dust to the air as the horses' legs churned through it. The sun pounded down with all its fury. José wiped at the sweat in his eyes, the sweat that trickled down endlessly from under his hat in spite of the wind whipping his face. He heard the train again, closer now, whistling to let the riders know it was still on the track. He could almost hear its iron wheels chugging, smell its black soot, feel its furnace-like nostrils breathing fire down his neck.

Up ahead, he saw two more horses through the dust. Hillman reached them and sprang from his horse, almost collapsing wearily before he could climb into the other saddle. José hung on grimly, wishing the other horse were only a short distance closer to him. But when he neared it he realized it wasn't even one of his. It must belong to one of the other riders.

He stared ahead, peering beyond the dust through the sweat in his eyes. Then he picked another horse out, still two hundred yards away. He spurred frantically, flailed the reins, forgetting his gentle way with horses. He felt the roan falter, thought it would go down. He gritted his teeth and prepared to jump and roll. But the roan caught itself, only for a moment.

Suddenly, it stumbled again and down it went, the ground flying up incredibly fast. José kicked his feet out of the stirrups, using his hands on the roan's neck to push himself away. They landed together, and José rolled and crashed dizzily, the brush careening past him.

He lay on his back, trying to catch his breath. A cloud of dust rolled about him, sticking to his sweaty skin. He heard the horse grunting laboriously, heard its hooves paw the ground. He turned in time to see it lunge shakily to its feet, looking around as bewildered as he was. It shook itself, rattling the saddle and bridle, spraying the air with white lather from its sides, neck, and mouth. A cloud of dust drifted off it, and it rolled its eyes warily at the man on the ground.

With great effort, José pushed against the earth, rising to a sitting position, and took in a great breath. The breath was more dust than air, and he broke into a fit of coughing, then wiped at his mouth as he sat wearily letting the sweat trickle down his cheeks and neck.

He turned his head at the sound of hoofbeats. Looking up, he saw a horse bearing down on him from the direction of Blackfoot. It stopped just shy of him, and its rider fairly flew from the saddle, running to him.

"Get up, José!" the young man yelled. It was Jim White, the last of his relay men. "Get on an' go!" White stared at José, then raised his eyes to look back in the direction of the train. He looked again at José with pleading in his eyes.

With a sigh, José glanced over at the approaching train, his body now throbbing with pain. Something in his mind clicked, and with White's help he struggled to his feet. He wouldn't let that train's passengers see José Olano on the ground. As the train flew past at fifty miles an hour they wouldn't see him lying down, but in the saddle, still riding stubbornly.

"Way t' go, José!" White yelled triumphantly as José staggered toward the waiting horse. White ran to it and grabbed the reins, then held the left stirrup for him as he clawed his way up onto its back.

"Now go!"

José heard White's voice only faintly over the sound of the train's whistle, now just a mile away. He rolled his spurs over this big bay's ribs, leaned forward and felt the horse sail out over the sagebrush, flying like a four-legged eagle. This horse was one of the best of the string, José knew immediately, at least for speed. It tore over the ground with reckless abandon, and in the exhilaration of the pounding ride José forgot his pain, forgot the sound of the train's whistle, saw only the distant gray form of Will Hillman and his horse galloping on with the great green masses of cottonwood which marked the site of Blackfoot appearing on the horizon.

The horse's hooves churned, the train bellowed its disdain, the road flew by with impressive speed. José's hat whipped about on its string, slapping his back as if egging him on. Gobs of saliva streamed from the corners of the straining horse's mouth.

And then the train was drawing past.

José didn't want to look, but human weakness pulled his eyes that way, and he saw with dismay the hundreds of bodies strung like a scattered sack of rags all over the eight cars of the train. Men rode the cartops, crowded the cars, stood eagerly on the platforms, the choicest places on the entire train, from which they could dismount easily and run for the land office. Some brave souls were even stretched out on the brake beams underneath the cars, holding on grimly as the rocks and heat of the railbed rushed dangerously past them.

It registered suddenly that the occupants of the train were yelling at him out the windows, from the platforms, from the roof, waving their hats in the air. At first, he thought they were jeering him, but with sudden elation he realized these were yells of encouragement, cheers! Grimly, José clenched his jaw and waved back, and the train chugged past. With one long last whistle, it shrieked back at him derisively, and he knew he had lost. But yet he had won.

Up ahead, the train bore down on Will Hillman. The little horseman spurred his horse grimly, ribbons fluttering behind him, ribbons that were to mark a victory. His horse churned its legs, its neck stretched out, trying for the town before the train could reach it. Hillman and his horse were so close now.

But it was as if they had stopped to watch the train go by.

The town came into view, its dusty gray buildings beautiful to the men on the train, but also a sign that the most important part of the race was about to commence. People thronged the broad, sandy street, moved around in the shade of the tall cottonwoods that sheltered the buildings. One building in particular swarmed with onlookers: the land office.

Will Hillman fell behind in the dust and smoke left by the train, but still he spurred for all he was worth, hoping to cross the track behind the train and beat its passengers to the line at the land office.

Before the train came to a stop, the unloading began. Men leaped through the air from the cartops, from the platforms, their coattails flying. They jumped from windows, more than one of them landing on his back in the dust as they misjudged the train's speed. They rolled from the brake beams with dust falling off of them, they plunged down the steps, not caring who got in their way. They yelled and pushed and scrambled, racing across the sandy street for the land office.

In less than half a minute, a line of people hundreds of feet long stretched along the street from the land office, and for most the race had ended. But then in came Will Hillman, his horse's sides heaving, his face grim, streaked with sweat. White dust coated his clothes from his head to his foot. And the little cowpuncher, usually happy-go-lucky, couldn't even look another man in the eye. His bright ribbons fluttered in the breeze as he walked up to the end of the line. Those ribbons waved merrily, as if they thought he had won.

A roar went up for the little rider, and men he didn't even know clapped him on the back, congratulating him on his incredible ride. At last, a weary smile lit his face, and he removed his hat and swept it in front of him, taking a bow.

José rode in two minutes behind Hillman, and a cheer went up for him, also. But in spite of the crowd's obvious admiration and respect, there was no place saved for him in line. All he had was the cheers and a handshake from little Will Hillman.

Up ahead in line, José saw the young miner, Ballister, talking excitedly with his friends. They looked happy. He spotted the dark-haired woman, too, at the same time she spotted him. Their eyes met, and they smiled. Reaching up, she removed her hat to him, and he had to laugh.

And then his eyes fell upon the old man with the haunted eyes. Somehow, miraculously, among the throng of younger people, he had found a place in line only a third of the way from the land office. José nodded and smiled to himself.

✳   ✳   ✳

The summer of 1902 passed, and fall came to Bannock County, stole in like a weasel in the chicken house before José knew it. The maple leaves turned wine red up Wagner Canyon, and gold washed the rustling leaves of the quaking aspens. There was a different feeling in the air, the strange sensation nature brings in her hour of greatest glory, just before she goes to sleep for another winter.

The nights were cold, with stars like distant, icy pools of water in the black sky. Some nights the moon hung like a huge, yellow dinner plate on top of the Portneuf Range. Frost grained up on the yellow grass in the mornings, melted slowly from the leaves as the sun crested Haystack Mountain. The scents of sage and juniper, cottonwood, aspen, and willow blended in the narrow passage of Wagner Canyon. Smells of fir, mahogany, and mountain laurel drifted down from farther up the canyon. The moose and mule deer gathered there, browsing, grazing, building up fat reserves for the approaching winter.

Summer birds seemed to disappear overnight, leaving only stragglers behind as they went on to warmer climes. The robins were gone, the bluebirds, the meadowlarks. José missed their cheerful songs. But he relished the smells of the fall, the cold, clear mornings, the rustle of the dying leaves. He loved the sound of the Portneuf when he rode along it between the Dempsey hotpools and McCammon. Its many falls glittered in early morning sunlight, with red dogwood tangled together along its banks like clumps of giant, rusted nails.

The fall roundup had just ended, and José had brought Ben Trombell's cattle back to the valley. He watched them graze peacefully across the grassy field. Haystack Mountain loomed behind them on the skyline, its high, flat top dropping off on the north into sheer white cliffs, the home of mule deer bucks with antlers so large they boggled the imagination.

José sat the saddle lazily, his eyes half closed, his bushy mustache and long hair rustling in the morning breeze. He rode back at a canter to the ranch house in Marsh Valley, watching blue smoke curl lazily from its chimney as he approached. The sweet scent of burning fir came to him on the breeze, and he drew it deep into his lungs and loosened his coat at the neck, letting the cool air flood down into his shirt. God had surely given him this morning as a gift.

After putting Duster away in the barn, José went quietly into the house. Rebecca was alone, for the children had gone to spend a couple of days with the couple they referred to affectionately as Grandma and Grandpa Bonn, at Dempsey. Rebecca started when she turned from the counter to see him standing there watching her. Her chestnut hair flew about as she whirled, and a strand of it strayed across her chin. She brushed it away and stood looking quietly at him, her green eyes sparkling with some secret thought.

They came together in a warm embrace, and their lips met passionately. Then Rebecca leaned back her head. "José, this morning is so beautiful," she beamed. "Don't you just love the sun on the mountains?"

José smiled. "I sure do. It reminds me of you." Before Rebecca could reply, he went on. "I rode up Wagner Canyon today. Saw a herd of mule deer there where I met that grizzly. Just as peaceful as can be up there."

"It is *now,*" Rebecca agreed. "Now that Mr. McAllister is gone."

The words stung José, and by the look in Rebecca's eyes she immediately regretted them. "I'm sorry, dear. I just can't forget the awful thing that happened over there."

"I know. There'll always be a ghost up Robbers Roost." José dropped his arms and started to retreat, but when Rebecca held onto him and insistently drew him back to her, he sighed and put his arms around her again. "I'm just glad those other fellas lost it. Looks like some good, honest folks ended up with it." He smiled and put the palm of his hand along her cheek, gazing into her eyes. "I do love you, Rebecca, you know that? More than anything."

"And I love you," she said and kissed him again. "I hope we can live happily up there."

"We will," José assured her. "I'll make you the happiest woman in the world."

"I already am." With a mischievous smile, Rebecca took José by the hand and led him toward their bedroom.

The law of Bannock County had conducted a fruitless search for Robert McAllister after the killing of the sooner up Robbers Roost. José had reported the killing to Sheriff Martin Rice, leaving out the fact that he was a friend of McAllister's. He told the story as if he and McAllister had just happened to try for the same piece of land. José didn't like to lie, but he hadn't had any part in the killing, and he just wanted to wash his hands of it and do what was right. But even though they had employed him as tracker in their hunt, he did his best to throw them off McAllister's track. And since McAllister was doing his best, too, there was no way any white man was going to find the murderer. The guilt of letting McAllister go scot-free sometimes racked his soul, but hunting him down would have been like betraying his own father. He just couldn't let that posse capture the man to whom he owed his life.

They had eaten noon dinner, and José was sitting back in his chair to let the meal settle, when he heard the hooves of many horses approaching from afar. "Wonder who that is," he mused, looking over at Rebecca.

She looked at him questioningly, but then her face showed understanding when the sounds registered on her own ears. She shrugged and stood up quickly, pressing her dress down with her hands to straighten it, then pushing her hair back behind her shoulders.

José laughed and stood up, going around the table to put his arm around her. "You make yerself any prettier, I'm liable to have to fight them off yuh."

Rebecca rolled her eyes and giggled as he led her toward the door and pulled it open.

A group of riders pulled up before the house, grimly looking about them at the yard. Ben Trombell limped from his house and shaded his eyes with his hand, staring toward the horsemen.

The leader was a sharp-nosed, stern-looking man of average height but whose overpowering presence made him stand out from the group. A badge shone on the front of his sheepskin coat, and a pistol butt on his right hip pushed out insistently against his coattail. He, like all the rest, carried a rifle in a saddle scabbard under the stirrup leather. This was Bannock County's sheriff, Martin Rice.

"Morning, José. How are you?"

"Medium," José replied with a grin.

A smile crossed Rice's face, brightening his visage, but he was not a man given to levity, and the smile faded as quickly as it appeared.

Sensing something out of place, José's own habitual smile quickly died. He looked from Sheriff Rice to the group in general with open curiosity. "What brings you out so far?"

"Well, José, we need your help," Rice said bluntly. "They tell me roundup just ended, or I wouldn't bother you. But we just had a couple killings in town, and we've had a hell—" He stopped and glanced apologetically at Rebecca. "—a *heck* of a time keeping on the trail of the killer. He's a sharp one."

José's heart instantly jumped, and a sick feeling gripped his insides. "You know who it was?" he asked hesitantly.

Rice nodded. "Fellow named Frank Preston. Taylor, there saw him. He can identify him when we find him. But this fellow's like a mountain lion. He hardly leaves any trail at all."

Inwardly, José sighed with relief and hoped it didn't show on his face. Just for a moment, he had thought…Well, it didn't matter. It wasn't McAllister. That was all he cared about.

"Like I said, José, I hate to bother you. I know you have other things to do, but I could use your help. And if you can find him, there's a thousand dollar reward to be split between us."

José nodded, his interest perking up. "Got time fer coffee, Sheriff?" He and Rebecca didn't drink coffee, but they kept a pot on for visitors.

Rice started to shake his head, then paused and looked around him at the horses, who stood blowing and bowing their heads. "Well, I reckon we could stand to rest the horses. You have enough to go around?"

José shrugged, raising his hands. "Depends on how full we pour the cups." He laughed. "I'll have to saddle up anyway, an' that means I gotta catch another horse. Duster's already been out."

José stepped away from Rebecca, leaving her standing in the doorway. "Come out to the corral with me, Sheriff," he said. "You c'n tell me about it while I'm ropin' one out."

Stiffly, the sheriff swung out of his saddle and followed José out to the corral. José picked out a dun gelding and roped it on the first try, then tied it to the top corral rail and treated it to a double ration of oats while he brushed its back and threw his saddle on. As he worked and the posse drank coffee, he listened to Martin Rice's story.

Frank Preston had been in town a day or two, spending his time in one of the local saloons. He had seemed an ordinary saddle bum to those who met him, a drifter looking for a meal and a place to rest his head. Then, early that morning, he had gone into the First National Bank and robbed it of six thousand dollars, and while making his escape had killed a clerk and one bystander, a thirteen year-old boy who had come in to make a deposit for his father.

José grew sick at the story. It turned out he knew the dead boy and his family. They were good folks, owners of a boot and shoe store in Pocatello. The more he thought about it, the more determined he became to catch the killer. Anyone who would kill a child… José shuddered and slipped the bit into the dun's mouth, then pulled the headstall over its ears.

Rebecca had been preparing food for José as he readied the horse, and she had it waiting in his saddlebags with a full canteen when he returned to the house. He pulled his bedroll from behind the door and lashed the works on behind his saddle, tying his coat in front of the saddle horn. When he turned around, Rebecca was holding his rifle in her hands, a '94 Winchester .30-30 Ben Trombell had bought him for his thirtieth birthday. She thrust the rifle toward him, her eyes round and worried.

"I loaded it," she said.

José took the rifle and passed it over to Sheriff Rice, who held it while he swept Rebecca into his arms. He kissed her unabashedly in front of the posse, and she was blushing when he let her go. "I don't know when I'll be back. Just don't worry, Becca, an' tell the kids I'll be all right. This shouldn't take long."

Rebecca reached out and put her hand on his cheek, looking into his eyes searchingly. "I love you, José. You get home soon, you hear?"

With a reassuring smile, he bent and kissed her again, his long hair brushing her cheek.

They rode to McCammon, then left the road, crossed the river, and traveled to the mouth of a sagebrush-covered canyon in the hills where a lone man and horse awaited them. He was a posse member, left to mark the spot where they had lost the trail. To the posse's amazement, José quickly picked up the trail. The killer had masked it by tying rawhide shoes over his horse's hooves, Indian style. This man had ridden the outlaw trail before, or at least he knew something of it.

From there, the puzzling trail took them partway up one brushy canyon, then veered east and led them straight up the side of the canyon to its ridge. The trail followed the ridgetop for a ways, then left it at the oddest of places, where a deep cut had been eroded out of the soil by run-off, leaving a crevice in the earth three feet across and another three feet deep.

By careful scrutiny, José was able to find where the killer had jumped this, trying to throw off pursuit. He had then tied his horse's reins to a clump of sagebrush and gone back across the crevice to obliterate his sign, sweeping the tracks away on both sides, then sprinkling the area with loose soil and dead, rotted vegetation collected from several yards away, where its absence wouldn't be noticed. José smiled grimly, recalling the times McAllister had shown him tricks like this and told him some day he might run into others who knew the same tricks.

The trail went like this for two hours, leading them up several different canyons, never staying to one path. There would be no second-guessing this man. And even though it took him extra time to play this hide-the-trail game, the odds were in the killer's favor. He could hide his trail all day, then ride all night, but José could only trail him in the daylight.

As José followed the trail, he thanked McAllister silently for his unending patience, his desire to make him into a tracker. Without that, he never could have made out this trail. The irony was staggering, and once, while they were letting the horses catch their breath, José stood silently and stared south, at the distant, indented bulge of Oxford Peak. If Sheriff Martin Rice had any idea who was responsible for their being able to remain on this trail, what would he think? It would surely sicken him to know that only because of one killer were they able to find another.

This man they chased now was almost as good as McAllister. He used a few of the same tricks. José was apprehensive about what other ploys awaited them as the trail wore on. And when they did find this Frank Preston José had a feeling he wouldn't be taken easily. Not if he was like Robert McAllister in other ways, too. He had worked too hard to escape with his booty, and he had already killed for it twice. José was smart enough to know he wouldn't hesitate to kill again. Any man who would kill a boy had no qualms. Even as hard as McAllister had grown, José knew he would never kill a boy, not even to escape capture.

They found the first campsite that evening, and it was a dry one. The killer had bedded down in a tangle of sagebrush and grass, with junipers all around him, and he had tied his mount fifty yards below him in the brushy canyon. When José lost the trail leading away from the camp, it was growing dusk, and Sheriff Rice decided to call a halt there. It would be a dry camp.

Cold purple shadows slunk across the hillsides as the last of the orange sunlight drained behind Scout Mountain and Old Tom, and the posse members huddled silently on the hillside, lost in their own thoughts. José walked away from the group and stood at a lone, gnarled juniper, gazing at the dusky draws and mountains stretching out before them to fade into the sky. A nighthawk swung and circled above them, crying out raspily, diving to catch some insect, then slicing upward through the air just as it seemed inevitable it would smash to earth.

José listened to the crickets, saw the stars, like distant conchos, appear in the sky. He watched the light of a far-off train creep northward through the valley. He heard someone walking up to him, boots scuffing rocks and pants brushing against junipers. McAllister would have scoffed at them. José himself wore wool trousers, allowing him to go silently.

"What do you think, José?" It was Sheriff Rice. "Can you find the trail again?"

José took in a deep breath and let it out quickly, breaking a branch off the juniper next to him and flinging it down the slope. "I c'n find it. But he's still a ways ahead of us. What happens if he makes it out of the county?"

Rice's clothing stirred in the darkness as he shifted his weight. "He killed a man and a little boy, José. I suppose I'll keep chasing him until you can't take me any farther. A man has to ignore boundaries sometimes for the sake of justice."

José nodded. "I'll do my best to see it through then too, Sheriff. I just hope he doesn't decide to stop runnin' an' lay for us."

The silence stretched for a long moment while Rice digested that comment. Finally, his deep voice broke the stillness, its tone quiet. "You ever have to kill a man, José?"

José looked over sharply at the sheriff, then sighed and looked away. Rice's eyes were fixed across the canyon, not on José. "Yes, I killed a man once, Sheriff. He killed a friend of mine and tried to kill me. But I hope I never have to kill another."

Rice didn't give any indication of surprise, and José guessed he'd already known the answer to his own question. The older man was silent for a long minute, except for a faint sniffle once, then a cough. At last, he cleared his throat. "I've never killed anybody, José. I never fought a war and never had reason to do any man in. But I'm in a job where I always know I could have to take a man's life any day I go to work. I'm different than you that way. No one expects anything out of you, except that you find a fugitive. But you're at the head of the posse. When we get close, he'll see you tracking him, and he'll know we couldn't find him without you. José, he'll kill you if he can. You know that."

José swallowed hard, squinting his eyes up at the stars. Rebecca and the children flitted through his thoughts, but he pushed them away just as quickly. "Like I said, Sheriff. I had to kill a man once. I reckon you already knew that. I don't wanna ever kill another, but this fella killed a kid, and that coulda been my kid. If he killed once, he'll kill again. He's gotta be stopped."

Sheriff Rice cleared his throat. "I'm glad you're here, José. You've been a lot of help to this county through the years. But killing is my responsibility, if it comes to our life or his. All you have to do is hang back. I reckon I can do the rest."

José turned and stared at Rice in the darkness, feeling a sudden kinship with this big, stern man. "I said I didn't *want* to kill another man, Sheriff. But I've already killed one, an' I've been through the nights of torture because of it. Before I let any friend of mine go through what I went through, I'll do the killing myself."

A cold breeze swept up the hill, whispering in the juniper branches, and out across the canyon a coyote barked, a wild, eerie sound in the night. The nighthawk gave one last cry, and José made a wish when a falling star careened down the sky.

Chapter Thirty

José was up long before daylight, and by the sounds he knew several of the others were, too. But they were probably up due to the cold. José was used to sleeping out in unpleasant conditions. He was up because his churning mind refused to let him sleep. All he could think of was the trail ahead, and the knowledge he might have to take another life—or lose his own…

The wind had died down, and the night throbbed with quiet. Stars hung dazzlingly near in the heavens, and the air was so crisp it almost crackled, filling his nostrils with sweet mountain fragrance in every breath. He had pulled a grape lollipop out of his saddlebag—a surprise from Rebecca—and he sat sucking on it quietly. He shrugged deeper into his sheepskin coat and worked his hands farther into the pockets, the cold, hard soil beneath him numbing his backside.

What would this day bring? Would the killer become complacent, hiding his trail less diligently than the day before? Would he grow tired of stopping and working carefully to cover sign of his passage? Would he think he had left pursuit behind and decide to make tracks and get out of the country? Probably not. As tuned to detail as he had thus far proved himself, it was unlikely he would drop his tactics and ride pell-mell for safety. He must know word would be out over the telephone lines, and other law enforcement agencies would be searching for him, too. He couldn't afford to run reckless. He would have to watch everywhere now for pursuit, and while doing so he had just as well take the extra time to hide his trail. He must know it would pay off in the end.

José heard one of the posse members rubbing his hands together, and a whispered, "Damn, it's cold." A horse blew out its nostrils and stirred against a juniper, making the frosted branches crackle against saddle leather.

Sheriff Rice's words of the night before plucked persistently at José's nerves. There was a lot of truth to what the sheriff had said. José wasn't a very big man, but right now he was an important one, and to a good marksman he made a big target. José assumed the man he hunted was a good shot. As much an outdoorsman as he had thus far proved, he reminded José of himself and McAllister, so it naturally followed he would be proficient with a firearm, too. An outlaw couldn't survive long without that skill.

If and when they neared this killer, he would see José out ahead of the posse. He would see him reading the ground, then coming on steadily. The man could probably waylay the posse, kill them all off one by one, if he worked it right. But why should he?

The only one he really had to kill was José, for without him the posse was lost. They might as well read a newspaper in the dark as try to decipher this trail. José was painfully aware of that.

Why was he here anyway? He wasn't a lawman. He was just a cowboy. He belonged on the range with a herd of cattle or horses, or home in bed with Rebecca. He should be with his children, protecting them. But he guessed he *was* protecting his children, and others like them. Any innocent person. This man had killed before, and he wouldn't hesitate to do so again. To think he might reform just because he had six thousand dollars to live on would be pure folly. That money would disappear, and then he'd need more, and someone else would die. If not the next time, then the time after that, or the one after that. José was not a student of the criminal mind, but he was a man of common sense, and he had seen enough to know bad men were never satisfied. There would always be a next time.

A sudden realization struck José that hadn't come to him before. By being here he was fulfilling an obligation to society. There were men who kept others supplied with hats, with boots, with groceries, dry goods, and tools. There were men who put out fires, men who patched wounds and delivered babies, men who built houses. Others took care of the law of the courts, and still others kept bank accounts straight. But there was only one kind of man who could bring a wily killer such as Frank Preston to justice, and that was a tracker.

Lawmen were necessary, and most were competent, too. They could bring in ordinary lawbreakers with comforting regularity. But Frank Preston was no ordinary man. He was like a Robert McAllister. Or a José Olano. José had to grunt in sudden humor at that thought, but it was true. It took a special kind of mind to track down a man of the outdoors, an obvious survivor like Frank Preston. When a man has the natural ability of a tracker, and the desire, and when he sees his training through to its end, he sets himself apart. His is a field seldom entered by the common man, and if he is to live among civilized people and enjoy the protection of the laws of the land, he must play the part for which he has destined himself.

With a sense of awe, the cold fact struck José that he was the key to finding Frank Preston and bringing him to justice. He was the *only* key. By his skill and perserverence, the door to success could be opened. And likewise, by his lack of it the door could be locked forever. It was a horrible responsibility to bear, but one he was up to. He had let the law down when it came to McAllister, but only because he was so close to him. In the case of Frank Preston, he made the promise to himself: before he turned back, the killer would be in his hands.

José chuckled silently when he thought of McAllister, his teacher, his friend, his idol. What would he think of José today? Could he ever have imagined he would be using the skills he taught him to hunt a killer to the ground? Would he be proud, or ashamed? After all, to help bring a man such as this to justice was taking one big step toward civilization. But he knew McAllister would be beside him if he could. McAllister had killed, too, but he wouldn't kill a child. To him there was no worse kind of man. In a way, McAllister was now paying his debt to society, too—through José.

José heard the soft scuffing of pant legs rubbing together and gravel rattling on the slope behind him, and then Sheriff Rice stood beside him. He realized suddenly the dawn was upon them, and the stars were being pulled up out of the sky as if by giant ropes, disappearing one by one. His breath puffed into the air in thin silver clouds.

"How was your night, José?"

"Medium." The two men said it in unison this time, and Sheriff Rice chuckled dryly. "You never do have a good day or a bad one, do you? They're all medium. How long till you can start looking for the trail?"

"Not long," José answered. "Twenty minutes. Maybe half an hour."

"Did you sleep at all?" the sheriff queried.

José shook his head. "Not much."

Rice put a heavy hand on José's shoulder. "Remember, you always have an out. The killing's my job. I get paid to take that chance."

With a long sigh, José removed his hat and ran his gloved hand back over his head, feeling its cold leather against his retreating hairline. "I'll spare you from it if I can, Sheriff. You don't have to find out what it's like."

"Well..." Rice's voice trailed off, and he lowered his head. He cleared his throat as if to speak but didn't. He just clapped José twice on the shoulder, then walked off toward his horse.

José followed suit, going to the dun. Grass around the juniper where he had tied it was sparse, and the horse had long since cleared it. It stood watching José's approach, its ears pricked sharply forward. It tried to nuzzle him, but he pushed its head away gently and rubbed its broad back, removing dead juniper branches and straightening clumps of sweat-matted hair. He threw his blanket on, then his saddle, and after thumping the dun soundly in the ribs with his fist so it would expel the breath it was holding, he drew the cinch up tight.

There was little talk in the half-light, and what José heard was soft, in reverence for the dawn. José was amused by the strange tendency of man to speak quietly in places of low light, as if to keep from disturbing the slumbering earth. The posse members who weren't already saddled did so now, then took long drinks from their canteens. They stood beating their hands together or folding their arms, wishing the sun would rise.

When it grew light enough to track, José went immediately to work, and at last he found an over-turned rock, marking where the killer had started away. The trail was well-concealed, almost more so than that of yesterday, and for a time José wondered if he wouldn't lose it. It continued to run uphill, the way he expected, so he used that knowledge to look ahead for any sign that might show up better at a side angle than directly on top of it.

It was while looking ahead that he noticed the crushed grass.

He walked over closer to the clump of grass, crouching near it. It wasn't in line with the path he'd been following. In fact, it was *down*hill from the path, back north toward the Portneuf Valley. And the only reason he noticed it was because it was so dead the killer had had trouble making it stand back up. But it was obvious he had tried.

Curious, José walked farther along, and he began to find other bits of information. A turned-over pebble, its dark belly exposed to the sun, a partially demolished red ant hill someone had tried to sprinkle gravel back onto, and bits of a dead, fragmented balsamroot leaf.

Satisfied he had discovered a change of direction in the outlaw's route, José called Rice over. He indicated the signs, then pointed down toward the valley. "I don't know what he's about, but he appears to be headed back t'ward Pocatello. He's still hidin' his trail, but he's in a hurry. He shouldn't have missed scatterin' that broken leaf."

Rice shrugged. "Well, I guess we just keep on him. I hope he's not heading for the road or the train tracks. Or the river. He'll lose us there for sure."

That remark spurred José's pride, and he looked down the ridge, then back at Rice. "No, he won't. Not for good, anyway."

The trail led down the ridge. It crossed the railroad tracks, then continued on through the sage and grassland of ranch country. It almost lost them at the river, changing directions twice, but José's stubborn will paid off in the end. Preston would now surely find out what kind of tracker he was up against, one way or the other.

José felt the imaginary bull's eye on his chest start to grow.

They came to the wagon road, and here José paused, his heart thudding heavily. This would be the big test. This was a heavily traveled road, and Preston's tracks could be completely obliterated here. Or he might not have even taken the road.

As at the river, it took precious time, but at last José located the trail, this time heading up toward Harkness Canyon and the Portneuf Range. He turned to Sheriff Rice. "I have a feeling this is gonna be a long trail, Sheriff. You might wanna have some of yer men go load up on supplies and bring in a packhorse or three and some grain an' corn."

Rice agreed, sending two men off toward McCammon. The rest of them started north across a string of shallow canyons that led to the Portneuf Range.

Sign was well-hidden for two hundred yards from the road, but then Preston relaxed, and José was able to follow him from the back of his horse. This was grassland, and here the passage of a horse could no longer be hidden. The path was a definite line, weaving through the tightly interwoven, sometimes chest-high grass. At last, they dropped into Mullen Canyon. Once they climbed out, it was uphill all the way until they topped out on a rise, and there was Harkness Canyon, snaking east and west below them. A perennial creek of the same name gurgled cold and clear down its middle.

The north side of the canyon was covered with yellow grass, sagebrush, and some junipers, but the south side was heavily overgrown with maple and other red-leaved shrubs, rank grass, and white-trunked quaking aspens with their dollar-sized leaves rustling in the midmorning breeze.

They fought their way down through the thick aspen groves to the creek, where the horses thrust their noses in and sucked water voraciously. José had to laugh at Rice's horse. It stuck its nose in partway and sucked water as if intent on drawing everyone's attention to it. It was the noisiest drinking horse he had ever heard.

"I hope he doesn't get thirsty when we're sneakin' up on somebody," José said jokingly. "'Course it could be for the best. They'll think there's a whole army of us." That brought only an obligatory laugh from Rice, but José felt triumphant in his attempt at humor.

When the horses had drunk their fill, José left the others below and rode back up to the ridge where they had left the killer's trail. Through the thick growth it was hard for the killer to hide his sign, so he didn't try. José followed the path from horseback by the broken branches of the bushes and trees. When he had gone two or three hundred yards, descending toward the creek, the others started forward to meet him.

They came together again at the creek about five hundred yards from where they had watered. Here, the killer let his horse drink and relieve itself in the form of hard green droppings. José got off his horse and picked one of them up, breaking it open. "He's gainin' on us. He's three hours, maybe four ahead of us. Glad you came for me when you did. If he'd had any more of a start, I don't know if we'd ever have caught up."

Rice raised his brows and looked at José appraisingly. "Are you so sure we will now? Four hours is a long time, especially when we have to stop and read trail all the way."

José shrugged with his eyebrows, looking up the canyon. It was starting to steepen, and directly in front of them monstrous white cliffs reared up over the trail. The left side of the canyon started to turn more to mountain mahogany and maple, and the right sprouted stands of fir.

"I'll let you in on a secret, Sheriff. I've tried to ride up Harkness Canyon, and unless Preston takes a trail out of it before he reaches those cliffs, he won't make it. It couldn't be done on a horse. Unless he knows this area, half an hour from now he'll be at the head of a box canyon that no horse could climb out of."

They continued up the canyon bottom and before too much longer fir forest hung close by them on both sides. They splashed through the creek as it meandered across their way, and the trail was still fairly easy to read here. Preston probably figured he'd lost the posse by one of his ruses, and rightly so. No normal posse could have followed him. But normal posses didn't have José Olano at their head.

Soon, the white cliffs towered over the trail in front of them, and huge gray masses of boulders thrust up a hundred feet high on their right, the slabs of rock interspersed here and there with clumps of trees. The creekbed continued on east, up the canyon, and huge white boulders and downed timber littered its snaking length. To their left was another narrow watercourse, this one merely a break in a steep hillside. At its base, a spring trickled out of mossy rocks, guarded jealously by wasps.

On horseback, it didn't appear possible to continue east. And the only way José knew out of the canyon was south, a trail that led toward Crystal Springs, and which they had already passed. But the killer's tracks still went on before them, oblivious to the obstacles in the way. José smiled grimly to himself. Unless the killer left his horse and escaped on foot, they would find him somewhere not far ahead.

José rode ahead of the others, still able to follow the trail from horseback. He had an uneasy feeling in this narrow canyon, and he scanned the cliffs on his right carefully and watched the timber on the left. He half-expected at any moment to hear a rifle shot, to feel a bullet pound his body. His caution was extreme now, for he had ridden to the impasse ahead of them. There was no way out now for a man on horseback. Well, there were ways, but a man would be lucky to find them, and even luckier to survive them. He didn't think Preston would be so lucky. No, he would be waiting ahead like a cornered cat. José's instincts told him this.

Two hundred yards farther, the rocks ahead of him exploded.

With the sound of the crash, José's gun seemed to leap into his hand, and as the dun shied and started to buck he clutched the saddle horn and prepared to go down. Behind him, the other horses stopped abruptly, snorting and balking, staring ahead.

Although initially startled, the dun had been trained in the mountains, and José was able to calm it quickly, before either of them was hurt. Probably, the dun had also seen there was nothing to fear from the three mule deer bucks that ran a ways up toward the white cliffs and stopped.

The bucks had been hiding perfectly still behind a cluster of boulders, standing on a shale slide. They had made the crash he heard when they decided to bolt and head up the hill, scattering shale below them. But now they just stood and stared. Finally, the lead buck turned his ears back and started up the talus slope, and the second one followed. The third one waited a while longer, then moved to catch up.

The trio took the shale slide, faltering only now and then, up toward the white cliffs, then at last through a tiny notch in the wall. José paused for a moment to let his dun catch its breath, then with a sidelong glance back at the posse he started on.

But the trail made a sharp bend to the right, and José stared in disbelief, looking down at the tracks, then up the shale slide to the notch in the cliff wall.

"I'll be kicked by a burro," he breathed quietly.

For a moment, he thought Frank Preston had escaped through that notch in the wall. Otherwise, where was he? But he realized the impossibility of that before making the foolish attempt himself. He decided instead to search for another way out of the canyon.

As he searched, an uneasy feeling began to ring in his head. What if Preston hadn't continued this way at all? What if he had doubled back, and they had missed it? After all, the man was canny. And he had several hours on them. He should have discovered the box canyon by now. He should have been long gone before they reached this point.

José's mind churned; he turned the dun around and went to where he had seen the last sign of Preston, then he left the trail, leaving the dun ground-reined. On his hands and knees, he scanned the brush and rock beside the killer's trail. He put his face down close to the dirt, peering for some sign, any sign that would tell him what he believed, that Preston had somehow turned around and gone back down the canyon.

Then there it was, the tiniest of objects, and he picked it up delicately between his thumb and forefinger and held it up to look closer. It was a piece of rawhide. The killer had put the rawhide shoes back on his horse!

To be certain, José crawled along farther, and before long he discovered another piece, this one slightly larger. The rocks had begun to wear on the rawhide. It was a small clue, but it was all José needed. Preston had hidden his tracks back down the canyon by taking a tougher, more unlikely route over rocks and deadfall. But he hadn't counted on the bits of rawhide and José's keen eye. These would be his downfall.

José almost ran to Sheriff Rice and held the rawhide crumbs out to him. When Rice looked at him questioningly, he explained what they were. "He's turned around!" he shot out triumphantly. "He's headed down the canyon!"

The corners of Rice's eyes crinkled. "You really are amazing, José. They ought to write a book about you."

Embarrassed, José laughed, but he was pleased. A weight had been lifted from his shoulders, and he knew that, barring rain, snow, or some act of God, he would never lose Frank Preston's trail for good. Not as long as the ghost of McAllister was riding on his shoulder.

Certain as he was the outlaw had turned around, José led the posse back down the canyon. Fortunately, there was no place to leave the canyon again for some time, so they needn't waste time looking for a deviation in the path. As José rode, he let his mind wander back to McAllister. He imagined him beside him, urging him on, praising him. He would be proud of José this day. He truly would. José let the bittersweet memories carry him momentarily away.

The horse's boots were wearing out fast, and José knew he could thank God for that. He, too, rode with José that day. When they found Frank Preston's turn-off, José wasn't surprised. He had doubled back nearly a mile, then turned north along a game trail—toward Wagner Canyon. Starting a hundred yards up the trail, he made no further attempt to hide his sign. He even let the horse defecate once more and didn't dispose of it.

Along the trail they traveled, until just before descending into Wagner Canyon, where Preston's tracks veered east up the ridgeline. There was a dimmer game trail here that led up into timber, and eventually to Haystack Mountain, if they stuck to it. The rocky soil had worn the rawhide shoes from the killer's horse to the point that they soon found one of them lying in the brush. By the hoofmarks, José could see he had discarded them all. The killer was done hiding his trail. He must have figured by now he had lost any pursuit.

They climbed the ridge, negotiating tangled arms of mahogany and outcrops of rock. They entered a long stand of fir that dropped them into a saddle filled with golden-leaved aspens. Then out of this saddle they went into a thickly interwoven patch of serviceberry and buckbrush. They climbed and climbed, the southern-most portions of Haystack Mountain over a thousand feet above them. They rode out of timber and into sagebrush and grass, following the game trail where Preston's tracks were plainly marked. They wove along this trail that sometimes took them nerve-wrackingly near sharp drop-offs that would dump them in timber hundreds of feet down precarious slopes if they made a false step.

At last they prepared to leave the side of the canyon and top out on the ridge that would become Haystack Mountain. The only obstacle in their way now was a Douglas fir that had died and toppled across the trail, its thick, long branches sticking up and down like some massive centipede. José carefully picked his way over it, and the others followed.

All of the horses made it without incident until it came to Jeff Terry.

Jeff Terry was the youngest of the posse, a man with a joy for life and a driving desire to see justice served. He rode a cowhorse they said was good at following a cow, but when it came to crossing the log its short legs were a drawback. It sidled and fought Terry until he became frustrated and gave it one ferocious kick. Then it started over with a jump.

José heard the terrified squeal as a branch jammed into the horse's right side, and with a grunt it heaved itself to the left. Jeff Terry was a cowboy, and he'd ridden many a pitching bronc. But when the horse fell to the left it smashed Terry's leg between the stirrup leather and a huge branch, and Terry cried out in pain, kicking his other foot free of the stirrup.

The horse came over the log bucking, and Terry rode it for two bone-jarring landings. But on the third try it came down with its front hooves on a small log next to the bigger one that paralleled it. The horse squealed and started to go down, and Terry, unable to jump in time, went down with it. They came over on the left side, and the horse rolled over Terry, pinning him momentarily to the logs.

José reined his horse closer, jerking his lasso from the saddle horn. "Get a rope on the saddle!" he yelled. "Get that horse off him!"

Before they could do anything, the horse grunted and rolled, coming back off Terry, then lunging to its feet. It stood wild-eyed, ears back, and Jeff Terry lay crushed against the logs.

José leaped from his horse and ran to Terry, and the others crowded around him, too. Somebody said, "You all right, boy?" and Terry nodded feebly.

"Get back, get back!" Rice ordered, shoving the others away with the backs of his arms as he hovered over Terry. "Give him some air."

"How's my leg?" was the first thing Terry could utter.

Sheriff Rice cut his pant leg and looked at his calf. "It's broken." The lawman looked with a sickened expression at José, and José knew instinctively this manhunt was over. They would have to take Terry back to town.

Rice pried his eyes from José and looked back at Terry. "You want a drink, son?"

Terry nodded. "Yeah. Just a little one. I had plenty in me, but I think that damn hoss just scared it all down the front of me." He started to laugh at his humor, then winced, clutching Rice's arm. "Get me off these logs," he pleaded, teeth clenched. "They're powerful uncomf'table."

The posse members obliged, four of them lifting him off the logs and laying him out on the levelest ground they could find. Rice took the canteen one of the men brought and gave Terry a long drink, then popped the cork back into the container's mouth. "Just rest, kid," he said. "We'll get you out of here."

Rice turned to José, his face grim. "He's in bad shape, José. We have to go back. Maybe we'll get another chance at Preston. I sure appreciate your try. We would never have made it this far without you." The sheriff looked down the ridge, then met José's eyes again. "I'll see you get paid for this. As well as Bannock County *ever* pays."

José nodded wordlessly and looked down at Jeff Terry, whose jaw muscles were bunched up. A tear had found its way to the corner of Terry's hard-pressed eyes. "Tough kid," he mused.

Rice nodded. "Yeah, he reminds me of you."

José chuckled humorlessly and walked off by himself, looking across the box canyon where they had been earlier, to the rugged ranges stretching to the horizon, toward Wyoming. Sure, he was tough, all right. Tough enough to go on alone. He had sworn to see this trail through, and he would. Somewhere ahead rode a killer, and a thousand dollar reward that could add to a beautiful log house up Wagner Canyon.

José Olano was the only man who could collect them both.

Chapter Thirty-One

Can a man know when he is about to die? Is there a still voice that warns him, lets him know he will see no more sunrises, no more rainbows painted across a rain-dark sky? Is there a whisper that tells him he will never again watch the moonlight silhouette the geese on the lake or feel the pounding gallop of a horse between his legs? Does he feel a cold emptiness—a loss in his soul? Does he have a sudden, unexplained longing to hold his loved ones one last time? Does he see God at the end?

José Olano sat on a flat-topped granite boulder, a wind-tortured pine at his back, and watched the posse slowly make its way down the ridge. He held his hat in his hand, squeezing the brim, and let a cool breeze filter through his long hair, ruffling it around his cheeks. The warm sun beat down on his face, and he thought long and hard of how it would be to die alone.

José was not completely alone, however. Beside him stood two of the possemen, looking after Sheriff Rice and the others, holding their horses' reins quietly. None of them felt any desire to break the silence. The only sound was the whisper of the wind and the occasional crunching as the posse passed through heavy brush or over a pile of loose rocks.

Calvin Briggs was a tall, slender man, younger than José by ten years. He wore a Montana Peak, a narrow-brimmed hat with four even dents in its round crown. Generally a good-humored man, fond of practical jokes, he was quiet today. His jaw was clenched, and he held tightly to the handle of his Smith and Wesson revolver.

Les Muldoon was shorter than Briggs, and a year or two his elder. His skin was fair and freckled, and a shapeless gray hat shaded it against the elements. He was a friendly man but quiet, always willing to let others speak for him. He and José had been friends for years. He had held José's first mount in the great reservation run.

When the posse had disappeared along the timbered ridge, José stood up and looked at Muldoon, then shot a glance at Briggs. He couldn't swear they were about to die, but a cold emptiness was definitely in his chest.

"Well, boys, I'm glad to have you here. But I still wish you'd reconsider. I don't have a good feeling about this."

Muldoon seemed to read José's mind and tried to ease it. "Don't get feelin' responsible for us, José. We're here because we wanna be, not 'cause we feel obligated to you. If anything happens, it ain't yer fault. We're both growed men."

José nodded with a grim smile. "I know. I know. But still, I don't think three men c'n get any better edge on this feller than one. It just means more to get hurt."

When Muldoon and Briggs remained silent, watching him, José clamped his hat back on. "We'd best be movin' on, then."

Without another word, they climbed into their saddles and continued up the ridge, following Preston's plainly marked trail. Off to their right, the terrain dropped off sharply into the box end of Harkness Canyon. It was prettier from above than it had been inside its treacherous jaws. They finally topped out on the Hogsback. The going became slow here, for the top of the mountain was mostly rock, and the killer had stayed right with it. José occasionally found a partial hoofprint in dust. Otherwise, there was no sign.

They pushed along doggedly, sometimes having to ride single file because of the narrowness of the ridgetop. Then José lost the trail for ten minutes, and when he found it the tracks were headed at a swift descent toward the Portneuf River.

They rode down through the heavy timber, on a path José and McAllister had traveled many years ago. Preston no longer tried to hide his trail. Even if he had wanted to, the terrain was too steep, and if he could have returned his path to its natural state it wouldn't have been worth the time it would have cost him. José was glad for this, because he had plenty of work just staying in the saddle and keeping his horse on the safest route down the mountain. He pushed against his stirrups, gritted his teeth, and leaned back in the saddle, letting his horse pick its own way down the slope.

Evening was approaching quickly by the time they came down into the foothills. The soft blue shadows had begun to creep up Petticoat Peak, to the east, and all the sage and grassland before them was bathed in shade. Their faces and their horse's faces, chests, and legs were cut and bleeding in many places from the heavy timber and rocks they had passed through. It was good to be down in thinner timber again, moving on leveler ground through aspen woods.

They followed the trail to the river before it was too dark to see, and here they pitched camp. They were tired, but Briggs took the time to build a fire, and they brewed a pot of coffee and warmed up three cans of black beans. Not long after the fire died out, José was snoring.

José was awake before the sun, and he sat shivering in the dark, waiting for tracking light. He didn't need to awaken the others, for the cold had opened their eyes, too. They silently chewed on jerky and the last of the biscuits, and José wished he were home with Rebecca. He badly needed some restful sleep and a home-cooked meal.

When light had grown sufficient, José found where Preston's trail had gone into the river and shortly thereafter where it had come out on the other side. Preston had made no attempt to use the river to lose them.

The trail made a beeline toward Dempsey. José was certain the killer would cross there to make his way up Dempsey Creek toward Baldy and Sedgwick Peak. But suddenly the trail came to a stop. The tracks milled here for a while, then turned east.

They crossed the railroad tracks, then the road, and started up Hadley Canyon, the killer still leaving his trail wide open. José guessed the man wanted to stay out of sight in the mountains for a few more days before he attempted to cross populated country.

Hadley Canyon was steep and rugged, the lower slopes crowded with aspens, its ridges and gullies packed with maple and mountain mahogany on one side, juniper, then Douglas fir on the other as the sides of the canyon tilted sharply upward. Limestone outcroppings were numerous on the north side of the canyon, but the trail stuck to the south. They followed Preston by hoofprints and broken branches. They climbed until their horses heaved for breath and sweat ran down them in frothy streams.

Once, José came across horse droppings, and they were fresh enough they had to have been made by Preston's horse. But they were at least hours old, old enough José was certain Preston was far ahead, and he no longer let fear of ambush bother him. That worry could return when they found some sign they were closing in.

On the ascent, they let the horses stop in clearings now and then to catch their breath, then continued on, growing ever nearer the broken line of rocks and old growth fir that lined the ridgetop. José watched the ground, the broken tree branches, the crushed grass, making sure they kept to the trail. He stopped to look ahead every so often, carefully scanning the rocks and trees in case Preston had decided to stay and watch for pursuit.

They had just topped the ridge, and José was riding down into the cover of some huge firs when the shot rang out. A sharp cry issued from behind him. He flew from his horse, holding tight to one rein as he landed in the brush on his backside.

José pushed to a crouch, looking intently past Les Muldoon's terrified bay horse. It screamed and whipped its hindquarters this way and that, the whites of its eyes showing as it stared down at Muldoon. José's friend clutched his right shoulder, his face a grimace of pain. Blood had started to ooze between his fingers. Somehow, with his right hand, he'd managed to hang onto his McCarty, which, like José, he kept tucked under his belt.

Behind Muldoon, Calvin Briggs had wheeled his mount and ridden it out of sight. José heard it snort from a clump of trees. Cursing, he searched the ridgeline to see if he could tell where the shot had come from. He could see no one, and no gunsmoke.

"Get down!" José hissed at Muldoon. "Get yer horse into the trees. Hurry!"

Clenching his teeth in pain, Muldoon stumbled toward a stand of fir, his eyes shocked. The horse went with him, still snorting and rolling its eyes. Just as the horse was about to disappear in the trees, another shot rang out, clipping a branch behind it. The horse reared and lunged forward, nearly coming down on top of Muldoon as he dove out of the way. The man landed in the brush with a stifled cry, and his horse turned and trotted down through the woods, its heavy hooves making the brush crash and pop.

Even as Muldoon's horse was making its escape, José dragged the dun down farther into the trees. This time the killer didn't fire.

Now all was silent. José continued to search above him where he had heard the shot, but he saw nothing. Not a clue where the ambusher was concealed.

"Olano! Muldoon! You all right?" Briggs's frightened voice whispered through the trees.

José spoke back, hoping his voice wouldn't drift to the killer. "I'm all right, but I think Les took a bad one in the shoulder."

A long moment of silence followed, and then two sharp cracks from the ridge sent bullets clipping through the trees overhead. José crouched lower, his curses coloring the air. He had to fight now to hang onto the frightened dun.

"Les! How bad you hurt?" José asked Muldoon after he managed to calm the horse down.

When there was no answer, alarm gripped him, and he rose and dragged the horse toward where he had last seen Muldoon. "Les, where are you? Say somethin'."

"I'm here," Muldoon groaned weakly. "I'm bleedin' bad, José."

With a sigh of relief that Muldoon could still at least talk, José slipped the dun's horse hair McCarty from his belt and tied it to a nearby tree. Then he made his way over through the brush to Muldoon. The cowboy had dragged himself to a big tree and was leaned up against its trunk, gripping his shoulder, his eyes closed tightly. He looked up when José crouched over him.

He smiled weakly, then grimaced. "Son of a bitch don't play fair."

José grunted. "Nobody will be playin' fair t'day, cowboy. Preston thinks he's the only one around here that knows the woods, but we'll see who's the better Injun before this day winds up. Let's see yer shoulder," he said.

Reaching down, he unfastened the top four buttons of Muldoon's shirt. Carefully, he slid the material down past the wound. It was a nasty hole, but the bullet had gone clear through and didn't appear to have touched bone. "Thank yer stars, Les. This fella's not worth beans at shootin' folks, unless they're up close to him—like in the bank."

José called down to Briggs. "Get on up here, Briggs. On yer hands an' knees," he added emphatically.

Briggs came up the ridge. He had gone one step farther than José cautioned and was slithering on his belly like a snake. He sat up when he reached them and jerked his thumb behind him. "I tied my horse down there."

José nodded peremptorily. "Listen to me, Cal, an' listen close. You gotta take care of Les. You gotta get 'im outta here. I got no choice but to hunt this fella down before he kills somebody else. He just ain't gonna stop."

Briggs swallowed hard. "What do I do? I ain't no doctor."

"Make 'im a bandage out of yer shirt," José advised. "Just pad the wound with four or five layers of cloth. Then get 'im down to the nearest homestead. He'll be all right, but there's not a lot of time to waste."

José turned and stared up the hill, his eyes hardening. He turned back to the others. "If yer worried about the reward, don't. I'll see you two still get your share. Hell, you c'n have it all, for that matter. But I have to stop this fella before he kills somebody else."

After José left Briggs and Muldoon, he crawled up the hill on his belly, leaving the dun. If he had earlier felt that his death was possible, now he feared it imminent. His stomach felt like it had been stomped by a horse, and he had to force himself not to think of Rebecca and the children. He had to concentrate on the job at hand. If he lost his single-mindedness now, this man would kill him.

With infinite care, he crawled in the direction from which he thought the last two shots had come. Eyes wide, he searched every rock about him, every tree, every clump of grass or brush, every swell of the ground.

Then he saw the blood.

He stared for a long moment at the huge, dark splotches on the ground in front of him. Something, animal or human, was bleeding terribly, but he guessed the blood too old for it to be Preston's. As long ago as it had fallen and as heavily as it was concentrated, the man would have been dead by now.

Scanning the ground, José's eyes picked out a hoofprint, then another. Preston's horse. Where was it now? Had it been injured? Of course. There were no other tracks here, none except Preston's, which José now made out beside those of the horse.

The blood trail led up the ridge through the rocks, growing as it went. José followed it with his eyes, then suddenly stopped. There was a big tan boulder ahead of him about twenty yards, and its side was splashed with red. Beyond it was a dark object José mistook for a rock, at first glance. But it was too dark, too out of place among the broken tan rocks that lay everywhere else. José stared at it, then looked away for a moment to clear his vision. When he brought his eyes back to it again, it was clear.

It was the bottom of a shod horse's hoof.

Turning his head slowly this way and that, José searched for sign of Preston but saw nothing. With a deep breath, he pulled himself forward with his elbows. Once, twice, three times. On and on he moved, ever so slowly, his Colt in his fist.

As he crawled closer, the hoof came more into view until it materialized into an entire horse's leg, then a horse. José crawled next to it and stopped. Its head was downhill, but he could see its throat had been cut, and one leg was twisted and obviously broken. *Tough country on horses.*

José waited ten minutes here, his eyes carefully picking the terrain apart. Frank Preston was on foot now. He would be harder to find and more dangerous than ever. When he saw no sign and heard no other clue that Preston was near, he began to circle uphill away from the horse. He crept up the ridgetop, where he would have hidden himself had he wished to ambush someone, and within minutes he discovered where Preston had lain to fire at him and the others. It was between two large boulders with brush in-between them. José turned and looked down the ridge. There was a perfect line of fire from there to where they had been riding. In fact, the outlaw had probably watched them for several hundred yards as they came up the slope.

Suddenly, a rifle report cracked across the ridge, and the bullet spat into the rock next to José's face, showering him with rock fragments. With a gasp, he rolled to the side, right into one of the boulders. José's side was now to the killer, and he lunged forward, clearing the brush pile and landing three feet down the slope on his shoulder.

He rolled to a stop, still clutching the Colt, and jerked his head around to stare back up the hill. Another shot, and this time he saw the puff of white smoke from the trees above at almost the same instant dirt and gravel spat up in front of his face, blinding him.

Slamming his eyes shut, he threw himself sideways, landing in a pile of sagebrush that jammed into his shoulder. He felt as helpless as a worm in a coffee can. He couldn't see anything. His eyes burned horribly, and with his free hand he rubbed at them, brushing dirt and bloody rock fragments away.

He stumbled to his feet, starting down the hill in a serpentine run. He could see just enough out of one eye to keep from going off a steep incline, but not enough to keep out of the rocks, and just as he tripped and fell forward the rifle exploded again behind him.

He fully expected the bullet to take him in the back, but it must have gone high when he fell forward. He landed half on his shoulder and half on his head, then rolled, over and over, down the steep slope. It seemed like he tumbled forever, and then finally he slammed up against a boulder embedded in the earth. It knocked the air out of him, and he lay gasping for breath, wondering if the rifle sights were still lined on him. Miraculously, he could still feel the Colt in his clenched fist.

One thing he knew for sure: he had to return to his horse and grab his rifle. He was completely outgunned with only the pistol. This killer was far too smart to let him get near.

Just as tears of pain cleared his vision enough to view his surroundings, José pushed away from the boulder and slid backwards down the hill on his hands and knees, the sharp rocks biting into his skin. He came up short against the solid trunk of a mountain mahogany and sucked in a deep breath.

The mountain was silent again, and looking up the ridge he could no longer see the place the killer had been firing from. For the moment, he was safe, until he headed for his rifle. And even the place where his horse was concealed might be out of the killer's view now, from his new position.

Looking to the left, José saw he was now slightly downhill from where he had left the horse. He would have to crawl up past a jumble of rocks and a tangled cluster of brush, then scramble across an open, gravelly clearing to reach the cover of the trees. But he had to have his rifle if he was to match Frank Preston. And then he could best him, for it was obvious Preston hadn't been schooled in the precise manner of marksmanship of Robert McAllister.

Wiping carefully one last time at his eyes, José sucked in a deep breath, let it out, then drew another. When he exhaled and breathed in again, he shoved away from the tree and clawed his way up through the rocks and brush. At the clearing, he didn't hesitate but ran as fast as he could up the slope.

Two shots bellowed in the morning, clipping rocks close behind his feet. One whined away vehemently as José reached the level and dove, hitting hard on his stomach. Oblivious to the pain, he rolled to the left, soon dropping off the edge of the ridge and thumping against the big, gnarled trunk of a fir.

Exhausted, he lay on his back, clutching his dusty pistol to him. His body was battered, his hands scraped and bleeding horribly. Blood oozed from many tiny cuts in his face and a bad cut in the lobe of his right ear, and he brushed at that unconsciously, gasping for air. His head throbbed, along with the rest of his body, and he was covered with sweat and dirt from head to foot.

At last, he rolled onto his stomach and thrust the Colt into its holster. He moved at a crouch through the trees, passing the spot where Briggs's horse had been, then where Muldoon had lain. They had already left him. For an instant, José felt a pang of loneliness. He would have been angry with Briggs and Muldoon if they *hadn't* gone, but the fact that they had made him feel deserted.

The dun nickered softly as he came near, and it rolled its eyes. It shifted about as he tried to touch it, unsure of his intentions and wondering what all the noise was about. He soothed the gelding with quiet words and caressed its neck, then drew the Winchester out of the scabbard. "I'll be comin' back for you, fella," he said reassuringly. "You c'n bet on it." But he wasn't as sure as he tried to sound.

When he started back up the hill, it was with confidence yet with a strange dread that filled his chest and seemed to compress his heart and windpipe. Whatever became of him before this afternoon ended, he would be sorry. He didn't want to die, but he didn't want to kill, either. Not that the man above him hadn't asked for a generous helping of death, but José wished somebody else could do him the favor. He had killed one man, and that was enough for a lifetime. *More* than enough.

He moved slowly through the rocks, stopping every now and then, keeping cover between himself and where he had seen the last puff of smoke. But of course the killer would have moved. He was a hunted man. It was plain he had been before. He wasn't fool enough to shoot, then stay in the same location. So where would he have gone?

The question had no more than flashed through José's mind when he heard the click of a rifle's hammer behind him.

The sound was shockingly close. *Too* close. The man meant to kill José, and now he would. A wild thought raced through José's mind. He could whirl and fire. It was his only chance. Frank Preston intended to shoot him anyway. José waited for the man to speak, but he didn't. And then he waited no more. With a lung-filling breath, he drew back the hammer of his rifle and whirled.

He didn't even have time to fire. He had only time to glimpse a bearded face looking at him over the top of a boulder, and then a large chunk of granite struck him hard in the stomach, sending a shudder through him and crushing the air from his lungs. His mouth fell open, and he gagged for air, the rifle useless in his hands. It might as well have been back on his saddle.

As he glanced up again, his eyes touched fleetingly on Frank Preston's face, and a strangled cry tore at his throat.

With the swiftness and agility of a cougar, Preston leaped out from behind the rock and charged José, kicking the rifle out of his hands. The blow's momentum spun José around and knocked him to his knees, and before he could react the man had stepped around in front of him, his rifle leveled in his face.

José leaned forward, retching. He didn't try to think, for he knew that was too late, but thoughts of death lurked in his head of their own volition. He rammed his eyes shut while he fought for breath. When he opened them, saliva hung in a long stream from the corner of his mouth, but he was too shaken to even wipe it off. He stared sickly at the rifle four feet away, and thought in horror of the man who towered over him, eyes full of icy fury.

"I tried to turn you back. I tried everything I could. But I guess you ain't made that way." The man's voice was gruff, and it came to José as if from a distance. His mind reeled as he tried to digest the words, as he tried to grasp the fact that this man stood before him with the bore of his rifle aimed at his head. Slowly, José raised his eyes and looked into the man's face, sinking back until he was sitting on his lower legs. He stared, unbelieving, at the leathery face before him.

"I named yuh Lucky," mused the voice. "But I guess yer luck just run out."

Frank Preston—Robert McAllister—cleared his throat and spat into the dust.

In a daze, José followed the spittle with his eyes. He couldn't quite grasp the turn of events. For two days he had chased a killer named Frank Preston, a man who had killed a bank clerk and a little boy in cold blood. But the trail had led him to a friend, a man he thought incapable of killing a child.

He looked back up at McAllister, and suddenly he started to laugh. He laughed drunkenly, then choked back a sudden rush of hot tears. He wiped his eyes and looked at McAllister, and it was like a veil slipped from before his eyes. He saw the entire thing so clearly. The description of the man they called Frank Preston. It fit McAllister. The incredible way in which he covered a trail. That was his old friend without question. The fact the killer didn't seem to be able to hit the broad side of a barn, although shooting a rifle and supposedly a man of the outdoors. He just didn't want to hurt José. His feelings for him ran too deep.

The staggering reality struck José like battering thunder, causing his head to spin with sick realization. He started to shake his head, now *wanting* the tears to come, and they wouldn't.

He struggled to his feet and stared at McAllister, who hadn't spoken a word in more than a minute. José was the one who broke the silence. "You killed a boy, Gray. I never thought…"

McAllister's eyes went half shut as if sick with the memory, and he quickly shook his head. "No. I never killed a boy, Lucky. The clerk tried to shoot me as I was runnin', an' he shot the boy instead. Hell, I didn't wanna kill nobody. I just needed a stake. I didn't even wanna kill the clerk, but when he shot that kid I just acted. It's made me sick ever since, thinkin' about that kid. I wish that clerk was a better shot an' got me instead."

José's eyes flickered to his rifle lying on the ground, then back to McAllister.

"Lucky," said the man with soft accusation. "You wouldn't use that on me. Would yuh?"

José was silent, staring. "Would *you?*" he asked at last, looking at McAllister's rifle.

McAllister swallowed. His eyes narrowed and he looked up the hill, then back at José. "I don't reckon I'd ever have to."

José cocked his head to the side. "What do you mean?"

"Now that yuh know it's me, an' yuh know I didn't kill that kid…" McAllister's voice trailed off as he looked into José's eyes with the closest thing to pleading José could ever imagine him showing.

José had to look away, and he wiped his mouth with his hand harshly, as if trying to scrape his mustache off. At last, feeling McAllister's eyes on his face, he looked back, and their gazes locked.

"It doesn't matter, Gray. I gotta take you back. If you didn't kill that kid, maybe…"

He didn't finish his thought.

A faraway look had come into McAllister's gray eyes, and he stared past José at the distant, timbered mountains. Finally, he looked back at José. "If I didn't kill that kid, what? I still killed the clerk an' robbed the bank, an' I'll still be hung just as dead."

"They might not hang you. The law ain't as anxious as it used to be to take a life fer a life. A lot of people get off with prison time or—" José stopped. Prison time? For Robert McAllister? Gray Eagle? He could never stand it. He would die in a prison, his spirit broken like the buckskin stallion. The stallion McAllister had mercifully put to death…

McAllister was looking sadly at José, a humorless smile touching the corners of his mouth. "I can't go to prison, Lucky. I'd ruther die."

Sickness washed over José in a powerful wave, and his face turned gray. His shoulders drooped. *Gray, please. Please don't do this.* These were the words which filled his head. "I can't let you go, Gray. I don't want you to kill anybody else. What happened to you? People's lives used to mean somethin' to you."

McAllister's eyes hardened. "There's no call fer that, boy. I told yuh what happened."

"Yeah. But if you hadn't been robbin' a bank an' been ready to kill you'd never 've had to."

McAllister nodded expressionlessly. "Maybe not. Well, I gotta go, kid. An' I'll have to take yer horse. I know it's a long way back, but yer tough. Besides, yuh got friends prob'ly right down below, there. They'll borrow yuh a horse."

José grunted. "The word's 'loan', not borrow."

A laugh softened McAllister's face. "Well, I never was no good at speakin', not like you. I never could fit inta this world you've worked yer way into so smooth. My place is out here." He waved a hand to indicate his surroundings. "Let me drift, Lucky. I'll never come back here. You'll never hear from me again."

José shook his head. "Maybe not you. Maybe Frank Preston. Or some other name."

"Like that?" McAllister chuckled suddenly. "Frank Preston? Got that from them two towns south of here. Franklin and Preston. Figgered that'd throw 'em off my track an' you'd never know it was me. But I never figgered they'd find yuh, not durin' roundup."

"They wouldn't 've. But roundup ended the day before you hit the bank. So you cost me a rest I really could've used," José said in mock reproach. "Now I gotta take you back. I can't just let yuh ride off."

McAllister's face was filled with a vast, awful sadness. The corner of his mouth twitched under his mustache, and he canted his head a little to one side, searching José's eyes. Then he took a deep breath and forced the sadness away. His voice lowered when he replied, and warning filled his eyes. "Ain't no way in hell yer takin' me back, Lucky. I can't go to prison. An' I won't be hung with a stinkin' black bag over my head. I'm leavin', an' I'm leavin' on yer horse. You wanna stop me, you'll have to kill me. An' remember who taught yuh to shoot."

With another deep breath, McAllister turned and started toward the dun.

José didn't have time to consider. He had to act, one way or the other. A friend of his was walking away, a friend who had taught him everything and had saved his life. A friend who had become a killer, and who would kill again.

With sickness in the pit of his stomach, José drew his Colt from its holster, cocking and lifting it as he spoke. Numbness filled his soul, and instinct made him speak. "Just stop, Gray!"

There must have been something in José's voice, something deadly, something frantic—something lost. There must have been something in his tone that said he was ready to kill for the cause of justice. He didn't even know it himself. But McAllister did.

The old man whirled and dropped into a crouch, and there came an inconspicuous click just before the pistol bucked against José's palm.

McAllister stumbled backward and landed on his back, his rifle rolling from his limp hand into a clump of grass. Fixed to his tracks, José stared, vision blurry, gun smoking in his still out-stretched hand. He wasn't standing there anymore, not in every sense of the word. Only his emotions and his body remained, for his consciousness seemed to have flown. He rushed forward, the deadly odor of acrid smoke stinging his nostrils.

José absently let the pistol drop from his hand as he reached McAllister and fell to his knees beside him, not feeling the rocks that jabbed him. He cradled his friend's head against the palm of his hand and lifted it. A tiny trickle of blood ran from the corner of McAllister's mouth, and a large, dark spot worked its way outward at the middle of his shirt.

A hot tear coursed down José's dusty, bloody cheek and into his whiskers, and for several moments he couldn't speak. He could barely see. Finally, he swallowed and shut his eyes tightly, forcing back the tears. He met McAllister's eyes.

"Gray! Gray, what the hell did you do? You had an empty under the hammer. You taught me better than that," he said, his voice quieting. He wiped at a wayward tear on his cheek.

McAllister gave a tiny, crooked smile, the canyons in his face deepening. "Hell, Lucky. I couldn't shoot you."

José's eyes became too blurred to see, filling up as quickly as he could dry them. He clenched his teeth and fought against the tears, trying to look again at his friend before it was too late. Then he felt McAllister relax against the side of his leg, and a breath of cool wind brushed against José's cheek, like a ghost taking flight.

José fought his eyes clear, staring at his friend. "Gray? Gray!" He grabbed him by the shirt and jerked him partly off the ground, but McAllister's head lolled back, unsupported. José shook his friend almost violently, staring in disbelief. "Gray! You can't do this! Gray!" His cry of anguish echoed through the trees.

Letting McAllister fall back to the ground, he took him by the sides of his head, his eyes fixed on the bearded face. McAllister's pupils were swelled far beyond normal size, heedless of the sun. José began to sob uncontrollably, looking around him as if someone might be there to help him, to bring back his friend, to wake him from the worst nightmare of his life.

"Please, Gray. Please…" Weeping, he lowered his head until it touched McAllister's bloody chest.

A sudden, sharp cry startled José, and he cringed and raised his head to look high over his shoulder. An eagle floated effortlessly on the air currents, crying out again with a lonesome sound that engulfed José's entire world.

José felt a chill in the autumn wind. He looked down at his battered hands. He couldn't stand up, so he sat and wept beside his friend.

He could have made it home, but he spent the night on the mountain, shivering in his bedroll. In the morning, the ground was hard with frost, and it sparkled brightly on the grass and trees and on the dead leaves on the ground.

Still numb, José loaded McAllister onto the reluctant dun, tied the body on, then picked up the bank's money sack and started toward the valley. He had to get back to Rebecca, to let her know he was alive. He had to feel her comforting arms around him.

The eagle appeared again and circled overhead, staying stubbornly with José's route, and as they came down the ridge over the jumbled rocks it lit in the snag of a giant fir towering among a stand of golden-leaved aspens. There was a huge, ragged nest in the snag.

José stopped the horse, staring at the great bird. It turned its head back and forth, watching him curiously. Then it took wing and began to circle, its smooth, perfect grace drawing lines of freedom across the sky.

José suddenly knew he couldn't take McAllister back. They couldn't know he had ever found him. The bank money? He'd turn it in and tell them the killer had lost it in his attempt to escape. He'd lay it on the counter, and that would be that. He didn't want the reward. He wanted no part of it. If they insisted, they could give it to Briggs and Muldoon. It was blood money, whether anyone else knew it or not.

José turned to his old friend with a sad smile and laid a hand across his back. He nodded, and a peaceful sigh escaped his lips. Gray Eagle would be proud of his decision.

He set to work. He unloaded McAllister's body from the dun, tied the horse to a nearby tree, and began to dig a grave with a sharp piece of shale, there beneath the giant fir. But then he remembered what McAllister had once told him about the Shoshone way of "burying." They laid their dead in a crevice in rocks, then filled in the crevice with brush and more rocks. *Who wants to be in the ground? Who wants dirt thrown in yer face?* McAllister had said. *Lay me in the mountain air. Let the wolves have me, if they will. Hell, I've had enough of them.* José paused and looked down at the stone in his hands. At last, he sighed and threw it away from him.

He laid McAllister to rest beneath the fir as the first of the black clouds billowed over the southern horizon. As his throat tightened and tears began to trickle down his cheeks, a single aspen leaf floated down near the outlaw's head and touched his gray hair. The wind gusted up and many more of the leaves broke free, twisting and plummeting to the ground like teardrops, falling silent on his friend's still form and on the frosted ground.

The eagle circled overhead, and its wild, shrill cry rang in the crisp autumn air, echoing down the canyon.

Death of an Eagle

He watches through the eyes of an eagle
The valley down below;
He soars on the wings of an eagle
While the sky is all aglow.

No one can see the true beauty
Of his mountains, his valleys, his sky;
No one can know of the treasures
That are seen through this eagle's eye.

And still, though surrounded by beauty,
He envies the ones with the gold;
He grows to covet their treasures,
For he knows he is growing old.

So he trespasses, knowing he shouldn't,
In the realm of those who go bad,
Forgetting the honor he's lived with,
And all of the freedom he's had.

High on the hill is a statue,
Standing so splendid and regal—
It turns into dust, as all of us must,
Gone with the death of an eagle.

About the Author

Kirby Frank Jonas was born in 1965 in Bozeman, Montana. He lived in a place called Bear Canyon, where sagebrush gave way to spruce and fir, and the wild country was forever ingrained in him. It was there he gained his love of the Old West, listening to his father tell stories and sing western ballads, and watching television programs such as Gunsmoke and The Virginian.

Jonas next lived in a remote farm in Virginia, and then in Shelley, Idaho, where he graduated from high school. He began writing at a young age, completing his first work in the sixth grade. He has since written four published novels and two which are forthcoming.

Besides his writing, he also paints wildlife and the West. He has done all of his cover art and hundreds of other pieces. He is a songwriter and guitar player and singer of old western ballads and trail songs. Jonas enjoys the joking title given to him by many of his friends: "The Renaissance Cowboy."

After living in Arizona to research his first two books, and nine countries in Europe, to see the world, Jonas settled permanently in Pocatello, Idaho. He has made a living fighting range fires for the Bureau of Land Management in five western states, worked for the Idaho Fish and Game Department, been a security guard and a guard for Wells Fargo in Phoenix, Arizona. He was employed as an officer for the Pocatello City police and currently works as a city firefighter. He and his wife, Debbie, enjoy traveling the West with their three children, Cheyenne Kaycee, Jacob Talon, and Clay Logan.

Author's Note

For those of you who wonder—yes, this book is real. At least in my mind it really took place. José Olano is real. He is a friend of mine, for which I am grateful. This story would never have been right without his inspiration. Clint Goss is real, and also a friend. Sheriff Hess, who was mentioned but never actually appeared, was my grandfather. He was sheriff of Bingham County, Idaho, for some twenty years until retiring in the 1970's. Like José and Clint, I placed him out of his time. And as for Sheriff Martin Rice, he really was sheriff in 1902, and later he became mayor of Pocatello. Police Chief Barnett McGarvey, also, was just that, in the year of the Pocatello Land Run. I took a great liberty in making Lauris José's daughter in the book, for in real life Lauris is José's lovely wife.

Not only were these people real, but the country is real. Perhaps some minor details are out of place, but as far as I could control it, every piece of country described in the book is a place I have been. As usual, I employed the modern names in many cases. But then, many times the origin of a name is lost to history, and who is to know when it came about, and who did the naming? As for Lava Hot Springs, of course the town didn't exist, but the settlement nearby was named Dempsey. Blackfoot was Grove City, but I chose to use the newer name for clarity. Some tell me Soda Springs was once called "The Soda Springs," but if it was it sounded awkward, and I only called it that once, in the beginning of the book. Bancroft wasn't founded until a while later, but some of you might have recognized it as the camping place by the train stop called "Squaw Creek."

To the best of my ability, I either hiked or rode the routes in the book, and I have camped and hunted in several of them, too. The weapons the characters used I have attempted to use, or at least their equivalent. For those of you who possess such fine historical weaponry, I hope the picture was real.

And to all of you who have had input in *Death of an Eagle* in any way, whether consciously or not, thank you. This story is for you.

Buy these books at your local bookstore, or use this handy coupon for ordering:

Howling Wolf Publishing,
P.O. Box 1045, Pocatello, Idaho 83204

Please send me:

❑ _____ copy/copies of: Death of an Eagle ($12.95)

❑ _____ copy/copies of: The Dansing Star ($10.95)

❑ _____ copy/copies of: Season of the Vigilante, Book I:
The Bloody Season ($8.95)

❑ _____ copy/copies of: Season of the Vigilante, Book II:
Season's End ($9.95)

Send check or money order—no cash or C.O.D.'s please.
Idaho residents add 5% sales tax
I am enclosing $_____.

Name _____

Address _____

City, State, Zip _____

Please allow three weeks for delivery.